JUN 2017

Sandpiper Cove

Center Point
Large Print

Also by Irene Hannon and available from
Center Point Large Print:

Thin Ice
Tangled Webs
Hope Harbor
Sea Rose Lane

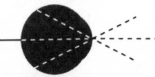

**This Large Print Book carries the
Seal of Approval of N.A.V.H.**

Sandpiper Cove

—A Hope Harbor Novel—

Irene Hannon

CENTER POINT LARGE PRINT
THORNDIKE, MAINE

This Center Point Large Print edition is published
in the year 2017 by arrangement with Revell,
a division of Baker Publishing Group.

This book is a work of fiction. Names, characters,
places, and incidents are the product of the author's
imagination or are used fictitiously.

The text of this Large Print edition is unabridged.
In other aspects, this book may vary
from the original edition.
Printed in the United States of America
on permanent paper.
Set in 16-point Times New Roman type.

ISBN: 978-1-68324-371-7

Library of Congress Cataloging-in-Publication Data

Names: Hannon, Irene, author.
Title: Sandpiper Cove / Irene Hannon.
Description: Center Point Large Print edition. | Thorndike, Maine :
Center Point Large Print, 2017. | Series: A Hope Harbor novel
Identifiers: LCCN 2017003218 | ISBN 9781683243717
        (hardcover : alk. paper)
Subjects: LCSH: Large type books. | GSAFD: Love stories. | Christian
fiction.
Classification: LCC PS3558.A4793 S26 2017b | DDC 813/.54—dc23
LC record available at https://lccn.loc.gov/2017003218

To my niece, Maureen Hannon,
as she graduates from eighth grade.

From the day I first held you in my arms,
you captured my heart—
and your sunny smile, warm hugs,
and contagious joie de vivre
have blessed my life ever since.

May your high school years be filled with
wonderful surprises, new friends,
and exciting opportunities
as you spread your wings and soar.

❧ 1 ❧

Not again.

Adam Stone slammed the door on his decrepit Kia, expelled a breath, and surveyed the damage.

The rustic, one-room cabin he called home appeared to be untouched this go-round. But it would take some serious sanding to get rid of the profanities spray-painted on the small outbuilding that housed his woodworking shop.

At least the vandals hadn't broken any windows this time.

But where was Clyde?

Breaking into a jog on the gravel drive, he scanned the surrounding woods that offered peeks at the pristine Oregon beach and choppy April sea a hundred yards away.

"Clyde!"

No response.

"Clyde! Come on out, boy. It's safe."

Silence, save for the distinctive trill of the sandpiper that gave this secluded cove its name.

He clamped his jaw shut. Damaged property, he could deal with. But if those thugs had done anything to . . .

A soft whimper came from the direction of the workshop, and the swinging door he'd rigged up for the adopted stray gave a slight shimmy.

Adam switched direction, digging out the keys to the shed as he goosed his jog to a sprint.

"I'm here, boy. Hang on." He fumbled the key as he inserted it in the lock, tremors sabotaging his fingers.

Clenching his teeth, he tried again. It was crazy to worry about a dumb mutt who hadn't had enough sense to move out of the path of a car. Letting yourself care for anyone—or anything—was an invitation for grief.

And he didn't need any more of that.

Yet walking away from a hurt, defenseless creature hadn't been an option on that foggy day by the side of Highway 101 when he'd found the injured pooch barely clinging to life.

The lock clicked, and he pushed the door open.

From the corner of the shop where he'd wedged himself behind some scrap wood, Clyde poked out his black nose. He whimpered again, his big, soulful brown eyes filled with fear.

Adam exhaled, his tension whooshing out like CO_2 being released from a soft drink can.

Clyde was scared—but okay.

Hunkering down, he held out his hand and gentled his voice. "You're safe, boy. Come on out."

Clyde didn't budge.

No problem.

Adam sat cross-legged on the rough-hewn floorboards and waited. Pushing any creature to trust if they weren't yet ready to do so could backfire—

no matter how well-intentioned the overture. The small white scar on his right hand from the night Clyde had mistaken a friendly reach for a threat proved that.

But these days, it didn't take long for the mangy mongrel to emerge from a hiding place.

Less than fifteen seconds later, Clyde crept out and inched toward him, limping on his bad leg.

As the dog approached, Adam fought the urge to pull the shaking mass of mottled fur into a comforting embrace.

Instead, he remained motionless until Clyde sniffed around, stuck a damp nose in his palm—and climbed into his lap.

All forty-three pounds of him.

Only then did Adam touch the dog.

"No one's going to hurt you, fella. Everything's fine." The last word hitched as he stroked the mutt. "I'm here, and I won't be leaving again until I go to work tomorrow morning. We'll spend the rest of Sunday together. I might even grill a burger for you too instead of making you eat that dog chow the vet recommended. How does some comfort food sound?"

Of course the stupid dog had no idea what he was saying—but his soothing tone seemed to calm the canine. Clyde's shakes subsided, and when their gazes connected, the mutt's eyes brimmed with adoration.

A sudden rush of warmth filled Adam's heart—

but he quickly squelched it. How pathetic, to be touched by a dog's affection.

Besides, it was all an illusion.

Dogs didn't feel emotions.

Without breaking eye contact, Clyde gave his fingers a quick, dry lick. As if to say, *Yes, we do. And I think you're great.*

Pressure built in Adam's throat as he smoothed a hand over Clyde's back, his fingertips feeling every ridge of scar tissue that had been there long before their lives had intersected sixteen months ago, when both of them had been in desperate need of a friend.

Okay. Fine.

Maybe he was reading too much into the dog's reaction.

Maybe he was being too sentimental.

But for today, he'd let himself believe the abused pooch *did* have deeper feelings.

Because while he'd made a few friends in Hope Harbor during the year and a half he'd lived here, the only one waiting for him in Sandpiper Cove at the end of each day was Clyde.

And without the canine companion who'd claimed a wedge of his heart, his life would be even lonelier.

"Happy Monday, Lexie. How's your week starting out?"

Hope Harbor police chief Lexie Graham leaned

a shoulder against the side of Charley's taco truck and considered the man's question as she gave the picturesque wharf a sweep.

Planters overflowing with colorful flowers served as a buffer between the sidewalk and the sloping pile of boulders that led to the water. Across the wide street from the marina, quaint storefronts adorned with bright awnings and flower boxes faced the sea. A white gazebo occupied the small park behind Charley's truck, where the two-block-long, crescent-shaped frontage road dead-ended at the river.

All was peaceful and predictable . . . as usual.

Just the way she liked it.

"So far, so good. Everything's been quiet."

"Looks can be deceiving, though. You ordering for one today?"

"Yes." She studied the taco-making artist, who hadn't changed one iota in all the years she'd known him. Same leathery, latte-colored skin. Same long gray hair pulled back into a ponytail. Same kindly, insightful eyes.

It was comforting to have one unchanging element in a world that liked to throw curves. The town sage and wisdom-dispenser could always be counted on to offer sound advice and brighten her day.

But his looks-can-be-deceiving comment didn't leave her feeling warm and fuzzy.

Squinting, she took another survey of Dockside

Drive. Nothing amiss in town, as far as she could see. Nor did there appear to be any issues meriting attention on the water. The long jetty on the left and the pair of rocky islands on the right that tamed the turbulent waves and protected the boats in the marina were as unchanging as the sea stacks on the beach outside of town.

Everything seemed normal.

Maybe Charley's comment had just been one of those philosophical observations he liked to throw out on occasion.

Whatever the impetus for his remark, she didn't intend to dwell on it.

"What kind of tacos are you making?"

"Cod's the star today." He pulled a handful of chopped red onions out of a cooler and tossed them on the griddle. The savory aroma set off a rumble in her stomach. "Enhanced by my grand-mother's secret lime cilantro cream sauce."

"Sounds great, as always."

"We aim to please." He flipped the fish on the grill and sprinkled some kind of seasoning over the ingredients on the griddle. "So did you find any clues out at Adam's place?"

At the non sequitur, she blinked. "What are you talking about?"

"The vandalism at Adam Stone's place yester-day." He stirred the onions. "Didn't he report it?"

"Not that I'm aware of." And she would know if he had. Every crime report landed on her desk.

"That surprises me, seeing as how this was his second hit."

There'd been *two* incidents of unreported vandalism inside the town limits?

"Well, I can't solve crimes if people don't report them." A prickle of irritation sharpened her tone.

"I suppose, given his history, he might prefer to stay off law enforcement's radar. You do know Adam, don't you?"

She called up an image of the man she'd seen only from a distance. Six-one or two, lean, muscled, dark hair worn longish and secured with a black bandana, bad-boy stubble, usually attired in jeans and a scuffed black leather jacket. She wouldn't be surprised if he sported a few tattoos too.

In other words, a guy who'd feel at home in a motorcycle gang—and who fit the hard-edged name everyone in town except Charley called him.

Stone.

"I know who he is." When an ex-con came to town, the police chief did her homework. "But we've never spoken."

"Is that right?" Charley set three corn tortillas on the counter beside him. "He's a regular at Grace Christian. I assumed your paths had crossed."

They might have if she still went to church.

Not a subject she was inclined to discuss over fish tacos on a public street.

Interesting that the guy went to services, though. She wouldn't have pegged him as a churchgoer.

"No. I work a lot of Sunday mornings." Like all of them. On purpose.

"Well, I hope you get a handle on this vandalism before it escalates to a lot worse than spray-painted graffiti, a few broken windows, and some uprooted flowers." He gestured to the planters along the wharf as he began assembling the tacos. "Rose and her garden club members spent hours salvaging what they could of the flowers after the last incident. And quite a few of the planters are damaged. They're being held together with spit and prayers."

"We're working the case as hard as we can, but whoever is doing this is picking times when no one is around. With our small force, we can't be everywhere at once 24/7."

"I hear you." He wrapped the tacos in white paper, slid them into a brown bag, and set them on the counter in front of her. "It's a shame about Adam's place, though. He's had too many tough breaks already."

"Not much I can do if he doesn't bother to file a report." She dug out her money.

"But there might be a clue out there." Charley counted out her change and passed it over.

And maybe you should check that out.

Charley didn't have to say the words for her to get his message. The man never pushed, but he had a gentle way of nudging people in directions he thought they should go.

Lexie sighed and shoved the coins into her pocket. "I suppose I could swing by his place."

"Couldn't hurt. But he won't be home until later."

Right.

He and the rest of BJ's construction crew were in the middle of building Tracy and Michael's house out at Harbor Point Cranberries. Given the small-town grapevine, showing up at the farm out of the blue to talk to him might not be the best plan. Who knew what people would think if law enforcement tracked him down? And a man who'd paid his debt to society didn't need any more hassles.

"I could stop by after work, on my way home." Not that there was much chance she'd find a clue lying around a day after the fact. "How do you know what happened out there, anyway?"

"Adam came by for tacos yesterday afternoon. I think a Sunday visit to my humble truck is his weekly splurge."

An order of tacos from Charley's was a splurge?

The man must not be saving much of the money he earned working for BJ.

Then again, if you were starting from scratch after spending five years in prison, it could take a while to refill the well.

"Thanks for lunch." Lexie picked up the bag, the tantalizing smell tickling her nose.

"Enjoy." Charley grinned, gave her a thumbs-up, and greeted the next customer in line.

Bag in hand, Lexie eyed the tempting benches arrayed along the curving wharf—but there was a mound of paperwork waiting on her desk, and she'd procrastinated too much already.

She picked up her pace. Maybe after dinner tonight, she and Matt could come down and watch the boats for a while. He always enjoyed that—and it would be a pleasant end to the day.

Especially if her official visit with police-shy Adam Stone turned out to be less than cordial.

Someone was coming down the road to his cabin.

As the crunch of tires on gravel echoed in the quiet cove, Adam stopped sanding.

He never had visitors.

Ever.

None were invited; none came . . . except for the vandal—or vandals.

But since this visitor wasn't attempting a stealth approach, it wasn't likely another attack.

Clyde edged closer and emitted an anxious whine.

"No worries, fella." He bent and gave the pooch a reassuring pat. "It might just be someone who took a wrong turn."

He hoped.

An unfamiliar Civic nosed out of the woods a hundred feet from the cabin. The car didn't set off any alarm bells—but the uniformed figure visible through the open driver's-side window did.

His heart stumbled.

Why was a cop paying him a visit?

As if sensing his sudden apprehension, Clyde rubbed against the leg of his jeans and gave another small whine.

He bent down to stroke the dog again, keeping a wary eye on the woman who emerged from behind the wheel.

Though they'd never exchanged a word, he knew who Lexie Graham was. Everyone in town did. Not only was she the police chief, but her stint with the State Department in some far-off hot spot lent her an intriguing air of mystery. Plus, she was Hollywood-worthy stunning.

Until now, however, he'd only seen her from a distance.

As much distance as possible.

No reason to tangle with a woman who was daunting even from far away . . . and who held a lot of power in her hands.

Up close, however, she was *much* more intimidating—in a different way.

As she approached, he tried not to pay too much attention to the sleek, lustrous dark hair pulled back at her nape. Or the lush lips and model-like cheekbones. Or the tall, willowy frame that had curves in all the right places.

But ignoring all those assets was difficult.

He might be an ex-con with an ugly background who had no hope of ever finding a decent woman willing to share his life, but he was also a man.

And no man who was still breathing would be immune to the chief's obvious charms.

When she stopped six feet away from him and removed her shades, the air whooshed out of his lungs.

Her eyes were as blue as the cobalt sea on a sunny day in Sandpiper Cove and fringed by dark, sweeping lashes that belonged in a mascara ad.

"Mr. Stone, I'm Lexie Graham. I don't believe we've met." Her voice was businesslike but pleasant, with a faint trace of huskiness.

He stared at the slender, graceful fingers she extended until a nudge on the leg from Clyde jump-started his brain.

In silence, he transferred the sandpaper to his left hand and gave her fingers a firm squeeze.

After a few moments, she arched an eyebrow and flicked a glance at their still-clasped hands.

Whoops.

He released her fingers at once.

"Sorry to bother you at home, but I understand you had some vandalism here yesterday—for the second time." She surveyed the side of the workshop, where remnants of the crude graffiti clung stubbornly to the wood despite his liberal application of elbow grease.

He frowned.

How in the world did she know his place had been targeted twice?

"Who told you that?"

"The source isn't important. I'm curious why you didn't report the damage."

"There wasn't much to report."

"Breaking the law is breaking the law."

"Look . . . I don't want any trouble."

"You've already had trouble. And whoever did this could come back again."

"If they do, I'll deal with it. This isn't high-end property. They can't break anything I can't fix."

She folded her arms and adopted the wide-legged stance police used to intimidate.

It did not endear her to him.

"Dealing with lawbreakers is the responsibility of law enforcement." Her voice was harder now, and there was steel in her eyes. "And you're not the only victim. There are quite a few others—all innocent citizens who don't deserve this kind of hassle. Some are older and far less capable than you of fixing the damage."

"I'm sorry for that, but I don't want to get involved." His response came out stiff. Defiant, almost.

Not a smart attitude to take with a cop.

But instead of getting mean and nasty with him, the chief uncrossed her arms . . . let out a slow breath . . . and angled toward the water visible through the trees.

Several silent seconds ticked by.

When she turned back, her features—and tone—were friendlier. "I can understand why you'd prefer to keep your distance from trouble. But we're getting nowhere solving this. I need more clues, and I hoped you might let me nose around and see if I can spot anything that could help us identify and apprehend the culprits before these minor annoyances ratchet up and someone gets hurt."

Her request wasn't unreasonable.

And as he'd learned in the school of hard knocks, being reasonable earned you brownie points—especially if you had nothing to hide.

"Fine." He flexed some of the tightness out of his shoulders. "Search all you want, but I doubt you'll find anything. I didn't."

"Thank you. Any other damage besides that?" She motioned toward his workshop.

"Not this visit. Three weeks ago, they broke a window in the cabin and tore out one of the steps to the porch while I was at work."

"They must not have been worried about anyone hearing them." She inspected the new riser, pristine and raw compared to the weathered gray wood around it.

"This is an out-of-the-way spot, and no one's here on weekdays except my dog, Clyde."

At the mention of his name, the canine peeked out from behind his legs.

The chief's manner warmed a few more degrees

as she dropped down to one knee and held out a hand. "Hey, Clyde."

"He's skittish around . . ."

Before Adam could finish the sentence, Clyde sidled out from behind his legs, sniffed the woman's hand, and moved close enough for her to pet him.

He even gave her fingers a lick.

Adam's jaw dropped.

"You are one handsome guy, you know that?" Clyde started wagging his tail, and she chuckled —a deep, throaty sound that set off an odd flutter in Adam's stomach. "Yeah. You know it." She lifted her chin. "What breed is he?"

"Uh . . . mutt."

"Hmm." She studied him. "I see a touch of terrier . . . a dash of beagle . . . a hint of lab. Let's go with mixed breed. It sounds nicer than mutt. Don't you think so, Clyde?"

The pup gave a happy yip.

His dog had bonded with a police chief?

Go figure.

"I agree." After ruffling his fur once more, she stood. "I don't suppose the vandals left any spray cans behind."

He forced himself to shift gears. "No."

"Too bad. I'll let you get back to that while I poke around." She nodded toward the sand-paper he was holding. "You have your work cut out for you trying to get that paint off."

"Any damaged board can be smoothed out and made new with work and patience."

A flicker of surprise sparked in her blue irises. "A thought worth pondering."

With that, she began a slow circuit of the shed—Clyde trotting along at her heels.

Adam went back to sanding . . . but the mindless task left his brain free to think about the visitor roaming around his property who'd befriended his skittish dog.

If Clyde trusted her, she must be worth trusting. Animals had sound instincts about people.

Not that you needed them with the chief. She had to be trustworthy if she'd worked for the State Department. That kind of job would require all sorts of high-level security clearances and background checks.

The kind he'd never pass.

One more reminder that his past mistakes would taint him for the rest of his life and limit his opportunities to do a lot of things.

Including meet a nice woman.

What decent woman would want to associate with him?

A cloud of depression settled over him despite the shafts of spring sun filling the clearing with brightness and light.

He gritted his teeth and sanded harder.

That kind of thinking wasn't healthy. Better to

take his new life one day at a time instead of worrying about—

"I don't see anything." The chief paused a few feet away from him, brushing off her hands as she inspected his work. "I'd say you're almost down to clean wood in that spot."

He surveyed the area he'd been sanding. Only faint traces of the obscenity remained.

Too bad it wasn't as easy to sand off the rough spots in a soul.

"Yeah. I'm getting there." With the shed, anyway.

"Are you certain you don't want to file an official report on the two incidents?"

"Yes. I took care of the damage, so the owner won't have to worry about an insurance claim."

"Suit yourself." She bent down and gave Clyde one last pat. "What happened to his leg?"

"I don't know. It was twisted like that when I found him. But he's learned to compensate."

"Smart dog. Adapting is the key to survival." A few beats of silence passed—and Adam had a feeling she wasn't thinking about Clyde. Yet once she straightened up, her professional demeanor was back in place. She dug out a card and extended it. "If you change your mind, or if anything else happens, feel free to contact me. See you around, Clyde."

With a wave, she returned to her car, Clyde following a few feet behind. After putting the Civic in gear, she turned around on the gravel pad and disappeared down the road that wove among the trees.

Not until the dust settled did Clyde return to his side, tail wagging, tongue hanging out in the goofy grin that often earned him a doggie treat.

"Since when did you decide to become an extrovert? I thought I was your best bud?"

Clyde sat on his haunches and rested one paw against Adam's leg.

Who could resist that impish face?

"Apology accepted. Now let's find you a treat."

The dog followed him into the cabin, scarfed down a biscuit, and hurried back to the open door to look around.

As if he was hoping their visitor would return.

Hard to blame him.

Another visit from Lexie Graham would be welcome—even if she *was* a police chief.

But as he replaced the box of dog treats in the cabinet, fingered the woman's card, and went back to cleaning up the shed, he recognized that thought for what it was.

A fanciful wish that had no more basis in reality than the fairy tales found in a children's storybook.

❧ 2 ❧

"Everything okay?"

Lexie slid a plate into the dishwasher and faced her mother. "Fine. Why?"

"You seemed distracted at dinner." Annette Clark stowed the butter in the fridge, leaned a hip against the counter, and folded her arms. "You asked Matt twice if he wanted to go down to the wharf later."

Whoops.

She should have paid more attention to the mealtime conversation instead of letting her thoughts wander to an ex-con who lived in a shack with only a dog for company.

"Lexie?"

At the prompt, she resumed loading the dishwasher. "I'm not distracted."

Not much, anyway.

"Well, something's up if you passed on these." Her mother selected a warm chocolate chip cookie off the plate on the counter and took a bite.

"I ate too much meatloaf."

"A piece and a half isn't even a full serving."

Busted.

"Fine. I'll have a cookie."

"I'm not trying to force one on you—but that

25

overactive mind of yours is stuck on some thorny topic. Want to tell me what it is?"

No, she did not.

Especially since she had no idea *why* Adam Stone was dominating her thoughts.

"Busy day." She shifted farther away from her mom and took extra care setting the glassware in the dishwasher.

"Is that why you were late?"

"Partly."

"No more vandalism, I hope."

"As far as I know, the culprits didn't strike today."

"So why were you late?"

Her mother should have been an interrogator with the CIA.

"I, uh, had to make a stop on the way home." She closed the dishwasher and braced for the inevitable follow-up question.

It didn't come.

She peeked over her shoulder—to find her mother giving her a speculative perusal. "What's wrong?"

"There's not a thing wrong with *me*." Her mom finished off the cookie. "You, on the other hand, are very reticent tonight. And given that you didn't offer any details on your after-work stop, I'm wondering if a man could be involved."

Good grief!

How had her mother arrived at *that* conclusion?

"That's a leap, isn't it?"

"Is it?"

Annette Clark's razor-sharp maternal instincts hadn't dulled one iota through the decades.

Better to come clean rather than let her mother's imagination take wing. It wasn't as if she was trying to hide some clandestine rendezvous, after all. Adam Stone might be on her mind, but the reason had nothing to do with romance. He was the victim of a crime—and he had a lovable dog.

His mesmerizing gold-flecked brown eyes had nothing to do with her distraction.

"No man was involved . . . at least not in the context you're thinking." She took a cookie she didn't want, bit into the gooey sweetness of warm dough and soft chocolate chips, and gave her mother a cursory account of her visit to Sandpiper Cove.

"That poor man. He's certainly had his share of misfortune."

"Most of it of his own making."

"I'm not condoning whatever he did to get sent to prison—but I suspect his troubles began long before that."

"Why would you think that?"

"I've exchanged a few words with him at church. He doesn't share much about his past, but from a few remarks he's made, I got the impression his family situation was the polar opposite of the Waltons. It appears to me he's trying to make a fresh start, though, and I'm sorry to hear someone is targeting him."

"He's not the only victim."

"I know—but I expect he's the one with the flimsiest support system."

Lexie couldn't dispute that. It was the same conclusion she'd drawn as she'd wandered around his isolated property this afternoon.

However, she had no intention of feeling sorry for him. He might not have come from an ideal background, but a life of crime was a choice.

"He could make friends if he wanted to."

"I imagine that's not easy for an ex-con. I'm sure prison life—let alone what came before—can reduce a man's self-esteem to rubble. And he'll always carry a certain stigma in some folks' minds."

That was true.

But it wasn't her problem.

Nor would she let it be . . . even if seeing him up close and personal with his lame dog and feeling his almost-palpable aloneness had bothered her more than she cared to admit.

"Mom, can we go now?" Matt zoomed into the room, bristling with the megawatt energy of an almost five-year-old that added life and joy to her days.

"I'm all set." She grabbed her purse and took his hand.

"Wait." He tugged free and swung toward the

counter. "Where's the bread for Floyd and Gladys, Mamaw?"

"Right here." Her mother pulled a plastic bag of scraps out of the pantry. "You tell those seagulls not to fight over this."

"They never fight. They're married."

Her mom's lips twitched. "How do you know that?"

"Charley told me."

"Ah. Then it must be true. That man has a sixth sense about all God's creatures. You two have fun."

"Me and Mom always have fun." Matt grinned at her.

Vision misting, she smoothed down the feisty cowlick he'd inherited from his father. Touched the tip of the aquiline nose that also came from paternal genes. Joe had always said it was a sign of aristocratic blood—and had promised to take her to visit the ruined castle in Scotland he claimed had been inhabited by his noble ancestors.

She'd never known for certain whether he was teasing about that trip or not.

Now she never would.

"Hey . . . Mom." Matt squeezed her fingers, his expression suddenly solemn. "Are you gonna cry?"

"No, of course not." She forced up the corners of her mouth and willed the pressure behind her eyes to subside. She'd shed her last tear more than two years ago. Made peace with the fact that love and romance weren't in her future. Learned to live with the loneliness that plagued her even here, in this house she shared with the two people she loved most.

There was no reason for this out-of-the-blue, sweeping surge of melancholy . . . and longing.

"Your face got kind of scrunchy." Matt tightened his grip on her fingers, his forehead knotted. "Kind of like Darcy's did at Sunday school when her dad was late to pick her up. I think she was 'fraid he wasn't gonna come. But you don't have to worry about being by yourself. You got me and Mamaw."

"I know that." She squeezed his fingers. "And what could be better than living in the same house with my two favorite people in all the world? You want another cookie for the road?"

"Yeah!"

"Here you go." Her mother handed him one, and Lexie let him pull her toward the door. "Be careful, you two."

"You want to come, Mom?" She tossed the invitation over her shoulder.

"No. I have an emergency garden club meeting tonight. We have to decide what to do about the damaged planters on the wharf."

They were back to the vandalism topic—reminding her again of the man she'd visited this afternoon.

"I have every confidence you enterprising ladies will come up with a solution."

"I hope so. And by the way . . . Matt's right. You do have the two of us in your corner—but there's always room for one more, should someone special come along."

"Let's go, Mom!" Matt gave her another tug.

She followed her son through the door without responding to her mother's comment.

Because the woman who'd nurtured her for thirty-five years was wrong.

There wasn't room for anyone else in her life.

Love was too risky.

Even if she felt lonelier tonight than she had since the early days after the tragedy that had changed her world forever.

"May I join you for lunch?"

From his perch on the dike surrounding one of the budding beds at Harbor Point Cranberries, Adam shaded his eyes and looked up at Luis Dominguez. "Sure. I didn't think you were working this afternoon."

"I finish early at school, so I come out. This is a big project, and I know BJ needs many hands. After all she has done for me, I do not wish to let her down."

"Yeah. I hear you." The construction firm owner had done no less for him than she had for the Cuban refugee who settled onto the dike two feet

31

away. More, in truth. Giving a job to an educated man like Luis, who'd led an upstanding life and endured great hardships through no fault of his own, was a lot less dicey than taking a chance on an ex-con. "How's school going?"

"Very well. The classes, they are not difficult. It is wonderful to be involved in medicine again."

Being a paramedic wasn't the same as being a doctor, though. It had to be tough for a prominent physician from Cuba to accept such a lesser role.

Yet the fortysomething immigrant never complained about his lot in life. Instead, he was grateful for any blessings that came his way.

There was a lesson to be learned there.

"Eleanor fixed you a great lunch." He motioned toward the man's hearty meat pie and generous slice of fudge cake. What a difference from the days when he'd packed an extra sandwich for cash-strapped Luis so the man would have more than a piece of fruit for lunch.

"Yes. She is a fine woman. I am fortunate to share her home." He moved aside some napkins in his lunch pail and extracted a second piece of cake. "She send some dessert for you too."

The elderly woman often did that—and her kindness toward a man she knew only through an occasional exchange of greetings at church never failed to surprise him.

"Thanks." He took the cake.

"I did not see BJ at the house site." Luis dove into his meat pastry.

"She was here all morning, but she had a dress fitting in Coos Bay at lunch. She said she might be a little late getting back."

"Ah, yes. The wedding dress. Her marriage is getting close."

"Yeah." Eleven days, to be precise. A week from Saturday.

"I am happy for her. Eric is a good man."

"He seems to be." He and BJ were at church every Sunday, but Adam never lingered long afterward. Charley spoke highly of him, though— and that counted for a lot.

"You would be welcome to ride to the wedding with Eleanor and me. We would not mind picking you up—and I expect BJ will put us at the same table for the dinner."

Adam ate the last bite of his sandwich and crumpled up the plastic wrap.

Just tell him, Stone. You knew this would come up eventually. Get it over with.

He took a swig from the bottle of water he refilled every morning from the tap and watched Shep and Ziggy chase bog rats in the adjacent bed, their barks echoing in the quiet air. "I'm not going to the wedding."

In the silence that followed, he could feel Luis watching him.

"You have told this to BJ?"

No. He'd been too much of a coward to decline the invitation to her face. And the response card was sitting on the table in his kitchen, the four-days-away due date staring at him accusingly every time he walked past.

"Not yet."

Nor had she asked him if he was coming—although she'd dropped plenty of hints she expected to see him there.

"She will be disappointed."

Like he didn't know that.

"No one will miss me in that crowd." The lame excuse sounded hollow even to his ears.

"Each person she invited is special to her. An important part of her life. She will notice you are not there."

And it will hurt her.

Luis didn't have to say the words for Adam to hear the man's implied rebuke.

There was no rebuttal to it, either. His coworker was right. Considering all BJ had done for him, he owed it to her to show up for her wedding.

But he wasn't fit for a high-class gathering like that.

"I do have a present for her." That counted for something, didn't it?

"A present is not the same as your presence."

The man's gentle reproach twisted his gut.

He opened the cake he no longer wanted, more to keep his fingers busy than because he had

34

any interest in the treat. "It's not my scene, Luis."

"You do not like weddings?"

"I've never been to one."

"Then how can you know it is not your scene?"

He broke off a piece of the cake and popped it in his mouth . . . but even Eleanor's sweet fudge frosting couldn't chase away the bitterness on his tongue.

"Look . . . there will be a lot of nice people there. I won't fit in."

"You see many of those people at church on Sundays, do you not?"

"This isn't the same. The reception is a social event, not a church service."

"You think they will treat you different at a wedding than they treat you at church?"

He had no idea—and he didn't want to find out.

"People might feel awkward if an ex-con shows up."

"You are an invited guest. Sometimes you must give people an opportunity to put the faith they express on Sundays into practice."

That sounded fine in theory—but Adam wasn't certain it would hold up in the real world.

And he'd had enough rejection to last ten life-times.

He switched to a practical argument.

"I don't have anything to wear to a fancy shindig like that. I've never owned a suit and tie, and I'm not about to buy duds like that to wear once."

"BJ will not care what you wear."

Maybe not, but others would judge him by his inappropriate attire.

"I can't go in jeans."

"Then get some new clothes. When I move in with Eleanor, I did not have much money. She wanted to buy me some better clothes, but my pride would not let me to accept her charity. She did not push—but she left a flyer for a Coos Bay resale shop in my room. They have good clothing at very cheap prices." He rattled off the name of the store.

Great. Now he was out of excuses.

Except for the real one.

And he wasn't going to admit he was afraid.

"I'll think about it."

"A wise choice." Luis started on his cake and motioned to the piece Adam had barely touched. "You must eat that. Eleanor will ask me how you liked it."

At Luis's prodding, he tried to do justice to the older woman's offering.

They ate in silence until both were down to crumbs.

"Please tell her I enjoyed it—and thank her for me." Adam stuffed the plastic wrap into the brown sack with the rest of his trash.

"I will do that. She may be old, with many limitations, but she still has gifts that can brighten people's lives. As we all do."

"Not all."

"Yes." Luis fixed him with an intent look. "All."

"I have nothing to offer." His voice rasped.

"That is not true. You have many fine qualities. Kindness. Compassion. Strength."

He snorted, crushing the bag into a tight ball. "Strength? How can you say that, with all the mistakes I've made? I'm weak, not strong."

"You survived those mistakes—and became a better person. That is strength." Luis's declaration rang with conviction. "As for compassion and kindness . . . I remember the man who gave me food he could not spare when I was hungry. Who saved a dog no one wanted and nursed him back to health. Who never says no if a charitable group like Helping Hands calls to tell him someone needs assistance."

"Anyone would do those things."

"No, my friend, you are wrong. And your actions say a lot about your character. If you give others a chance, they too will see what I see."

Reverend Baker had offered similar encouragement during their last conversation before he was released from prison.

Yet life had taught him a different lesson—and it was much easier . . . and safer . . . to continue with the solitary existence he'd carved out for himself.

But it was also lonely.

And getting lonelier every day.

"I will be happy to write out the directions to the resale shop for you." Luis wiped his fingers on a paper napkin and closed his lunch box.

Adam didn't respond.

Nor did his lunch companion mention the subject again as they worked together during the afternoon—but when Adam finished for the day and returned to his car, he found the carefully written directions tucked under his windshield wiper.

For a moment he was tempted to wad up the slip of paper and toss it into the trash can beside the drive.

But in the end, he tucked it in his pocket.

Just in case he had a change of heart.

❧ 3 ❧

That car was going way too fast.

Lexie caught no more than a glimpse of the vehicle in her rearview mirror as it zoomed past the intersection of Highway 101 and Sea Rose Lane on the outskirts of town, but she didn't need a radar gun to know the driver was paying zero attention to the posted speed limit.

Executing a tight U-turn, she hit her siren and lights and took off after the lawbreaker. Issuing a ticket hadn't been on the agenda for her final patrol this Thursday afternoon, but she couldn't ignore that kind of excessive speed. Some serious fog was rolling in, and the coastal highway would be more treacherous than usual.

She gained on the car ahead of her—but only after mashing the gas pedal to the floor. Forty . . . fifty . . . sixty . . . seventy . . . seventy-two.

Man.

This driver was about to get one hefty fine.

As she approached the car, it slowed. Eased to the side of the road. Stopped.

She pulled in behind it, noting the make and color through the swirls of fog.

A dark-blue Kia.

The same kind of car Adam Stone drove.

The left front door flew open. An instant later the driver shot out and raced toward her, his eyes frenzied.

Like he was on drugs.

It was Stone.

Nerves vibrating, she scrambled out of the patrol car and reached for her gun.

"Please . . . I need to get to Coos Bay. My dog's . . ." He lurched to a stop and slowly lifted his palms, eying her hand on the gun. "Chief Graham, I . . . the vandals came back. Clyde's hurt. I need to get him to my vet in Coos B-bay." He choked on the last word. "I know I was speeding, but it's an emergency."

The man was distraught but lucid, his agitation sourced from panic, not drugs.

Lexie relaxed her grip on the pistol and left it in its holster. "How bad is he?"

"I . . . I don't know. He has a gash on his head and he seems disoriented. He's on the front seat."

"Show me." She gestured for him to precede her. Her gut told her his story was true, but in this business, it was better to back up instincts with proof.

He led the way to the Kia, moving aside at the door to give her a view of the dog.

Clyde was on the passenger seat, as Stone had said. There was blood on the blanket cocooning him. As she peeked in, the dog whimpered. He was shivering so hard the whole blanket was shaking.

Beside her, she could feel Stone quivering almost as much as the injured dog.

The man was in no condition to drive.

"I can get you there faster. Lock your doors and put on your emergency flashers. Pick Clyde up and get in the back of the patrol car. Hold him as steady as possible."

Without a word, Stone followed her instructions.

He hesitated only once, at the door of the cruiser. As if he was recalling other unpleasant rides in the back of a police vehicle and was loath to revisit those memories.

But he straightened his shoulders and slid in anyway, cradling Clyde in his arms.

The trip to Coos Bay took twenty minutes— longer than she would have liked, but the best she could do in the fog. Lexie made no attempt to talk until they reached the veterinary clinic.

"Are you certain this place will still be open?" She tossed out the question as she swung into the parking lot.

"I called my vet as soon as I found Clyde. He said he'd wait."

As promised, the man greeted Stone at the door and ushered them inside. "You got here fast."

"I had some help."

"I see that." The man nodded to her. "Speed is always important in a medical emergency. Go ahead and take him back. First room on the right."

"Can I stay with him?"

"Absolutely. You and I have been down this road before. I think you can handle it."

Stone paused at the door that led to the examining rooms and turned to her. "You don't have to wait. This could take a while. I can call someone to pick me up."

That was a viable plan. There were people in town who would be glad to come to Stone's aid— Luis, BJ, Reverend Baker.

But somehow she knew he wouldn't ask any of them for help. Rather than impose, he'd spend his hard-earned money on an expensive cab ride back to his car.

"I always see every incident through to the end." She sat in one of the chairs in the waiting room to emphasize that point. "I'll be here when you and Clyde are ready to leave."

Several emotions passed through his eyes. Gratitude was among them—but it was colored with other feelings that came and went too fast to identify.

Whatever they were, though, they left her feeling breathless.

How weird was that?

As Stone disappeared down the hall and the vet closed the door behind them, she pulled out her cell. Her mom and Matt would have to eat without her . . . but unless she told her mother she was stopping for a bite elsewhere, there'd be a plate waiting in the oven for her, however late she arrived home.

A heaping dose of TLC had been one of the perks of moving back to Hope Harbor.

She keyed in the number and leaned back in the chair. As Stone had said, depending on the vet's assessment, this could be a long wait. And based on the bond between the man and his dog, he wasn't going to leave without Clyde.

But getting a statement about this latest incident of vandalism was important—and the fresher the incident, the more inclined he might be to file a report. So she had to wait.

Right.

At the skeptical retort from her conscience, she frowned. What was with that? She *did* have official business with the man.

Yeah—but that's not your only motive for sticking around.

She huffed out a breath.

Fine. She could admit the truth—to herself, anyway.

For some obscure reason, the man had touched her heart.

Maybe it was seeing that forlorn shack he called home.

Maybe it was discovering he'd adopted a lame dog—a fellow misfit in society.

Maybe it was the resignation in his demeanor when he'd told her there was no reason to report the vandalism . . . as if he deserved to be a target.

Maybe it was his frantic worry over Clyde tonight—and the soft words of comfort he'd offered as they'd sped toward Coos Bay.

Who knew why she was drawn to him?

One thing for sure, however. As much as she'd craved TLC when she'd come back to Hope Harbor, this man needed nurturing a lot more than she had.

And while she couldn't make everything right in his world, at least she could keep him company tonight so he didn't have to face this emergency alone.

"He should be fine, Stone." The vet stripped off his latex gloves and tossed them in a trash container in the examining room. "The gash will heal, and the concussion appears to be mild. Expect him to be a little wobbly at first, but that should pass fast."

"I'll watch over him. Thank you again for waiting around tonight." Adam pulled out his wallet.

"Goes with the job." The man waved away the cash he extracted. "Check with the office tomorrow on the fee. I leave money matters to my bookkeeper." He rummaged around in a drawer and pulled out some antibiotic samples. "These should hold you until I remove the stitches." He reached into another cabinet and gathered up several packets. "This is a topical ointment to keep the stitches from itching. We don't want Clyde to start scratching."

"Thanks." Every free sample helped. Who knew how much tonight's emergency would set him back? And he'd only last month finished paying off the bill for Clyde's close encounter with a car.

But the expense didn't matter as long as the dog recovered.

He followed the vet to the waiting room, a woozy Clyde in his arms.

Lexie stood as soon as he appeared in the doorway. "How is he?"

"The doc says he'll recover. He's got a . . ." His voice rasped.

"Concussion and eight stitches." The vet finished his sentence. "He should be good as new after a couple days of rest and some close observation over the next twenty-four hours."

"That's great news." Her features relaxed as she crossed to him and stroked Clyde's ear.

A faint fragrance wafted up to Adam's nose, much more appealing than the antiseptic odor that had permeated the examining room. It smelled like . . . not flowers exactly. More like freshness and dew and spring and . . .

". . . ever you're ready."

He blinked and tuned back into the conversation. "What?"

"I said, we can leave whenever you're ready." Lexie jingled her keys.

"I'm ready now."

After thanking the vet again, he followed her out.

"There's more room in the back, but if you can squeeze into the front with Clyde on your lap, you're welcome to sit up there." She motioned toward the passenger seat as she unlocked the car doors.

"We'll fit." If he never again rode in the back of a squad car it would be too soon.

And he had a feeling this woman knew that.

"I'll get the door." She circled around the car ahead of him and pulled it wide.

Keeping a firm grip on Clyde, he lowered himself gingerly into the seat. The dog snuffled and snuggled against him but otherwise made no sound as Lexie pulled out the seat belt for him, waiting while he adjusted it.

Once he was strapped in, she disappeared around the rear of the cruiser. Ten seconds later she took her place behind the wheel and started the engine.

"Sorry to keep you out this late." He squinted at the clock on the dashboard as she pulled out of the parking lot. "Seven thirty must be long past your quitting time."

"Like being a vet, this job isn't nine-to-five." She pointed the car toward 101. "Have you had dinner?"

"Not yet."

"Me neither. I need to fill out some paperwork on this latest incident. We can do that over a pizza at your place, if you don't mind calling in the order while I drive. There's a great place south of Bandon. Looks like a hole in the wall, but Frank has a magic touch. You *are* going to file a report on this incident, aren't you?"

It wasn't really a question—not that she'd have to twist his arm. Whoever was wreaking havoc in the town could mess with his stuff all they liked, but they'd crossed a line when they'd hurt his dog.

"Yeah. I am. I can fix myself some dinner after you leave, though."

"Suit yourself, but my stomach isn't willing to wait for dinner." She pulled her cell off her belt. "Half of it—or more—will go to waste if you don't help me eat it . . . unless you don't like pizza?"

"I like it fine." Restaurant food wasn't a treat his tight budget accommodated very often, but he could spring for half a pizza.

"Order whatever you like. I'm not too picky." She held out the phone and rattled off the number. "But if you need a suggestion, the supreme lives up to its name."

He tapped in the number and followed her recommendation on the order, hesitating at the request for a credit card number. "Um . . . can we pay cash?"

"Is that Frank?" Lexie glanced over at him.

He repeated her question into the phone.

"Yeah. Who's asking?" The gruff-voiced man didn't sound any too friendly.

"I'm with Lexie Graham. The police chief in—"

"This order's for Lexie?" The man's tone did an about-face. "When do you need it?"

"Fifteen minutes?"

"It'll be waiting." The line went dead.

"I take it you're a friend of Frank's." He handed her back the phone.

"More like a longtime customer. Back in high school, I used to hang out at his place with my friends if Charley's was closed." She slipped the phone back onto her belt.

"He sounds like a grouch."

"It's only an act. Under that crusty exterior, he has a heart of gold."

"A reminder not to judge a book by its cover, I suppose."

"Yeah." She shifted in her seat. "So . . . do you have any idea what happened to Clyde?"

"No. He was semiconscious when I found him halfway between the woods and the shed. I'm guessing he heard or saw strangers and tried to get to his swinging door. The vet thinks someone might have thrown a rock at him." His voice hardened.

"Any other damage?"

"I don't know. That wasn't my priority."

"I'll do a quick sweep tonight, but darkness hides a lot. I'll come back in the morning and do a more thorough search."

"Fine with me. But I'm not optimistic. They haven't left any clues up until now."

"If people commit enough crimes, they eventually make a mistake."

She fell silent, and Adam didn't attempt to keep the conversation going. What was there to talk about beyond the vandalism? They had nothing in common. While she'd been going to pizza parties with her friends and checking out colleges and planning for the high school prom, he'd been on the street laying the groundwork for a prison sentence.

Holding Clyde close, he tried not to let that bother him as they drove through the foggy night.

But he couldn't shake the heavy cloak of regret that weighed him down.

Ten minutes later, she pulled into a parking lot beside a small, rustic building that sported a neon sign. "What kind of soda do you like?"

"Sprite. Regular. But I can drink water."

"With pizza?" She gave him a get-real look. "Sit tight."

Ten minutes later, she was back. After stowing the flat box and a brown bag on the back seat, she retook her place behind the wheel.

A savory aroma filled the car, setting off a rumble in his stomach.

Even Clyde lifted his nose and sniffed.

When had he last had a decent piece of pizza? The cardboard-crust stuff they'd served in prison didn't count . . . and before that? It had to be years.

This treat would be worth every penny it siphoned out of his budget.

"Your car's coming up, but I'd suggest we leave it for now and get Clyde home." Lexie waved a hand toward the opposite shoulder as she guided the cruiser down the dark highway. "I can have an officer ride back with me after we're finished to pick it up."

"I don't want to put anyone out."

"Part of our job is helping citizens in emergencies. This qualifies. Besides, you live in Hope Harbor—and in case you haven't figured it out by now, we take care of our own."

Yeah, he'd noticed that.

Except he wasn't one of them. He was an outsider who lived on the fringes of the small community.

But if she was willing to help him out tonight, he'd accept her generosity—for Clyde's sake. "Thanks."

She acknowledged his acceptance with a nod and continued past his car . . . past the mist-enshrouded town . . . finally turning off 101 to follow the gravel one-lane road that led to his cabin.

"Stay put. I'll get your door." She set the brake, slid out of the car, and circled around to his side.

As soon as she opened the door, he released his seat belt and swung his legs out, trying not to jostle the dog. Clyde shifted in his arms, emitting a tiny whimper.

"It's okay, buddy. We're home."

He stood as smoothly as he could with forty-three pounds of limp fur in his arms, then started toward the door, Lexie on his heels and . . .

Wait.

Lexie on his heels?

His step faltered.

No woman had ever visited his cabin—and

50

living alone, with only a dog for company, didn't give a man much incentive to keep his space neat and tidy.

What kind of stuff had he left lying around?

"Where's your key?" Lexie stopped beside the door.

Uh-oh.

Another concern took priority.

His arms were full, and he didn't want to set Clyde on the ground.

"It's, uh, in my pocket. I'll need to set Clyde down and—"

"Which one?"

"Front right. But I can—"

Without waiting for him to finish, she slipped a couple of fingers into the pocket he'd indicated, wiggled them around until she snagged his keys, and pulled out the ring.

The maneuver took all of four seconds.

Four up-close-and-personal seconds.

But if the cozy contact had any effect on her, it wasn't apparent. She seemed cool and calm as she inserted the key in the lock, twisted it, and pushed the door open.

What else could he do except walk through— and try to beat back a raging surge of testosterone?

"I'll grab the pizza and do a fast circuit of the cabin and shed." She closed the door, leaving him alone to grapple with his hormones.

After settling Clyde into his basket next to the

double bed that was tucked into a corner of the one-room cabin, he stood and took several long, slow breaths.

Get a grip, Stone. You're acting like an adolescent.

Forcing his lungs to keep expanding and contracting, he gave the place a cursory scan. The bed was made—sort of—and there weren't any dirty dishes in the sink. A bowl of cereal and a cup of coffee didn't create much mess at breakfast. The basket of dirty clothes over by the wall, waiting to go to the Laundromat, wasn't too offensive. At least there was no underwear strewn around.

The small wooden table held the most clutter.

He gathered up the loose sheets of paper, pencils, rulers, and sketches as Lexie reappeared in the doorway with their dinner.

"You can put that here." He bent to brush off the table with his palm.

No.

Bad move.

He should wash his hands, after all he'd been through with Clyde tonight.

"Let me, uh, wipe it down first."

He set the papers aside, moved to the sink, and scrubbed his hands with a bar of soap. Then he dampened a paper towel with hot water, scoured the top of the scratched wooden table, and pulled out one of the two chairs.

"Thanks." She dropped into it, set the pizza down, and began unpacking the brown bag. "Frank threw in some plates and napkins along with our sodas."

That was helpful. He had only two chipped dinner plates, no soda, and paper towels that did double duty as napkins and dishcloths.

He took the chair across from her, staring as she flipped up the top of the flat box.

Wow.

That was a pizza.

"Dig in." She helped herself to a piece.

He didn't need a second invitation.

The first bite was a taste of heaven. So was the second . . . and third . . . and every mouthful that followed.

This was the best pizza he'd ever eaten.

"I'll have to tell Frank he has a new fan."

As he claimed his third piece, he surfaced from his gastronomic euphoria long enough to notice Lexie's amused expression.

He counted how many slices were missing from the box.

Four.

Meaning she'd only taken one—and part of it was still on her plate.

Had he chowed down in record time . . . or was she a slow eater?

"Take as much as you want." She picked up her can of soda. "No matter how hungry I am, I can never manage more than two or three pieces of Frank's supreme. It's super filling."

For her, maybe.

He could easily down three-fourths of the pizza.

But he didn't want to make a pig of himself.

Better slow the pace. Give some of the food he'd ingested a chance to reach his stomach and take the edge off his hunger.

"It's also amazing." He took a more measured bite of the piece he'd picked up.

"I agree. So tell me about this place." She swept a hand around the cabin. "I know it belongs to some guy from Eugene who used to come out on weekends. How did you end up here?"

"Reverend Baker lined it up for me. The owner's job took him to Europe for a few years." He wiped his lips on a napkin. "I signed a lease, and I pay rent. It's legit."

A flicker of distress sparked in her irises. "I didn't mean to suggest it wasn't. I was just making small talk while you finish your dinner."

Small talk.

Yeah, he'd heard of that.

But it wasn't one of his skills.

Classy, cultured people—like this woman— probably perfected the art of chitchat early on . . . about the age he'd been learning to dodge his old man's vile temper and pilfer cash from unattended purses.

One more indication he was out of his element with this woman.

"Sorry." He picked up a stray mushroom and put it on top of his pizza. "Most of the people in uniform who've asked me questions in the past had an ulterior motive. I'm not used to being on the other side of the law."

"But that's where you've been since you came to town, as far as I know."

Was that a question . . . or was he overreacting again?

Best not to take any chances.

"That's where I've been—and it's where I plan to stay." He met her gaze straight on.

"I assumed that." Her eyes were steady too. "And it's one of the reasons I'm especially angry you've been hit by vandalism multiple times."

"My location makes me an easy target."

"I think it's more than that."

Some of his appetite evaporated.

It was one thing to know deep inside that he'd never escape his past; it was another to be constantly reminded of it.

He picked up his can of soda, the aluminum crinkling beneath his fingers. "I can't change my history."

"None of us can." Her features contorted for a brief moment before she composed her face. "But people who are trying to follow the rules have a right to live without fear. Tell me what happened tonight." She dug a notebook out of her uniform pocket.

He surveyed her plate. For someone who'd claimed to be hungry, she hadn't eaten much. Did a single piece of pizza even qualify as a dinner?

"There isn't much to tell. We finished up at work a little early, and I got home about five. I called Clyde. He didn't come, which set off a red alert. He never wanders far from the house and shed, and he's always waiting for me at the end of the day. I didn't see any sign of vandalism, but I was getting bad vibes. Less than a minute later, I found him. I called the vet and took off. You know the rest."

"Is there anyone in the area who could be trying to settle a score with you?"

"No. Other than going to work and church, I keep to myself—and everyone I've met has been friendly."

She furrowed her brow and took another piece of pizza.

He did too. Despite his flagging appetite, it was too good to waste.

But when Clyde whimpered a moment later, Adam sprang to his feet and crossed the room in a few long strides.

"Is he all right?" Lexie rose too.

He bent down. Clyde had already drifted back to sleep.

"I think so. The vet gave me a list of signs to

watch for over the next twenty-four hours, and he hasn't shown any of them yet." He scrubbed a hand down his face and rejoined her. "I can keep a close eye on him tonight, but I may need to call BJ in the morning and see if she can spare me tomorrow." The loss of a day's wages would hurt, but what choice did he have?

"There might be another option."

A slight nuance in Lexie's tone put him on alert. She sounded kind of . . . nervous.

Not an emotion he'd have expected from this strong, in-charge woman.

"Like what?" Caution colored his question.

"Well . . ." She wiped a smear of tomato sauce off her hand with her napkin, giving the task more attention than it deserved. "My son loves animals. So does my mom. They have nothing on their agenda tomorrow. I called them while I was outside, and they'd be happy to watch Clyde while you're at work." Her offer came out a bit breathless and unsteady.

Kind of like how he felt as he mulled over the unexpected suggestion.

Why was the police chief's family willing to watch his dog? Wasn't she worried about having an ex-con in her house? Exposing her son to someone with his background? Offending her neighbors?

Hard as he tried to absorb this surprising turn of events, it wouldn't compute.

"Why?" The question was out before he could stop it.

"Why not?"

"I'm not . . . most people don't . . . no one's ever . . ." His voice trailed off.

"I told you earlier—here in Hope Harbor, we take care of our own."

"I'm not one of your own."

"You live here. You work here. You go to church here. You're one of us—and you belong."

An odd tightness gripped his chest as her firm but gentle assurance seeped into his soul.

He'd never belonged anywhere. Never been wanted—by anyone.

The temptation to accept was strong . . . but her kindness was more than he deserved.

As if sensing his imminent refusal, the chief spoke again.

"My son would consider it a treat. A dog has been on his wish list for months. This would be the next best thing." She linked her fingers on the table and watched him. "Unless you're looking for an excuse to take a day off."

He'd love a day off—but not without pay. Even if BJ balked at docking him, he couldn't take money for work he didn't do.

"For the record, there aren't any strings attached —or ulterior motives."

As Lexie tossed his earlier comment back at him, heat crept up his cheeks.

Don't labor over this, Stone. Be grateful and take the help.

"All right. Thank you." His acceptance came out stiff.

"You've just made a little boy's day." Lexie stood. If she noticed his lack of graciousness, she gave no indication. "What time do you want to come by?"

"I'm supposed to be out at the farm by seven thirty." He rose too. "Is seven too early?"

"No. I'm always up by six. And I doubt my son is going to get a lot of sleep tonight once he knows for sure a dog is coming to visit tomorrow. He's already a bundle of energy; now he'll be hyper."

An alarm bell rang in his mind.

Hyper kid.

Injured, gun-shy dog.

Maybe not the best combination.

"Umm . . . your son is about four, right?" From the bits and pieces of town scuttlebutt he'd picked up, it sounded as if she'd come home to Hope Harbor three or four years ago with an infant in tow.

"Almost five."

"Clyde won't be up to playing—and he's very cautious around strangers. Based on his scars, I think his original owner abused him. This might not be the best fit."

Her eyes softened. "I'll have a long talk with

Matt tonight—and my mom's a diligent supervisor. She'll keep a close watch on everything. Clyde will be in safe hands. Trust me."

A police officer was asking *him* to trust *her*.

Shouldn't it be the other way around?

Why did his world suddenly feel out of kilter?

"Hey . . . it'll be fine." She touched the knuckles he'd clenched around the back of his chair.

His chest tightened again as he focused on her graceful fingers, warm against his skin.

"Okay." He choked out his assent.

She broke contact and walked to the door. "I'll see you tomorrow."

A few seconds later, the lock clicked. A minute after that, an engine started. Gravel crunched. Car lights swept across the cabin.

Then everything returned to normal.

Except his heart.

For in the deepest, darkest corner, an ember of hope sprang to life . . . and the shadows that had filled his life for as long as he could remember receded a tiny bit.

Hands braced on the table, Adam lowered himself into his chair. Was there a chance this town might actually live up to its name? Might he find hope here . . . and a new beginning?

Given his history, that would be a miracle.

But for the first time since he'd walked out of the prison gate eighteen months ago, he allowed himself to believe in that possibility.

❧ 4 ❧

"When's he gonna get here, Mom?" Matt hopped from one foot to the other in front of the kitchen window, leaning sideways to catch a glimpse of the street.

"Not for a few minutes. Come and eat your breakfast." Lexie added a dash of cinnamon to her son's oatmeal.

"I want to watch for him."

"Watching won't make him get here any faster." Her mom walked over, took his hand, and towed him toward the table as Lexie set the bowl in his place.

"I want to be ready."

"Matt." Lexie telegraphed a silent warning.

He stuck out his lower lip . . . but gave up the fight and climbed onto the chair.

"Besides, you're more than ready. You've been up for an hour." She poured him a glass of juice and stifled a yawn.

"Tired?" Her mother patted her shoulder as she passed.

"Short night. Someone in this house didn't drift off until almost midnight."

"I remember those days." Grinning, her mother lifted the empty coffee mug Lexie had set on the counter while she finished making Matt's oatmeal. "Want a refill?"

"Yes. Thanks."

"Can I go look out the window again?" Matt wiggled around on his chair and gave her a hopeful glance.

"After you finish your oatmeal and juice."

"Aww, Mom."

"Eat."

He sighed—but began shoveling in the contents of his bowl and gulping down the juice at warp speed.

"Hey! Slow down. I don't want to have to practice the Heimlich maneuver this morning."

"What's the Heim—"

A car door banged.

Matt vaulted out of his chair and raced toward the living room.

Breakfast was over.

"We'll make it up with a midmorning snack and hearty lunch." Her mom patted her arm and sipped her own coffee. "Never try to suppress the enthusiasm of youth. It's a blessing."

"Ya think?"

"From the perspective of grandmotherhood . . . yes." She winked.

"He's coming! He's coming!" Matt's pitch rose to a squeal.

"I better do a fast refresher on the ground rules." Lexie set her cup on the table and joined her son at the front window. "You remember what we talked about last night, right? Clyde got hurt and doesn't feel too good. He needs to rest and stay quiet today. Mr. Stone said he's shy too, so you have to give him some space until he gets used to you."

"I 'member." He started hopping from one foot to the other again, excitement pinging off him.

Oh, brother.

Maybe this hadn't been such a bright idea after all.

"And those folks in Washington claim we have an energy crisis." Her mother strolled in and smiled at her grandson.

"Not in this house."

Lexie leaned over her son's head and peeked out the window. Stone was walking up the path to the front door, Clyde cradled in his arms. Only one of the dog's ears was visible among the folds of the blanket wrapped around him.

"I'll get the door." Her mother detoured that direction.

By the time Stone arrived at the threshold, all three of them were waiting in the foyer.

He hesitated, his gaze shifting from Lexie to her mother and son, recognition dawning in his eyes.

"Nice to see you, Stone." Her mother swept a hand toward the foyer, ushering him in.

"We've met at church."

"Yes. Annette and Matt. We're happy to welcome you to our home."

"I didn't realize you all were . . . that you were related to Annette and Matt." Stone directed the last part of the comment to Lexie as he entered.

"I guess I should have mentioned it last night." Frowning, she flicked a speck of lint off her knife-creased uniform slacks. Of course she should have mentioned it. Stone would have felt more comfortable knowing his dog would be spending the day with people he'd already met.

But once she'd reached into his pocket to retrieve those keys and encountered solid muscle a layer of denim couldn't disguise, the left side of her brain had short-circuited.

And that moment when she'd touched his strong, lean fingers to reassure him Clyde would be safe with a rambunctious youngster?

Whew.

Her own fingers had tingled all the way home.

All of which was nuts.

This man was *not* her type. He was a felon, for pity's sake. On top of that, the dark, brooding, shaggy-haired look wasn't her style. Give her a clean-cut, spit-and-polish guy any day.

Like Joe.

So what was with the unnerving vibes she got whenever she saw—or thought about—the man standing in their foyer?

"Mom!"

A tug on her hand, and the frustration in her son's voice, pulled her back to the present.

"What?"

"Mr. Stone asked you where he should put Clyde."

"Oh." Everyone was watching her, and heat rose on her cheeks. "The kitchen might be best. Mom's in there a lot and can keep tabs on him. Does that work for you?" She angled toward her mother.

"Sounds like a plan."

Lexie ignored the subtle twinkle in the older woman's eyes and led the group back to the kitchen, stopping en route to pull a small throw rug out of the coat closet in the foyer.

Once in the kitchen, she set the rug in the corner of the bright room, out of the path of traffic but close to the action. Then she moved aside.

Stone took her place, lowered himself to one knee, and gently set down his blanket-wrapped bundle.

Clyde poked his head out and surveyed his audience.

"Oh, wow!" Matt squatted down beside Stone, his voice hushed. "What a great dog." He reached out to pet the pooch.

Clyde whined and burrowed back under the blanket.

Her son's face fell.

"Honey . . . remember what I told you." Lexie dropped down next to him on the other side. "He's very shy. You have to give him a chance to get used to you before you can make friends."

"This should help." Stone pulled a dog biscuit from his pocket. "He likes these a lot. I have a few more in the car I'll bring in. If you give him three or four over the next couple of hours, you'll be friends forever. Want me to show you how to do it so he doesn't get scared?"

"Yeah!"

"Hang on to this for a second."

Her son took the biscuit and clutched it tight.

"Clyde . . . come on out, boy. You're among friends. Let us see that handsome face again. I have a treat for you."

At the word *treat,* the dog peeked out and sniffed.

"It's right here, boy. Matt, hold it out a little bit farther."

Her son complied . . . and the dog retreated under the blanket.

"I don't think he likes me." Matt's lower lip quivered.

"He's going to like you fine after he gets to know you. He's just scared. His last owner wasn't very nice to him, and when he meets new people, he's afraid they might be mean too."

Lexie gave the man a surreptitious scan over her son's head. He might be talking about Clyde, but she had a feeling that summed up his own mind-set too.

"He doesn't have to be 'fraid. I won't be mean to him."

"I know. Let's try it again. This time, hold it here"—Stone positioned her son's hand—"and let him come to you. He'll probably sniff your fingers first. Stay real still while he does that. If he takes the treat, don't try to pet him unless he comes close to you, okay?"

"Okay."

Stone sat cross-legged on the floor. Matt followed the man's example, imitating him move for move.

Lexie rose and eased back. No need to hover. Stone had this under control.

"Come on, boy. We've got a treat for you."

The blanket twitched—and once again Clyde nosed aside the folds.

"Good boy. Come on out."

Clyde inspected the treat Matt was holding . . . looked at Stone . . . and stayed where he was.

"I don't think he's gonna come out." Matt's whisper was laced with disappointment.

"Give him another minute."

Ten seconds dragged by.

Fifteen.

Twenty.

Uh-oh.

Lexie knew her son's patience threshold—and it was about to be breached.

But much to her surprise, he remained motion-less, emulating the man beside him.

Half a minute in, their persistence paid off.

Belly to the ground, Clyde crept toward the treat inch by inch, the off-center dressing on his head giving him an endearing, rakish appearance.

He blinked at Matt.

Stretched his neck to sniff her son's hand.

Snatched the treat from his fingers.

Matt didn't flex a muscle . . . and Clyde didn't retreat. They just watched each other while the dog chomped down the biscuit.

Either her son had a lot more self-restraint than she'd given him credit for, or the example of the stock-still man beside him had made a deep impression.

Clyde finished chewing, scooched closer to Matt—and licked his fingers.

A sharp, indrawn breath . . . followed by an ear-to-ear smile . . . were the only reactions from her son.

"You did great, Matt." Stone scratched behind Clyde's ear. "See what I'm doing? He likes this. Lift your hand slow and take my place."

He did as Stone directed. With a blissful sigh, the dog rested his chin on Matt's knee and closed his eyes.

"Is he my friend now?"

"Yep. All you have to do is watch him for cues. If he's tired and wants to sleep, leave him alone. If he comes over to you and wants to be petted, pet him. Move slow so he doesn't get scared.

And feed him a few more of those treats." Stone stood. "I'll run out and get them, along with his other stuff."

"Do you need some help?" Lexie stepped forward.

"I can manage. Thanks."

With one last glance at boy and dog, he strode out of the room.

"Impressive." Her mother watched him leave.

Instead of responding, Lexie took a sip of her coffee. Grimaced. It had grown cold while the little drama played out in her kitchen.

"Need a refill?" Her mother lifted the pot.

"Yeah." She crossed the room and held out her cup.

"That man has a way with kids."

"Seems to."

"And dogs."

"Yeah." Could her mother pour the coffee any slower?

"Does he have younger brothers or sisters?"

"I have no idea."

"Mmm. Could just be natural ability." Her mother dropped her voice as she finished topping off the mug. "Did you notice how Matt took to him right off?"

Yes, she had.

But she had no intention of following where her mother was leading.

"He wanted to make friends with the dog." She

backed away. "Stone was his ticket to do that."

"No. There's more to that man than meets the eye. Anyone who rescues dogs, knows how to deal with children, volunteers to help shore up our crumbling lighthouse, and pitches in to repair planters destroyed by vandals is worth getting to know better."

Ignoring her mom's less-than-subtle implication, she homed in on her last comment.

"What's the story on the planters?"

"Stone's name came up at our garden club meeting. Apparently he's a very skilled carpenter. Rose called and asked him if he'd help us out, and he said yes. I think he's planning to tackle the job this weekend or next. BJ's going to donate the lumber from job-site scraps. He's done a lot of under-the-radar good deeds like that since he's been here, according to Reverend Baker."

The man was full of surprises.

She turned as he reentered the room toting a small corrugated box, a water bowl balanced on top.

"Why don't you put that over there and give me a rundown on what I need to do today?" Her mother motioned toward a spot near the back door.

While the two of them sorted through the contents, Lexie returned to her son's side.

As she dropped down on one knee, Clyde lifted his eyelids and watched her.

"Hey, boy. Welcome to our house." She started to reach for him, but Matt grabbed her hand.

"Remember, you have to go real slow till he gets used to you. Like Mr. Stone said."

"Right." She moderated her pace.

Clyde sniffed her fingers, gave her a doggy grin, and licked her hand.

"I think he likes us, don't you, Mom?"

"Yes."

"Maybe after he's all better, I can play with him."

"That won't be today."

"I know. But Mr. Stone could bring him back sometime, couldn't he?"

"We'll see." She wasn't about to make any promises she might not be able to keep. Stone was a loner. He needed them today . . . but once he got past this crisis, he might retreat back into his protective shell.

"I bet he'd come again if we asked him."

"Maybe. For now, let's be happy Clyde's here today."

The mutinous set of her son's chin told her he wasn't satisfied with that answer.

Stone and her mother finished their discussion, and she rose as they crossed the room toward her.

"I need to get going." Stone hunkered down beside Matt again and gave the dog a pat. "Be polite, Clyde. I'll be back tonight."

"Me and Mamaw will take real good care of him, Mr. Stone."

At Matt's earnest expression, one corner of Stone's mouth twitched. "I know you will. I gave your grandma my cell number, and you can call me if you have any questions. Otherwise, I'll see you at dinnertime."

"Okay. Hey . . ." Matt's face lit up. "Why don't you eat with us? We always have a bunch of food."

Before Lexie could step in, her mother spoke. "I already asked, honey. He says he can't stay tonight."

Lexie had no trouble interpreting the pointed look her mom directed at her—or the message behind it.

If you ask too, we might convince him.

But the notion of Stone joining them for a cozy supper in the home that had always been her safe haven kind of . . . scared her for some reason.

When the silence lengthened, Stone rose. "Thanks again for doing this."

"It's our pleasure." Her mom scowled her direction. "And if you change your mind, the invitation is open. I'm making stew, and we always have a lot left over."

"Thank you."

"Lexie—walk him out, would you, while I fill up Clyde's water bowl?" She pivoted on her heel and marched toward the sink.

Sheesh.

It seemed Clyde wasn't the only one in the doghouse today—metaphorically speaking.

She led the way to the foyer, Stone following close behind.

At the door, she turned to find he had his wallet in hand. "I need to settle up for last night."

"For what?"

"The pizza and soda." He extracted a ten-dollar bill and held it out. "Is this enough to cover my share?"

He wanted to pay for his dinner?

She shook her head. "You don't owe me any-thing."

"You paid for the pizza and sodas. I don't take charity."

"It wasn't charity. It was a . . . a business expense. A working dinner."

"I ate most of the pizza."

"I needed food. The town budget has an allowance for meals if we work overtime."

That was true—though she wasn't planning to tap into it. Her choice to extend the evening had been based on personal as well as professional reasons.

But Stone didn't need to know that.

"Are you certain?"

"Absolutely."

He hesitated . . . then put the ten back in his wallet. "Are you going out to my place?"

"First item on my agenda. It will be a lot easier to search in daylight than it was last night."

"Good luck."

"Thanks."

He moved past her, leaving a faint, woodsy scent in his wake that was masculine . . . rugged . . . and very appealing.

Clamping her lips together, she closed the door behind him.

She was *not* going there.

Maybe she couldn't control the unsettling attraction that had sprung up between them—on her end, anyway.

Maybe she couldn't completely erase thoughts of the tall, dark loner from her mind.

Maybe she couldn't figure out why she was intrigued by a man who should be off-limits—for a lot of reasons.

But she *could* carry on as if everything was normal. That was one skill she'd perfected over the past few years. No one would ever suspect that under the cool, composed, in-control façade she presented to the world, her heart was like a broken-winged bird that would never soar again.

"Well?" Her mother appeared in the doorway to the foyer, wiping her hands on a dish towel.

She shoved her melancholy reflection aside. "Well what?"

"Did you ask him?"

"No." Why pretend she didn't understand the question?

"Hmm."

"What's that supposed to mean?"

"What do you think it means?"

"I don't have time for riddles this morning." She edged past her mother and escaped down the hall.

"It's not a riddle when you know the answer."

She kept walking . . . but that didn't deter her mom.

"He's a kind, decent man. Remember—never judge a book by its cover."

The same sentiment Stone had expressed to her last night about Frank.

It had bothered her then.

It bothered her now.

Because she'd been guilty of doing that with him—until her visit on Monday began chipping away at the motorcycle-gang image she'd formed of him.

But even if he *was* more than he seemed, the whole notion that they might have enough in common to sustain any kind of relationship was ludicrous.

An ex-con and a police chief were like oil and water. There was no possibility of anything developing between them.

Period.

No matter what her mother might think—or hope.

⚜ 5 ⚜

"Brian! You're gonna miss the bus!"

Brenda Hutton yelled the warning to her son from her bedroom as she finished buttoning her uniform shirt. If she didn't hurry herself, she'd be late for her breakfast shift at the diner—especially if fog played hide-and-seek with the road again, like it had last night after her three-to-eleven stint.

She secured her salt-sprinkled brown hair at her nape with a barrette, grimacing at the image in the mirror. Forty-seven was too young to have this much gray—but life hadn't exactly been easy.

And raising a fifteen-year-old alone wasn't making it any easier.

"Brian!" She toed a fraying edge of the mobile home's carpet back under the cheap baseboard, crossed the narrow hall outside her room, and knocked on his door. "You're gonna miss the bus!"

Silence.

The boy was getting harder to deal with every day.

"Brian! Answer me!"

"I'm not going to school today."

His voice was muffled, his words distorted. Like he had his head under the blanket.

She stood up straighter. "Yes, you are. You're

finishing high school and you're going to college. You're not making the same mistakes I did."

"It's my life. I can do what I want."

She swallowed past the tightness in her throat. She might hate conflict—but she was *not* going to let her son throw his life away, like she had. Maybe she hadn't had much backbone when Jerry was around. Maybe she still didn't. However, on this one point she would stand firm.

"Brian!" She tried to twist the knob.

It was locked.

"Open up. Now."

"I'm not going to school!"

"I don't have time for a debate. I'm already running late for work. Open up."

She waited, hands clenched. What if he didn't comply? At five-seven, he was bigger than she was now. One of these days, he was going to defy her outright . . . and then what would she do?

Please, let that not happen today!

The knob rattled, and her shoulders relaxed a hair. At least this was one battle she wouldn't have to . . .

Sweet mercy!

Her stomach bottomed out as she took in her son's black eye, swollen jaw, and puffy, split lip.

No wonder his speech had sounded slurred.

"Oh, Brian!" She reached out to him, but when he backed off, she let her hand drop to her side. "What happened?"

"I got into a fight."

And came out the loser, by all appearances.

"Are you hurt anywhere else?"

"No."

His halfhearted answer wasn't convincing.

She took his arm, propelled him toward the twin bed in the small room, and urged him down onto the mattress. "What else is wrong?"

He shrugged.

"Answer me."

"I have a bruise." He touched his side.

She leaned over, lifted the edge of his T-shirt . . . and sucked in a breath.

A black and blue contusion as large as her hand stretched around his torso, its angry fingers extending toward his ribs.

"Oh, baby." She let the shirt drop back into place and gently touched his uninjured cheek. "Who did this to you?"

"I'm fine, Mom."

"You're not fine. I need to get you to a doctor."

"No. I'm putting ice on it." He gestured to a makeshift ice pack he'd rigged up from a towel and a Ziploc bag. "Once the swelling goes down, I'll be okay. But I'm not going to school today."

In light of his condition, she gave up that fight.

"Fine. Missing one day won't hurt." She twisted her wrist. No way around it—she was going to be late.

"Go to work. I have this under control."

"If you're getting into fistfights, you don't have it under control. What started this?"

"I got into an argument with someone. It's no big deal."

"No big deal? Have you looked in a mirror?" She planted her hands on her hips. "Who did this?"

"It doesn't matter."

"Yes, it does. Was it another student at school?"

"I don't want to talk about it."

"Well, I do. I can't stand by and let someone hurt you like this."

"Why not? You let Dad hurt *you*—and he was your *husband*. This guy was just a friend." He glared at her.

"Your father never beat me up like this."

"He slapped you around."

"Only at the end."

"But he beat you up in other ways. He slept around, Mom—and instead of confronting him, you buried your head in the sand."

That was true.

It was not, however, a subject she wanted to discuss with her son.

"That's history."

"He'd still be doing it if he hadn't walked out after he found someone with more money—and you'd be letting him."

"That's enough, Brian."

"You should have thrown him out years ago."

"A boy needs a father." The excuse sounded pathetic even to *her* ears.

Disgust flattened Brian's features. "That is so lame. He sucked as a father. You just didn't have the guts to tell him to get lost." He gingerly stretched out on the bed. "Go to work."

"We'll talk when I get home."

"Right."

"Do you need anything before I leave?"

He closed his eyes. "Nothing you can give me."

The edges of the scene in front of her blurred, and she turned away. Stumbled toward the door. Fled the decrepit trailer they called home.

But as she climbed behind the wheel of her car and drove toward Coos Bay on autopilot, she admitted the truth.

Her son was right—about everything.

She should have dumped Jerry as soon as she recognized him for the callous con man he was.

Better still, she should have listened to the persistent warning that kept looping through her mind while they'd been dating.

So what if you're thirty years old and no beauty queen? So what if there aren't any other husband prospects beating a path to your door? Don't be desperate. Don't settle for a smooth talker who makes you feel like somebody until you know what he's like inside. Don't let him rush you.

Had she taken that sound advice?

No.

And she'd been paying the price for her mistake ever since.

She blinked to clear her vision. If only she'd been smarter and stronger. If only she'd taken Brian and left long ago. Maybe that happy-go-lucky little boy with the perennial smile wouldn't have grown into a surly teen who got into street fights. Maybe they could have done a lot better on their own.

If, if, if.

Maybe, maybe, maybe.

The story of her life.

But it was too late to change the past. All she could do was try and cope with the mess she'd made of everything.

So tonight she'd talk to her son, ask him again to answer the questions he'd evaded a few minutes ago.

And if that didn't work?

She didn't have a clue.

Two miles north of Hope Harbor, Lexie slowed the patrol car at Randolph Road and hung a right off 101, heading inland. During her tenure as chief, they'd had a few peace-disturbance calls from the low-end mobile home development at the far edge of town, but none had escalated to serious charges. For the most part, no one who lived there had caused any serious trouble.

Until now.

One mile in, she turned right again, past the trailer park entrance sign that was missing a few letters.

Ocean Breeze?

Not even close.

The ocean was miles away.

She maneuvered the car down the asphalt road, scanning addresses while she dodged potholes. It had taken her a good part of the day to decipher the scribbled first name on the jagged-edged scrap of paper she'd found caught in a bush at Stone's place. Longer still to realize it was a fragment from a ripped-up math test. But at the high school, the principal had hooked her up with some teachers and she'd hit pay dirt. One of them had given her a pretty solid ID.

And the other item she'd discovered at Stone's place could clinch the deal.

She pulled to the side of the road in front of a trailer well past its prime. An older-model Nissan was parked in the single slot beside it.

Someone was home.

Preferably mother *and* son.

As she left the cruiser behind and walked to the door, she stayed on high alert. The trailer park appeared to be deserted, but eyes were no doubt watching her from behind the slats in window blinds. And while she didn't expect trouble, it was always better to be prepared for it.

At the door, she leaned forward and knocked.

Seconds later, a woman answered. She was dressed in waitress attire—black slacks and red uniform blouse emblazoned with the name of the diner where she worked. Her gray-flecked hair was pulled back, her face was makeup free except for some faint, lingering specks of color on her lips, and she was carrying some extra pounds on her five-foot-fourish frame.

"Brenda Hutton?"

"Yes." Twin grooves dented the woman's brow.

"Chief Lexie Graham from Hope Harbor. Is your son home?"

A flicker of fear darted across her face. "Yes."

"I'd like to speak with both of you."

"What's wrong?"

"May I come in?"

"Yeah. I . . . I guess so." She eased the door open.

Lexie crossed the threshold and gave the living room a quick sweep. The furnishings were old, but the place appeared to be clean and there was little clutter.

No sign of Brian, though.

"Would you ask your son to join us, please?"

"He's . . . uh . . . resting. He got hurt in a fight."

That would explain his absence from school today.

"We can talk in his room if he'd rather stay in bed."

83

"No! Let me . . . uh . . . see how he's feeling. I'm sure he can come out. Give me a minute." She scurried away.

While she waited, Lexie circled the room. There were several photos of Brian at various ages but no family shots.

That would suggest an absentee father, as the teacher who'd identified the handwriting had speculated.

And missing fathers were one of the contributors to delinquency.

The murmur of voices from down the hall ceased, and a door opened.

Moments later, Brenda appeared, her mouth grim. A gangly teen, sporting a shiner and a split lip, shuffled after her, chin to chest.

"Why don't we sit?" Lexie motioned to the kitchen table, visible through a doorway.

The boy hesitated, but his mother nudged him forward.

Once they were all seated, Lexie pulled out the copy of the piece of paper she'd found at Stone's place and set it on the table.

"Do you recognize this, Brian?"

His complexion lost a few shades of color.

"I . . . I don't know."

"One of the teachers at your school identified your handwriting."

He didn't say anything.

"What's going on?" Brenda twisted her fingers

together on the table and looked back and forth between the two of them.

"Do you want to tell her, Brian, or shall I?"

The teen stared at the table and remained mute.

"I'll take that as a no." Lexie transferred her attention to Brenda. "As you may have heard, Hope Harbor has had some vandalism over the past few weeks. One place was hit for the third time yesterday. This go-round, the resident's dog was injured. I found the original of this during a search of the property this morning." Lexie tapped the paper.

Brenda's knuckles whitened. "My son would never hurt an animal."

"Someone did. Is that your son's handwriting?"

She squinted at it. "I think so . . . but . . . couldn't it have been planted there to make him seem guilty?"

"Who would do that?"

"I don't know." Brenda wrapped her fingers around Brian's arm. "Talk to us. *Were* you involved in these vandalism incidents?"

"No."

Lexie pulled a clear evidence bag out of her pocket and set it beside the piece of paper. "I found this too. Look familiar?"

Mother and son regarded the unusual button.

"Oh, Brian." The older woman's features crumpled.

"Chill out, Mom." His skin grew mottled. "Lots

of people have coats with that kind of button."

"But I suspect this will have your fingerprints on it." Lexie tucked the envelope back in her pocket.

The kid's Adam's apple bobbed.

"Should I get a lawyer?" Brenda's voice shook.

"We can't afford a lawyer, Mom."

"I can't let you go to jail."

"I'm not gonna go to jail. I'm just a kid."

"Is that true?" Brenda sent her a hopeful glance.

"Before we get into that discussion . . . is there another parent who should sit in on this?"

"My husband is . . . he's no longer part of our lives. Hasn't been for six months."

Suspicion confirmed.

"Then let me explain where we are with this. As far as I could tell from a quick search, your son hasn't had any previous brushes with the law. That works to his advantage. However, hurting an animal is a much worse offense than minor vandalism. Animal abuse in the second degree is a Class B Misdemeanor with a fine of up to two thousand dollars and/or imprisonment for up to six months."

Any color that remained in the two faces across from her leached out.

"But . . . but Brian is a minor."

"That's why the juvenile court will handle this—if it goes that far."

"Look . . . I didn't hurt that dog, okay?" The defiance in the teen's demeanor morphed into fear.

"Are you saying there was someone else with you?"

"I'm not saying anything." His surliness surged back.

"Then here's what happens next." Lexie folded her hands and locked gazes with him. "Because there have been multiple offenses during this vandalism spree, and because I have evidence you were on a victim's property, I'm going to send a report to the county juvenile department. A counselor will be assigned to your case. He or she will meet with you and your mom and decide whether to proceed informally or to press charges. You may or may not end up in front of a judge."

Tension radiated off mother and son.

"This is a nightmare." Brenda kneaded her forehead. "How could you do this, Brian?"

"I didn't say I did. And what do you care?" The quiver in his voice undermined his attempt at bravado. "You're never around. You're always at that diner."

"I have to work."

"You wouldn't have to work as much if you hadn't let Dad spend all our money and sink us into debt."

"I'll admit I made some mistakes, but—"

"Hold on." Lexie stepped in before the exchange degenerated into a shouting match. "At the moment, we need to focus on the current situation."

"That stuff you found . . . it's all circumstantial." Beads of sweat popped out on Brian's brow. "You can't prove I did anything wrong."

"At the very least I can cite you for trespassing."

"That's not as bad as the other stuff."

They were getting nowhere with this discussion. Time to switch tactics.

"What happened to your face?"

"I . . . I had a fight."

"When?"

"Yesterday."

"Why?"

Silence.

"Brian . . ." Brenda leaned toward him, posture taut. "Don't make this worse than it already is. Answer the chief's questions."

More silence.

But the boy's hands were shaking.

That was a positive sign. The kids who weren't afraid were much harder to reach—and help.

"You know, Brian"—she adopted a more conversational manner—"attitude is a big factor in how juveniles are dealt with. Cooperation will work in your favor. You can wait and talk to the counselor instead of me—but I'll be having a conversation with whoever is assigned to you, and they'll take into consideration what I tell them about our exchange."

"Brian." His mother touched his hand again, features strained, tone urgent. "Be honest. Don't dig yourself any deeper into a hole or go farther down the road that led to that." She swept a hand toward his bruises. "If you did wrong, admit it and take the consequences. You're young enough to start fresh. This doesn't have to ruin your life."

A shadow of indecision darkened his irises—and Lexie held her breath.

When his shoulders slumped, she exhaled.

"Okay. Yeah. I was involved in all those incidents. But I didn't hurt that dog. It was an accident. The guy I was with was trying to scare him, and the rock ricocheted off the ground. I wanted to take him to a vet, but my friend said we couldn't or we'd get into trouble. I said I was going to anyway. We had a fight. He won." Brian swallowed. "Is the dog all right?"

"Yes. A vet treated him last night. Who's the other kid?"

"I can't tell you that."

"So you're going to take the rap alone—and let a guy who says he's your friend get away with beating you up? There are consequences for assault too, if you want to press charges."

His lips remained locked together.

Fine. She had what she needed for today. The juvenile counselor might have more success getting an ID on the other kid.

"Why did you do this, Brian?" Brenda searched his face.

"My friend . . . he said it would be fun."

"Was it?"

Brian hung his head. "No. It felt wrong to wreck stuff and leave other people to clean up the mess."

"So why did you keep doing it?"

"I didn't want him to think I was a dork—and I didn't want him to dump me."

"Dumping you would have been a favor. You don't need friends like that."

"He was nice to me, okay? All of the kids were already in groups when we moved here. But he talked to me, and after that, other kids did too. I don't want to sit by myself at lunch anymore."

"Oh, honey." Brenda laid her hand over his, her features contorting. "I'm sorry the move's been hard on you. I thought it would be better if we started over in a new place. I guess that was a mistake."

"Seems like all we do is make mistakes." His voice wavered.

This was what Lexie had been hoping to get— insight into the kid's motivation, and some sign of remorse. Those would be in her report too . . . and hopefully, the counselor would go the informal route and give Brian a chance to make restitution.

She had some ideas on that score too, which she intended to pass on.

"Mistakes can be corrected." Lexie rose. "I don't need anything else today. Expect to hear from the counselor as early as Monday. I'm going to ask them to expedite this."

"I'll walk you out." Brenda stood too and followed her to the door, closing it gently behind her after they stepped onto the stoop. "For the record, I didn't know about the fight until this morning." She wrung her hands. "He's in serious trouble, isn't he?"

"He's in trouble, yes. Whether it becomes serious is up to him. The counselor will emphasize that too."

"I hope he listens better to him or her than he listens to me. Ever since his dad walked out, he's been one angry kid. I can't blame him. Neither of us have been great parents—or role models."

"You seem to be doing your best to keep things together now."

"Too little too late."

"It's never too late."

"I hope that's true." Her eyes moistened, and she swiped the back of her hand across them. "But I wish I could turn back the clock ten years."

Lexie could relate.

Except she'd settle for six.

"Expect a call from the juvenile counselor. In the meantime, tell Brian to keep his nose clean. I'll do what I can to help him, but any further incidents will exacerbate his problems."

"I'll pass that on."

The woman remained where she was while Lexie returned to her car, climbed behind the wheel, and retraced her route down the bumpy road.

She was still there when the road curved and Lexie lost sight of the trailer. As if she didn't want to go back in and deal with the difficulties waiting for her on the other side of the door.

No surprise there.

The task that lay before her wasn't an easy one. Dealing with rebellious teens—especially angry ones—wasn't a chore for the fainthearted. And while Brian's mother might be trying her best now, the woman didn't strike her as bold or brave.

But the counselor might be able to talk some sense into the boy. There were also options she could suggest that might help him get his life back on track—in particular the one that had popped into her mind as her meeting with the boy and his mother wound down. It was a bit off the wall . . . and none of the parties involved might go for it . . . but it had the potential to have a huge impact.

She couldn't propose it, though, until she talked to one of the key players.

Adam Stone.

She tightened her grip on the wheel. Was she nuts to consider involving him?

The counselor might think so.

Stone might think so.

Yet her gut said it was an inspired idea.

Who better to dissuade a kid from a life of crime than a man who'd been there? Who'd taken the hard knocks and was now trying to rebuild his life with the odds stacked against him? There could be no more credible voice in this debate . . . *if* he was willing to take this on.

She had only an hour to come up with a convincing argument—unless she bought herself some time by persuading him to stay for dinner.

Pressing on the accelerator, she watched the speedometer needle rise. She needed to contact the juvenile department, deal with any issues at the office, and make a few phone calls first—and Stone wasn't likely to hang around the house once he came to retrieve Clyde. She needed to be there when he arrived.

And if her instincts were correct . . . if he was hiding a tender heart beneath the taciturn, reclusive façade he presented to the world . . . perhaps he'd be willing to help a young man who was hovering on the edge of disaster avoid the same mistakes he'd made.

✺ 6 ✺

Man.

Adam slowly inhaled another lungful of the savory aroma wafting through the air as he approached Lexie's front door.

If that had been coming from a restaurant, patrons would be lined up halfway down the block.

But he wasn't going to get even a taste.

Yeah, Annette had invited him for dinner. So

had Matt. But they'd already gone above and beyond by watching Clyde all day. He couldn't eat their food too.

Especially since Lexie hadn't seemed all that keen on him staying, despite the obvious prompt from her mother to endorse the invitation.

He stepped onto the porch, brushed off his jeans to dislodge any clinging sawdust, and pressed the bell. Maybe he should have swung by his cabin and cleaned up . . . but why bother for such a fast visit? It wouldn't take him more than three minutes to collect Clyde, thank Annette and Matt, and be on his way.

The door opened—and Lexie gave him a warm smile. "Hi."

"Hi." He managed to croak out the return greeting as he tried to regroup. What was she doing home from work already? Given the kind of hours she'd referenced last night, he hadn't expected to meet up with her tonight. "I . . . uh . . . came to pick up Clyde."

Real smooth, Stone. Like she doesn't know why you're here.

Heat crept up his neck.

"He's in the family room with Matt. You have to see this." She motioned him in. If she thought his comment was dumb, she kept it to herself.

"What are they doing?" He crossed the threshold.

"Follow me."

She tiptoed down the hall, and he fell in behind

her. Funny. Even though she was in her official cop attire, she seemed somehow . . . different . . . tonight. More approachable. Softer. More feminine.

Before he could figure out what had changed, she arrived at the doorway to the family room and motioned toward the far side.

On the rug in front of the fireplace, where flickering gas logs were taking the chill off the forty-nine-degree afternoon, Matt and Clyde were out for the count. The little boy was curled on his side, one arm over his new friend as they slept almost nose-to-nose.

Any worries he'd had about leaving his dog in the care of a rambunctious almost-five-year-old had obviously been unwarranted.

But touching as the hearth scene was, the woman beside him had a bigger impact on his heart.

Lexie was in profile as she watched boy and dog, her generous lips bowed into a gentle curve, the tenderness in her face giving her complexion a glow no cosmetic could ever achieve.

This was Lexie, the loving mother.

It was also Lexie, the alluring woman. At this proximity, inches from her silky dark hair, that same fresh, dewy fragrance he'd noticed at the vet's office tickled his nose again—putting ideas in his head that didn't belong there.

"Mom says they've been inseparable all day."

Her soft words were little more than a puff of warmth against his cheek.

He tried to respond.

Failed.

She tipped her chin up a fraction, lifting those sinfully long eyelashes. Her smile wavered, and an emotion that read as longing flashed through her eyes. But it came and went so fast . . . had he misinterpreted it?

Of course he had. A smart, accomplished woman like Lexie could have her pick of first-class men. She'd never give the likes of him a second look.

"I think they've bonded." Her statement came out husky—as if she was as much affected by their closeness as he was.

In your dreams, Stone.

"Yeah." Somehow he convinced his vocal cords to kick back in. "Looks like they also wore each other out."

Faint parallel creases dented her brow. "Don't worry . . . Mom kept tabs on the situation. She wouldn't have let Matt get carried away or do—"

"Whoa." He held up a hand. "I wasn't being critical. I'm glad they had fun together—and that Clyde felt safe enough here to go to sleep."

"Oh." The tension faded from her features. "Well, I'm glad too. As for wearing each other out . . . Matt always takes a nap. Mom says he's been conked out for close to two hours, which doesn't surprise me. He was so excited about having a dog in the house he didn't drift off until close to midnight last night, and he was up at the crack of dawn."

Meaning she had been too.

"I'm sorry the dog-sitting gig disrupted everyone's sleep."

"Not an issue." She waved a hand in dismissal. "I get up early every day."

"After a full night's sleep."

"I'll catch up tonight. So . . . do you have plans for this evening?"

He did a double take. "Why?"

"I wondered if you'd reconsider staying for dinner. I have something I'd like to discuss with you."

"About the vandalism?" When she'd answered the door, he'd had a fleeting thought to ask about her trip to his place—until the right side of his brain shut down.

"Yes."

"Did you find some clues?"

"Yes, and they were very helpful. I talked with one of the perpetrators today, and I had an idea I wanted to run by you. It's a bit . . ."

"Did you ask him?" Her mother poked her head into the room.

"Yes—but I don't have an answer yet." Lexie angled toward him.

He hesitated. Sharing a meal with the three people who called this cozy place home would be a treat. But breaking bread with this close, loving family, making small talk, would also be like visiting a foreign country where you didn't know the language or the customs. He'd surely commit a gaffe.

"I'm not, uh, dressed for dinner." He swept a hand down his work jeans.

"Don't be silly." Annette waved a spatula at him. "You should see what we wear to the table sometimes. This isn't a formal affair. Come on in and make yourself comfortable. I'm putting the food out now. Clyde did great all day, in case you're wondering. He appears to be making a rapid recovery." She disappeared back into the kitchen.

"Mom is a force to be reckoned with." One side of Lexie's mouth lifted. "Don't let her steamroll you if you don't want to stay . . . but I'd appreciate it if you would. Otherwise dinner will have to wait while we have our conversation—and Mom isn't too happy with people who let food she works hard to prepare get cold."

Put like that . . .

"Since I don't want to find myself in your mother's bad graces, I accept."

"Good. Shall we wake up the new buddies?"

Without waiting for him to respond, she crossed the room and knelt beside her son.

He dropped down on the balls of his feet next to her.

"Matt . . . dinner's ready." She gave his shoulder a gentle shake.

Her son blinked his eyes open, oriented himself, and felt around for Clyde.

The pup lifted his head, licked her son's hand, gave his owner a quick scan—and stayed where he was.

"I guess that puts me in my place." Adam scratched behind the dog's ear.

"We had a real fun day, Mr. Stone." Matt sat up, and Clyde scooted closer to him.

"I can tell."

"Come on. Let's eat." Lexie rose, held out her hand for Matt, and led him to the table.

"Is Mr. Stone staying?"

"Uh-huh."

"Awesome!"

Adam followed, Clyde at his heels—but on the threshold of the kitchen, he came to an abrupt halt.

If Annette considered this a casual dinner, they weren't operating from the same dictionary.

Sunny yellow placemats were topped with matching blue plates. Ceramic, not paper. Gleaming silverware flanked the plates. Metal, not plastic. Beside the knife and fork, crisp yellow napkins stood at attention. Cloth, not paper. The water at each place was in crystal goblets. Glass, not plastic. And the table was laden with food—

a huge tureen of stew, a basket of what appeared to be homemade rolls, a bowl of salad.

This was a close runner-up to the Thanksgiving dinner BJ had insisted he attend at Seabird Inn last fall, where her fiancé's father had served up a fabulous meal with a view to match from a bluff overlooking Hope Harbor.

"You can sit here, Mr. Stone." Matt jogged over to a chair at one end of the table and pulled it out.

"I'm not taking anyone's place, am I?"

"Nah. This chair's almost always empty."

Brushing at his jeans again, he entered the room and slid onto the seat.

"Stone, would you like to lead us in a blessing?" Annette shook out her napkin and laid it across her lap. "We always invite our guests to do that if they're churchgoing people."

"Um . . . I don't do formal prayers, like at church."

"We don't either. We just praise from the heart."

They all bowed their heads.

Apparently the matter was settled.

He took a deep breath. Reverend Baker had often asked him to lead the prayers for the prison Bible study group, but for whatever reason, this was scarier.

Best to begin with a silent entreaty.

Please give me the proper words for this occasion, God.

Folding his hands, he dived in.

100

"Lord, we thank you for the food we are about to eat. It smells great, and we ask your blessing on the hands that prepared it. We also thank you for the gifts of generosity and kindness—and for Clyde's recovery. I know he's only a dog, but friends come in all shapes and sizes. Please keep us all safe, and help us remember that even when clouds hide the sun, it keeps on shining— just like your light. Amen."

He lifted his head to find the two women watching him as Matt snagged a roll from the basket on the table.

"That was beautiful, Stone." Annette beamed at him from the other end of the table.

His cheeks warmed. "It wasn't very fancy."

"Neither was Jesus." She gestured to the tureen in the middle of the table. "Help yourself."

Lexie was still watching him with an expression he couldn't read . . . but the instant he looked her way she transferred her attention to the bowl of salad.

"You have to try these, Mr. Stone. Mamaw makes awesome rolls." Matt set the basket next to him.

"I plan to do that, buddy. I haven't had home-made bread in . . . well, maybe never."

"Never?" The boy's eyes grew round as saucers. "Mamaw makes a lot of homemade stuff. Mom does too when she's not working. She made brownies last night. Do you like brownies?"

"They're one of my favorites."

"Mine too. We're having them for dessert."

Clyde wandered over to his chair and dropped down between him and Lexie. If he was at home, he'd pet the dog . . . but that might not be the best idea here. A lot of people didn't think animals and food mixed. It was hard to know what to do in polite society after growing up in a . . .

"Hey, Clyde. You're much more chipper tonight." Lexie ruffled his fur.

O-kay. Petting an animal at the table must be acceptable—in this house, anyway.

Maybe he'd get through this dinner unscathed . . . as long as he held up his end of the conversation.

As it happened, that wasn't difficult. Between Annette and Matt, there was never a lag in the chitchat. Lexie didn't say a lot, but she did her part to draw him into the lively discussion.

By the end of the meal, he'd not only eaten two helpings of stew, a heaping plate of salad, and three rolls, he was actually relaxed.

"Let's get those brownies going." Annette stood and removed his wiped-clean plate.

Lexie rose too and picked up Matt's plate as well as her own. "We like to heat them up and serve them with vanilla ice cream, but you can have yours plain if you prefer."

"They're better hot with ice cream," Matt offered. "They get kind of gooey inside and the ice cream melts into little puddles."

"I'll go with that recommendation." He gave the chatty tyke a high five.

"Coffee?" Annette hefted a mug.

"Yes. Thank you. Black."

Matt propped his elbow on the table and rested his chin in his palm. "What's a biker dude?"

"Biker dude?" Lexie stopped cutting the brownies and frowned at her son from the counter. "Where in the world did you pick up that term?"

"Did I say a bad word?" Matt stopped playing with his spoon.

"No. I just . . . where did you hear it?"

"From Daniel in Sunday school. He said Mr. Stone is a biker dude."

The two women sent their visitor a quick, embarrassed look.

Adam shifted in his seat, the subtle tension that had been part of his life for as long as he could remember creeping back.

Matt's only saying what everyone in town probably thinks, Stone. Get over it and try to put these gracious people at ease.

Forcing up the corners of his lips, he tried to keep his posture relaxed. "A biker dude is a guy who rides a motorcycle. Usually they wear black leather jackets. A lot of them have longer hair and wear bandanas." He touched the one covering his own dark locks, which hadn't seen a barber in far too long. "Most wear boots. Some have tattoos."

"Awesome!" Matt tucked his legs under him

and leaned close, elbows on the table as he spoke in a hushed tone. "Do you have a tattoo?"

"Matt!" Lexie zoomed over and resettled her son in his chair. "That's a personal question." She refocused on him, her expression contrite. "Sorry about that."

"It's okay. And I don't mind answering. No, I don't have a tattoo—or a motorcycle."

"Maybe you could get one." Matt poked his spoon into the ice cream Lexie set in front of him.

"I don't see that happening. Motorcycles cost a lot of money."

"Oh." Matt's face fell. "I thought if you got one you might take me for a ride sometime. I've never been on a motorcycle. Have you, Mom?"

Lexie finished distributing the dessert and retook her seat. "Yes."

"Yeah? When?"

"Before you were born."

"Did my dad have one?"

"Yes." She focused on scooping up some ice cream and a bite of brownie from her plate. "Mom, did you add a different seasoning to the stew tonight? It had an extra zing."

She didn't want to talk about her late husband—at least not in front of strangers.

Too bad. He'd like to learn more than the few scraps he'd picked up here and there about her history. All he knew was that she'd married while she was overseas and her husband had died not long afterward. No one in town seemed to have a clue about what had happened to him.

Given the exchange taking place between mother and daughter about seasoning and spices, however, his curiosity wasn't going to be satisfied tonight.

Matt was too busy devouring his dessert to add much to the conversation, so Adam followed his example and gave the warm, tender brownie covered in melting ice cream the attention it deserved.

"Would you like another one?"

At Lexie's question, he tuned back into the table conversation.

"No, thanks. But it was delicious."

"Can I have some more, Mom?" Matt cast her a hopeful look.

"Let's give what you ate a chance to get to your stomach first. If you're hungry in half an hour, you can have another half."

"Okay." Sighing, he pushed his plate back, surveyed the table, and gave Adam a toothy smile. "I like you sitting in the empty place. It feels . . . fuller."

"I agree. I prefer a full table myself." Annette's comment sounded innocent, but Adam caught the light-speed squint Lexie directed at the older woman.

"If you leave everything, I'll stack the dishwasher later." Lexie stood. "I need to talk to our guest for a few minutes."

"Take your time. Matt and I will clear the table and keep Clyde company in here. Right, Matt?"

"Right!"

And no doubt try to pilfer another brownie out of his grandmother, who Adam suspected was a softer touch than his mother.

Taking Lexie's cue, Adam rose.

She motioned toward the family room. "Let's sit in there. It's quiet—and private."

He followed her, taking a seat in the corner of the couch she indicated while she claimed an adjacent chair.

"Let me fill you in on what I found today at your place, and what happened next." She was back in official mode.

Good.

It was easier to concentrate when she was Chief Graham.

He listened without interrupting as she described the events of the day, no less angry that Clyde had been hurt, but feeling more sympathy than he expected for the fifteen-year-old whose home situation sounded anything but ideal.

Especially after Lexie told him she was handing Brian over to a juvenile court counselor.

"I hope that works out for him." In addition to his own experience, he'd heard too many horror stories from fellow inmates to have much confidence in the system.

"That's what I wanted to talk to you about. I think Brian is sorry he got involved in all this, and I know he feels bad about the damage and about Clyde. I'd like to give him every possible chance to straighten out."

"What does that have to do with me?"

"I had an idea this afternoon that I ran by the counselor who's been assigned to the case. No names, just a concept. He thought it had merit— but it all hinges on you."

A quiver of unease snaked up his spine. "I'm trying to steer clear of anything related to crime."

"I can understand that—except this would put you on the other side of the law. Will you at least listen to my idea?"

After all she and her family had done for Clyde —and him—he owed her that much. "I can listen."

She leaned close, her expression earnest. "I don't know your whole story, Stone. Only what's in the police record. I don't have access to social service files from your younger days. But I suspect you may have come from a tough home situation."

"That would be an understatement."

"Brian isn't in the best environment, either. I think his mother is trying, but his father took off six months ago. Between you and me, he sounds like a user—and a deadbeat. I don't know if there was any physical abuse, but that's not the only way to make someone's life miserable."

She paused, as if waiting for him to offer some insights based on his own experience.

Not happening.

He never talked about his past except in vague detail, and he wasn't about to spill his guts now.

Lexie apparently got that message.

"Bottom line, I don't think there's ever been a solid role model in Brian's life." She clasped her hands together as she continued. "Being new at school here, trying to break into established cliques, has been tough—and he ended up connecting with the wrong person. He's teetering on the edge at this very minute. I can give him a second chance . . . but I can't give him a role model or a father figure. Neither can the juvenile counselor. Nor can we talk to him, or offer any wisdom, with the voice of direct experience."

As Adam caught the drift of where this was leading, his jaw went slack. "You're seeing *me* in that role?"

"That's part of our idea."

"You've got to be kidding."

"I'm dead serious."

"Let me get this straight." He spoke slowly, trying to make sense of her suggestion. "You want to hook this kid up with a felon who spent five years in prison, has a juvenile record, came from a worse background than he has, and who's only been walking the straight and narrow for eighteen months?"

"The plan is more fleshed out than that, but you've nailed the gist of it."

The whole notion still wasn't computing.

"I can't believe anyone in the juvenile system would agree to this."

"On paper, I don't think they would have. With a personal recommendation from a police chief the counselor knows—it was an easy sell."

"You vouched for me?" Had he slipped into an alternate universe?

"I've met you. I've watched you. I have sound instincts, and they're telling me you're a safe bet. But I've also talked to people in town who know you—BJ, Reverend Baker, Luis. The picture that emerges is one of a model citizen. A man who's made mistakes but who's doing everything he can to turn his life around. I imagine it's a tough road—and I'd like to keep Brian from having to tread it. Who better to convince him to stay on this side of the law in the future than a man who crossed the line . . . and faced the consequences?"

The tautness of her posture, the urgency in her tone, her obvious commitment to do the best she could for this troubled kid were compelling.

Too bad someone hadn't cared half as much for him in those early days, before he'd taken the wrong fork in the road.

It was impossible to fault the logic of her

plan . . . but the whole premise left him feeling as shaky and scared as he'd been the first time he'd broken the law.

"I don't have any experience at this kind of thing."

"The main job requirements are compassion and persistence. If you're half as adept with Brian as you've been with Matt today, I think he'll listen to what you have to say."

"And if he doesn't?"

"We'll have done our best to give him a chance —and that's all anyone can do." She leaned forward again. "During the meeting on Monday with Brian and his mother, the counselor will do a risk assessment screen and develop a case plan. Since there are no priors, I'm expecting the matter will be handled informally. That means there could be a fine, restitution for victims, letters of apology . . . along with community service."

"Where would I fit into all that?"

"Two places—restitution and community service. Mom told me you agreed to repair the flower boxes on the wharf that were damaged in one of the vandalism incidents. If Brian was assigned to help you with that job, he'd be partially ful-filling both of those obligations . . . and learning some useful skills too. What do you think?"

He had no idea.

No one had ever asked for his help with anything this . . . important.

What if he failed?

But if he didn't try, this kid might lose his one chance to have a decent life—and some of the blame would fall on him.

His stomach knotted.

As if he'd sensed his benefactor's distress from the next room, Clyde trotted in and wedged himself next to his leg.

When he reached down to pet the dog, his fingers were trembling.

"You can do this, Stone."

At Lexie's firm, quiet comment, he scrutinized her. If she had any doubts about her plan, he could see no signs of them.

"I wish I had your confidence."

"I have plenty for both of us. But I can offer you a safety net, if that helps. Should this become burdensome, or should you change your mind, we can regroup and modify the plan."

She was making it hard to say no.

A suffocating sense of panic, the kind he'd always felt when he was cornered, closed in on him.

"Do I have to decide now?"

"No. The counselor does need some time to prepare a proposal before he meets with Brian and his mother, though, so the sooner you can give me an answer, the better."

"Can I call you tomorrow morning?"

"That works."

A reprieve. Not much of one, but enough to get him back to Sandpiper Cove, where the fresh air might clear the muddle from his brain.

"Thanks again for your help today with Clyde." He rose.

"It was a treat for Matt." She stood too.

"Are you leaving, Mr. Stone?" Matt stuck his head around the doorway.

"Yes."

"Mamaw!" the boy hollered over his shoulder. "He's leaving!"

"Hey! No shouting in the house." Lexie shot him a stern look.

A home with no shouting?

Out of his realm of experience.

Annette appeared in the doorway, the box of dog supplies in her arms.

"I can take those." Adam started toward her.

"You worry about Clyde. I've got this. Lexie, would you get the bag on the kitchen table? I made up a human doggie bag for you, Stone. We have a week's worth of stew. I gave you a portion, along with some rolls and a few brownies."

"That's very generous, but you've already been more than kind."

"Don't argue with Mom about food." Lexie grinned and set off for the kitchen. "She loves to feed people."

"Then I accept—with pleasure." He bent and hefted Clyde into his arms.

"Matt, would you open the door for our guest?" Annette motioned toward the foyer with the box.

The tyke trotted ahead of them and pulled the door wide as Lexie appeared from the kitchen.

"We'll help you carry all this stuff out." Annette started down the path, Lexie and Matt following in her wake.

Adam closed the door behind him as best he could with his foot and brought up the rear of the parade to his car.

After sitting Clyde on the backseat, he relieved Lexie of her bag and deposited it on the front passenger seat. They all followed him around to the trunk, where he stowed the box Annette was holding.

"Thank you again for taking such great care of Clyde and for the wonderful dinner." He closed the lid.

"It was our pleasure. And you're welcome for a meal anytime." Annette held out her hand.

He returned her firm clasp.

"We could watch Clyde for you again some-time." Matt peeked in the back window at the dog. "Me and him had a lot of fun. After he's all better, we could play outside in the backyard. I bet he'd like that."

"I bet he would." Adam fingered his car keys, making no promises. Tonight had been great—but social interaction wasn't his forte. "Well . . ."

"Say good night, Matt." Annette took the boy's hand.

"Good night."

"We'll see you inside, Lexie." With that, she led the boy back up the path, through the door, and out of sight.

"I'll say good night too." Lexie took a step back. "My cell number is on the card I gave you during my first trip to your place. That will be the best way to reach me tomorrow. Do you need another one?"

"No. I kept the one you gave me." It had been front and center on his kitchen counter since the night of her visit.

"Okay. And please think hard about what I asked. It could transform a young boy's life."

"I will." He edged away, climbed behind the wheel, and put the car in gear.

At the end of the cul-de-sac, he executed a wide turn and drove again past her house.

She wasn't standing in front anymore, but warm light spilled from the windows.

A surge of yearning swept over him, so strong that for a moment his foot eased back on the gas pedal. What would it be like to call a place like this, filled with warmth and light and laughter and love, home?

Gritting his teeth, he forced himself to press harder.

This wasn't where he belonged.

He needed to be satisfied with the small, isolated cabin that was his lot—and the companionship of a loyal dog.

Like he'd been before a lovely woman had unexpectedly entered his life and asked a favor that would pull him out of his isolation and stretch his comfort level to the limits.

He'd bought himself a few hours to think it through—yet as he drove through the night toward Sandpiper Cove, he already knew that however daunting her request might be, come morning he was going to agree.

Because saying no to a woman like Lexie Graham wasn't an option.

🕊 7 🕊

Eleven forty-five—and no decision from Stone.

Bummer.

Lexie pulled out her phone and scrolled through her messages on the off chance she'd missed his call.

Zilch.

Sighing, she stowed her cell and shaded her eyes, watching from the bench she'd claimed on the wharf as Matt tried to lure two wary seagulls close enough to take some bread from his fingers.

His quest appeared to be as fruitless as her

efforts to persuade Stone to bond with a juvenile delinquent.

"Morning, Lexie."

She swiveled around. Charley lifted a hand in greeting and strolled down the wharf toward her, attired in his usual jeans and a Ducks baseball cap.

"Good morning. Tell me you're opening up. Matt and I were hoping to have fish tacos for lunch."

"That's my plan. Mind if I sit for a few minutes first?"

"Not at all." She slid over to open up more space for the tall, spare man who'd been a town fixture for as long as she could remember. "How's everything going?"

"No complaints."

His standard answer. Charley took life as it came, made the best of everything, and always maintained a placid demeanor.

"You know . . . you should teach a master class on finding inner harmony. You'd make a fortune."

"Fortunes are overrated—and there's no secret to inner harmony." The noonday sun highlighted the lines creasing his weathered face as he did a slow sweep of the tranquil harbor. "You just have to keep your priorities straight."

Easier said than done—but she wasn't up for a philosophical discussion this morning.

"What are you working on at the studio?"

Sometimes it was hard to believe the humble, low-key taco maker was an acclaimed artist whose work sold for hefty prices all over the country.

"A seascape. It's coming along . . . but I got a sudden urge to cook. As my grandmother always used to say, listen to your inner voice—if you've been raised well, it will never lead you astray. So here I am." He motioned toward Matt. "The little one is growing fast."

"Tell me about it."

She watched her son, who was persisting in his attempt to befriend the pair of seagulls . . . and showing remarkable patience. The result of Stone's tutoring with Clyde, perhaps?

Very possible.

Matt seemed totally enamored with the man who'd shared their table last night. Despite the bad home situation Stone had alluded to, which likely hadn't offered a role-model father, he'd managed to bond with her son and . . .

"I imagine it is difficult to raise a young boy alone. It's always best to have a father in the home."

She blinked.

How odd for Charley to bring up that subject while Stone's image was front and center in her mind.

"My mom's a great help."

"I have no doubt of that. Annette is a wonderful

woman. Still . . . it's not the same as having a father in the picture."

Coming from anyone else, that comment would have raised her hackles. But somehow, delivered by Charley in his gentle, sympathetic manner, it didn't put her on the defensive.

"It is what it is."

"Things can change."

"I hope not. Change is too disruptive. I'm fine with the status quo."

"Not all change is bad. Some of it transforms. But we can't recognize possibilities unless we're open to them . . . and they can often come in unexpected forms. How's Clyde doing?"

It took her a moment to switch gears after his abrupt change of subject.

"Fine, as far as I know." She cocked her head. "How did you know about that?"

He treated her to a flash of brilliant white teeth. "In a town this size, there are few secrets." A sudden flap of wings drew his attention, and he leaned forward to look past her. "Floyd . . . Gladys . . . make friends with Matt. He won't hurt you."

Stifling a smile, Lexie checked on the pair of seagulls. Leave it to Charley to know the name of every Hope Harbor resident—human and nonhuman. Not that the gulls would pay one bit of attention to . . .

Wings tucked, the two birds hopped closer to

Matt and began taking scraps of bread from his fingers, much to her son's delight.

"How did you get them to do that?" Lexie stared at the gulls.

"The simple act of paying attention and offering reassurance can often have a remarkable impact on behavior. Now tell me about the vandalism. You've solved the case?"

"Uh . . . I think so. Part of it, anyway." She continued to watch the suddenly cooperative birds.

Weird.

"It's a shame when someone young starts down a wrong path."

She transferred her attention to Charley. "I didn't mention an age."

"Isn't vandalism often the work of troubled teens?"

"Yes."

"A logical assumption, then. I imagine Adam would attest to the folly of such behavior."

This conversation was all over the place.

"You mean Stone?"

"Adam Stone—yes."

"You're the only person I know who uses his first name."

"Stone doesn't suit him. It might have once, but not anymore. It's too tough . . . too hard . . . too coarse. That name doesn't fit a man whose rough edges have been smoothed and refined—and it cements an incorrect image."

"Don't you think you're giving too much importance to a name?"

"Am I? As I recall, you didn't like your nickname as a child. What was it again?"

"Metal Mouth." After almost two decades, it still made her cringe. Those braces had been the bane of her existence for two agonizing years as a freshman and sophomore in high school.

"Ah yes. I remember. You kept up a brave front and tried to laugh off the teasing when you and your friends came by for tacos, but in your eyes there was hurt. A name is a mighty thing. One that has the power to mold and shape."

"I suppose that could be true." The Metal Mouth moniker had definitely undermined her self-confidence, despite her popularity and healthy self-esteem. "Did he ask you to call him Adam?"

"No—but a wounded man doesn't always know to ask for the things he needs most."

As she mulled that over, her phone began to vibrate. After retrieving it from her shoulder bag, she scanned the screen.

Stone.

The man was cutting it close, but he'd kept his promise to call this morning—barely.

"I need to take this."

"And I need to open the stand. I'll get your tacos going."

"Three orders. I'm taking some home for Mom."

"Got it." Charley stood and wandered toward

his truck, pausing for a brief exchange with Matt as he passed.

Lexie put the cell to her ear. "Morning."

"With two minutes to spare." His resonant baritone came over the line, creating an entirely different image than the Hell's Angels face he presented to the world. The name Stone did *not* fit that deep, smooth voice. "Sorry I'm so late. It's been a difficult decision."

"I had a feeling you might be struggling with it." Fingers tightening on the phone, she fought the temptation to push. If Stone . . . Adam . . . chose to tackle this project, she wanted him on board because of commitment, not coercion.

"As long as there's an escape hatch if the situation goes south, I'll give it a shot."

Thank you, God!

"That's great news."

"I hope you don't change your mind once we get rolling."

"I'm not expecting to. How's Clyde this morning?"

"Acting as if nothing ever happened."

"I'm glad to hear that. Matt had a great time with him yesterday. He couldn't stop talking about—"

"Mom!"

"Hang on a sec." She shifted toward her son. He was clutching the empty bag of bread scraps and flanked by the two seagulls. "What?"

"Is that Mr. Stone?"

"Yes."

"Can I talk to him?"

She put the phone back to her ear. "The youngest member of my household would like to speak with you, if you have a minute."

"Sure."

She passed the phone over.

"Hi, Mr. Stone. How's Clyde?" He shook out the bag while he listened, watching as the gulls pecked up the crumbs. "I miss *him* too. What's he doing? . . . Yeah. I take naps too . . . We're down by Charley's. I've been feeding Floyd and Gladys . . . No, they're seagulls . . . Uh-uh. Charley told me their names . . . I don't know. I guess he asked them."

Lexie stood and motioned for him to hand the phone back.

"Mom says I need to go. Will you be at church tomorrow? . . . Yeah . . ." He aimed a look her direction. "I don't think so . . . Okay, that would be cool. Here's Mom."

She took the phone while Matt wandered off, the seagulls waddling along behind him.

"Thanks again for your help with Brian. I'll be back in touch as soon as the counselor gives us the green light."

"No hurry on my end."

"Thanks for being patient with Matt too. A lot of people don't bother with children."

"He's a great kid. Also quite a conversationalist for his age."

"He does have strong language skills. Some days that's a blessing . . . other days not so much."

"I can imagine." A rich, husky chuckle came over the line—along with a surge of electricity.

She groped for the edge of the bench and sank back down.

"Chief Graham? Are you still there?"

"Uh . . . yes." *Get your brain in gear, Lexie!* "Listen . . . since we're going to be working together on the project with Brian, let's . . . uh . . . skip the formalities. Just call me Lexie."

Now there was silence on his end.

She waited.

"Okay. I think I can do that—but I'm not used to being on a first-name basis with law enforcement."

"Things can change."

"Most of the changes in my life haven't been for the better until the past couple of years." All humor vanished from his inflection.

"There's no reason that positive trend won't continue. Not all change is bad."

She frowned as the words of encouragement spilled out. Hadn't Charley said the same thing to her not ten minutes ago? And hadn't she blown off that notion?

"I hope you're right. I'll wait to hear from you about next steps with Brian. Enjoy your weekend."

"Thanks. You too."

Lowering the phone from her ear, Lexie inhaled a lungful of the fresh, salt air. Released it.

Her fingertips continued to tingle.

This was crazy.

She'd seen Stone . . . Adam . . . around town for months. Not once had she given him more than a passing glance. Not once had she harbored any secret fantasies about him. Not once had she thought of the two of them together in any context other than police chief and ex-con.

Now she couldn't get the man out of her mind.

It was bizarre.

Pocketing her cell, she leaned back on the bench to watch as a boat left the protected harbor, heading for open sea—and unknown perils.

What was that old saying? Something about ships in the harbor being safe . . . but that's not what ships were built for.

Once upon a time she'd believed that. Adventure had been her middle name.

Not anymore.

These days, the very notion of leaving safety behind and striking out on a new voyage was—

"Hey, Mom!" Matt raced over. "Charley's cooking. Are we eating?"

The perfect diversion.

"Yes." She stood and took his hand.

"Mr. Stone said he'd bring Clyde to church tomorrow and I could pet him afterward."

"Reverend Baker lets dogs into church?"

"No." Matt giggled, skipping along beside her. "Clyde's going to wait in the car. Hey, Mom?"

She braced at the familiar, quizzical tone that told her a thorny question was coming. "What?"

"How come you don't go to church with me and Mamaw?"

An old and sore subject.

"We've talked about this before. I work on Sunday morning."

"How come you have to work *every* Sunday?"

Because it gives me an excuse to skip church.

Not an acceptable answer.

"This is a small town. We don't have a lot of police officers. Someone has to work."

"How come you don't take turns, like we do at preschool?"

Not only did her son have superior language skills, his analytical ability was improving every day. Soon, he and her mom would be tag-teaming the campaign to get her back to church.

"For a lot of reasons."

"Like what?"

"Here we are, Charley." She picked up her pace, tugging Matt along with her to the window of the truck. "Is our order ready?"

"Yep." He slid the white butcher-paper packets into a brown bag.

"Hey, Charley, if I draw you a picture of Floyd

and Gladys, would you put it up back there?" Matt pointed to the rear wall, which was covered with layers of children's artwork.

"I'd be honored." Charley winked at her son as Lexie counted out the money.

"Drat. I'm low on cash. I need to run to the ATM."

"Don't bother. Pay the rest next visit."

"You know . . . it would help if you took credit cards."

He tucked the bills into a box below the counter. "I like doing business the old-fashioned way."

"Aren't you the one who told me to be open to change?" She picked up their order.

"I was talking about constructive change. Credit cards don't qualify." Grinning, Charley lifted his hand in farewell and moved on to the next customer in the rapidly forming line.

"Grandma will enjoy these, won't she?" Lexie took Matt's hand again as they walked toward the car.

"Yeah. Do you think Mr. Stone likes tacos?"

"Adam came by for tacos after church yesterday. I think it's his weekly splurge."

As Charley's comment from a few days ago echoed in her mind, she picked up her pace. "I think so."

"Why don't you call him back and ask him to have lunch with us?"

"Not today. I only bought enough tacos for you and me and Grandma."

"We could share."

Another concept he was beginning to understand—and embrace.

"Not today."

"Why not?"

"Mr. Stone might be busy."

"We could ask, couldn't we?"

She popped the locks on the car as they approached. "Tomorrow isn't very far away. You can wait that long to see him and Clyde."

"But dinner was fun last night with Mr. Stone there. It felt kind of like I had a dad." Matt gave a wistful sigh. "All the other kids at Sunday school have dads. I wish I had one too."

"It's always best to have a father in the home."

As another Charley quote replayed in her mind, she exhaled. The man was right. And maybe if she'd stayed in San Francisco after returning from overseas, she'd have met someone who could banish the sadness from her heart and convince her to take a second chance on love. The pool of eligible men was certainly much larger there than in Hope Harbor.

But she'd never regretted her decision to come home, even if the meager supply of bachelors limited her options in the romance department.

The sole downside was the one Charley—and Matt—had highlighted.

Her son would grow up without a father in their home.

"Mom?"

"Yes?" She pulled open the car door, deposited the sack of tacos, and helped him into the car seat.

"Does Mr. Stone have any kids?"

"Not that I know of."

"Why not?"

"He isn't married." That didn't stop a lot of people these days from having a family—but at least Matt wasn't old enough to question her answer.

"You aren't married, either."

"Not anymore. But I was." She adjusted the strap on his restraints.

"Would my dad up in heaven be mad if you got married again?"

A melancholy smile whispered at her lips. Joe, with his go-for-the-gusto, live-every-day-to-the-hilt mentality, mad? No way. He'd loved her too much to want her to spend the rest of her life alone. There hadn't been a selfish bone in his body.

As he'd proven the day he died.

Her mouth flattened.

"No. He wouldn't be mad."

"Are you sure?" He studied her, forehead knotted. " 'Cause you got real sad."

She finished securing his belt and forced herself

128

to lighten up. "How could I be sad? I'm with my best buddy." She kissed the top of his head and stood. "Let's go eat those tacos before they get cold."

He didn't mention Adam or remarriage again during the short drive home. *Thank you, Lord!* Instead, he chattered about the fun he'd had with Clyde yesterday, his new friends Floyd and Gladys, and the picture he was going to draw for Charley's collection.

But as she guided the car through the small town, listening with half her brain to his enthusiastic monologue, the other half was occupied with thoughts of a tall, lean ex-con who'd taken up residence in Hope Harbor—and was beginning to make inroads on her heart.

And that was *not* good. Even in laid-back small towns, police chiefs didn't get involved with felons. There were proprieties to consider.

So she needed to be logical about this. Maintain a professional distance and wait for the electricity to run its course and fizzle out. As it would. A guy who wore a bandana and sported a bad-boy look wasn't her type. Until five days ago, she hadn't had the least interest in him. It was some wacky aberration—and it would go away.

It had to.

Because in a life already filled with challenges, she didn't need the complications a man like Adam Stone would add.

● ● ●

"Adam!"

Clutching his bag of purchases from the Coos Bay resale shop, Adam turned away from the window of the hair salon as Charley closed the distance between them.

"What are you doing up here?" Adam fished his car keys out. "There must be a lot of disappointed taco lovers in Hope Harbor on a beautiful Saturday afternoon like this."

"I was open for a while, but I had a few errands to run. Been doing some shopping?"

"Yeah. I decided at the last minute to go to BJ's wedding and I didn't want to show up in jeans. Luis told me about a resale place here."

"It must have worked out well for you." Charley inspected the bulging bag.

"I kind of had to start from scratch on formal stuff. You're going to the wedding, aren't you?"

"Wouldn't miss it. BJ's a wonderful woman, and I've known Eric since he was younger than Lexie's boy. In fact, Matt kind of reminds me of him at that age. You've met Matt, haven't you?"

"Yes. He and his grandmother watched Clyde for me yesterday while I was at work. The vet wanted someone to monitor him for twenty-four hours."

"That sounds like them. Where's Clyde today?"

"Waiting for me in the car." He motioned down the block.

"Ah. Then you won't want to linger here." He inspected the hair salon.

Adam gave an indifferent shrug. "I wasn't planning to, anyway."

"No? I thought you might be thinking about changing your look for the wedding, now that you have all those fancy new clothes."

"New clothes and a new hairstyle won't change what's inside."

"True . . . but they might better reflect it."

He squinted at the man. "What does that mean?"

"Well, take lawyers, for instance. When one of them is hoping to impress new clients or a judge, you can bet he or she will be well-groomed and well-dressed. They want to convey self-respect and self-confidence—because if they don't believe in themselves, how can they expect anyone else to?"

That made sense. He might not have had the best upbringing, but he understood image stuff. Understood why people in town assumed he was a biker dude. Understood what that implied.

Until the past few days, however, he hadn't cared a lick what people thought.

Then he'd met Lexie . . . and everything had changed. It had been like a window opening, letting a fresh breeze into a long-shuttered room filled with stale air.

As for what that meant for his future . . . he had no idea.

"Are you suggesting I need a haircut?" He tried for a light, teasing tone.

"Nope." Good-natured creases fanned out from the corners of Charley's eyes. "You can tell from my ponytail I don't frequent salons. The trick is to make certain the image you present to the world reflects what's in here." He tapped the left side of his chest. "If there's a disconnect, it confuses people. I'm not saying people can't overcome that . . . but it takes a lot more work."

"You don't like my image?" Adam swept a hand down his body, forcing up the corners of his lips.

"Do you?"

"This is how I've looked for almost twenty years. It's what I'm used to."

"Habits are comfortable—and often hard to break. But you've done a fine job creating a new life since you came to town. I don't think the Adam Stone who moved here eighteen months ago is the same man who went to prison for second-degree robbery . . . do you?"

"No."

"But he looks the same on the outside." Charley let a few beats pass as he perused the sky. "Couldn't ask for a finer day on the Oregon coast. What are your plans for the afternoon?"

"I was going to inspect the planters on the wharf, get a feel for how much repair work needs to be done."

"A worthwhile endeavor. Stop by for a taco after

church tomorrow, if I'm cooking—and enjoy the rest of your day."

Lifting his hand, he wandered down the street.

Adam watched him for a few moments . . . gave the salon one last survey . . . and continued toward his car. If he hadn't happened to pass a styling shop, a haircut wouldn't have crossed his mind.

Yet now that Charley had brought it up, he had to admit the idea had some merit. Shaggy locks and a bandana didn't exactly go with a suit and tie—or his post-prison life. And his dozen amateurish attempts to prune his own hair these past few months had left it pretty hacked up.

Today, however, he had other priorities.

After depositing his purchases in the trunk, he took his place behind the wheel and patted Clyde, who was curled up on the seat beside him.

"Hey, boy. Miss me?"

The pooch gave a little yip and licked his fingers.

"I'll take that as a yes." He twisted the key in the ignition and pulled into traffic.

Clyde edged closer, watching him with bright, happy eyes. Judging him not by his appearance or his history, but by his behavior now. Today.

Too bad people weren't always as open and accepting.

Of course, he hadn't helped matters by reinforcing certain stereotypes with his appearance. If he believed he was a different man than the one who'd gone to prison, as Charley had implied, shouldn't he look like a different man too?

It was definitely a question to ponder during the drive back to Hope Harbor . . . and in the days ahead.

❦ 8 ❦

His Kia was here—meaning Adam was home.

Pulse spiking, Lexie mashed down the brakes on the squad car.

Maybe she should back up to 101 and continue to town. She didn't have to talk to Adam in person. Their business could be handled with a phone call.

Except she'd tried that, and he hadn't answered his cell.

You could have left a message, Lexie.

Yeah, yeah.

But then she wouldn't have had an excuse to drop by.

Kneading her forehead, she blew out a breath and admitted the truth.

She liked being around Adam Stone. However, that didn't mean she had to let it go any further. After all, if you understood the inherent dangers in a situation like this—and she did—you could sidestep them.

As long as she was here, and as long as she remained on alert, why not follow through with this in-person visit?

Decision made, she depressed the gas pedal again, nosed in beside his car, and shut off the engine.

In the sudden quiet, classical jazz drifted toward her from the shed, filling the woods with mellow notes and achingly tender riffs that took "Somewhere Over the Rainbow" to a whole new level.

For half a minute, as the sun dipped low over the sheltered waters of Sandpiper Cove and the late-afternoon light filtered through the majestic fir and spruce trees, she sat unmoving. Adam might not live in the plushest accommodations, but he had a world-class setting—with a soundtrack to match.

After one last, lingering sweep of the collage of sea views framed by tree boughs, she slid out from behind the wheel and left the safety of the cruiser behind.

As she walked toward the shed, the volume of the music increased. No wonder he hadn't heard the crunch of gravel from her car.

At the open door of the outbuilding, she paused. Adam was angled away from her, rubbing a curved piece of wood with a cloth, the impressive muscles below the sleeves of his T-shirt bunching with each stroke. Clyde lay sleeping on a rug in the corner, chin on paws. On a workbench off to the side, a plate held dinner remnants—a crust of bread, a scattering of potato chip fragments, the browning core of an apple.

All at once, Clyde lifted his head, sniffed, and scurried over to the door as fast as his bum leg allowed, tail wagging, tongue hanging out.

Adam swung toward her, posture tautening.

"Sorry. I didn't mean to startle you." She bent to scratch Clyde's ear.

He exhaled, the rigid line of his shoulders easing. "And I didn't mean to overreact. I don't get many unexpected visitors—and recent ones haven't been friendly."

"I tried to call earlier, but your phone rolled to voicemail."

"I should have warned you about that when I gave you my number. Since I don't make many calls, I just have a throwaway for emergencies. In the morning and evening, I check messages. I would have gotten yours later."

"I didn't leave one. I knew I'd be ending the day with a patrol in this area and decided it would be simpler to stop by. I wanted to bring you up to speed on Brian."

"Let me turn down the volume." He crossed to the bench and adjusted a switch on an inexpensive CD player.

"I like your taste in music." Even if it surprised her.

As if he'd read her mind, one side of his mouth

rose. His eyes, however, were resigned rather than amused. "It's more cultured than the heavy metal a biker dude should prefer, right?"

"I didn't say that."

"You didn't have to. Acid rock goes with the look. But I've learned to appreciate some of the finer things in life." He tossed the rag he'd been using onto the workbench. "It's kind of cluttered in here. Why don't we talk outside?"

She gave the space another scan, homing in on a Windsor-style rocking chair. The piece had a warm, rich patina in the late afternoon light spilling through the wide door, along with a graceful back and a polished seat embellished by a gentle hourglass curve on each side. It occupied the workbench in the center of the room and . . .

Wait.

Workbench?

She took a rapid inventory. Lengths of raw wood, bottles of stain, tape measure, clamps, saws . . . and a bunch of equipment she didn't recognize but that appeared to be suited to woodworking.

The pieces fell into place.

"You made that." She gaped at the chair.

"Yeah."

"Wow." She moved closer to it. You didn't have to be a furniture expert to recognize the quality workmanship that had gone into the crafting of the stunning rocker. "It's gorgeous."

"You're being generous—but it's not a bad effort for a beginner."

"Beginner?" She transferred her attention to him. He was standing in the doorway, the dipping sun behind him leaving his face in shadows, masking his expression. "This is *not* a beginner effort. How did you learn to do this?"

"Happenstance. I took a carpentry course in prison and found out I had some natural abilities. After BJ hired Luis, he showed me a bunch of woodworking stuff his father taught him in Cuba while he was growing up. The rest I learned from books—and practice. BJ gets me scrap lumber from the sawmill where she buys her wood. Any spare cash I accumulate goes into equipment."

"Your pieces are made from scrap lumber?" She examined the chair again.

"Yeah. All of them have a few defects."

"I don't see any in this chair."

"You would if you looked close enough—but most flaws can be smoothed out with a little effort. I'm able to salvage a lot of the leftovers the mill thinks are worthless."

"Well, speaking as someone who doesn't have a creative bone in her body, I'm awed. You have a real talent for this. What do you do with the pieces you make?"

"I've only finished a few. The rocking chair is one of a pair I made for BJ and Eric as a wedding gift."

"That's some gift."

"I'm sure they'll get a lot of presents more valuable than mine."

"Some guests may spend more cash on their gifts—but money isn't the only measure of value." She stroked a hand down the satin finish on the curved rocker. "Have you ever thought about selling your work?"

"It's just a hobby."

"You might be able to build it into more than that. Quality handcrafted goods command high prices. If Tracy can sell her Harbor Point cranberry nut cake all over the country for top dollar, there's no reason you couldn't do the same with your furniture."

"I already have a job."

"But you make furniture anyway on the side."

"For my soul, not for money. Working with wood gives me . . . I don't know. Joy, I guess. And a feeling of freedom. Creating beauty out of discards, turning rejects and scraps into something functional, it's . . ." His voice rasped, and he pivoted away. "Sorry. You didn't come out here to discuss furniture. Let's find a comfortable place to sit and you can tell me about Brian."

He disappeared out the door.

Lexie waited a few moments. He needed a chance to regain his composure—and she needed to try and assimilate all the disconnects he kept throwing at her. The raw emotion on his face and in his voice as he'd attempted to express what woodworking meant to him did *not* fit the image of a hardened ex-con that his physical appearance and usual taciturn manner projected to the world.

This was a man of great passion, who felt deeply. His heart might be tattered and his soul wounded from all the dark experiences in his life, but deep inside an ember of his better nature had continued to glimmer, waiting to be coaxed back to life.

Here in Hope Harbor, it seemed that ember was finding its spark.

What other surprises did this man hold?

Still pondering that, she emerged from the shed. Adam was waiting in the shadows, watching Clyde chase a squirrel.

"Would you like to go into the cabin while we talk?" He motioned toward the rustic structure.

That made sense. The table where they'd shared pizza would be an appropriate place for a business discussion. She should take his suggestion.

Instead, she looked through the trees toward the water and heard different words tumble out of her mouth. "Is there anywhere to sit on the beach?"

He appeared to be as surprised by the question as she was.

"Some rocks. They're not that comfortable."

He was giving her an out.

She should take it.

"Works for me."

What in creation . . . ?

That wasn't what she'd intended to say.

"You might get your uniform dirty."

"It's been up close and personal with a lot worse than dirt and sand. Unless you'd rather stay up here?" Maybe he'd save her from herself.

No such luck.

"The cove is one of my favorite spots. I like to end my day down there with a cup of coffee while the sun sets. Clyde and I have the place to ourselves unless Casper stops by."

"Casper?"

"A silver-white harbor seal that used to hang out near BJ's house. She named him. Lately he's been showing up here on the rocks offshore." He rubbed his palms down his jeans. "It's too early for my sunset ritual . . . but I'd be happy to brew a pot of coffee if you'd like a cup while we talk."

The urge to accept was strong—but she'd already crossed a line by suggesting they hold their meeting down by the water. Sharing convivial cups of coffee on a secluded beach might be pushing it too far.

"Scratch that." Adam shoved his fingers in his back pockets and gave her a grin that seemed forced. "It's dinnertime, and I remember what you said about your mom's reaction to delayed meals."

The man had obviously picked up her hesitation.

"I was exaggerating a little." *Quit stalling, Lexie. Take the out he's offered.* "Mom knows I

141

often have to work late. If I'm running behind, she puts a plate in the oven for me."

"For real?" He shook his head. "It must be nice to have people in your life who care that much."

Though his tone was conversational, the subtle yet unmistakable note of longing deep-sixed her lingering qualms about holding their meeting on the water. "I'd love a cup of coffee."

He did a double take—but recovered quickly.

"Great." He indicated a narrow path that led through the woods. "That will take you to the beach. I'll bring the coffee down as soon as it's ready—but I don't have any cream. Is milk okay?"

He'd noticed how she'd doctored her java on Friday?

A tingle of pleasure rippled through her.

"Milk is fine."

"Go ahead and find a spot. There's not a bad seat in the house." He snapped his fingers, and Clyde scampered over. "Beach, boy?"

The dog's ears perked up.

"Hang on a sec." Adam disappeared into the shed again, returning a few seconds later with a rubber ball. "Clyde loves retrieving this. I've been holding off since he got hurt, but a few short throws would make him happy."

She took the ball, her fingers brushing his during the handoff.

Mercy!

It was tingle city all over again.

She backed off a few paces. "I'll, uh, see you down there. Come on, Clyde."

Before the fresh doubts that were crashing over her like waves on a stormy Oregon day could undercut her decision, Lexie strode away, Clyde prancing at her feet.

Maybe she'd live to regret this lapse in prudence.

Maybe she was playing with fire.

Maybe this was a mistake that would come back to bite her.

But when she emerged onto the generous crescent of sand where the sheltered blue-green waves lapped gently at the shore, being here felt right.

And for this moment, she was going to take Charley's advice, listen to the inner voice urging her to stay—and trust it hadn't led her astray.

What in heaven's name were you thinking, Stone?

As the aroma of brewing coffee filled the cabin, Adam extracted the two mismatched mugs from the kitchen cabinet and weighed them in his hands.

Telling Lexie Graham about his evening ritual—and incorporating her into it—had been flat-out dumb. He should have let her conduct her business and leave instead of trying to find ways to extend her visit.

But whatever impulse had spawned his ill-advised invitation, he was stuck now. She was waiting for him.

Which led to two questions.

Why had she accepted his offer of coffee . . . and why had she suggested holding their meeting on the beach in the first place?

He pulled out the carton of milk, mulling over the conundrum.

Came up blank.

There was no reason for her to spend any more time than necessary with an ex-con. She'd no doubt put in a long, busy day, and there was a hot meal waiting for her at home . . . along with a son who would be eager to see her.

The coffeemaker sputtered, and he moved toward it.

Whatever her motivation, he wasn't likely to figure it out in the next few minutes. The best plan would be to tread with caution . . . let her take the lead . . . and do nothing to further detain her the minute she indicated she was ready to leave.

Armed with that plan, he poured their coffee and followed the familiar path to the beach.

Emerging from the woods less than a minute later, he spotted her off to the right. She was sitting on the sand, her back against a large rock, legs stretched out in front of her, ankles crossed, Clyde's head in her lap as she stroked his fur.

As he approached, his steps silent on the sand, the two of them were the picture of contentment.

Except for the uniform, Lexie could be any young woman who'd stopped to admire the view while out for a walk on the beach with her dog.

And it was a great view.

Better than ever tonight, thanks to her presence.

He shortened his stride, engraving the scene on his mind—but slow as he walked, the distance between them disappeared too fast.

Only after he lowered himself beside her and held out her coffee did she glance toward him.

"Thanks." She wrapped her fingers around the mug. "You have a beautiful spot here." Sipping the brew, she gazed out over the tranquil water, toward the shimmering golden orb hovering over the horizon. "It's so peaceful."

"Yeah, it is." He rested his back against the boulder too, keeping a respectable distance between them. "Whenever I'm down here, all my worries fall away. In the sunset and the water and the expanse of sky and clouds, I can feel God's presence. Sometimes even more than in church—though I'd appreciate it if you wouldn't share that with Reverend Baker."

"An easy promise to make. I don't see him much."

"I noticed you don't attend services with your mom and Matt." He positioned his comment as a statement rather than a question. If she didn't want to talk about her faith, he wasn't going to push. But he *was* curious. She'd obviously been raised in a Christian home and had no objections to her son attending church with her mother. There had to be a reason she stayed away.

Silent seconds ticked by, one after another, until he was certain she was going to ignore his remark.

Then she surprised him.

"I stopped going to church after my husband died." Her inflection was matter-of-fact, but a tiny thread of hostility and anger wove through it.

"Why?"

The question slipped out before he could stop it . . . and it didn't go over well. Although she continued to stroke Clyde, he could feel her subtle withdrawal.

"Look . . . I'm sorry. I didn't mean to pry. Forget I asked."

She pulled out a pair of sunglasses and slid them over her nose. "I just don't talk much about that subject. It's not a pretty story."

"I can appreciate not wanting to dwell on ugliness." He spoke slowly, choosing his words with care. "In my case, though, that leaves only a very small window of time to talk about. Unlike you, I didn't have a great childhood. The best part of my life didn't start until I went to prison."

"You mean until you were *released* from prison?"

"No. While I was *in* prison. One of the guys convinced me to join the Bible study Reverend Baker led every week, and that changed my life."

"He's a good man."

"I agree. But it was the message, not the messenger, that made the difference."

"Mmm."

At her noncommittal reply, he took a slug of his coffee. If he stepped outside his comfort level and opened up a little, might she reciprocate—if not tonight, one day soon?

It was worth a gamble.

Gripping his mug, he focused on the dark depths of the coffee. "The message was a tough sell at first, though."

"I imagine you had plenty of reasons to resist."

"Yeah, I did. My life had been a train wreck for as long as I could remember. God was invisible all those years while my dad was drinking and knocking me around and taking every opportunity to tell me I was a worthless piece of . . ."—he cleared his throat—"trash."

"Didn't your mother intervene . . . or wasn't she around?" Dismay underscored her gentle question.

"She was there." He swallowed past the hint of bitterness that curdled on his tongue. "But she just disappeared whenever the punching and kicking started. So I ran away when I was sixteen. Kids that age aren't equipped for street life, no matter how tough they think they are. I hooked up with the wrong people, did what I had to do to survive . . . and everything went downhill from there."

Shifting toward him, she removed her glasses. The warmth and compassion in her eyes seeped straight into his heart. "I'm sorry, Adam. I can't begin to imagine how hard it must have been to grow up in that kind of environment."

His fingers tightened again on his mug.

She'd called him Adam.

Since he was sixteen, no one other than Charley had ever called him anything but Stone. He'd never asked the taco-making artist to use his first name, but it had sounded right coming from him . . . and it sounded right coming from Lexie too.

"Don't try. You don't want to go there. I'm glad you had it better than I did."

"It's not fair, though."

"Lots of things aren't."

"True." She leaned back against the rock, her features hardening. "That's one of my issues with God. I don't understand how a kind and loving deity can let innocent people suffer."

"I didn't either—until Reverend Baker pointed me to a passage in Isaiah that helped me deal with that disconnect. 'For my thoughts are not your thoughts, neither are your ways my ways, saith the Lord. For as the heavens are higher than the earth, so are my ways higher than your ways, and my thoughts than your thoughts.' "

"In other words, don't try to figure it out?"

"That about sums it up. We're human; he's God. To assume we can grasp his mind is actually a form of arrogance."

She continued to stroke Clyde, a slight frown creasing her brow. "I never thought of it quite that way."

"I hadn't, either. In the end, it comes down to trust. We have to accept that God understands why things happen, even if we don't—and try to learn and grow from our misfortunes. We also have to remember that he never promised us a perfect life on earth, only a perfect eternity—if we follow his teachings. Although it sounds like your childhood was close to perfect."

"It was. As my parents' sole offspring, I was the apple of their eye—pardon the cliché."

"What happened to your dad?"

She lifted a handful of sand. Let it drift through her fingers. "He died of a massive heart attack four years ago."

"I'm sorry."

"Thanks. I still miss him every day. But that loss did help me realize it was time to let go of a life that no longer held any allure. Not long after that, I came home."

"Home from where?"

"San Francisco. I worked in a field office for the Bureau of Diplomatic Security. It was close enough to Hope Harbor so I could get back here often."

"And you've never thought about going to church since you came home?"

"No." She slipped the glasses back on.

Once again, he'd overstepped. And her abrupt *no* hadn't given him a lot to work with in terms of trying to salvage the situation.

He'd have to do the best with what he had . . . and tread carefully.

"Well, church has been a blessing for me. Ever since Reverend Baker convinced me I wasn't as alone and unloved as I'd always thought, I haven't missed a week. Maybe my parents didn't care about me, but God did—despite all the bad stuff I'd done. The whole concept that I didn't have to earn his love, that he gave it freely, blew me away. But once I accepted that, I vowed to stay the course and rebuild my life after I got out of prison —whatever it took."

"Seems like you're achieving that."

"So far, so good."

"I admire how you've turned your life around without any kind of family support." She patted Clyde's head, avoiding the injured area. "Did you ever have any contact with your parents after you left home?"

"None that I initiated. My mother did track me down in prison and wrote to tell me my dad had died—and to apologize for not being a better mother and protecting me."

"Did you write back?"

"Not for a while." He watched an egg-shaped mole crab scurry along the wet sand at the edge of the water, then vanish beneath the surface in a flurry of digging. "Reverend Baker encouraged me to pray on it, and months later I did respond. But my letter came back as undeliverable."

"Maybe she moved."

"No. After I was released, I did some research and found out she'd died of a drug overdose." He took a sip of his tepid coffee. "I'm glad I made the effort, but to be honest, I'm not sorry we didn't connect. I doubt there would have been a happy ending."

"Yeah. Happy endings are hard to come by." The muscles in her throat contracted, and when she continued, her tone was more businesslike. "You ready to talk about Brian?"

"Yes." More than. He'd already told Lexie almost as much about his background as he'd shared with Reverend Baker.

"The counselor said he and his mother were receptive to the remedial steps he outlined. Those include making restitution for any material damage—like your vet bills for Clyde—and sixty hours of community service for Brian, beginning with the planter project. Given their financial situation, no fine was imposed for this first offense."

"Did he identify the other kid who was involved?"

"Not yet—but the counselor will continue to press for that information in his meetings with the family."

"So what happens next?"

"Brian's mother will be expecting a call from you this week to discuss the planter project. You can work out the details by phone or in person. Here's her number." She pulled a slip of paper from her pocket and handed it to him. "She has rotating hours at her waitress job, so it may take a few tries for the two of you to connect. Have you tackled the project yet?"

"No. It's the main item on my weekend agenda, other than BJ and Eric's wedding."

"Ah, yes. The social event of the year." The breeze freed a few strands of Lexie's hair, and she tucked them behind her ear. "I've been meaning to get up to the Seabird Inn for a tour, and the reception gives me the perfect excuse to poke around. I heard the remodel turned out great, thanks to BJ's design and the hard work you all put into it."

"John was happy with it. And Eric told BJ it's booked solid." At room prices that boggled his mind. "Do you think there will be a lot of people at the wedding?"

"I expect most of the town is invited. As a native, Eric knows almost everyone. BJ might be a recent transplant, but she's endeared herself to the community. I'm glad they found each other." She peered at her watch. "It's getting late. Will you let me know once you touch base with the Huttons? The counselor is running the show now, but I'd like to keep tabs on how the arrangement is progressing."

"Sure."

She tipped her head back to finish her coffee, giving him a perfect view of the graceful arch of her neck.

"Thanks for this." She handed him her mug and ruffled Clyde's ear, gently urging him off her lap. "I hate to disturb you, boy, but I have to go home."

With what sounded like a disappointed snuffle, the pup stood.

Adam could relate. He was sorry to see her go too.

In one lithe movement, she rose to her feet—leaving him no choice but to follow.

"I'll walk you to your car."

"No need. Stay and enjoy the sunset. I have a feeling it's going to be spectacular tonight, and I don't want to mess up your evening routine. Talk to you soon."

He watched as she crossed the beach and entered the woods, catching occasional glimpses of her through the trees. As far as he could tell, she never looked back.

Just as well.

She might not appreciate being gawked at.

Two minutes after she disappeared from view, he heard the faint hum of an engine. Slowly it faded away.

She was gone.

Leaning against the boulder where they'd propped their backs, he traced the faint outline of lipstick clinging to the rim of her mug . . . the only visible proof she'd briefly occupied this private part of his world.

Maybe he wouldn't wash it.

As that absurd notion popped into his mind, he snorted.

Clyde sent him a quizzical look, then grabbed the rubber ball and trotted over. As if he knew his friend needed distracting.

"You're a good buddy, you know that?" He set the lipstick-imprinted mug on the boulder and bent down to take the ball. "One last toss until the doc gives us the green light for more."

He sent the ball arcing through the air as Clyde raced ahead as fast as his bum leg allowed, anticipating the throw, his paws flinging sand in all directions.

A loud belch echoed across the water, and Adam shaded his eyes. Casper had returned to his perch on the rocky outcrop fifty yards offshore. As if he too sensed the man who lived in this isolated place needed company.

He rolled his eyes. What a bunch of nonsense.

Clyde just wanted to play, and the seal's appearance was a fluke.

But he had to admit, the animals did help ease the loneliness that had intensified since a certain police chief appeared on his doorstep a week ago.

Odd how he'd been content to come home to this solitary cove for months with no one but Clyde to greet him, yet now he felt restless. Like some essential element was missing from his life.

And after spending time with Lexie, he knew exactly what that element was.

The companionship of a woman with whom he could share laughter and tears, joys and sorrows, sunsets on the beach, quiet dinners, late-night confidences, hugs and touches.

But as the two of them had discussed less than fifteen minutes ago, happy endings were in short supply—especially the romantic kind. He could overcome a lot, start fresh in many ways, but he could never erase his prison record . . . and no woman who had any other options would settle for a man like him.

God—and Clyde—might be able to offer him unconditional love, but humans weren't as forgiving about unsavory baggage.

And he was loaded down with it.

Clyde ran back, compensating for his lameness with an odd but efficient lope that was all his own, and dropped the ball at his feet.

"I think we're done for tonight, fella. Try this instead." He dug a treat out of his pocket and bent down.

The pooch downed it in one gulp, licked his lips, and set off to nose around the water's edge.

In the distance, the sun was dipping lower . . .

but it wouldn't vanish beneath the horizon for at least an hour, hour and a half. He could finish the rocking chair and be back with another cup of coffee in time to see it. A sound plan, since he wanted to deliver the chairs to the reception site tomorrow rather than tote them over there the night of the wedding while wearing his fancy duds.

Adam picked up Lexie's mug from the rock and retrieved his from the sand. Hers was in much better shape than the nicked-up model he'd claimed for himself. Glaze pristine instead of chipped. Inside unblemished versus stained. Finish smooth rather than riddled with hairline cracks.

Not a bad analogy for the differences between the two of them.

Still . . . she'd stayed tonight. Given him a memory of a pleasant interlude on a beach with a beautiful woman.

That was a gift to cherish.

And as he whistled for Clyde and trekked back up the trail in the waning light of this ordinary Tuesday, the day no longer felt the least bit mundane or routine. Nor did the fading radiance of the sun dim the glow Lexie had generated in his heart.

Perhaps, come morning, this feeling of . . . hope was the only way to describe it . . . would be gone.

But for now, he was going to hold on tight to it—and thank God for an evening he would long remember.

❧ 9 ❧

"I thought we were done with all this." Planting his fists on his hips, Officer Jim Gleason surveyed the broken statue and crushed plantings in the meditation garden Father Murphy had created behind St. Francis church. "Instead, they're targeting God."

"Or St. Francis." Lexie inspected the damaged statue of the monk. "More likely our vandal—or vandals—just picked a spot they knew wouldn't be occupied on a Tuesday night after dark."

"You think the Hutton kid was in on this?"

"My instincts say no. Both the juvenile counselor and I laid it on the line with him. He knows he's getting off easy for a first offense, and that if he screws up, his case will escalate to a judge. I'm betting it's the work of his partner in crime, acting alone or with a new accomplice."

"Too bad the Hutton boy didn't identify him."

"That may be about to change."

"You going to pay him another visit?"

"His case is in the counselor's hands now, but this merits an in-person follow-up interview—and I intend to tag along."

A car swung into the parking lot . . . started toward the rectory . . . then changed direction mid-course and barreled toward them. Reverend

Baker waved through the open window, screeched to a stop, and hopped out.

"I just heard about this." He called out the greeting while he hustled over, distress etched on his features as he scanned the damage. "My word. Who would commit such a senseless act? Kevin must be devastated. This little piece of heaven is his pride and joy."

"I only had a couple of minutes to speak with him before the six-thirty Mass, but yeah, he's upset. That's why I called the chief. I thought she might want to poke around while we waited for the padre to finish." Jim's radio crackled to life, and he retreated to listen in.

"Such a waste." Reverend Baker shook his head. "I was hoping we'd seen the end of our town's little crime spree, now that you've identified one of the perpetrators, but it appears this isn't over yet."

"It may be, if we can convince the guilty teen to reveal the name of his accomplice."

"I hope you succeed—but boys that age can have a warped sense of loyalty."

"Maybe his self-preservation instincts will kick in if we exert some pressure."

"I'll pray for that outcome. We don't need this kind of hooliganism in Hope Harbor. Kevin!" He lifted a hand in greeting as the priest exited the back door of the church and crossed the grass to join the group in the garden. "I'm so sorry about this." Reverend Baker clasped the priest's hand between both of his.

The other man managed a smile. "Thank you. It was a shock—but spending the past half hour with the Lord helped restore my perspective. Flowers can be replanted and statues replaced. It's like my grandmother used to say whenever we complained about our tribulations—no one died, it could be worse, and it can be fixed, so stop bellyaching."

"A sound philosophy."

"She was a smart woman." Father Murphy did another sweep of the garden. "Still . . . I pray for the soul of whoever did this. It must be sorely troubled."

"I agree. But despite the mess, I think we can get this back into shape with a few hours of elbow grease, don't you?"

"We?"

"Some extra physical activity beyond our Thursday golf games would be beneficial to my waistline." The minister patted his stomach. "What's on your agenda today?"

"Sick calls and homily prep for Sunday."

"Do the sick calls this morning and I'll help you with the homily prep while we work in the garden this afternoon. You might actually have some Bible citations in there for once."

"Hey . . . I quote the Bible."

"So you keep telling me. But at Grace Christian,

we've taken to heart a very important passage from the Good Book: 'All Scripture is given by inspiration of God, and is profitable for doctrine, for reproof, for correction, for instruction in righteousness.' "

"Catholics believe that too."

"So you're familiar with the quote?"

"I do have a passing acquaintance with the Bible."

"Including that quote?"

Father Murphy huffed out a breath. "I'm not playing name that verse with you anymore."

"I can understand that. It's hard to catch up when you're so far behind." The corners of the minister's mouth twitched.

"Fine. Second Timothy, chapter 3."

"Incomplete . . . but not bad. You neglected to mention the verse. For future reference, it's seventeen."

"Sixteen."

Reverend Baker squinted at him. "I don't think so."

"Look it up. You can apologize tomorrow during our golf game. As for reading the Bible, I'll have you know we—"

"Gentlemen . . ." Lexie tried to flatten the bow of her lips. The good-natured banter between the clerics was always a hoot. "Officer Gleason needs to get a more complete statement. I'll pay our known vandal another visit today—and try again to convince him to give us the other boy's name."

"I'll pray for that," Revered Baker offered.

"As will I." Father Murphy made the sign of the cross.

"All assistance—human and divine—is welcome."

"I'll include a special prayer for a quick resolution to this unfortunate situation during Sunday services too. You could join us if you like." Reverend Baker touched her arm. "Where two or three and all that."

"Or if you'd like a change of ecclesiastical scene, you'd be welcome at St. Francis. I'll put a prayer in our petitions this weekend as well." Father Murphy winked at her.

"Trying to steal my congregants again, I see." The Grace Christian pastor gave a mock huff.

"Not at all. But we *have* taken a page from your playbook and are instituting a social after Mass once a month. With homemade doughnuts, not those store-bought belly bombers you serve."

"You manage to find excuses often enough to stop by after our services to sample those belly bombers."

"Pure coincidence. I never—"

Lexie cleared her throat, and both clerics angled toward her. "I need to run. Jim, keep me in the loop. Nothing jumped out at me, but do another walk-through. If you spot anything useful, give me a call."

"Roger."

Leaving the officer to deal with the statement—and fighting a yawn—Lexie returned to her car. After going to bed at ten, she shouldn't be this tired, despite the early wake-up call from Jim.

On the other hand, she *had* spent half the night tossing while she relived her impromptu coffee date with Adam.

The man was an enigma for sure, busting one ex-con stereotype after another . . . except for his biker appearance. Every single thing she'd learned about him in the past nine days had been positive. One facet at a time, he was emerging as a diamond instead of a piece of coal.

And getting to know him better—off the job—was becoming more and more tempting.

It would be dangerous to follow that inclination, however. What would the people in town think about their police chief fraternizing with an ex-con?

Hard to say . . . but it might not be pretty.

Sighing, she slid behind the wheel and stuck the key in the ignition. Being attracted to a felon was a complication she did *not* need. She liked her life just as it was—simple, safe, predictable, uneventful. In other words, perfect.

The only negative was the loneliness that plagued her in the wee hours of the morning if sleep was elusive.

She could live with that, though. It was a small

price to pay for all the benefits she'd gained by moving home.

Or that was what she'd believed until Adam Stone had crossed her path and reminded her she was more than a mom and a daughter and a police chief.

She was also a woman.

Releasing the brake, she put the car in gear and rolled forward through the dissipating morning fog. Soon the sun would banish the last of the obscuring wisps, and clear skies would emerge. Visibility would increase, giving drivers an unobstructed view as they navigated the twists and turns on 101.

Too bad she didn't have as clear a view of the road that lay ahead of *her*.

Once upon a time, in a sticky situation like this, she'd have sought guidance from the Almighty. But he hadn't been on her radar for more than five years. Not since anger at the injustice of life had pushed him off.

Strange how adversity could turn some people away from God yet lead others to him.

Like Adam.

The man's faith appeared to be sincere . . . but where had God been during his childhood in an abusive home? Where had he been in *her* life, during those tragic days that had left her soul dry and her spirit broken?

I am with you always.

Fingers tightening on the wheel, she frowned. What in the world had prompted *that?* It was a quote from somewhere in the Bible—but she wouldn't win any prizes in a game of name that verse, either. Her last brush with Scripture had been at Joe's funeral, when the minister uttered some nonsense about the Lord being close to the brokenhearted.

Right.

If that was true, why hadn't she ever felt his presence during those first traumatic months . . . or in all the years that followed?

And why were Bible verses suddenly popping into her head, anyway?

Mashing her lips together, she tapped a finger on the wheel. The friendly jibing between the clerics could have prompted the aberration. Or Adam's confession last night about how his faith had changed his life.

But whatever the reason, she didn't intend to dwell on God. The top item on her agenda today was contacting the juvenile counselor to set up a meeting with Brian and his mother.

If the boy was smart, he'd pass on the name of his fellow vandal and they could wrap up this case —assuming he hadn't been involved in last night's garden party at St. Francis.

Lexie braked at the main crossroads on Dockside Drive, the aroma of fresh-baked cinnamon rolls from Sweet Dreams Bakery setting off a rumble in her stomach. Go home and have a hot breakfast, or continue to the office?

Despite her hunger, the decision was a no-brainer. The office.

She continued straight down the street. Her mom would be up by now, rested and ready to pick up the questioning where she'd left off last night after Lexie mentioned her stop at Adam's place. Dodging the nonstop queries had almost given her a case of whiplash. Thank goodness she hadn't shared anything about their impromptu coffee klatch on the beach. Based on the gleam in her mother's eye whenever Adam's name came up, she was already veering into matchmaking territory.

Better to swing by the Myrtle Café in an hour or two for takeout and avoid another interrogation until this evening. If fate was kind, by then her mom would be fixated on some issue other than the lack of romance in a certain police chief's life.

Unfortunately, the odds of that could be summed up in two words.

Fat chance.

Adam maneuvered around another set of potholes and double-checked the address he'd scribbled down while talking to Brenda Hutton.

The decrepit mobile home coming up on the right was his destination.

As he slowed the car, a nauseating sense of

déjà vu swept over him. Roll the clock back twenty years, this could have been his home. Half his early life had been spent in a rusted-out trailer that could be this one's twin.

For a fleeting moment, the temptation to put the car in reverse and hightail it away from here as fast as he could overpowered him. This was the life he'd walked away from, and he wanted no part of it ever again.

Except he'd promised Lexie he'd work with Brian.

And it wasn't as if he was going back to his old ways. He was trying to keep another young boy hovering on the brink from making the same mistakes he had. After he finished this lunch-hour meeting, he could return to the new life he'd created and leave this world behind.

Sucking in a lungful of air, he braked, killed the engine, and forced himself to walk to the front door.

The woman who answered on the second ring sent another shock wave rippling through him.

Brenda Hutton didn't bear the least physical resemblance to his mother, but she had the same beaten-down, submissive demeanor. The same premature gray in her hair. The same victim-like aura.

All of which stirred up the simmering anger deep in his gut that he thought he'd put to rest long ago.

"You must be Adam Stone." The woman gave him a quick, wary once-over, unease radiating from her as her gaze lingered on the longish hair and bandana.

It appeared the negative first impression went both ways.

"Yes."

"I'm Brenda Hutton." She held out her hand.

He gave her limp fingers a quick squeeze.

The instant he released them, she stepped back. "Please, come in."

He crossed the threshold, into the living room. At least the interior didn't stir up any unpleasant memories. The furniture was threadbare, the carpet worn, the paint faded—but there wasn't any clutter and the place was clean. Nothing like the sty he'd called home.

"Thank you for meeting me on your lunch hour." She followed him to the center of the room, twisting her hands together. "Working nights can be difficult, and with Brian only having half a day of school today, I thought it might be better to get together now rather than wait until I'm on days next week."

"This is fine. Where's Brian?"

"I'll get him. Have a seat." She gave a vague wave around the living room and disappeared down the hall.

He remained standing. It was always better to begin from a dominant position, and unless Brian was a basketball player, he'd have the height advantage.

In less than a minute, a door opened somewhere down the hall. Moments later, Brenda reappeared, Brian behind her. At the doorway to the living room, she moved aside, took his arm, and urged him forward.

"Brian, this is Adam Stone."

The kid gave him the same head-to-toe his mother had.

Adam reciprocated.

The boy was about five-seven and skinny, hands in pockets in the typical slouch posture kids his age favored, sandy hair a tad too long, and the remnants of some serious bruises fading to yellow on his cheek and around his eye.

A slight, belligerent tilt to his chin was a warning flag, but he'd give the kid the benefit of the doubt.

"Hello, Brian." Adam held out his hand.

The boy seemed surprised by the gesture but leaned forward and clasped his fingers. "Hi."

"I understand you're willing to help me repair the flower boxes on the wharf."

"Yeah. I guess."

His lack of enthusiasm wasn't encouraging.

"I'm starting on Saturday. Are you available?"

"Yes." Brenda answered for him. "What time?"

"I have a commitment later that day, so I want to be rolling by seven."

"Seriously?" Brian grimaced. "I always sleep in on Saturday."

"You can sleep in again after you finish the program the counselor laid out." Brenda shot her son a stern look. "He'll be there."

"Aw, Mom, can't I go later?"

"No, you can't." She faced him, hands clenched at her sides. "You're lucky to get off as easy as you did. You will do exactly what everyone tells you and be grateful for this second chance. Is that understood?"

Adam raised an eyebrow.

When it came to her son, Brenda had some backbone after all.

Too bad his own mother hadn't cared this much about *his* welfare.

"Yeah." The kid hung his head.

"What time would you like me to drop him at the wharf?" Brenda swiveled away from Brian.

If the woman was working a late shift at the diner in Coos Bay, it wasn't likely she'd get home until ten or eleven. No sense making her get up early too.

"I can pick him up. Six forty-five."

"Oh, geez." Brian rolled his eyes. "I'll be dead by noon."

"Do your homework and go to bed early Friday night. You're grounded anyway. What else do you have to do?"

The kid gave her a mutinous stare.

"Okay . . . we need to get something straight here." Adam waited until Brian looked at him. "I have a job to do on the wharf. This is not a babysitting gig. If you're not committed to this plan, we can ask the counselor to come up with an alternative. I want a partner on this job who's willing to learn and intends to work hard, not someone I have to prod every step of the way. If that doesn't describe how you're approaching this, I'm out of here. You decide."

"He's going to—"

Adam lifted his hand to cut Brenda off, never breaking eye contact with Brian. He appreciated the woman's desire to help her son, but he needed buy-in from the boy too or the whole plan would be a bust.

Several seconds ticked by in the silent trailer, a parade of emotions passing through Brian's eyes. Hostility . . . anger . . . frustration . . . capitulation . . . resolve . . . and the hint of respect Adam had been waiting for.

"I'm in."

"Fine. Expect me at six forty-five. I plan to work until about—"

The doorbell rang.

Twin furrows creasing her brow, Brenda walked toward it. "Excuse me. I wasn't expecting anyone else. Give me a minute and we can . . ." As she pulled open the door, her words died.

Lexie and some guy in a sport coat stood on the stoop.

"Good afternoon, Mrs. Hutton." The guy extended his hand. "The chief and I would like to talk with you and Brian for a few minutes. I understand school let out at noon today."

"Yes. Sure. Come in." She backed up.

As she entered, Lexie looked his direction. "Hi, Adam. We saw your car outside."

"A noon meeting worked best for all of us."

"Let me introduce you to Brian's juvenile counselor."

He shook hands with the guy as she did so. If the man found his biker appearance off-putting, he gave no indication of it.

"May we sit down?" The counselor indicated the couch.

"Yes. Of course." Brenda was back to hand twisting. "Um . . . is there a problem?"

"I'm hoping Brian will tell us that."

"I was just leaving . . ." Adam took a step toward the door.

"You might want to wait, if you have the time." Lexie sat on the couch. "Depending on the outcome of this discussion, the arrangements could change."

"I can spare five minutes." He propped a shoulder against the wall and folded his arms, remaining in the background. Whatever was about to go down didn't require his active participation.

The counselor sat beside Lexie while mother and son claimed side-by-side chairs.

"Chief, why don't you give them the background?" The counselor opened a file as he deferred to Lexie.

She got straight to the heart of the matter.

"We had another vandalism incident in town last night, at St. Francis church. A statue was broken and flowers were uprooted. It's similar in style to the previous incidents, which leads us to believe it was done by the same perpetrators."

While she talked, Adam watched Brian. The boy lost a few shades of color, and his knuckles whitened on the arms of his chair.

"We need to know if you were involved, Brian." The counselor's posture remained relaxed, but his tone was somber.

"No! I had nothing to do with that! I was here all night."

"Was anyone with you?"

"No. My mom was at work." A hint of panic hiked the pitch of his voice. "But I was here. I'm not lying. I swear!"

Brenda leaned forward, posture taut, her own complexion pale. "If he says he was here, he was."

"We'd like to believe that." The counselor's tone remained calm and nonjudgmental. "But it would help if you told us who else is involved in these vandalism incidents. Protecting lawbreakers isn't in your best interest."

Brian was shaking his head even before the man finished speaking. "I can't do that. We made a pact."

"Why would you honor a promise you made to a kid who beat you up?" Brenda gripped his arm.

A muscle clenched in his jaw, but he remained silent.

Adam checked his watch. The kid wasn't going to budge, and he had to leave. Besides, after dealing with plenty of criminals, he'd already reached his own conclusions about Brian.

The boy hadn't been involved in last night's incidents.

As far as he was concerned, their arrangement stood.

"Excuse me . . ." All heads swiveled his direction. "I have to get back to work. If anyone needs to contact me, you all have my number. Brian, I'll see you on Saturday. Wear old clothes. I'll let myself out."

Without waiting for a response, he slipped through the door.

Once behind the wheel of his car, he glanced back at the trailer. The meeting wasn't going to last much longer . . . because Brian wasn't going to talk. Not today. Not with people he didn't know and trust.

If the two of them could develop some rapport while they worked on the planters, however, it was possible he might be able to convince the boy that revealing the name of his partner was the right thing to do.

Then again, he had zilch experience working with adolescents and no fatherly role model from his own youth to follow. For all he knew, the kid might decide to go the silent treatment route while they worked.

But he'd give their partnership his best shot—and with a little assist from above, maybe he'd find a way to connect with the troubled teen and save him from making any more mistakes he'd live to regret.

❧ 10 ❧

"This is a total waste of time." Lexie stopped flipping through the rack of clothing at the boutique in Coos Bay her mother had dragged her to. "I do not need a new dress. You found what you came for. Let's go home."

"Are you planning to wear your uniform to BJ and Eric's wedding?"

"You know better." She scowled as her mother pulled a chiffony creation off the rack and gave it a critical survey.

"Well, what *are* you going to wear? The wedding is the day after tomorrow."

"I have dresses in my closet."

"All five years old—minimum."

"They still fit."

"That's not the point."

Lexie snatched her mother's hand before she could pull out another garment. "Mom . . . no one's going to be paying any attention to me. I'm not the bride."

"And you never will be if you keep hiding all your assets under that badge and uniform."

Lexie narrowed her eyes. It had been simple to sidestep the subtle hints about romance her mom had begun dropping, but this new direct approach required an equally direct response. "For the record, I'm not in the market for a husband."

"I got that message—but things can change."

Hadn't Charley said the same thing to her less than a week ago?

Why was everyone fixated on change all of a sudden?

"I'm fine with the status quo."

Her mother bent down to examine the hand-kerchief hem of a dress, muttering something that sounded like "more's the pity."

Lexie folded her arms and retreated a step from the rack of party dresses in which she had zero interest. If her mother hadn't badgered her into this shopping trip—and arranged babysitting for Matt—she could be spending a quiet Thursday night at home with her son, watching a Disney movie.

She was beginning to smell a rat in her mother's

lament about having nothing to wear to the wedding and needing her daughter's advice about what to buy.

"Now this is a dress." Her mother spun around to display a form-fitting, cobalt-blue silk sheath. "It's sophisticated and classy, and I love the subtle pattern in the fabric. See how it shimmers? Best of all, it's your size. You should try it on."

"I told you—I don't need a new dress." Though if she was going to buy one, Lexie had to admit this was a stunner.

"At least try it on." Her mother held it out.

Lexie locked her arms across her chest. "Mom . . . we came to find you a dress. We found one. We're done. Let's go."

"Oh, sweetie, come on." She wiggled the hanger. "Try it on for me. Like you used to do on our shopping trips when you were a teenager. I miss those days, and the fashion show you used to give me after hauling an armload of clothes to the dressing room."

Great.

Now her mother was resorting to the always-effective guilt-trip strategy.

"Fine." She plucked the hanger from her mother's fingers. "After I try it on, we can leave—right?"

"Of course. I'll wait over there." She motioned toward a grouping of plush chairs near a tall three-way mirror.

Turning her back, Lexie barreled toward the dressing room. If she hurried, they could be out of here in ten minutes. Five, if she really hustled.

Once behind a closed door, she changed at light speed. Zipped up the dress as best she could without assistance. Turned back to the mirror.

Froze.

Oh. My. Word.

Lips parting, she studied her reflection. The dress fit as if it had been designed for her. The soft silk hugged her curves, the V neckline revealed a modest hint of cleavage, the color was an exact match for her eyes.

Gone was Lexie the no-nonsense police chief.

Gone was Lexie the loving mom.

Gone was Lexie the accommodating daughter.

This was Lexie the alluring woman.

What would Adam think if he saw her in this dress?

A delicious shiver ran through her as she imagined his reaction. Or what she *hoped* his reaction would be.

Which was bad, bad, bad.

Hadn't she been telling everyone she liked her life fine as it was? Hadn't she warned herself that seeing an ex-con on a social basis could be tricky? Hadn't she decided it was smarter to be cautious, to keep her distance?

Yes, yes, and yes.

Still she'd love to see Adam's reaction to this dress.

Dare she buy it and indulge herself?

She took a deep breath. Let it out slowly as she tried to engage the left side of her brain. Maybe she was overthinking this. She was talking about a dress here, not a lifetime commitment. After all, buying a sexy outfit to impress a man wasn't against the law. Women did it all the time. It didn't mean she was trolling for a boyfriend— or even a date.

Stop rationalizing, Lexie. Leave the dress behind. You're flirting with danger.

Prudent advice.

"Lexie? Do you need help with the zipper?"

She spun around as her mother's voice came through the louvered door, not more than two feet away.

"No. I've, uh, got it."

"Does it fit?"

Oh, man, did it fit.

"Yes."

"Are you going to let me see it?"

"Uh-huh. I'll be out in a minute. Meet you by the mirror."

She delayed as long as she could, shoring up her resolve to leave the dress behind despite the pressure her mother would surely put on her to buy it. But at last she braced and left the dressing room.

Her mother was waiting by the larger-than-life mirror that tripled the impact of the dress.

"Oh, my." Her mom pressed a hand to her chest. "You look beautiful. Come over here, in the middle, so you can get the full effect."

Lexie didn't need the full effect to appreciate the dress. It had been fabulous in the cramped dressing room's narrow full-length mirror.

She did a slow pirouette, examining the sheath from all perspectives.

"Perfect." Her mother beamed at her. "You have to buy it. That dress was made for you."

"It's too expensive."

"There's a 20-percent-off sale."

"It's still too expensive."

"You deserve a splurge. When's the last time you indulged yourself?"

Hard as she tried to come up with a reply, she couldn't pull one example from her memory.

"See? You owe yourself a treat."

"I'll never wear this again." She fingered the subtly patterned silk. It *was* a beautiful dress.

"You don't know that. A dress like that is very versatile."

"It's too fancy. It doesn't fit my lifestyle."

"Then change your lifestyle. There's more to life than work and motherhood, you know. You're starting to become a stick-in-the-mud."

Lexie blinked. "Gee, why don't you tell me what you *really* think?"

"Oh, honey." Her mother gave her a hug. "You know I have your best interests at heart. I just hate to see you frittering your youth away in a bland life without making any attempt to add some spice."

"You mean romance."

"That would do the trick."

"Nope. Been there, done that. I have no interest in going down that road again."

Brow puckered, her mother adjusted one shoulder of the dress. "I know you've had a rough ride these past few years. If I could take away the pain, I would. But grieving forever won't bring Joe back. And from everything you've told me about him, he'd want you to love again if the opportunity came along."

Yeah, he would.

But grief wasn't the main impediment to a new romance.

Guilt was also holding her back—though she'd never shared that part of the story with her mother.

"He would. But opportunities are few and far between in a town the size of Hope Harbor."

"True. However, they do come along now and then. For example . . . Adam Stone is single. He's also nice, available—and interested."

Lexie's mouth dropped open. "How in the world did you arrive at that absurd conclusion?"

"I watched his eyes the night he came for dinner. Every time he looked at you, they heated up."

"You're kidding, right?"

"No. And for the record, the heat went both ways."

"That's crazy." Cheeks warming, Lexie spun away and walked closer to the mirror on the pretense of giving the dress a closer inspection. Maybe her mom would let the subject drop.

"I'll make just one more comment."

So much for wishful thinking.

"I'll be the first to admit that when I first met Stone at church I wasn't impressed. That biker-dude image Matt mentioned was a bit off-putting. Plus, he never smiled, and he didn't mingle. I almost wrote him off . . . until I remembered a quote I'd once read."

Silence.

Lexie rolled her eyes. Her mother should have been a mystery writer, with her knack for leaving listeners hanging. Much as she didn't want to continue this conversation, curiosity got the better of her.

"Are you going to share it?"

" 'Those who smile the least are often the ones who need smiles the most.' " Her mother sat in one of the chairs. "So I began smiling at him every Sunday. Now, on occasion, I manage to get a tiny uptick of the lips—although Matt's better at eliciting that than I am. The two of them hit it off while Clyde was at the house, in case you didn't notice."

"I noticed." Lexie smoothed a hand down the silky skirt of the dress. "However . . . even if I was interested in a new romance, Adam wouldn't be the best person for a police chief to date."

"He's paid his dues to society, and as far as I can see, he's leading an exemplary life. He quietly helps whenever help is needed, has a steady job, attends church. He's also respectful and kind and intelligent. If anyone in this town had an issue with you seeing Stone, I'd say it's their problem, not yours."

If only life were that simple.

"You're more open-minded than a lot of people. Besides, he might already be dating someone."

"Nope. If he was, I'd know about it. It's hard to keep secrets in a town the size of Hope Harbor."

"Could be he's not interested in dating at the moment."

"Or he is but doesn't think the woman who's caught his eye would want anything to do with him. I imagine a man in his position might have issues with self-esteem. Given all the mistakes he's made, he might not feel worthy of a woman like you."

"I'm not perfect, either."

"That might be worth communicating. In the meantime, buy the dress. It will give your ego a boost, if nothing else."

"I'll think about it while I change."

"You know . . . sometimes a person can think too much."

Hadn't the very same notion occurred to her in the dressing room mere minutes ago?

Lexie shot her a wry look. "I'll keep that in mind."

"Do that. I'll wait here." Her mother picked up a fashion magazine and began to page through it.

Back in the dressing room, Lexie did one more twirl in front of the mirror, then exchanged the glitzy party frock for her comfy jeans and sweatshirt. Once the silk confection was back on its hanger, she stroked a finger down the sleek skirt.

She did like the dress—but she didn't need it to provide an ego boost, despite the rationale her mom had offered to justify the purchase. Her ego was in fine shape.

There was only one reason she'd indulge in an expensive splurge like this.

To impress Adam Stone.

She touched the dress again. It was tempting.

Very tempting.

So why not buy the dress, watch Adam's reaction, and keep her distance? That would be safe—and it wouldn't send any wrong messages.

But she had a feeling that if she saw what she expected to see in his eyes, keeping her distance was going to take far more willpower than she might be able to muster.

She lifted the hanger off the hook, opened the louvered door, and left the dressing room behind.

Decision time.

And she had only the forty or fifty steps to the checkout counter to make a choice that might rock the placid, calm waters of the life she'd created in Hope Harbor.

"Let's take a break." Adam wiped his forehead on the sleeve of his sweatshirt and motioned toward the cooler he'd brought from home. "There's water and soda in there. Grab a Sprite for me and help yourself."

Brian laid down the electric screwdriver he'd been wielding with far more skill than Adam had expected, retrieved two cans of soda, and passed one to him.

Adam popped the top and sat on the nearby bench that faced the wharf. After a few moments, Brian claimed the other end.

Taking a long slug of his soda, he assessed the kid in his peripheral vision. Three hours in, he didn't have any major complaints about his temporary partner. Brian had been waiting outside the trailer at six forty-five and had done everything he'd been asked to do. He was a fast learner, and he had a knack with tools.

But he sure wasn't a talker. At most, he'd uttered two or three full sentences since they'd arrived at the wharf.

At this rate, while the kid might clock his community service hours, he wasn't going to reap whatever benefit Lexie and the counselor had hoped to achieve by pairing him with an ex-con.

Not unless the ex-con could break through the kid's wall.

Thumbing off a tear of sweat from the side of his soda can, Adam angled toward the boy. "So . . . have you ever done any carpentry?"

"No."

"You have some natural ability."

Silence, other than the caw of a seagull and the slap of water against the dock.

Sheesh.

This was almost as painful as digging out the splinters he'd gotten after trying to work with some Douglas fir early in his furniture-making career, before he realized how mercilessly the local timber dispensed them.

"Did someone teach you a few basics, though?"

"Like who?"

"I don't know . . . your dad, maybe."

"Are you kidding?" The boy barked out a humorless laugh. "He had more important stuff to do."

Adam's stomach clenched. Man, he was making a mess of this. He was so not equipped to deal with *any* teenager, let alone a troubled one. What had Lexie been thinking?

On the other hand, the boy *had* responded with

two full, complete sentences. That was progress . . . wasn't it?

He inhaled a lungful of the salty air and scanned the mist-shrouded horizon. Too bad this gig hadn't come with operating instructions.

Since it hadn't . . . why not follow the same strategy he'd used with Lexie? Be honest and share some of his background. Brian might lower his defenses a bit, as she had.

It was worth a try, anyway. At this point, what did he have to lose?

Adam took another swig of soda. "I'm sorry your dad wasn't there for you. I've been in your shoes, and it stinks."

He felt the boy's glance as he rested one arm on the back of the bench and continued to sip his soda.

Please, God, help me out here. I'm trying—but I could use a hand.

"Did your dad steal your money and run off too?"

"No. I was the one who ran off. I got tired of being a punching bag and took off when I was sixteen."

A few beats passed while the kid digested that. "Dads are supposed to care about their kids."

"That's true—but at least your mom cares about you."

"Didn't yours?"

A spot in his heart smarted, like a prod to a

forgotten bruise. "If she did, she never showed it. All those years my father was beating up on me, she looked the other way."

"My mom did that too—about my dad cheating on her, not about being beat up. He didn't start hitting her until the last month."

"Did he hit you too?" Adam kept his inflection neutral, despite the sudden churning in his gut. Anyone who picked on the defenseless deserved to rot in prison.

"No. He tried to once, but Mom stopped him." The can crinkled beneath the kid's fingers. "I'm glad he left. I hated him. He was a user."

He was worse than that, but no need to add fuel to the fury already consuming the boy.

"Do you ever hear from him?"

"No. We moved away from Medford after he left." Brian toed a loose pebble on the sidewalk. "The sick thing is, even after everything he'd done, I think Mom kind of hoped he'd come after us."

"Did you?"

"No way. I thought she was nuts." He kicked the pebble, watching as it bounced down the large boulders that separated the sidewalk from the water, his mouth tight. "I hope we never see him again."

His tone was bitter and angry—but underneath Adam picked up remnants of little-boy hurt.

Brian might be glad to be rid of his father, yet

a tiny part of him wished their relationship had been different. Better. More normal.

Adam could relate. He'd been down that road.

Hopefully, the boy beside him would learn to deal with his anger better than he had.

For now, though, that anger—along with the challenge of adjusting to a new town and school—was driving him to make some serious mistakes that could escalate unless he got with the program the juvenile counselor and Lexie had outlined.

"I never wanted to see my dad . . . or mom either . . . after I left." Adam finished off his soda.

"Did you?"

"No. I've been on my own since I was your age."

"I wish I was. It would be cool to be free." He crushed his empty soda can in his fingers. "I'm tired of everyone telling me what to do."

"You'd have less freedom in prison."

"I'm not planning to go there."

"I wasn't, either." Adam shifted toward him, keeping his tone conversational. "But surviving on your own at sixteen is tough. I hooked up with the wrong people. Vandalism led to petty theft, which led to shoplifting, which led to robbery. Your life can spiral out of control before you realize what's happening. All of a sudden you're behind bars with no freedom at all and a record that will follow you for the rest of your life."

"You seem like you're doing okay now."

"I am, thanks to Reverend Baker from Grace Christian here in town. His prison ministry changed my life. But a lot of opportunities are closed to me because of my record."

"That's not fair."

He shrugged. "Choices have consequences. I made the wrong ones, now I'm paying the price. If I'd been offered a second chance like the one you've been given, my story could have turned out very differently. I wish I'd been as lucky."

The boy focused on the crushed can in his hand. "I've never felt very lucky."

"Depends on your perspective, I guess. From where I sit, you seem pretty lucky."

"Morning, Adam. Brian. You're making headway on the planters, I see."

Adam swung around as Charley strolled up behind them. "It's a start, anyway. You opening up the taco stand?"

"That's the plan. I don't want to disappoint the lunch crowd. I'll have a couple of orders with your names on them whenever you get hungry."

"Um . . ." Adam did a mental inventory of the cash in his wallet. There was enough to pay for the items on his noontime to-do list, but no extra to cover two orders of tacos. "Tacos were on my menu for tomorrow."

"Come then too. Today's lunch is my contribution to repairing the planters. I have no skill with a hammer, but I wield a mean spatula. The least I can do is feed the workmen." The man winked and addressed Brian. "You and your mom stop by the stand sometime. We need to get better acquainted—and the first order for newcomers in town is always on the house. See you around." He lifted a hand and strolled off.

"We need to get back to work too." Adam stood.

"Hey . . ." Brian rose more slowly, tracking Charley's progress toward the stand. "How did he know my name?"

"Charley knows everybody." Adam headed back toward the planter they'd been repairing.

"But . . . how did he know it was just me and my mom? I mean . . . I've never talked to him." Brian fell in beside him.

"Charley knows more about this town—and the people in it—than anybody. Don't ask me how. I quit trying to figure it out. But he's a great guy. You and your mom should stop by for those tacos he mentioned." He picked up a length of wood. "Let's give this another hour and call it a day. I have some errands to run and a wedding to attend later. Are you available tomorrow afternoon?"

"You work on Sunday?"

"I don't make it a habit, but I'm losing half of today. Are you already booked for tomorrow?"

"No. I can help for a while."

"I'll pick you up at one."

"My mom could bring me down."

"I don't mind swinging by your place."

"Why would you bother? I mean, what's in it for you? Nobody's paying you to do any of this."

It was a serious question—and it deserved a serious answer.

He set the wood down and gave Brian his full attention. "Because I've been in your shoes. I know how easy it is to mess up your life. I can't change my history, but if I can keep someone else from going down the wrong path, maybe that will help make amends for all my past mistakes. On top of all that, it's the right thing to do. After I got out of prison, I vowed never to turn away from those in need. That's what the Bible teaches, and I'm trying my best to follow that rule."

Brian picked up the screwdriver and weighed it in his hand. "You don't seem like the kind of guy who would go to church or talk about God stuff."

One side of Adam's mouth hitched up. "So I've been told."

"My mom used to take me to church back in Medford, when I was a little kid."

"Why did you stop going?"

"My dad didn't like it."

Another strike against the man.

"Well, he's gone now. Reverend Baker would be happy to have you both at Grace Christian. Why don't you mention that to your mom?"

"I might. So what do you want me to work on next?"

The deeper conversation was over for today.

Yet the walls between them continued to fall as Adam showed Brian how to shim one side of the damaged planter and the conversation transitioned to more general topics.

Maybe Lexie's idea had merit after all.

And barring any major glitches, maybe, just maybe, Brian would weather his ill-advised detour off the straight and narrow without any further complications.

❧ 11 ☙

He wasn't going to show.

A glass of soda in each hand, Lexie wove through the crowd under the lawn tent at Seabird Inn and gave the milling reception throng another sweep.

No sign of Adam—and the cocktail hour was winding down. Dinner would be served soon.

Swallowing past her disappointment, she continued toward the table she, her mom, and Matt were sharing with Marci Weber, editor of the *Hope Harbor Herald*, and an older couple the groom knew from his corporate law days in Portland.

"Here you go." She set the sodas in front of her mom and Matt and retook her seat.

"When are we gonna eat? I'm hungry." Matt slurped the sugary drink through his straw.

"Why don't you try some of the appetizers I

192

got for you?" Lexie tapped the untouched plate in front of him.

He wrinkled his nose at the cocktail shrimp, bruschetta, mini crab cake, and bite-sized quiche. "Yuck. I want real food."

"Dinner will be served soon." Thank goodness BJ and Eric had been kind enough to offer a children's menu for the few young ones in attendance. "You'll like the chicken strips and fries."

"Yeah!" He continued to guzzle the soda.

"Better drink slower. We're switching to water after that's gone."

"But it's a party."

"One glass of soda. That's it. We talked about this at home."

He gave her a disgruntled pout and started to fidget.

Great.

If he was bored after thirty minutes, what would he be like by the end of the dinner and toasts?

This was going to be a long evening.

On Matt's other side, her mother was engaged in an animated conversation with the only woman at the table close to her age. The two of them were laughing and chatting as if they'd known each other for years.

At least one person in the family was having fun at this wedding.

"It's a beautiful setting, isn't it? Very romantic."

As Marci spoke, she gave the decorations her full attention.

Yeah, it was.

The interior of the tent was lit with muted chandeliers and plenty of soft candlelight. Crisp white linen cloths covered the round tables, burnished silverware gleaming at each place. In the center of each table, arrangements of hydrangeas, roses, and delphiniums spilled from cut-glass bowls onto the pristine linen. Beside the dance floor, a quartet of instrumentalists played classic love songs.

"It *is* beautiful."

"And don't you love BJ's dress? She told me it belonged to her grandmother—and her great-grandmother also wore it. They don't make dresses like that anymore, do they?"

Lexie scanned the crowd again, homing in on the bride. She'd noticed the vintage gown at the church, but here, in the evening candlelight, the elaborate beadwork on the bodice, long sleeves that tapered to a point on the back of each hand, and sweeping satin skirt were even more beautiful. For once BJ's hair wasn't pulled into its customary ponytail but had been coiffed into an elaborate upsweep featuring a cluster of flowers and a long, trailing wisp of tulle.

The ensemble was nothing like the simple white sundress and barrette of flowers she'd worn for her own impromptu wedding.

"No, they don't. Are you going to do a write-up in the *Herald* about the wedding?"

"Of course! It's the social event of the season next to the cranberry festival." Marci winked. "Oh, look! They're getting ready to cut the cake!" She reached for her camera and jumped to her feet. "I've already got plenty of pictures, but I can't resist a cake shot. Be back in a sec."

The editor dashed off toward the happy couple.

A smile tugged at Lexie's mouth. Marci was a go-getter for sure. It had been a lucky day for the town when she'd arrived last year after inheriting her great-aunt's summer cottage. Not only had she revived the newspaper, she'd launched a successful PR firm that was drawing clients from across the state.

Curious that someone so attractive, upbeat, and friendly seemed, in her free time, to be almost as much of a loner as Adam.

Adam.

Lips drooping, she fingered the hem of the silky fabric above her knee. What a waste of money this dress had been.

Flashbulbs went off, followed by laughter, as the bride and groom cut into their wedding cake, creating memories they would carry their whole life.

A pang echoed in her heart. Too bad she didn't have memories of a beautiful day like this tucked away to sustain her. The simple ceremony that had united her and Joe as man and wife had held none of the elegance or romance or glamor of today's event. Nor had it been memorable.

But they'd had each other—and absolute confidence they'd have a lifetime together to create special memories.

Who could have predicted that lifetime would be cut so very short?

"What're they doin', Mom?" Matt attempted to climb onto the seat of his chair for a better view of the excitement around the cake.

"Whoa! These folding chairs weren't designed for gymnastics."

She stood and swept him into her arms, this son she'd cuddled and cradled. He was her best tangible memory of her short but happy marriage —all thirty-nine pounds of him. Yet soon he'd be too heavy to lift . . . and life would change again, no matter how hard she tried to maintain the status quo.

"What're they doin'?" He craned his neck.

Blinking back the film of moisture in her eyes, she held him tighter. "They're cutting their wedding cake."

"Oooh! Do we get a piece?"

"After dinner."

"Oh." His face fell. "So when're we gonna eat?"

"Ladies and gentlemen, if you'll take your seats, dinner is about to be served."

As the keyboard player spoke into the microphone, Lexie set Matt down and ruffled his hair. "There's your answer."

Her son climbed back into his chair, the combo resumed playing, and waiters began parading through the tent with trays of salads.

Lexie retook her own seat. If the dinner was half as delicious as the appetizers Matt had turned his nose up at, the meal would be memorable. The music was superb too. As soon as BJ and Eric finished their first dance, the portable floor was going to get crowded.

It was a great party.

Nevertheless, Lexie was counting the minutes until she could go home, slip out of her Cinderella dress, and let her life turn back into a pumpkin.

He'd arrived at the perfect time.

Adam surveyed the interior of the tent. With the lights dim and the waiters busy delivering salads to the tables, no one would notice his late entrance —just as no one had noticed him slipping into the church moments before BJ walked down the aisle. And by claiming a seat in the last pew, he'd been able to escape the minute the bridal party paraded out.

Even so, the few people who'd spotted him had done a double take.

It had not been a comfortable experience.

And it wasn't likely to get any better.

He peered at the card he'd found at the entrance

to the tent with his name and table number written in fancy script. How was he supposed to find his seat in this dim light, short of making a very conspicuous circuit of the room?

Maybe a waiter could point him in the right direction.

He waylaid the first one who came close. The man indicated the general direction of his table, and as he started toward it, Luis stood and motioned to him.

Saved.

Staying at the edge of the tent, he skirted the tables and kept his gaze fixed on his destination.

"You are here." Luis grasped his hand. "I thought you might have changed your mind."

"I told BJ I'd come. I always keep my word."

"You were at the church too?"

"In the back."

"Front . . . back . . . it does not matter. In God's house, every seat is equal. I saved you a place. This new image"—he made an all-encompassing gesture—"it suits you."

Adam fiddled with his tie. "It feels strange. Like I'm pretending to be somebody else."

"You *are* somebody else. Now you are dressing the part. Sit." He pulled out the chair between his own and Eleanor Cooper's, insulating him from any unwanted social interaction.

Thank you, God, for a friend like Luis.

"Good evening, Stone. You're very polished

tonight." Eleanor Cooper touched his hand as he sat.

"Thanks." He managed a smile for the soon-to-turn-eighty-nine-year-old widow who'd given Luis a home when he needed one most—though the living arrangement had ended up being a blessing for both of them.

"You missed some fine hors d'oeuvres . . . but we saved you a few to sample." She set a small plate in front of him.

As usual, the kindness of this woman who barely knew him tightened his throat. "I appreciate that."

"Not at all." She waved his thanks aside and draped her napkin over her lap. "How is your dog doing?"

"Improving every day."

"Wonderful news. I know how upset I'd be if anyone hurt my dear Methuselah."

As he scarfed down the appetizers, Adam tried to pay attention to the story Eleanor launched into about her cat—but the food was a huge distraction. Compared to the canned and frozen stuff he subsisted on, this was like state dinner fare.

The waiter whisked away his small plate the instant he finished and replaced it with a salad.

He devoured that as well.

"The food is tasty, yes?" Luis motioned toward his empty plate. Not one speck of lettuce remained.

"Yeah. It's great."

He checked out the other guests at the table. Most of them were only halfway through their salad course.

Better put the brakes on. Obviously, the proper behavior at an event like this was to savor the flavors in slow motion.

Now that the edge was off his hunger, he might be able to exercise some restraint.

"The small orchestra is excellent too." Luis indicated the combo off to the side of the dance floor. "Not like the loud noise that passes for music these days. I imagine many people will be dancing tonight."

"I guess." Not on his agenda, though. Dancing, like small talk, hadn't been among the social niceties he'd learned during his youth. Nor was it a skill easily mimicked—like slowing down his food intake.

The waiter set a plate in front of him, the food arranged like a work of art, a fresh flower tucked beside . . . was that filet mignon?

"My. This is almost too pretty to eat, isn't it?" Eleanor examined her own entrée.

Since she didn't seem to expect an answer, he continued to ogle the piece of meat.

"You do not like beef?" Luis leaned closer.

"I like it fine. But my beef is always the ground kind. Is this filet mignon?"

"I believe it is. BJ told me they were having

a . . . what did she call it? Ah. A surf and turf dinner. There is salmon too."

"Wow."

"It is a very nice meal."

Like the nicest one he'd ever had.

Although the temptation to chow down at top speed was strong, Adam paced himself by keeping tabs on Luis's progress. Eating slower did have one benefit—it gave him longer to enjoy the best meal of his life.

He finished a bite or two ahead of the man beside him, and once again the waiter whisked away an empty plate.

"And now it is time for the first dance." Luis motioned toward the portable floor in front of the head table.

Adam shifted around as Eric swept BJ into his arms and began to sway to an oldie but goodie—"It Had to Be You." One of his favorite CDs had a striking jazz arrangement of that song.

"They look good together, do they not?" Luis spoke softly, his focus on the newlyweds.

"Yes. BJ cleans up real . . ."

His words trailed off as he caught sight of a stunning, dark-haired woman in his peripheral vision. She was angled away from him, talking to Tracy Hunter, BJ's matron of honor. Tracy had traded her usual cranberry-farm attire of jeans and baseball cap for a swirly pink dress—but it paled in comparison to the silky blue number the other woman was . . .

The brunette turned, and Adam's heart skipped a beat.

Lexie?!

"She is very different tonight too, isn't she?" Luis motioned toward the women.

"Yeah, I . . ." His voice rasped, and he swallowed. "I've never seen her in anything but her uniform."

"Ah. You are talking about our police chief. I was referring to Tracy. But they are both lovely."

Adam kept his head averted to hide the heat creeping up his neck. Bad faux pas. He didn't want his friend thinking he had any foolish aspirations. "I didn't even realize it was her at first. It was kind of a disconnect."

"Yes. Seeing people out of context can be confusing."

Tracy's husband came up beside her and slipped an arm around her waist. After another brief exchange, Lexie lifted two plates of cake he hadn't noticed she was holding and wove back through the tables while Tracy and Michael moved onto the dance floor. Near as he could tell before he lost sight of her, she was sitting on the far side of the room.

Did she have a date?

Possible. She'd been carrying two plates of cake.

He stretched his neck, but to no avail. It was too

dim and there were too many people between them—including the couples on the dance floor. Short of standing up and calling attention to himself, he wasn't going to find out who her companion was unless the two of them ventured out to dance.

But it was very likely a date. Most people brought one to events like this, and with her beauty and intelligence and numerous other assets, Lexie would have her pick of men.

Though he tried to tamp it down, a foolish surge of disappointment swept over him.

And hanging around to watch Lexie in someone else's arms held no appeal.

It was time to go.

He'd honored his promise to BJ. Attended the wedding, stayed for all the important parts of the reception. There was no reason to linger.

He pushed his chair back.

"Oh, Stone, if you're getting up, would you mind bringing me a piece of wedding cake? I believe it's on that table over there, near the band." Eleanor smiled at him.

A word not fit for polite company flashed through his mind.

He wanted out. Now.

But refusing the kindly older woman's request wasn't an option.

Besides, how long could it take to retrieve and deliver one piece of cake?

"I'd be happy to. It won't come close to your fudge cake, though. Are you sure you want second best?" His flattery was sincere—but maybe she'd change her mind if she thought about the comparison?

Pink spots appeared on the older woman's cheeks, and she touched his hand. "You're very kind. But wedding cake is special. Call me fanciful, but I can always taste the love inside. You should have some too."

He was stuck.

"I might do that in a little while. Luis, would you like a piece?"

"Yes. I'll go with you. It would be hard to juggle three plates."

"That's okay, I can . . ."

"Coffee, anyone?" A waiter stopped beside their table and lifted a silver pot.

"Yes. Three here." Luis indicated their cups. "Let's go get that cake."

Apparently he was staying for dessert after all.

Adam trailed after Luis, circling the dance floor in the opposite direction from where Lexie had disappeared. If he stayed among the crowd, there wasn't much chance she'd notice him.

And once he returned to his seat, he was going to ignore the protocols on speed-eating, wolf down his cake, leave this gracious and elegant world behind, and hightail it back to his rustic cabin.

Where he belonged.

ᴺ 12 ᴸ

"This is good cake, Mom." With the side of his fork, Matt scraped up the remnants of icing on his plate with the diligence of a miner pulling gold flakes out of a panning sieve. "Are you gonna eat the rest of yours?" He cast a hopeful glance at the piece on her plate, untouched except for one bite.

"I might."

"Don't you like it?"

"Yes. I'm letting my dinner settle before I eat any more."

"If you're too full, I can help you finish it."

"I'll let you know." After cajoling her into another half glass of soda, he did *not* need any additional sugar. "You want to look at one of the books I brought?"

"I guess." He leaned back and swung his legs, watching the swaying couples while she dug a picture book out of her oversized purse. "Are you gonna dance, Mom?"

"No."

"Why not?"

"I didn't bring anyone to dance with." She handed him one of his favorite books and picked up her cup.

"Maybe you could . . . hey!" He sat up straighter. "Is that Mr. Stone?"

The black liquid sloshed close to the edge, and she gripped her cup with both hands to steady it. "Where?"

"Over there." He vaulted to his feet and stood on tiptoes, pointing in the direction of the cake. "I don't see him now. He was with Mr. Luis."

"You mean Mr. Dominguez?"

"Yeah—but I can't say that name good, so he told me to call him Mr. Luis. See . . . there they are again!"

Keeping a tight grip on her cup, Lexie took a cautious peek over her shoulder. If the man *was* here, she didn't want him to think she was spying on him.

No need for concern on that front. She couldn't see either of the men through the crowd on the dance floor. How had Matt managed to spot them?

Then again . . . perhaps he hadn't. The light was dim. Or romantic, as Marci would no doubt describe it.

"Honey, I don't think you . . ."

Wait.

Luis *was* over there, talking to some woman she didn't recognize.

"Do you see them?" Matt knelt on his chair.

"Sit down or you'll drop your book." She resettled him in his seat and peered through the crowd until she found Luis again. "I see Mr. Dominguez, but I don't think Mr. Stone is with . . ." Her voice trailed off.

There *was* a guy standing a couple of feet behind Luis, his back to her. Tall, wearing a suit jacket that emphasized his broad shoulders, dark hair neatly trimmed. She squinted. It was too dim to get a clear view, and dancers kept blocking her line of sight, but it *could* be Adam—if he'd made a major image adjustment.

Had he?

"Is it Mr. Stone, Mom?"

"I'm not sure."

"Me neither. He looks different."

No kidding—assuming it was him.

"Can we go say hi?"

"No." She swiveled back to the table.

"Why not?"

Why not, indeed? Hadn't she wanted Adam to see her in her new dress? What was with the sudden case of cold feet?

"He might, uh, be with some friends."

"We're his friends too, aren't we?"

"Yes. Maybe later. Read your book for now."

"I don't wanna read my book. I wanna go see Mr. Stone." He clamped his arms over his chest and stuck out his chin.

"You keep that up, young man, and we'll be going home instead."

"Everything okay?" Her mother interrupted her chat with her neighbor to join the conversation.

"The natives are getting restless." She grabbed the book before it slid off Matt's lap.

"Weddings aren't much fun for young ones." Her mom tousled his hair. "We don't have to stay late."

"I don't want to leave until I say hi to Mr. Stone."

"Is he here?" Her mother searched the crowd, interest sparking in her eyes.

"We're not certain. Matt thinks he . . ."

"Good evening, folks." Charley appeared beside their table, his standard jeans replaced with an elegant dark suit and string tie. "Lexie, may I have this dance?"

She did a double take. Never in a million years would she have pegged Charley as a dancer.

"Um . . . I haven't danced in ages—and I was never very adept at it. I'd probably step all over your feet."

"I don't think so. Those routines you cheer-leaders did at the high school during games were impressive."

"That was years ago—and they were choreo-graphed. Making it up as you go along on a dance floor is a lot harder."

"You don't have to make it up. That's my job. Just follow where I lead." He held out his hand. "This music is too superb to waste."

Hard as she tried, she couldn't think of another reason to refuse.

"Okay . . . but you may regret this." She stood and took his hand.

"I'll take my chances."

He led her to the dance floor, assumed the

classic dance position—and before she knew it, they were moving in time to the music, her feet following his with nary a blunder.

By a dozen measures in, she'd relaxed and was enjoying herself. "You're a great dancer—and you lead well."

"You follow well. Now, if we were both trying to lead, this might be awkward. But as long as people are clear on their roles—in dancing or any other endeavor—they can usually find their rhythm without stumbling or missing a beat."

When the music at last wound down, Lexie smiled up at him. "Thank you. That was fun."

"It was my pleasure. I'll walk you back to your table, but give me a minute to say hello to a few friends while we're close."

Taking her arm, he guided her off the dance floor, toward a nearby table.

Luis rose as they approached . . . as did the broad-shouldered man she'd spotted from across the room.

Her step faltered . . . but Charley kept walking, urging her along with him.

It *was* Adam—but a new and improved version . . . in the looks department, anyway.

Gone was the bandana

Gone were the shaggy locks.

Gone was the bad-boy stubble.

The clean-shaven man in the suit and tie standing a few feet away could be a model for *GQ*.

Her breath hitched.

If the old version had rattled her, the new one sent her pulse off the charts.

Somewhere in the background she heard a conversation taking place between Charley and the two men. On autopilot, she returned Eleanor Cooper's greeting and asked about Methuselah. Responded to Charley's comment about the dance they'd shared. Sidestepped a waiter bearing down on her with a loaded tray of empty cake plates.

But 99.9 percent of her focus was on Adam.

And her tunnel vision appeared to be mutual.

No longer did she have to speculate about his reaction to her Cinderella dress. It was all there in his eyes. Locked on her, they consumed. Darkened. And communicated one word.

Wow.

No question about it—the splurge had been worth every penny.

". . . find a new partner for this next dance?"

As the last part of Charley's question registered, she tore her gaze away from Adam. "What?"

"I said, I'll walk you back to your table— unless you want to find a new partner for the next dance." He motioned toward Adam. "It's a great song. Old but timeless."

She tuned in to the music. The strains of "Unforgettable" floated through the tent, prompting a rush to the dance floor.

Once more she homed in on the tall man inches

away. Interesting that Charley had put the ball in her court, rather than Adam's, for initiating a dance. As if he too believed what her mother had implied the day of their shopping trip—that Adam might not think himself worthy of her.

That was baloney.

And how better to prove it than by asking him to dance?

Yet if she did that, she'd better be prepared for the consequences. The Hope Harbor residents present tonight might be shocked to see their police chief in the arms of a felon. Adam could follow up with a request for a date. Was she ready to deal with those possible outcomes?

If the answer to both of those questions was yes . . . another important one loomed.

Was she ready to let go of the past and take a chance on a future that could be fraught with challenges—and change?

The music swelled. Seconds ticked by. Her heart began to race.

What should she do?

Lexie had no idea.

But she knew what her mom would suggest. Adam too, given all he'd shared with her over coffee at the cove. And in the face of no other options, it wasn't bad advice.

So in desperation, Lexie did something she hadn't done in a very long while.

She prayed for guidance.

● ● ●

Adam could read the conflict in Lexie's eyes.

She didn't want to ask him to dance—yet she didn't want to hurt his feelings.

He needed to give her a way out now that Charley had put her on the spot.

He also needed to save himself. Despite the potent appeal of holding her close and swaying to that romantic tune, he'd be in over his head. What passed for dancing at the bars he'd once frequented had been more clutch and grind, while the moves Charley and Lexie had been doing were *Dancing with the Stars* caliber.

It would be a disaster if he got out on the dance floor.

"I'm afraid I could never live up to you, Charley. Where'd you learn to dance like that? I saw some fancy footwork out there." He tried for a teasing tone as he broke the charged silence.

"There's no secret to dancing. If you can hear the rhythm, you can move with the music."

"That is correct." Luis put a hand on his shoulder. "I was never much of a dancer until I met my wife, Elena. But she said if I listened with my heart to the music, my feet would know what to do. She said that was true about many things—and she was right. The key in any situation is to listen with the heart . . . and follow where it leads."

"While all of you are standing here talking,

you're missing a wonderful tune." Eleanor swayed with the music in her seat. "Why, if I didn't have that stupid walker, I'd be out there myself."

Adam rejoined the conversation, trying to silently communicate to Lexie that he didn't expect her to follow up on Charley's ridiculous suggestion. "Don't worry about it. I wouldn't want to have to run you to the emergency room with a broken toe." He managed to hike up one side of his mouth. "Would anyone like a refill on coffee? I can try to round up the waiter and—"

"I'm not much of a dancer, either. Charley made me seem better than I am. But if you want to try and struggle through this song together, I'm game." Lexie wrapped her fingers around the back of the empty chair beside her, her voice a bit breathless.

The air whooshed out of Adam's lungs . . . and panic set in.

"Um . . . I haven't had a lot of opportunity to learn how to dance."

"Join the club. No one does much more than shuffle around these days . . ."—she motioned toward the dance floor—"except Charley. He can actually dance. I may end up stepping on *your* feet."

"Go on. Dance with the lady." Luis gave him a tiny shove.

"By all means," Eleanor seconded. "I'd claim a

dance myself if I could manage it. There's nothing like dancing to a romantic tune with a handsome man."

"You have nothing to lose . . . and much to gain." Charley smiled at him.

Four against one.

He was doomed.

"I'll give it a shot—but don't say I didn't warn you. And it's not too late to change your mind." He directed the latter comment to Lexie, hoping . . . he had no idea what. Part of him yearned to hold her in his arms, part of him was terrified he'd fall on his face on the dance floor.

Perhaps literally.

"I'm not letting you off the hook at this stage." Lexie sounded more confident now.

Then she held out her hand.

It took another nudge from Luis to prod him into action.

Instead of trying to speak, he simply took her hand and let her lead him to the dance floor.

When she turned into his arms, it felt like the most natural thing in the world to rest his hand at her waist and wrap her fingers in his.

"Ready?" She looked up at him, her throat working as she swallowed.

And was that a tremor in her fingers?

Was she as nervous about this as he was?

For some reason, the notion that he wasn't alone in his terror helped calm him.

"Or not. Do you mind the audience? I assume they're watching." He tipped his head toward the threesome on the sidelines.

She spared the trio a quick peek. "They are—but we can blend into the crowd once we're dancing."

"I wasn't kidding about being a rookie at this." Some of his nerves returned.

"It's not rocket science. All you have to do is sway to the music." She did so, taking him along with her. "Then just lift your feet and set them down somewhere else in time to the beat. I'll follow."

She made it sound easy.

Too easy.

Yet strangely enough . . . it was. Everyone around them was doing the very kind of maneuver she'd described, and it wasn't at all difficult to imitate.

In fact, it was almost as easy as watching Luis for cues on which fork to use at dinner and how to pace his intake.

"See? It's not that hard, is it?" Lexie squeezed his fingers.

"No. I guess not."

"So get rid of that frown, relax, and let's enjoy the music."

Great advice.

Except now that he had his sea legs—or dance legs—he was going to enjoy more than the music.

He was going to enjoy the woman in his arms.

Inching his hand farther around her waist, he splayed his fingers against the smooth fabric of her dress and urged her a hair closer.

She came without protest.

He dipped his chin until her soft, silky hair brushed his jaw, inhaling her enticing fresh scent.

She rested her cheek against his shoulder.

He brushed his thumb over the soft skin on the back of her hand.

She squeezed his fingers.

No one could have scored the scene better—for these few unforgettable minutes with Lexie in his arms would be indelibly etched on his mind. Forever.

When the last, lingering notes died away, Adam forced himself to release her. "Thank you for the dance. I'm sorry Charley put you on the spot like that."

Her gaze caught—and held—his. "I'm not."

Couples brushed past them, clearing the floor for the next dance, but Adam didn't budge. The husky note in Lexie's voice, the intensity of her blue irises, locked him in place.

Was she *glad* Charley had pushed them together—or was his imagination working overtime?

The band launched into the next song. A Gershwin classic.

There was one way to find out.

"Would you like to dance again?"

"I thought you'd never ask." Without further ado, she stepped back into his arms.

Adam lost track of how many dances they shared. Only after the band upped the tempo with a swing number did the magic spell come to an end.

"This one's beyond me." Lexie watched a nearby couple execute some intricate footwork and twirls.

"I'm with you. Let me walk you back to your table."

He fell in beside her, one hand instinctively moving to the small of her back as he guided her around an exuberant couple whose arms were extending beyond the edges of the dance floor with every spin.

It was simple to spot her table, because Annette stood up and waved at them as they approached.

"There you are! I've been trying to spot you for . . ." Her mother blinked. "Stone?"

"Yes."

"My. I didn't recognize you. I like the new image." Lexie's mother shifted her attention to her daughter. "Were you two together?"

"We were dancing." Lexie took control of the conversation. "Why were you looking for me?"

Her mother blinked. "Oh. Right. It's Matt." She eased aside to reveal the little boy, whose head was propped on his arms on the table. "He says his stomach hurts."

Lexie edged past her mother, dropped into the chair beside her son, and felt his forehead.

"I already did that. Cool as a cucumber." Annette seemed more interested in her daughter's dance partner than in her grandson's upset stomach, based on the speculative gleam in her eye.

"What did he eat while I was gone?" When Annette didn't respond, Lexie tried again. "Mom!"

The older woman refocused on her daughter. "What?"

"What did he eat while I was gone?"

"I gave him the rest of my wedding cake."

"Uh-oh." A guilty flush spread over Marci's cheeks. "I gave him some of mine too. I didn't realize he'd also had part of your mom's."

"And mine." Lexie tapped an empty plate at her place. "That's a glass and a half of soda and three pieces of cake. I think I know what the problem is."

"I wanna go home." Matt lifted his head.

The poor kid looked like he was going to puke.

"That's your next stop. But you are in big trouble, young man. We'll discuss that tomorrow, after you recover from your sugar orgy." Lexie stood. "Let me say good-bye to the bride and—"

"No need for you to leave. I'm winding down myself. I'll take Matt home." Annette circled around behind the youngster and picked up her purse.

"That won't work, Mom. We all rode together."

"Oh." The older woman's face fell . . . but brightened again as she turned to him. "Unless you could get a ride with someone."

Adam wasted no time picking up her cue—even if it carried another risk of rejection.

"I'd be glad to take you home later, if you'd like to stay awhile."

Lexie caught her lower lip between her teeth. "I wouldn't want to inconvenience you."

"I don't mind." He tried for a smile. "The band probably has a few slow dances left, and it would be a shame to let them go to waste."

There. He'd taken the leap and laid his cards on the table. The ball was in her court. All clichés —but all true.

"Why don't you stay, Lexie?" Her mother helped Matt to his feet. "I can handle a cake-stuffed kid."

"Hi, Mr. Stone." Matt leaned against his grand-mother's leg and held onto his stomach. "I don't feel so good."

"That's what I heard." He hunkered down in front of the boy, who was a tad green around the gills, buying Lexie a few seconds to consider his invitation—and come up with an excuse to leave, if that was her choice. "Too much cake, huh?"

"I 'spose. How's Clyde?"

"Feeling much better."

"I wish I could see him again. Do you think I could?"

How did you say no to a hurting little kid with big, beseeching blue eyes?

"We might be able to arrange that."

"Awesome. Were you dancing with my mom?"

"Uh-huh."

"You gonna dance some more?"

"That's up to her."

"Let's go, young man." The older woman took his hand.

Adam rose and faced Lexie. Her expression gave him no clue how this was going to play out.

But as he waited for her decision, he sent a silent prayer heavenward—asking not for a positive response but for the right response. Whatever that might be.

And if it was no?

Well, at least he could add a handful of romantic dances to the memories he'd carefully preserved from their impromptu coffee date in the cove.

Which was far beyond anything he'd ever expected—even if it had only whetted his appetite for more.

❧ 13 ☙

By eleven thirty, they had the dance floor to themselves except for one other dallying couple. Even the bride and groom had departed.

But now the party was over.

As the final song wound down . . . as Lexie rested her forehead against the curve of Adam's neck . . . as the music swirled around them like an insulating force field keeping the world at bay . . . she sighed. If only this night could go on forever.

"I think we shut the place down." Adam's soft words were a whisper of warmth against her ear.

"Mmm." She closed her eyes, sucking every last drop of pleasure from this night that had started out disappointing and ended up ranking as one of the most memorable of her life.

He didn't say anything else, just pressed her closer during the wistful, waning notes of the final song. Beneath her ear, his heart beat steady and strong. The woodsy scent of his aftershave teased her nose. Against her temple, the beginning bristle of a five o'clock shadow on his newly shaven chin nuzzled her skin.

For this one moment in time, the world was perfect—and uncomplicated.

But all too soon it ended.

He held her for half a dozen extra beats after the music faded away . . . then eased back an inch or two. Just far enough for her hand to slide from his shoulder to his impressive biceps. The man might be lean, but his muscles were rock hard—a fact that had become crystal clear during the dances she'd spent in his arms.

Fingers entwined with hers, he remained where he was while the band began to put away instruments and music books. As if he too hated for this magical night to end.

"I guess we need to leave." She had to force out the words.

"I guess we do." His throat worked. "I had a great time tonight. Maybe the best time of my life."

The raw honesty in his hoarse voice and the intensity in his dark brown eyes short-circuited her lungs.

"Me too."

The lights blinked, and one corner of his mouth twitched. "A not-so-subtle hint for us to leave."

"Let me get my purse and shawl."

He followed her to her table, draping the shawl over her shoulders when she fumbled her own attempt while juggling her purse.

"Thanks."

"Happy to help—though I hate to cover up that dress. You look ama . . ." He cleared his throat. "It's beautiful."

A warm rush of pleasure surged through her. "My mom convinced me to buy it."

"Thank her for me." The lights blinked again, and he took her arm. "We better go or we'll be stumbling around in the dark."

He guided her out of the tent and across the lawn, toward the street. Overhead, the full moon played hide-and-seek with the clouds. In the distance, a buoy bell gave a sonorous bong. Tendrils of fog swirled through the air.

It was a typical night in Hope Harbor.

Yet the electrified air around them made it feel anything but typical.

And for a woman whose last brush with romance had been more than five years ago, it was heady stuff.

Too heady.

She needed to get a grip on her emotions and focus on lighter, less personal topics . . . like tonight's event.

"BJ and Eric did a great job with the wedding, didn't they? I love all the small touches they incorporated, like those." She motioned to the votive candles in raffia-ribboned mason jars that lined the drive, striving for a bright, perky tone. "And the miniature loaves of Harbor Point cranberry nut cake at each place were perfect favors. Tracy was so sweet to provide them."

Ugh.

Too gushy.

She needed to tone down the artificial animation.

"It was a first-class wedding—not that I have anything to compare it to."

Lexie jolted to a stop. "You've never been to a wedding?"

"No. As a matter of fact, I experienced a lot of firsts tonight." He urged her forward again before she could dwell on his husky comment, stopping at the end of the drive. "I was the last to arrive, and the closest parking spot I could find was a couple of blocks away. It might be a hike in those high heels. Would you like to wait here while I get the car?"

And give up five or ten extra minutes in his company?

Not a chance.

"If I can dance for hours, I can walk to your car."

"Okay—but the pavement may be uneven and the overhead lighting isn't great. Why don't you take my arm?"

A fine suggestion.

She slid her hand into the crook of his elbow—and held on tight.

Although he shortened his stride to match hers and their pace was unhurried, his Kia came into sight much too soon. And once they got into it, she'd be home in five minutes.

She was so not ready for this evening to end.

Could she convince him to come in for a while when he dropped her off? Matt and her mom would have gone to bed long ago. Why not reciprocate his offer of coffee—and throw in an invitation for some food? The back porch would be a great spot for a late-night snack if she turned on the gas logs in the chiminea.

"How did your feet hold up?" Adam stopped beside the car and pulled out his keys.

"Fine." Sort of. Her protesting toes definitely preferred her comfy uniform shoes over fancy pumps.

He held the door while she slid inside, then circled the hood and took his place behind the wheel.

If she wanted to postpone their parting, this was the moment to make her pitch.

Her pulse picked up as a wave of doubt assailed her. Maybe this was a bad idea. Being alone on a porch was a lot different than swaying on a crowded dance floor. What if he . . .

"I don't know about you, but after all that dancing I'm hungry. Dinner was hours ago. Are you up for some food?"

Well . . . how about that? They were on the same wavelength.

Yet the tiny ripple in his question suggested he too was nervous about extending their evening.

Good.

If they were both a bit on edge, they'd proceed with caution as they tested the waters. Nothing would get out of hand.

Decision made.

"Food sounds fine."

"Great." He started the engine. "I don't think anything is open this late in Hope Harbor, but we could try Bandon."

"I know a spot closer to home where we could have omelets—unless you're after heartier fare."

"An omelet would be perfect. What's the name of the restaurant?"

"When I said closer to home, I meant that literally." Her heart began banging against her rib cage, and she clenched her fingers around her purse. "My house. I don't cook much these days, since my mom loves to putter around in the kitchen. But I make a mean omelet. Even Matt likes them—and he's a picky eater. Of course, it won't be world-class cuisine. I can't top tonight's meal." Her words came out in a staccato, pell-mell rush. Like she was flustered.

Which she was.

Stop talking, Lexie, before you make a total fool of yourself.

Sound advice.

She clamped her lips together.

Several beats ticked by, the silence broken only by the hum of the engine. It was too dark to read Adam's shadowed profile, and after several futile attempts she quit trying.

At last he put the car in gear and pulled away from the curb. "I'm not used to world-class food, anyway. Omelets are more my style. Your place sounds fine."

Slowly she exhaled. One hurdle cleared.

But who knew how many more might rear up before this night was over?

Banishing that unsettling worry, she chitchatted during the short drive, asking about his woodworking and Clyde's recovery and Tracy and Michael's construction project at the cranberry farm. Not until they pulled up in front of her house did she pause for breath.

"That was quick." She adjusted her shawl and picked up her purse.

He killed the engine and angled toward her. "Lexie."

Some nuance in his inflection put her on alert. "Yes?"

"If you want to change your mind about me staying, it's okay."

What?

Was he having second thoughts?

Her stomach bottomed out.

"Why would I want to do that?" She pulled the shawl tighter around her shoulders.

"You seem nervous—and I totally get that. The two of us . . . we live in different worlds. The reception tonight was a party. This is real life. You're well-educated, well-grounded, well-adjusted. I'm an ex-con. Aside from the dances we shared, we don't have much in common. I'm flattered by your invitation, but if it was just a polite gesture, you won't hurt my feelings if you retract it."

"You think I was just being polite?" She squinted at him in the darkness, his features too dim to decipher.

"I think good manners are in your DNA. I

brought up food. Offering a snack could be a way to repay me for the ride home. If that's the case, I appreciate the thought—but it's not necessary."

A few of the kinks in her stomach loosened. As usual, her mom had nailed it. Adam's self-esteem needed a serious boost.

If that meant she needed to step out of her comfort zone—so be it.

"Can I be honest with you?"

She could sense his slight stiffening—as if he was bracing for rejection.

"Yes."

"Before you asked me about food, I was planning to offer some. I enjoyed our evening and didn't want it to end. Am I nervous? Yes—but it has nothing to do with you. It's all about me. I've been out of the dating game so long I'm not even sure I remember how to play it—or if I should. With anyone. But I'm not retracting my offer."

There. She couldn't be much more direct than that. If he had any doubts about how she viewed this after-reception get-together, the D-word should take care of them.

This time he didn't hesitate.

"Then I'm staying. Let me get your door."

She waited as he circled the car, the buzz of attraction vibrating in her fingertips. Like it used to around Joe.

But look where that had led her.

Another wave of panic swept over her. Was she

being foolish? Setting herself up for more heartache and . . .

Her door opened, and Adam extended his hand. She hesitated for a second, but once she took it, her trepidation vanished. There was strength in his lean, firm fingers . . . and warmth . . . and a surprising gentleness.

All of which set off a flutter in her stomach as they walked toward her front door—and it had nothing to do with panic.

Inside the foyer, she shrugged out of her shawl and lowered her voice. "This house has been around for decades. They built them sturdy back in the day, with thick walls. Once we're in the kitchen, we won't have to worry about our conversation waking anyone up."

Taking her cue, he remained silent while he followed her to the back of the house. Only after she flipped on the light did he speak, keeping his volume low despite her reassurance.

"Can I help with anything?"

"Omelets don't require a lot of effort—but you can start a pot of coffee, if you like." She pulled an apron out of a drawer and slipped it over her dress. Not very chic, but this baby deserved protecting. "I do have one favor to ask, though."

"Name it."

"Do you mind if I ditch these shoes? My toes are threatening anarchy."

"No—as long as you don't mind if I ditch this

tie. I haven't worn one in . . . maybe never. Whoever invented these things should be strung up by his thumbs."

"Shoes for tie . . . sounds like a fair trade." She stepped out of her heels, pulled a bag of coffee from the fridge, and handed it to him. "My husband hated ties too."

As the casual comment spilled out of her mouth, the floor seemed to shift slightly beneath her feet.

Where had *that* come from?

She never talked about Joe. On the few occasions his name had surfaced in conversation, she'd changed the subject as fast as possible, before a fresh wave of sorrow could swamp her.

But tonight *she'd* brought him up. And instead of the usual debilitating grief, she felt only a vague, melancholy sadness.

Strange.

"Smart man." Adam loosened his tie, unclasped the top button on his shirt, and went about making the coffee. If he thought the mention of her late husband odd, he gave no indication of it.

"Uh-huh." The less said the better until she figured out what was going on.

In silence, she removed some eggs from the fridge and began cracking them into a bowl.

"So what did he do for a living?"

The egg in her hand shattered as her fingers compressed.

Great.

Dumping the gooey mess in the sink, she nudged the faucet on with her elbow.

Calm down, Lexie. It's a logical follow-up question. Adam doesn't know this is an off-limits topic.

She dried her hands and began whipping the eggs already in the bowl into a froth. "He worked in security."

Keeping her back to him, she chopped some ham. Pulled a bag of grated cheese from the fridge. Sliced a few mushrooms and tossed them into a pan of sizzling butter.

The kitchen remained silent.

As the minutes ticked by, some of her tension evaporated. Her terse answer and body language had obviously communicated that this was not a subject she wanted to discuss.

But maybe you should.

Lexie froze at the out-of-the-blue prompt. It was the same advice the counselor she'd been forced to talk to after the incident had offered. Sharing the memories would help her find closure, the woman had said.

Back then, she'd blown her off. Talking wouldn't bring Joe back.

It still wouldn't.

Yet with the perspective of distance, she could see how the counselor might be right. How giving voice to the grief and guilt she'd been carrying all these years could help her put it to rest and move on.

But why the sudden realization? And why wasn't the thought of sharing the story—the whole story—with someone other than the official government debriefers twisting her stomach into a knot, as usual?

As the eggs firmed and solidified from the steady warmth of the stove, she peeked at Adam. He was leaning against the counter by the coffee-maker, gazing out the window into the darkness, brow furrowed.

He was the reason she'd reached this point. The impetus to open up had come not from the mother she loved or the professional counselor who was paid to help people deal with feelings, but from a man she'd met less than two weeks ago.

Based on his posture and expression, however, he wasn't going to broach the subject again. If she wanted to talk about Joe, it would be up to her to reintroduce the topic.

Did she?

Could she trust her secrets with this man who'd known plenty of trauma himself—or would she regret taking such a risk?

The butter spattered, and she turned back to the task at hand, layering the filling over the eggs. Soon she'd fold the omelet over, hiding what was inside . . . as she'd carefully hidden what was in her heart after Joe died.

But you couldn't appreciate an omelet until you poked around under the surface.

And maybe that was true for people too. Like Adam. You had to dig a little, get past the biker-dude image he'd sported since arriving in town, to discover there was a lot more to the ex-con than a prison record.

Just as there was a lot more to her than the competent police chief image she projected around town.

"Coffee's ready."

Her fingers spasmed, and she almost dropped the spatula.

"The food is too. Let's eat on the porch. There's a lamp outside the door, on the left. I'll join you in a minute."

While he found mugs and poured the coffee, she cut the omelet in half. Slid it onto two plates. Added some fresh fruit.

Behind her, the door opened. Closed.

He was waiting for her.

Fingers trembling, she took off her apron . . . picked up the plates . . . walked toward the porch.

And made her decision.

❧ 14 ❧

He was lucky she hadn't thrown him out.

Adam set Lexie's coffee on the low-slung table in front of a wicker sofa and took a fortifying sip of his own.

Asking about her husband had been a huge mistake. He'd heard the town scuttlebutt, knew she didn't talk about the man she'd married . . . or her past. The locals might be curious and chat about it among themselves, but they respected her privacy—as he should have.

All he could do was hope she wouldn't hold his nosiness against him, since he hadn't been a local for long.

She pushed the door open with her shoulder, juggling two plates, and he moved across the room to hold it for her.

"Thanks." She gave him a strained smile.

Not a positive sign.

"I put your coffee over there." He indicated the table. "I didn't know where you'd want to sit."

"That's fine." She set their plates down and crossed to a contraption that looked kind of like the wood stove he relied on for most of his winter heat . . . but fancier. A flip of a switch set gas logs burning, chasing away the late-night coolness and adding instant warmth to the cozy porch. From a wicker basket beside the stove, she pulled out a pair of fuzzy slippers and a sweater. "Not very stylish, but these will keep me warm."

He could think of better ways to do that—but squelched the inappropriate thought. "Sometimes practical is better than stylish."

"Not according to the fashion world—but who cares?" She slid her arms into the sleeves of the sweater, sat on the settee, and pulled on the slippers. "Make yourself comfortable."

"The omelets smell great." He claimed the opposite end of the small sofa, set his coffee down, and picked up a plate.

"It's an easy late-night snack—or an anytime fast meal. When I worked overseas, I often put in irregular hours. Omelets were a quick dinner."

He cut off a bite of the egg dish. Why had she brought up her past again if she didn't want to talk about it?

Be careful, Stone. Approach with caution.

"Was that while you worked for the Bureau of Diplomatic Security?" She'd mentioned her job once, so that question ought to be safe.

"Yes." She sipped her coffee and picked up her own plate. "I learned to eat a lot of strange fare in some of the places the State Department sent me, but omelets were always my go-to comfort food." She took a miniscule bite. "Joe—my husband—liked them too."

They were back to the man she'd married . . . and now she'd offered a name.

Had he misinterpreted her reaction in the kitchen —or had she decided to share some background with him after all?

"How did you two meet?" That simple, standard question shouldn't elicit any pushback . . . but he broached it with the tentativeness of an explosives expert defusing a bomb.

"On the job—in Turkey." She forked another bite of omelet and motioned to his plate. "You better eat. Cold pizza is fine. Cold omelets, not so much."

In silence, he followed her suggestion. If she chose to say more, fine. If she didn't, he was done asking questions. The last thing he wanted to do was end this evening on a sour note.

It didn't take long to finish the tasty egg dish, though Lexie still had half of hers left as he ate his last bite. Same dilemma he'd had at the reception. He was going to have to do a better job pacing himself if he wanted to fit into polite—

"Joe worked for a US defense contractor. I was stationed at the embassy as a regional security officer." She continued to pick at her food while she threw out a few more tidbits. "DS is the law enforcement arm of the Department of State. We provided security for department personnel. But in a lot of hot spots, like Turkey, our ranks were supplemented by contractors."

"It sounds like dangerous work."

"It can be."

He waited, but when she didn't continue, he took a chance and asked what he hoped was an innocuous question. "How did you get interested in that kind of work? Was it a family tradition?"

"No." She snagged a renegade mushroom. "My dad and grandfather worked for the lumber mill outside of town their whole life. I don't know where my fascination with law enforcement came from, but it goes back to my childhood. While other girls were playing with dolls and dreaming about getting married, I hung around our police chief, Sam Martin. Eventually he made me an honorary deputy and encouraged my interest."

"Yet you went into diplomatic security instead."

"Same field, only bigger league and more exotic settings. I figured if I was going to be in law enforcement, why not get a job that would give me a chance to travel and experience the world? After the glamour wore off, I could always find a position like the one I have now."

"Is that what happened? The glamour wore off?"

"No. I liked the job." She laid down her fork, picked up her mug, and dispensed with any pretense of eating. "My five-year plan was to work for DS in a couple more overseas locations and reevaluate at that stage. Romance was *not* on my agenda. Then I met Joe, and everything changed . . . including my priorities."

Brow puckered, she tucked her feet under her and thumbed off a lipstick smudge on the rim of her mug. Like the one on the mug back at his cabin.

The one he'd planned to wash off every day since her visit but never had.

Thank goodness no one other than him and Clyde knew about that—and his canine friend wouldn't be talking.

He studied the creases on her forehead. "You weren't happy about falling in love?"

"Not at first. It disrupted my plans. But Joe was such an incredible man." Her throat contracted. "I know this is going to sound cliché, but it was love at first sight."

"That's how it works in a lot of movies too."

"Movies don't always depict real life—but our romance *was* kind of like a Hollywood story." Her last word wavered, and she drew in a breath. Let it out. "I fought the attraction at first but finally realized I was being a fool. Joe was the real deal. Smart, funny, high-energy, principled, enthusiastic, committed, brave . . . I could keep going, but you get the picture. He'd had a long career as a Navy SEAL before his contracting gig."

She'd been married to a Navy SEAL?

His spirits tanked.

Those guys were the cream of the crop. The best the nation had to offer, with impeccable credentials and spotless backgrounds.

He was totally hosed.

Adam took a sip of coffee and tried to think of some appropriate reply.

Lexie saved him the effort by picking up the story. "Joe was also very single-minded. If he wanted something, he went after it."

"Like you?" Adam took one last swallow of coffee and set the mug down. It was cold now, anyway.

"Yes. However, since romances among staff members—contractors included—were frowned upon, we conducted ours under the radar. But he got tired of that fast and wanted to get married."

"Did you?"

"Not right away. After we got serious, I bid on a special agent assignment in San Francisco, which I was assured was a slam dunk. As soon as that came through, Joe planned to leave his job and open a domestic security firm in San Francisco. After we were both stateside, we'd get married here in Hope Harbor. A year later, I'd resign from government service and join him in the firm. We had everything worked out."

And then Joe died.

But how? Where? As far as he knew, no one in town had ever met Lexie's husband. That would suggest they'd married ahead of schedule. Why?

Adam bit back the questions tripping over his tongue and asked a different, less intrusive one.

"Did you both come back?"

"No. My assignment was confirmed, but they extended my stay in Turkey for three months until my replacement could get there. Joe didn't want to wait four or five more months to have a wedding in Hope Harbor."

"So you got married over there?"

"Yes. On the QT. I didn't even wear my wedding ring at work. We stole what hours we could together. It wasn't ideal, but we had our sights on

San Francisco, and a vow renewal and reception here. It was supposed to be a short-term inconvenience. Except it ended up being a lot shorter than either of us e-expected." She leaned forward to set her mug down. With both hands.

Because she'd begun to shake.

Badly.

Adam's gut clenched. Every instinct in his body urged him to tug her against his chest, stroke her cheek . . . and try to make everything better.

But he couldn't fix whatever had gone horribly wrong in her life—and he had no experience consoling a grieving woman. He was out of his league here. *She* was out of his league.

He fisted his hands and closed his eyes.

God, what should I do? Please tell me!

The Almighty remained silent as Lexie's almost tangible anguish seeped into his soul.

Then, all at once, Luis's comment from earlier in the evening echoed in his mind.

"The key in any situation is to listen with the heart . . . and follow where it leads."

If that was true, Lexie wouldn't be sitting there alone in her sorrow. She'd be wrapped in his arms.

But he was no Joe, with a pedigree worthy of this woman. Overstepping bounds could be a fatal mistake. Just because she'd told him her story didn't mean she'd welcome a . . .

He froze as a tiny, choked sob ruptured the stillness.

She was trying not to cry. To be strong. To lock her emotions inside and maintain the act-together image she presented to the world as the town police chief.

But she didn't have to do that with him.

Quashing his fear, he twined her cold, quivering fingers with his. Not as bold as a hug—but better than nothing.

"It's okay, Lexie. Tears aren't a sign of weakness. I shed plenty myself over the past few years." True . . . though only Reverend Baker and God had witnessed them.

"I don't c-cry anymore. I'm past that."

Not if the vise grip she had on his hand and the shimmer in her blue irises were any indication.

And they'd come too far now to back away from the hard stuff.

"Do you want to tell me what happened?"

"It's not pretty."

"I'm used to ugly."

A few beats passed. "This might be hard. I've never told my story to anyone except State Department personnel."

"What about your mom?" Surely, as close as they were, Lexie had shared the details with her.

"No. She knows the bare facts, but nothing about the . . . the guilt."

Guilt?

"I don't understand."

"You would, if you knew the story." She examined their clasped hands.

"You know I'll keep whatever you tell me in confidence."

"Yes—or I wouldn't even have told you this much."

He didn't say anything else. The decision to share more had to come from within, not from outside pressure.

"Okay. Let me see how far I get." She moistened her lips, and a pulse began to throb in the hollow of her throat. "Two weeks before we were scheduled to come home, a crowd of protestors gathered in front of the embassy. Joe and his crew were summoned to supplement our team on the off chance we might need additional support. We'd had similar situations, and groups like that always dispersed after a while."

"I take it this one was different."

"Yes. After it got dark, the protest turned violent. A rocket-propelled grenade hit the main building. Hand grenades came flying over the walls. A huge group of armed militants surged out of the crowd, rushed the Marine security guards, and broke through the gates. It was chaos." A shudder rippled through her.

Adam edged closer and draped his free arm around her shoulders.

She didn't pull away.

"This isn't a great bedtime s-story." Tremors shook her body as well as her words.

"Don't worry. I know life isn't a fairy tale. I don't expect happy endings . . . and I've learned to deal with nightmares."

A full minute passed in silence. But he could sense her shoring up her resolve to continue.

At last she did, tightening her grip on his hand. "While I and some of my colleagues secured embassy personnel in the safe room, Joe and his crew fought back the militants alongside our own security people and the Marines. After our people were as safe as we could make them, most of us dispersed to assist in the fight while we waited for additional help to arrive."

Adam tried to wrap his mind around Lexie going head-to-head with a rabid terrorist. Abandoned the effort. The whole notion freaked him out.

Better to focus on logistics.

"How fast did you get help?"

"Fast. There were injuries and massive destruction on our side, but only one person died. And it was . . . it was m-my fault."

Adam's pulse stuttered.

Lexie thought her husband's death was her fault?

No way.

"I don't believe that."

"It's true." She looked up at him, her eyes dark pools of misery. "After I went outside, I ran into

243

Joe. He told me to go back in and guard the ambassador in the safe room. That he and his team were better equipped to deal with the situation."

"Were they?"

"Yes. I was trained for hostile situations—but I'd never had that training tested in the field. He was a veteran of hundreds of SEAL missions in enemy territory. Most of his colleagues were ex-military too. But I didn't think it was fair to duck the fight. Instead of going back in, I stayed outside and lurked around the edges, ready to provide support if they needed me. I thought that was my job."

"It was—wasn't it?"

"Yes . . . but Joe and his team were doing fine on their own, and the embassy staff *was* a priority. The safe room wasn't infallible."

"*Did* they end up needing you outside?"

"No. After a while, I accepted the logic of Joe's suggestion and started back toward the main building. I was almost there when a terrorist came barreling around the corner not fifty feet in front of me."

Adam's heart lurched again. "What happened?"

"I shot at him . . . and missed. I knew I wouldn't get a second chance. The guy had an AK-47."

A word from his rougher days almost slipped out.

He hadn't lied about learning to deal with nightmares, but he had a feeling this one was going to haunt him for a very long time.

Yet Lexie had survived. That was what mattered.

"What happened?"

"Out of nowhere, someone took him out. Joe, I found out later. But as the militant fell, he squeezed the trigger. His gun was in full automatic mode, and in the spray of bullets I got clipped in the leg."

Dear God.

Lexie had been shot!

Despite his seedy past and the bad characters who'd peopled his world for most of his life, she'd come closer to death than he ever had.

"How badly were you hurt?" He could barely squeeze out the question.

"Not as badly as I could have been. Two operations and some intense physical therapy got me back on my feet faster than I expected. Joe wasn't as lucky."

Right.

This was supposed to be about Joe.

"What happened?"

"As I was lying on the pavement, I saw him running across the courtyard. He yelled, 'Hang on. Everything's going to be fine.' More shots were fired. He twisted. Fell over. There was a barrage of gunfire—and everything after that is a blur. But I do know if I'd done what he asked in the beginning, he'd be alive today. He died trying to help me." A tear brimmed on her lower lid. Spilled over. Trailed down.

Adam drew in a lungful of air. She hadn't lied. Her story wasn't pretty.

No wonder she shied away from talking about it.

"I'm so sorry." Lame—but what else was there to say in the face of such tragedy?

"Me too. Joe was a good man. And he would have been a great father. Maybe . . . maybe if we'd known I was pregnant, we both would have been more careful that day."

Another shock wave reverberated through him. "You didn't know?"

"No. I found out while I was in the hospital being treated for the wounds in my leg."

In the silence that followed, Adam ticked through all the traumas Lexie had endured. She'd lost her new husband—and blamed herself for his death. Suffered gunshot wounds. Discovered she was carrying a baby who would never know his father. Watched all her plans for the future disintegrate in seconds.

Most people would have folded under one or two of those setbacks.

Yet she'd not only survived, but carried on. She'd built a new life, taken on a responsible job, and was doing a fine job raising her son as a single parent.

That took guts. And courage. And grace.

"You're sorry you asked, aren't you?" She watched him, her tone tentative.

"No. I'm trying to absorb everything." He exhaled. "And I thought life had dealt me some tough blows."

"It has—and spread out over a much longer period."

"Nothing like what you've been through, though. I never lost anyone I loved."

"I hope you never do. But bad as that is, the guilt compounds it."

He narrowed his eyes. Now that he was beginning to digest her story, a couple of pieces weren't fitting—including the guilt.

"You know, I think you're being too hard on yourself. You were doing what you believed your job required. It took a lot of courage to go outside in the midst of that kind of danger—and stay there after Joe told you to go back inside."

"No." She shook her head. "It was my duty to protect embassy personnel. Courage is walking into danger by choice."

"Were you scared?"

"Yes."

"But you went anyway—and stayed longer than you had to. I call that brave."

"Joe didn't agree. He said it was crazy."

"He was in love with you. In his place, I would have said and done the same." And that brought him to the other piece that didn't fit. She might not like what he had to say, but if she hadn't considered it, she needed to. "To tell you the truth, I have a feeling it was more his distraction than your foolishness that led to disaster."

"What do you mean?"

"After you went down, it sounds as if he acted like a man in love rather than an ex-SEAL trained to evaluate danger before taking action. If you had been a stranger to him, do you think he would have rushed out into the open like that, toward you?"

She bit her bottom lip. "I . . . don't know."

"My guess is he would have stayed under cover until he was certain the danger was gone. Or tried to get to you by hugging the edge of the building and working his way over."

"Even if that's true, had I gone back inside, it wouldn't have happened."

"But that wasn't what you were trained to do. Did your superiors—or any of your husband's colleagues—blame you?"

"No."

"How did the media position his death?"

"They reported it as a nameless casualty in the initial stories. While the details were being sorted out, a much bigger incident at one of our diplomatic compounds in Libya usurped their attention. In comparison to that, the death of one contractor didn't matter enough to merit further coverage." A twinge of resentment crept into her voice.

So the world hadn't noticed—or honored—her husband's sacrifice.

Another bitter pill to swallow.

"I'm sorry, Lexie. For everything. I wish I could offer more than trite sentiments."

Her eyes began to shimmer again. "Trite sentiments help when they're sincere. Thanks for listening."

"Thank *you* for sharing."

"It felt like the right thing to do." She played with a button on her sweater. Smoothed a hand down her skirt. "It's kind of strange. We haven't known each other long, but I feel a strong connection between us."

"I do too." He stroked his thumb across the back of her hand. "Charley told me once that while he was growing up in Mexico, his grandmother called immediate connections like this heaven-sent links."

"You think God had a hand in our meeting?" Her fingers stilled.

"I don't know—but I do view it as a blessing . . . for however long it lasts." No sense hiding his head in the sand about this idyllic interlude.

She blinked. "What does that mean?"

"Like I said earlier, we don't have a lot in common. One of these days, some man from your world will come along and . . ." His voice scraped, and he swallowed. "You have a lot to offer."

"So do you."

"Lexie—I'm a convicted felon. I spent five years in prison. I have a GED, not a college degree. I'm a carpenter with very little money in the bank and few tangible assets. I have nothing to offer someone like you."

"That's not true! You have great instincts, superb people skills, a steady job, and an extraordinary gift with woodworking. You're also kind and generous and a wonderful listener. Those are huge assets."

The conviction in her voice was gratifying . . . but it didn't change the reality.

"What would people say if we—as you suggested earlier—began dating? A police chief and an ex-con. Not the best combination."

Her chin firmed. "My mother always told me you should never worry about what other people think as long as you know what you're doing is right. I've lived by that rule my whole life. Have I thought about the challenges that might come up if people see us together? Yes. I'm a realist. But with every day that passes, I'm caring less about possible complications and more about you." She squeezed his fingers. "I don't know where this might lead—but I'm willing to test the waters."

She wanted to go out with him?

In public?

"You mean . . . you actually want to go on a real date?"

"Yes."

"I haven't been transported to some alternate universe, have I?"

The corners of her mouth rose. "If you have, I'm along for the ride—but I think we should take it slow and easy. I'm rusty at this game."

"Not as rusty as I am."

"Maybe we can relearn it together." Her smile broadened.

His gaze dropped to it—and got stuck there. She had beautiful lips. Generous. Soft-looking. Kissable.

Very kissable.

He leaned closer.

She'd said slow and easy—and this wasn't even an official first date—but surely it would be acceptable to—

"Mommy?"

He jerked back.

"Mommy . . . I threw up again."

At the tear-laced announcement, she shifted around.

Scratch romance for tonight.

Over her shoulder, Matt was framed in the door-way, a tattered blanket trailing from one hand, pajamas reeking with a distinctive, vile smell.

As Lexie rose and crossed to the little boy, he stood too.

"What do you mean, again?" She dropped to one knee in front of her son.

"I threw up in the bathroom at the party too.

Mamaw helped me there. But she's snoring real loud now, so I went to your room. Then I saw the light in here. My pajamas stink!"

"No kidding. Let's get you cleaned up and back in the sack." She took Matt's hand. "I'm sorry, Adam. This isn't the best end to our evening. Can you let yourself out?"

"I'd rather stay and help you deal with the mess."

"This kind of stuff isn't fun."

"I've dealt with worse. Let's see what needs to be done."

After a nanosecond hesitation, she led the way through the kitchen, down the hall, and into a bedroom lined with shelves filled with picture books and toys and stuffed animals.

The stench was stronger in here.

"I need to change the bedding." As she did a fast assessment, Lexie pulled a new pair of pajamas out of the dresser. "Do you think you could clean Matt up while I do that? The bath is next door, and there are towels on the rack."

"I can handle that." Adam held out his hand. "Come on, buddy. We'll get you into some fresh pjs."

Lexie was already stripping the bed as they left the room, her practiced efficiency suggesting she'd mastered this drill long ago.

Once in the bathroom, Adam went to work on the stink bomb. Disposing of the clothes helped, and a few scrubs with a washcloth took care of the smell clinging to the youngster's skin.

As he redressed the boy, Matt gave a sleepy yawn. "I guess I ate too much cake."

"I guess you did."

"It tasted real good going down."

"It always does."

"Do you like cake?"

"Yep."

"Did you ever eat too much and get sick?"

"No—but it's easy to eat too much of something tasty."

"Could you tell my mom that? She's gonna be mad at me tomorrow. I wasn't 'sposed to eat extra cake."

"I'll see what I can do."

"Thanks! Are you staying all night?"

"No." He took the boy's hand. Better be crystal clear on that point. "I drove your mom home from the party. I'll be leaving in a few minutes."

"Oh. Are you gonna be at church tomorrow?"

"That's the plan. You want me to bring Clyde again?"

"Yeah!"

"I'll wait for you after the service."

He retraced their steps down the hall. Lexie was folding back the new bedding when they entered.

"All set, young man. Climb in." She motioned her son over.

Adam released him and he trotted to the bed, the ratty blanket clutched in one hand.

"Do I need to throw that in the wash?" Lexie tweaked the worn square of cloth.

"No. It escaped the eruption."

"Good. We have a hard time falling asleep without it." She gave Matt a boost onto the mattress, tucked him in, and leaned down for a kiss. "You feeling better now?"

"Uh-huh. Mr. Stone is going to bring Clyde to church again tomorrow. I guess it was kinda lucky I threw up, or he might not have thought about doing that, huh?" He gave her a hopeful look.

"Throwing up is never lucky."

His face fell.

Lexie retreated to the door, and as she reached for the light switch, Adam gave the kid a thumbs-up behind her back. Matt rewarded him with a wide grin.

"Good night, sweetie." She flipped off the light.

" 'Night."

Putting her fingers to her lips as they exited, Lexie gestured to a room across the dim hall, where the cracked door couldn't muffle the loud snores.

He remained silent as he followed her to the front door. She pulled it open and stepped outside, closing it again after he crossed the threshold.

"Sorry for the inauspicious end to our evening." She stifled a yawn. "Sorry for that too."

"Don't be sorry—for either. It's late. And try not to be too hard on Matt about the cake. At his age, those kinds of temptations are hard to resist."

"He put you up to that plea for mercy, didn't he?" She folded her arms and arched an eyebrow.

"I don't know if I should answer that."

"You don't have to. I know my son. He tries to enlist allies whenever he's in trouble. However, in light of the source of this request, I'll let him off with a stern warning. Besides . . . between you and me, I pulled the same stunt once as a kid. Being sick was punishment enough—and taught me a lesson without the need for any further penalty from my parents."

"I think Matt learned his lesson too. So . . . can I call you this week to set up a date for next weekend?"

"I'd like that."

"No second thoughts?"

"None." Another yawn snuck up on her, and she clapped a hand over her mouth. "Sorry again! It's not the company."

"No offense taken."

Say good night, Stone. She's tired, and there's no reason to linger.

True—yet just walking away after all that had happened tonight didn't feel right.

The romantic moment on the screened porch was gone, diminishing the temptation to attempt a real kiss . . . but he could do the next best thing.

Without giving himself a chance to weigh the pros and cons, he rested his hands on her shoulders, leaned down, and brushed his lips over her forehead. "Sleep well."

"You t-too."

He released her, turned, and forced his legs to carry him to his car.

From behind the wheel, he glanced back. Lexie was still on the porch, bathed in the warm glow of the porch light, holding on to the railing. As if she needed the support.

He could relate. Tonight had sent a shock wave through him too. Opened a door he'd never allowed himself to believe existed. Filled his world with sweet possibilities that only yesterday had been no more than the stuff of dreams.

And as he drove back to the isolated cove he called home, a tiny ember of hope for a future that included more than a loyal, lovable dog for a companion began to glow in a long-dark corner of his heart.

✑ 15 ✑

"My. You're up early. I thought you'd sleep in today after all that dancing. What time did you get home, anyway?" Annette paused in the doorway to the kitchen, fussing with the button on the side of her skirt. "I've either been indulging in too many cinnamon rolls from Sweet Dreams Bakery or this shrank in the last washing."

Lexie stirred Matt's oatmeal, lowered the heat on the burner, and tried to tamp down her jitters. If she ignored the first question, perhaps her mom would forget about it.

"You've weighed the same for the past twenty years."

"I don't know. This feels snug." She moved to the cabinet and pulled out a mug. "So . . . when did you get home?"

There was no escaping *that* topic, it seemed.

"A little before midnight."

"You must have stayed until the end." Her mother sounded altogether too pleased.

"The band was great."

"The company wasn't too shabby, either. Who knew a hunk was hidden under that scruffy veneer?"

"Mom!"

"What? I can't notice a handsome man? You did, or you wouldn't have stayed so late."

"We had a very enjoyable evening. In fact . . ." Her voice faltered.

Oh, for pity's sake.

Spit it out, Lexie. Matt will tell her Adam was here last night if you don't.

She took a deep breath and tried again. "In fact, after he brought me home, we—"

"Is breakfast ready?" Matt bounded into the room. "I'm hungry."

"Well. You're much more chipper today." Her mom tousled his hair.

"I felt a lot better after I threw up again."

"Again?"

"Yeah. In the middle of the night." Matt climbed onto his chair. "But Mom and Mr. Stone cleaned me all up. I'm real sorry about eating all that cake, Mom." He gave her a contrite look.

"Are you ever going to do it again?" She could feel her mother watching her.

"No. Throwing up is yucky."

"I hope you remember that."

"I will. I promise. Can I have some cinnamon toast?"

"We'll see after you finish your oatmeal."

"Hold on. Back up a minute." Her mother propped her hands on her hips. "Stone helped you clean up Matt?"

Of course her mom would home in on that piece of news.

"Yes—but it wasn't the middle of the night." Better clarify that pronto. She turned off the stove and spooned the oatmeal into a bowl. "We were both hungry, and I made us omelets after we got back here."

"You *cooked* for him?"

At her mother's reverent tone, she rolled her eyes. "Don't get carried away. An omelet isn't a gourmet meal."

"The menu doesn't matter. It's the principle."

O-kay. Time to drop her second bombshell. It might divert attention from her impromptu late-night meal with Adam—and it was easier to talk about than her feelings for a man whose simple kiss on the forehead had kept her tossing half the night.

"What time are you leaving for services?"

"Nine thirty, like always. Why?"

"I think I'll join you today."

Her mother choked on her coffee.

"Are you okay, Mamaw?" Matt half rose from his chair.

"Fine." The assurance was more wheeze than word, but at least there weren't any life-threatening issues with her windpipe.

"Are you really going to church with us, Mom?" Matt sank back into his seat and swirled his spoon through the oatmeal she set in front of him.

"Yes. I didn't schedule myself at work today. I thought I might be tired after the wedding, but I woke up early. Do you want milk or orange juice?"

"Juice."

"Lexie."

Bracing, she retrieved the juice from the fridge and swiveled toward her mother, trying for a don't-mess-with-me expression. "Yes?"

After an assessing sweep, her mother stuck a bagel in the toaster oven. "I'm glad you're joining us."

Mission accomplished. Her mom had concluded

it was better to be glad her wayward daughter was returning to the fold than ask questions that might drive her away again.

"Mr. Stone said he'd bring Clyde today." Matt began shoveling in his oatmeal.

"Speaking of Stone . . . what did the two of you talk about while you ate?" The casual, conversational tone didn't jibe with the avid interest in her mom's eyes.

"Lots of things. Unfortunately, our meal was cut short by my puking son."

"Oh. Right." Her mother grimaced. "I suppose that would put a damper on . . . conversation. You can always get together again and pick up where you left off."

"Maybe."

More like definitely . . . and in the not-too-distant future.

That, however, was a bombshell for another day.

But before she dropped it, she needed to figure out a way to downplay their date so her mom wouldn't jump to all sorts of fanciful, romantic conclusions.

Because foolish though it might be, she was already doing that—and one starry-eyed conclusion-jumper in the family was more than enough.

Adam swung onto Dockside Drive and checked on his passenger.

Brian was staring straight ahead, silent as a clam—same as he'd been for the entire eight-minute drive.

No surprise, given his round-eyed double take once he'd gotten an eyeful of his mentor.

The kid was thrown by the new look. Perhaps even feeling blindsided. Yesterday, he'd started to open up to one Adam Stone, and today a different one had picked him up.

They were going to be back to square one unless he did some fast damage control.

"In case you haven't noticed, I changed my image." He pulled into a parking spot near Sweet Dreams, shut off the engine, and faced the kid. No sense beating around the bush. "For the record, inside I'm the same guy I was yesterday."

Darting him a quick peek, Brian fiddled with his seat belt. "Then why did you get rid of the hair and bandana and . . . stuff?"

"The look I used to have belonged to someone who doesn't exist anymore. The town thinks I'm a biker dude—despite the fact that I don't have a motorcycle. That's not me anymore, but I never bothered to change the image. Now the outside matches the inside."

"So what's your new image supposed to be?"

Excellent question—and one he needed to answer for himself as well.

"I want to be seen as a responsible, law-abiding citizen." He spoke slowly, carefully composing his reply. "Someone whose appearance doesn't send people running the other way. I want everyone in Hope Harbor to think of me as an ordinary, hard-working guy who does his best and is willing to lend a hand when it's needed. I want to be someone others would like to have for a friend."

A few beats ticked by while Brian mulled that over. "I guess that makes sense." He shrugged, and faint pink spots appeared on his cheeks. "I thought you might be trying to impress a girl or something."

That too.

But the whole concept of dating Lexie was too new . . . and too tenuous . . . to discuss with his fifteen-year-old protégé.

"I'd like to impress *everyone* in town—so they want to get to know me better. My life's been pretty lonely for a long time."

"Yeah." The boy's shoulders slumped. "I know how that feels."

Right. Lexie had said the friend issue was a big deal for Brian. It had come up during her first visit with the mother and son. Being dropped into a new school midyear was tough, and it was easy to see how a lonely teen, desperate to fit in, might hook up with the wrong kid if there was a chance it would give him entrée to a group of friends.

"You know, school isn't the only place to find friends. We have a teen group at church that has activities every week."

"What kind of activities?" Brian didn't attempt to hide his skepticism.

He tried to recall some of the events that had been mentioned in the bulletin. "Pizza nights, road trip to a Ducks game, crabbing, camping, some charitable community outreach—that's all I can remember off the top of my head."

"Some of those sound okay."

"I'd be happy to find out more about the group for you, if you're interested. Did you talk to your mom about coming to services some week?"

"Yeah. She said we've been away too long, and that God might be mad at her for not standing up to Dad instead of caving after he told us to stay home on Sunday."

"God doesn't work that way."

"Maybe you could tell her that. She might listen to you."

Not a chore he relished. He'd had his fill of wimpy mothers . . . though Brenda did seem to care about her son, even if she'd let her husband run her life.

"Will she be there when I take you home?"

"No. She's working a double shift today. Tomorrow she's back to nights again."

Reprieved.

"Next time I see her, I'll try to bring up the subject. You ready to work on planters?"

"Yeah." He pushed the door open and got out of the car.

Adam joined him at the trunk. Once the supplies were unloaded, they crossed the street and headed toward the next container slated for repair.

"Stone!"

He stopped as John Nash waved at him from down the street.

"Go ahead and put all the stuff over by that planter." Adam motioned toward it. "I'll be there in a minute."

"I'm glad I caught you." John hurried over and extended his hand.

Adam put down his toolbox and returned the man's hearty clasp. "How's the father of the groom?"

"Couldn't be better. They make a handsome couple, don't they?"

"Yes. It was a great wedding."

"I noticed you and our police chief were enjoying the orchestra." He grinned.

"The music was great." He tried to curb the flush creeping up his neck.

"Yes, it was. Did you enjoy the meal?"

"It was great."

As the words left his mouth, he stifled a groan.

He sounded like one of those annoying parrots with a limited vocabulary that repeats the same phrase over and over again.

"Well, I won't keep you from your work—and thank you for taking on this repair project for the town, by the way—but I wanted to pass this on." He retrieved a business card from his pocket and held it out.

Adam took it and read the type. Rebecca Oliver, owner, Oliver Design—a Portland business specializing in distinctive décor, according to the tag line.

He shot John a puzzled glance.

"She and her husband were at the inn for a few days last week, and she saw the rocking chairs you delivered for BJ and Eric. At breakfast one morning she asked about them, and she was very excited to hear they were handmade in town. Apparently a lot of her clients want commissioned, handcrafted pieces, and she's always on the lookout for new sources. She asked me to give you that and tell you she'd appreciate a call."

Adam fingered the fancy, embossed card that communicated class, high-society connections, big bucks—all the things he lacked. "Does she know my background?"

"She asked. I told her about the meticulous work you did on the inn remodel and how you make furniture in your spare time."

"Did you tell her I'm an ex-con?"

"Why would I tell her that?" He appeared to be genuinely puzzled.

"It might make a difference."

"Why?"

"Clients of a firm like this"—he lifted the card

—"might not want furniture made by someone like me."

"Stone." John grasped his upper arm. "There isn't a person in this town who wouldn't vouch for you. You may not have sought friends, but everyone knows about the good deeds you do behind the scenes. And they'd *like* to be your friend. You're part of Hope Harbor now. If you want to tell this woman your history, that's your choice. But remember—it *is* history . . . and I think it bothers you a lot more than it bothers any of us."

Pressure built in his throat. "Thanks."

"Don't thank me. You've earned your place here over the past eighteen months. We consider you an asset to the town." He removed his hand and sniffed the air. "Mmm. Charley's cooking. My next stop. See you soon."

With a jaunty wave, he continued down the wharf toward the colorful taco stand.

Adam picked up his toolbox and wandered to the planter where Brian was already hard at work.

Could what John said be true? *Did* people in town want to be his friend?

It was possible.

From the beginning, Annette and Matt had sought him out at church to offer a pleasant greeting. Luis and BJ had always been kind to him. Eleanor Cooper often sent him fudge cake. Charley had befriended him on day one. John had given him a standing invitation to drop by the inn any time he was in the mood for one of the gourmet breakfasts he'd enjoyed there while working on the remodel project.

And now there was Lexie.

His mouth flexed up. Of all the blessings he'd received during his months in Hope Harbor, she was the best.

"Did you win the lottery or something?"

At Brian's query, he redirected his attention to the teen. "Why?"

"I don't know." The boy studied him. "You look kind of like it's Christmas morning and you just walked into a room full of presents."

An apt analogy.

"No gift-wrapped presents, but I've had an eventful twenty-four hours—capped off with some unexpected news. I'll tell you about it while we work."

Adam followed through on that promise, answering Brian's many questions about wood-working before they branched out to other topics.

And throughout the day, as they hammered and sawed and nailed and sanded, his mood remained elevated. Buoyant, almost.

It was a new sensation . . . and 180 degrees from how he'd felt the day he'd rolled into this town, fresh out of prison.

That had been a scary moment.

Despite Reverend Baker's assurances that Hope

Harbor would offer him both a haven and a fresh start, he'd been dubious—and nervous. He was tainted merchandise, after all. Why would any decent person want to have anything to do with him?

Yet quite a few had made welcoming overtures, despite his reserved manner.

Now a lovely woman wanted to date him—and his woodworking hobby was on the verge of becoming much more than a pleasant pastime.

Adam drew in a lungful of the fresh sea air and looked past the boats bobbing in the water to the distant horizon, shrouded in fog on this April day.

Kind of like the future.

No one knew what tomorrow held—even those who had it all planned out. Lexie was proof of that.

But for the first time, he was beginning to believe that, barring any unforeseen glitches, his life was finally, truly, on a permanent upswing.

"Hey, Brian. What's up?"

Stomach knotting, Brian watched Lucas Fisher stroll toward him and prop a shoulder against the wall next to his locker. The high school football hero hadn't talked to him since . . . the incident . . . and whatever the reason for this contact, he had a feeling his Tuesday was about to go downhill.

"I got your note." He shoved his geometry book onto a shelf and pulled out his lunch. "I thought you said it would be better if we weren't seen together until the cops got off my back."

"Yeah . . . but that's dying down." Scanning the hall, he winked at a passing cheerleader. She moved on with a giggle, and he dropped his volume. "You haven't mentioned my name to anyone, have you?"

"No. We made a pledge. I keep my word."

"Good, good. Listen . . ." He leaned closer. "I had an idea for some . . . entertainment. I could do it alone, but it's more fun with two people. You in?"

The ball of nerves in his stomach tightened. "I can't. I'm already in trouble. If I get caught again, they're gonna put me in front of a judge. I could end up in jail."

"Oh, give me a break. The jails are already too crowded with real criminals. Nobody cares about this kind of stuff."

"That's not what the police chief said . . . or that juvenile counselor."

"They're just trying to scare you."

"Yeah? Well, it's working."

Lucas narrowed his eyes. "I'm beginning to think you're a wimp."

"No. I'm not." His fingers crimped the lunch bag.

"Prove it."

"I can't." His throat tightened. "Not how you want me to."

"You know"—Lucas's features hardened—"you

wouldn't have any friends in this place if it wasn't for me. Nobody talked to you until I did."

"I can find friends somewhere else if I have to." The assertion was brave, but the crack in his voice betrayed him.

"I wouldn't count on that. This is a small town. Everyone goes to school here. If you want . . ." He smiled and straightened up. "Hey, Coach."

"Fisher." As Brian shifted his weight, the man spared him a disinterested glace. Like he was nobody. Brian mashed his lips together to keep them from trembling while the coach refocused on Lucas. "Stop by my office later. I want to talk to you about some ideas for next season."

"Sure thing."

A bell rang, and the coach strode away. The noise level in the hallway rose immediately as classrooms disgorged antsy students.

Lucas turned his back on the surging throng. "One last chance, Brian. Are you in or out?"

"Look . . . I don't want any more trouble. We almost got caught the *first* time." Hard as he tried to contain it, a thread of desperation slipped in.

"That's because the planters were too public. We don't pick those kinds of places anymore. If it hadn't been for that stupid dog at the cove, we wouldn't have had any trouble there, either. Think about it and let me know by the end of the day. But remember . . ." He tapped the lunch bag. "You'll be eating alone from now on if you don't come through. I don't hang with losers."

He pivoted away and joined a passing group of students.

Brian sagged against the locker, gut churning. If he hooked back up with Lucas, he'd never have to worry about sitting by himself in the cafeteria again. He'd have friends and a social life.

But there was a risk.

A big one.

He'd used up his second chance, and if he got caught again, it would be bad. Real bad.

Muttering a word his mother wouldn't approve of, he threw his lunch back in the locker and slammed the door shut.

Why wasn't anything ever easy?

Why couldn't they have stayed in Medford, where he'd had friends?

Why did his father have to be such a jerk?

Why was he the one who'd gotten caught instead of Lucas?

Why did some kids live in homes with real foundations and have fathers who hung around?

His whole life sucked.

And it wasn't like he could talk to his mom about this stuff. She'd tell him to stick with the program and keep his nose clean.

But she didn't know how hard it had been in the beginning, until Lucas came to his rescue.

He couldn't go back to that lonely place.

Another bell rang, prompting him into action.

Since he wasn't eating lunch, he'd find a quiet spot in the library, pretend to study . . . and try to figure out what he was going to do to avoid making a bigger mess of his life.

Adam hadn't called.

Maybe he wasn't going to.

Spirits sinking, Lexie scrolled through her messages again in case she'd missed a call while she helped Matt with his bath and read him a bedtime story.

Nothing.

But it was only eight thirty. It was possible her phone might ring any minute. He *had* promised to call, and unless her instincts were failing, Adam would honor that promise. Tuesday wasn't too late to set up a weekend date. Tomorrow wouldn't be, either.

Waiting, however, was hard.

She wandered out to the screened porch, where her mom was ensconced with an afghan and a suspense novel, wicker rocking chair pulled up beside the flickering flames in the chiminea.

"Matt down for the count?" Her mom glanced at her over the top of her reading glasses.

"I hope so. He's a little fidgety tonight."

"He's not alone."

"What does that mean?"

"You've been jittery and distracted yourself for the past two days."

"No I haven't."

"Shall I present the evidence?" Her mother closed her book and removed her glasses. "You knocked over a glass of juice yesterday morning. Almost left the house without your gun this morning. Completely lost the thread of conversation at dinner tonight. Are there issues at work?"

"No." If only it were that simple.

"Are you coming down with some kind of bug?"

"No." There were cures for most of those.

"Then it must be man trouble."

She folded her arms. "That's a leap, isn't it?"

"Nope. A logical conclusion." Her mother motioned to the wicker chair beside her. "I put that in front of the fire in case you wanted to join me. Dug out your sweater and slippers too."

Lexie checked the seat of the chair. Everything was there, inviting her to sit . . . and continue the conversation she'd been trying to avoid.

Talking to her mom might not be such a bad idea, though. She was going to find out about the coming date soon—assuming Adam followed through. It might be helpful to get her mother's take on this new, unsettling complication in her placid life.

"I'll sit for a few minutes." She crossed to the chair, pushed her arms through the sleeves of the sweater, and pulled on the slippers.

Like she'd done the night Adam had shared this cozy spot with her.

But she felt alone tonight, even though her mom was sitting four feet away.

"It's not the same as sitting here with Adam, is it?"

Was her mother a mind reader or what?

Then again, since her days of high school crushes and fleeting college romances, her mom had always had uncanny intuition—and she'd been a great sounding board on matters of the heart.

"No." She buttoned the sweater, giving the task more attention than it deserved.

"He's a fine man."

"Yes, he is."

"He likes you, Lexie."

"I like him too. As a matter of fact . . . he said he was going to call me about a date for this weekend."

"And you're not certain you want to go?"

"No! I definitely want to go. But . . . he hasn't called yet."

"The week is young."

"I suppose so, but . . ." She pulled the sweater tighter around her.

"You'd like to at least hear his voice."

"Yes. Silly, isn't it?"

"Not at all. While we were dating, the day seemed incomplete if your dad didn't call. I felt like that almost from the moment we met—a strong indication he was the one. You probably had the same experience with Joe."

"No. That was different. I saw him every day—often more than once. I never had a chance to miss him. But I'm sure I would have if I hadn't seen him as much. I felt most alive when I was with him."

"Is that how you feel around Adam?"

"Yes—and it's kind of . . . unnerving." She picked at some lint on the sweater. "I wasn't in the market for another romance."

"That's how God often works. He sends possibilities our way—often in unexpected forms."

"Charley offered a similar opinion not long ago."

"He's a very wise man." Her mother began a slow, gentle rock. "You know, I'm wondering if Adam is struggling to come up with somewhere to take you."

Huh.

Now her mom was calling him Adam too.

Interesting.

"Why would it be hard to pick a date spot?"

"I assume he doesn't have a lot of cash. That leaves out a first-class restaurant—often a man's strategy to impress a woman on a first date. He might also be wondering how comfortable a police chief would feel being seen in public with an ex-con. And other than dancing, he may not have a sense yet for activities you enjoy."

"I've already told him I'm comfortable dating

him, I don't need a fancy dinner and he could ask if he wants to know my other interests."

"Or you could tell him."

"You think I should initiate the call?"

"It's an option. Last I heard, women were a lot more liberated about such matters these days."

"Yes . . . but he said he'd call—and I'm used to guys doing the pursuing. Like Joe did."

"Adam's not Joe. Rules change with different players." The phone in the kitchen trilled. "That will be Rose to talk about the next garden club meeting. Will you turn off the chiminea when you come in?"

"Sure."

Her mother disappeared through the door, and Lexie leaned back in her chair, watching the flames that warmed and brightened the room.

The same things Adam was doing for her life.

Her mom could be right about his foot-dragging. It might have more to do with self-esteem issues, which her super-confident husband had never dealt with, than a change of heart.

Why not come up with a few date options that took into account his limited financial resources and give him a call? He might be grateful for her input . . . and it would be better than sitting around waiting—and hoping—for him to make the first move.

She rose and flipped off the gas logs, the tension that had plagued her shoulders for the past forty-eight hours easing as her plan firmed in her mind. She'd give him another day or so to initiate contact. If he didn't, she would.

Because no way was she letting a possible case of cold feet derail what she hoped would be the first of many dates with the nicest guy she'd met in a long, long time.

❧ 16 ❧

Adam pressed the off button on his cell, weighed the phone in his hand, and looked over at Clyde, who was nosing through some wood scraps in the corner of the workshop.

"Well . . . how about that, my friend?"

The pup turned toward him and wagged his tail.

"You think I should go into the furniture-making business?"

He gave a little woof that was hard to interpret and went back to foraging.

"Thanks. That helps a lot." Grinning, he patted the pooch and wandered outside. Through the trees, the sun was beginning to dip toward the sea on this Wednesday night. Too early for the sunset show on the beach, which was fine. He needed some time to think through his surreal conversation with Rebecca Oliver.

He raked a hand through his hair, trying to process all the high-end interior designer had said. Not only hadn't she given a hoot about his prison background, she'd gone so far as to say the notion of helping someone get a fresh start appealed to her—and would appeal to her clients too. Plus, her compliments about the rocking chairs had been lavish enough to make him blush.

As for the price she said her clients would pay for pieces like that—his head was still spinning.

She was even going to drive back to Hope Harbor next week to meet him and discuss a couple of projects.

Incredible.

And the ego boost had been just what he needed before he placed his next, more difficult call.

To Lexie.

He sat on a tree stump, sweat breaking out on his temples. The whole date thing had been driving him nuts since Saturday. Distracting him during the day, keeping him awake at night. Where did you begin when planning a date with a classy woman like her?

His stop at the Bandon library after work last night had solved that challenge, though. After a search on one of the public computers, he'd found several elegant, refined, upscale restaurants in Coos Bay. She would be comfortable at any of them. There was also less chance they'd run into anyone from Hope Harbor there. If their evening flopped, at least she wouldn't have tongues wagging in town about her one date with an ex-con.

However . . . those expensive spots were going to set him back some serious money. Lexie was worth it, of course—but he wouldn't be able to pull off too many dates like that back-to-back.

And he didn't want to wait until he refilled the coffers to see her again. Assuming she wanted to see *him* again.

But maybe he should put that in God's hands and see where the first date led. He might discover there were some activities she enjoyed that didn't cost a lot.

Drawing in a lungful of air, he started to tap in her number.

Froze after three digits.

Something—or someone—was walking down the gravel road.

Moving quickly, he secured the shed door to keep Clyde inside, melted into the shadows behind a few trees at the edge of the clearing—and kept his phone at the ready in case he needed to call 911.

The volume of crunching gravel increased. Produced by a human, based on the steady, purposeful pace. The black-tailed deer that were frequent visitors tended to generate less noise and meander rather than follow a straight line.

He remained where he was, unmoving, every muscle poised for action. Like in the bad old days.

Once the lone figure came into view around the

bend in the road, however, his taut posture relaxed.

It was Brian.

No danger here.

But why was the teen paying this unexpected visit?

And how had he gotten here? It was five miles, door-to-door.

Pocketing his phone, he moved out of the shadows.

The instant Brian spotted him, his step faltered. "Hi." He lifted a tentative hand in greeting.

"Hi. Welcome." He waited while the kid picked up his pace again and descended the slightly sloping road to join him in the clearing. "This is a surprise."

"I would have called if I had your number."

"No worries. I don't keep my phone on, anyway. What's up?"

"You said last Sunday you'd show me your woodworking stuff sometime. I finished my homework, so I decided to come over. If you're busy, we could do it a different day."

"No. This is fine. But . . . did you walk here?" He must have, with his mother working nights this week.

"Yeah."

"That's a long trip. Want a soda?"

"Sure . . . if it's no bother."

"I was going to have a drink myself." Coffee, not soda—but caffeine was caffeine. "Come on in." He strolled toward the cabin, stopping as a whimper came from inside the shed.

"Is that your dog?" Brian surveyed the structure.

"Yeah. He doesn't like to be left out of activities, though he tends to stay on the sidelines." Adam switched direction.

"Why does he do that?" Brian fell in behind him.

"I suspect his first owner abused him. It takes him a while to warm up to strangers. Let him set the pace if you value your fingers."

Brian came to an abrupt halt. "I'll wait here. I got bit by a stray dog once and had to get shots. It wasn't fun."

"I bet it wasn't."

Adam opened the door, and Clyde tumbled out—then scurried back and hid behind his leg once he saw the teen.

"Chill out, boy." Adam patted the dog. "Brian's a friend."

"Is his head healed?"

"Yes. The vet gave him a clean bill of health the day he took out the stitches." He walked toward the house and called over his shoulder, "You coming, Clyde?"

The dog sat on his haunches.

"I guess not. Let's get those sodas."

Keeping a wary eye on the canine, the boy followed him inside.

While Adam got their drinks, Brian sized up the place.

"Not very fancy, is it?" Adam retrieved two Sprites from the fridge.

"No—but it's not rusty . . . and it's private . . . and you're by the ocean. That's cool."

Adam handed him a can of soda. "It works for me. Come on out and I'll show you the shop."

As they approached the shed, Clyde retreated a few yards.

"He's really scared, isn't he?" Brian's pace slowed.

"That can happen if you've been mistreated. It can take a long time for trust to build up again."

"Yeah. I get that. Do you think . . . is there a trick to making friends with him?"

"Slow and easy is the key. He'll wander in while we're in the shed. If he works his way over to you, let him sniff around. He'll let you know if he wants to be petted."

Once they were inside, Adam gave him a tour of the small space—workbench tools, reference books, in-progress pieces. Brian asked a few questions, but it didn't take long to realize the kid hadn't hiked to Sandpiper Cove to talk about woodworking.

He had something else on his mind.

Cutting the tour short, Adam motioned toward a roughed-in bench against the wall. "Why don't we sit there while we finish our sodas? But watch for splinters."

Brian followed him to the bench in silence, faint furrows creasing his brow.

The kid was definitely dealing with some knotty dilemma.

Since he'd trekked out here, he must want to talk—but it might take some subtle prompting to open the spigot.

"How's your mom doing?" Adam swigged his soda, establishing a casual mood. That might be the safest topic—unless Brian and his mother had had an argument.

"Hanging in." He toed a wood shaving. "She works too hard, and they don't treat her great at the diner. She's an awesome cook, but all they let her do is wait tables. We need the money, though. Dad bled us dry." He stomped his heel on the shaving, cracking it into pieces.

The fact that Brian wasn't happy about the situation with his father was old news. Whatever had triggered tonight's hike was a new glitch.

"How's school?"

The boy's can crinkled beneath his fingers.

Bingo.

A few seconds ticked by while the teen watched Clyde peek at him from under the workbench and inch closer.

"I think he's getting comfortable with me."

"Uh-huh."

"Maybe we'll be friends before I leave."

"That could happen."

"I hope so. I could use another friend." His Adam's apple bobbed. "Now that I'm about to lose the ones I have at school."

This was the crisis that had compelled him to make the long hike to Sandpiper Cove.

"Why would that happen?" Adam kept his tone conversational. If he pushed, the boy would shut down.

"They all take their cues from Lu . . . from the guy who invited me to sit with his group at lunch."

Adam opened his mouth to ask if this was the so-called friend who'd convinced him that vandalism would be fun—and beat him up.

Shut it.

Phrasing it like that could put the kid on the defensive. Better to position it so Brian came to his own conclusions about his partner in crime.

"Is this the friend who hurt Clyde?"

At the mention of his name, the dog cocked his head, tongue hanging out. Adam snapped his fingers, and Clyde trotted over, staying on his far side but peeking around his legs at their visitor. As if he too wanted to know the answer to that question.

Brian regarded the lovable dog. "He didn't mean to hurt him."

"But he left him behind—bleeding and woozy."

"Yeah." Brian crumpled the empty can in his fingers. "I knew it was bad news when he stopped by my locker today."

"What happened?"

"He's got another idea for some entertainment. His phrase, not mine."

More vandalism was planned?

Great.

Lexie would have another incident to investigate —and someone else in town would be left with a mess to clean up.

Unless Brian was willing to offer some details.

"When is this entertainment supposed to happen?" He maintained an even tone.

"I don't know. We got interrupted. He said I had to let him know whether I was in by the end of the day."

"Did you?"

"No. I avoided him—but that gave him his answer."

"You ready to share his name yet?"

A few beats passed while Brian mulled that over.

"I . . . I don't think so." He blew out a breath and scrubbed a hand down his face. "Why does everything have to be hard?"

Because that's how life works sometimes.

Adam had arrived at that simple truth after asking himself the same question too often to count through the years.

But it wasn't what the kid needed to hear tonight.

Nor was pushing going to help him build rapport with the boy—his primary objective.

Better back off and focus on his main goal.

"That's how I felt while I was in prison." As well as many times before—and since—but that didn't need to be said. "Life seemed totally unfair. Most of the bad stuff that had happened to me as a kid wasn't my fault."

"Yeah. I get that."

"Except I used that as an excuse to abdicate responsibility."

"What do you mean?" Brian gave him a wary look.

"I figured that if life was going to treat me like dirt, I'd do whatever I had to do to survive—right or wrong. So I made a lot of bad decisions . . . and always put the blame somewhere else if I got in trouble."

"But . . . the bad stuff that happened *wasn't* your fault, was it?"

"The circumstances weren't, but the decisions were mine—and those have consequences. Once I accepted that life isn't always fair, I learned to stick with my principles even on days when I'm discouraged or lonely or tempted to give up. I also learned that if you stay the course, sooner or later there will be an upswing."

Brian used the side of his sport shoe to sweep some wood shavings into a pile. "There hasn't been an upswing in my life in ages."

That wasn't true. The day his father had walked out, leaving him and his mother to flounder—but ultimately to create a new and better life—was a positive change, as far as Adam could see. They were better off without that user.

Yet often the good in traumatic events like that could only be appreciated in hindsight by those who were closest to the situation.

"Then I'd say you're about due." Adam angled toward the boy. "And just like we often create our own problems by making bad decisions, we can also create an upswing by making smart ones—like the one you made today to walk away from more vandalism."

"Losing all my friends doesn't sound like an upswing to me."

"You haven't lost all of them." He laid a hand on the boy's shoulder. "One of your newest ones is sitting right here."

The boy slanted him a look, swallowed, and went back to studying the floor. "Thanks."

"I'm also available any time you want to talk." He retrieved a pencil from his pocket and jotted his cell number on a scrap of paper. "I check my messages twice a day, and I always return calls."

The boy took the slip. "I appreciate that."

"This is what friends do. They support and encourage and want what's best for the other person." Hopefully the boy would see the contrast between this type of friendship and the kind the vandal at school was offering. "So . . . I haven't had dessert yet. Want to join me on the beach for a brownie while I watch the sunset? It's a nightly ritual here in the cove."

"I like brownies. My mom used to make great ones, but she's too busy to bake now."

"These are store-bought—but they're better than nothing."

"Sure. Thanks."

He rose . . . and Clyde scuttled back to huddle under the bench.

"He must still be scared." Brian stood too.

"Be patient. He'll come around."

As they trooped back to the cabin, Clyde emerged from the workshop and once again dropped to his haunches outside the door.

He was in the same spot a few minutes later when they emerged with the brownies, the last can of soda from the fridge, and a cup of coffee . . . but he followed them down to the beach.

Adam didn't broach any more heavy subjects for the next forty-five minutes, and neither did Brian. Yet as the sun dipped below the horizon, officially ending the day, the boy appeared to be calmer—and more at peace with his decision.

"I think that's a wrap." Adam picked up his empty mug from the sand beside him. "I'll give you a ride home."

"I can walk."

"Not on 101 in the dark. Too dangerous. That's what sidelined my friend here a year and a half ago." He patted Clyde, who was cuddled up beside him on the sand. "I found him in bad shape on the side of the road one night not long after I got here."

"Sounds like he's had his share of tough breaks too."

"More than. But he keeps bouncing back—and responding to love."

As if taking a cue, the dog lifted his head in the fading light, looked up at him—then rose and edged closer to Brian. He gave a tentative sniff . . . crept in another few inches and sniffed again . . . and repeated the process until he was almost nose to nose with the boy. Tongue hanging out, he watched the motionless teen.

"Do you think he wants me to pet him?" Brian's lips barely stirred.

"That's my take."

"He won't bite, will he?"

"Not if you're slow and careful." Adam repeated the same advice he'd given Matt not long ago on how to approach the dog.

Brian took it to heart. In fact, he moved at such a snail's pace Adam had to struggle to rein in a smile.

But when he at last offered the dog his hand, Clyde gave his fingers a dry lick.

One more connection made tonight between two beings wary from previous hurts yet finding the courage to try again.

A lesson for him too perhaps.

Which reminded him—he owed Lexie a call.

"Ready to go home?" He emptied the dregs of his coffee into the sand.

"Could we sit here a little longer, now that Clyde's warming up to me?"

"Sure."

The little longer turned into an hour, but Adam didn't mind. He had nothing pressing to do other than call Lexie, and teen and dog were enjoying themselves.

Finally Brian ruffled Clyde's ears while the dog soaked up the attention. "I guess I better go home. It's getting late."

"Yeah. It's after nine. Clyde, want to go for a ride?"

The dog yipped and wagged his tail.

"That means yes. Watch your step going through the woods in the dark."

Once back at the clearing, they piled into the car for the quick drive to the trailer park.

As they pulled up in front of his address, the teen leaned around to give the dog another pat.

"Thanks for the ride."

"Anytime."

The boy grasped the door handle. Hesitated.

"Everything okay?" The area was too dimly lit to read his face, but Adam was picking up some odd vibes.

"Yeah." He opened the door and stuck one leg

out. "I just want to say thanks again and . . . and that I wish I'd had a dad like you."

Before Adam could recover enough to respond, the boy sprang from the car, shut the door, and jogged toward the trailer. A moment later he disappeared inside.

Second after silent second passed as Adam sat frozen behind the wheel—until at last a cold nose against his neck nudged him into action.

Moving on autopilot, he put the car into drive, executed a U-turn, and bumped back toward the main road while Brian's last comment replayed over and over again in his mind.

"I wish I'd had a dad like you."

At the entrance to the trailer park, he braked, blinking to clear his blurry view of the dashboard.

Who could ever have predicted an outcome like this the night Lexie approached him about taking on the job of mentoring Brian? He had no fancy degrees or credentials that qualified him to work with a troubled teen. This could have been a disaster.

Yet from the beginning, she'd assured him that compassion and persistence were the keys to reaching the boy . . . and it appeared her instincts had been spot-on.

But he'd done more than reach him, based on that parting comment. He'd touched the kid deep inside in a way no one—least of all him—had expected. Never in his wildest dreams could he have envisioned being a father figure. How could he, when he'd had no role model to emulate?

Clyde nudged him again.

"Fine. I get the message." He patted the canine and pulled onto the road to begin the drive to Sandpiper Cove.

Yet as the dark miles passed, one after another, light filled his heart—and his soul.

For Brian wasn't the only one who'd benefitted from the arrangement Lexie had orchestrated. Not by a long shot.

One more blessing to add to his growing list.

He gave a contented sigh—and Clyde nuzzled his neck.

Keeping a firm grip on the wheel with one hand, he scratched behind the mutt's ear with the other.

"You're on that list too, boy. You were one of my first friends in this town . . . but now you're one among many."

And for a man whose best hope had once been to lead a quiet life of solitude in his adopted town, all the new connections—and possibilities—that were materializing boggled his mind.

He just hoped he didn't wake up one morning to discover it had all been nothing more than a dream.

✿ 17 ✿

It was too early for the phone to ring.

Fumbling in the dark for her cell, Lexie squinted at the clock on the bedside table.

Six eighteen.

Definitely too early for a Thursday morning.

Scooting into a sitting position, she peered at the screen in the dim room.

Jim Gleason.

This must mean trouble.

"Morning, Jim." She pushed her hair back and tried to clear the haze from her brain.

"Sorry to bother you this early, Chief. I know you got pulled into that pileup outside of town last night that took hours to sort out."

"I'll survive." True—but the meager five hours of sleep she'd clocked were going to make for a very long, tiring day. "What's up?"

"We've had another vandalism incident."

The last vestiges of fogginess vanished from her mind and she swung her legs out of bed. "Any injuries?"

"No."

"What happened?"

"Someone slashed Marci Weber's tires and keyed both sides of her car."

She blew out a breath. Why anyone would get

their jollies by targeting one innocent person after another was beyond her.

"Are you at her house?" She strode to her closet.

"Yes."

"I'll be there in twenty minutes."

After throwing on her clothes, she tiptoed into the hallway. No time to brew any java this morning. She'd have to grab a cup at Sweet Dreams or the café later.

She cast a longing glance at the coffeemaker on the kitchen counter as she passed—but pulled up short at the note attached to it.

Changing direction, she hurried over, pulled the taped sheet off, and tilted it toward the dawn light filtering through the window.

Adam stopped by last night to see you. I told him you'd be late because of that accident on 101. He said he'd call you tomorrow. You might want to give him a ring if you get a chance. He seemed anxious to talk to you. ☺

Mom

Lexie shoved the note into her pocket. Apparently she wouldn't have to initiate the call about their date after all.

But she did have some ideas to offer.

For the moment, though, her full focus needed to be on this latest vandalism incident.

Less than ten minutes after leaving the house,

she pulled into the driveway of the cottage on Pelican Point that Marci had inherited from her great-aunt. Gone was the eyesore it had become over the past few years as the dwelling fell into disrepair. The Hope Harbor newbie had done a superb restoration job—fresh paint, restored gardens, rebuilt gazebo in back.

She did *not* deserve this kind of mess.

Jim was waiting for her at the rear of the driveway, next to the damaged car.

Too bad Marci hadn't yet gotten around to building the detached garage that would replace the decaying potting shed. That would have protected her car.

Not that it should need protecting. Hope Harbor was supposed to be safe.

And it would be again as soon as she nailed the culprit.

"I already got a statement and took pictures." Jim shifted out of her path as she circled the car to assess the damage.

Nasty.

It was going to need a total paint job, and all the tires would have to be replaced. Not huge bucks—but sufficient to make this the most expensive act of vandalism to date.

Lexie stopped beside the officer. "Give me a topline."

"According to Marci, the car's been in the driveway since she got home from work last night about six. She did hear some minor noise around nine o'clock, but not enough to alarm her. However, this is what she found this morning."

"Anything else damaged?"

"No. But she's really shook up."

"Who wouldn't be?"

"No—I mean *really* shook up."

"Define that." She gave Jim her full attention.

"White as a sheet and shaking. I know this is upsetting and a hassle to deal with, but it's not like anybody got hurt."

"I'll talk to her in a minute. Did you find anything helpful in the area?"

"Yeah."

He walked over to the cruiser, retrieved a small, clear evidence bag, and passed it to her in silence.

Inside was a flash drive.

"I take it you found this near the car?"

"Yes. I plugged it in my computer. It's full of PowerPoint presentations and school papers belonging to Brian Hutton."

The bottom fell out of her stomach.

She'd taken a chance on the boy, convinced he'd cling to the lifeline they'd thrown him and keep his nose clean.

Her usually sound instincts must have failed her.

"Where did you find it?"

"Next to the car." Jim indicated the spot.

Hmm.

Very convenient.

"No chance we'd miss that." She pocketed the bag.

"Nope. It was front and center. In plain sight."

They were tracking on the same page.

"This read as a setup to you?"

"It has all the earmarks."

"Agreed." It appeared her worries about her instincts might have been premature. "I'll contact the juvenile counselor and we'll pay Brian another visit. This might persuade him to give us the name of his partner in crime." Jim's radio crackled to life, and she motioned toward it. "Go ahead and handle that while I talk to Marci."

Leaving him to deal with the dispatcher, Lexie ascended the single step to the back door and knocked.

Marci answered at once.

The officer's assessment had been on the mark. She was too pale even for a redhead, and she had a death grip on the edge of the door.

"Are you all right?" Lexie gentled her voice.

"Yes. Fine. A little spooked."

More than a little, based on her pallor.

"We found a clue we're going to follow up on. If you need a recommendation for a body shop, Marv's is—"

"I already called him. Do you know who did this?"

"It appears to be the work of the same vandals

who've been plaguing the town for the past few weeks."

"Then you don't think I was personally targeted?"

Lexie blinked. "No. Should I?"

"No. Just . . . asking." She checked her watch. "If you have everything you need from me, I have a client call I need to prep for."

"That's fine. I'll let you know what we find out."

"Thanks." She looked over at the damaged car, brow puckering. "You know, when I moved here I assumed it would be a safe place to live. Small town, friendly people who had each other's backs . . . But I guess nowhere is really safe, is it?" She sighed and eased the door toward the shut position. "Thanks again for getting out here so fast."

"That's our job."

Click.

Lexie frowned at the closed door. What had *that* been all about? In all the months she'd been in town, Marci had never been anything but upbeat and chatty.

Strange.

On a positive note, however, she wasn't hurt and the car could be fixed.

As for the woman's assumption that Hope Harbor would be a safe place to live . . . Lexie straightened her shoulders. That was her responsibility. She needed to get a handle on this vandalism spree and shut it down ASAP.

It was time to put more pressure on Brian.

"Mom, you don't have to get up and cook for me on school days after you work the late shift. I can eat cereal."

Brenda turned the bacon in the frying pan, stirred the pancake batter, and conjured up a weary smile for her son. "I don't mind. I want you to start the day with a hearty breakfast—and this is the only chance I get to see you when I'm on nights. If I'm tired later, I'll take a nap. How's everything at school?"

"Same old."

"That doesn't sound very positive." She poked at the sizzling bacon, fighting back a wave of panic. "You're not still hanging around with that kid who dragged you into vandalism, are you?"

"He didn't drag me. I chose to go. And no, I'm not hanging around with him anymore."

"Good." She exhaled. "Are you working on the planters again this Saturday with Mr. Stone?"

"Yes."

"How's that going? You haven't said much about it."

"It's fine. He's an okay guy." Brian poured a glass of juice. "That youth group at his church sounds kind of cool. Do you think we could go there some Sunday, scope out the place?"

"Like I told you before, I don't know if God would be that happy to see me after all the mistakes I've made." The bacon spattered, burning her hand, and she snatched it back. "I could take you, though, if you want to try it."

"Mr. Stone said that's not how God works."

"That may be true, but I'd rather have my act more together before I set foot in his house. Why don't you . . ."

At the ring of the doorbell, she froze. Who would come calling on a Thursday morning at—she angled toward the clock on the counter—seven twenty-five?

"Are you expecting someone?" Brian sent her a puzzled look.

"No. Here . . ." She handed him the fork. "Watch the bacon."

Shoving her uncombed hair into a semblance of order, she went to answer the summons.

Lord, please let this not be more trouble.

The plea came unbidden, surprising her as much as it probably surprised God. Must have been triggered by the power of suggestion, since she and Brian had been talking about church.

In any case, based on a quick peek through the peephole, it appeared the Almighty wasn't tuned in to her wavelength. The police chief and juvenile counselor wouldn't be on her doorstep at this hour of the morning unless there was *big* trouble.

Heart pounding, she braced herself and opened the door.

"Good morning, Mrs. Hutton. Sorry to drop in this early, but we have an urgent matter to discuss with you and Brian." The chief's demeanor was cordial but businesslike—and serious. "He hasn't left for school yet, has he?"

"No. Come in." She stepped back to give them access and called over her shoulder, "Brian!"

As the chief and counselor entered the living room, her son rounded the corner from the kitchen. He froze, shock and confusion widening his eyes.

The very reaction she'd hoped to see.

He had no idea why the law-enforcement duo was here.

"Why don't we all sit for a few minutes?" The chief indicated the couch and side chairs.

"Brian." Brenda motioned for him to join her on the couch.

He crossed to her with a wooden gait and sank onto the cushions, never taking his gaze off the two people who claimed chairs on the other side of the coffee table.

"We've had another vandalism incident." The chief directed the comment to Brian without any preamble.

"Oh, sh—"

"Brian!" She'd raised her son better than to use that kind of language, despite the poor example he'd had from his father.

"You know about this?" Chief Graham continued to watch him.

"No. I mean, I knew something *might* happen. I didn't know when. Or if it would, for sure."

"Were you involved?"

"No!"

"Where were you last night around nine o'clock?"

"With Mr. Stone. At his place."

Brenda frowned. "Why don't I know about that?"

"It wasn't planned. After I finished my homework, I decided to go out there. He said he'd show me his woodworking stuff sometime . . . and I didn't have anything else to do."

"How did you get there?" Brenda gripped his arm. "You didn't hitch, did you?"

"No. I walked."

"That has to be five or six miles." The chief continued to scrutinize him.

"It was better than sitting here all alone."

Brenda's stomach knotted. "Oh, baby, I'm sorry I have to work nights so much and leave you by yourself." Maybe if she had a regular job that left her evenings and weekends free, Brian wouldn't have gone down the wrong road.

No matter how hard she tried, she couldn't seem to do anything right.

"What time did you get home?" The chief consulted a notebook in her lap.

"About nine thirty, I think. Mr. Stone would know."

The chief pulled out a clear plastic bag. "Brian . . . the officer investigating the incident found this at the scene. It has your schoolwork on it."

As the flash drive dangled in front of them, Brenda turned to her son. All the color had leached from his complexion. "Brian? Is that yours?"

"I-I think so." His words came out choked—and laced with fear. "I gave the other guy my locker combination after . . . after I got caught in case he wanted to pass notes to me. He didn't think we should be seen together."

"But you weren't involved in this new vandalism . . . right?" Brenda seized his hand and held on tight, forcing him to look at her. "Just tell the truth. You need to tell the truth."

"That's sound advice, Brian." The counselor joined the conversation. "If the person you're trying to protect set you up, he doesn't deserve your loyalty. You don't do this to a friend."

"Oh, man." He dropped his head into his hands.

"Talk to them, Brian." Brenda squeezed his arm. "You've done everything the way you should up to now. Tell them what they need to know. Give them this boy's name."

She waited, stomach quivering, while endless silent seconds ticked by.

Please . . . please . . . let the morality I tried to

instill in him triumph over the example of his deadbeat dad.

At last Brian dropped his hands and raised his chin. "Lucas Fisher."

Thank you, God!

"Lucas Fisher?" Surprise flattened the police chief's features. "The son of Martin Fisher, who owns Fisher Lumber Company?"

"Yes."

After considering Brian, the woman slid the plastic bag back into her pocket. "I have some calls to make. What's next from your end?" She passed the baton back to the counselor.

"Brian goes to school, you make your calls, we regroup later today and pay a visit to the Fishers."

"That works." The chief rose and pulled out her keys. "That's all we need for now. Sorry again for the early visit."

Brenda showed them to the door, then hurried back to Brian.

"It's gonna be fine, honey." She rested a hand on his slumped shoulder. "You did the right thing."

"I hope so."

"I know so. Life's gonna get better, you'll see." It had to.

He lifted his head. "That's what Mr. Stone said."

"There you go." At least he had a worthy adult male role model now. "We're all on the same page. Come on. I'll finish your breakfast and drive you to school after you eat. The bus is long gone."

He stood, but as she turned to go back to the kitchen, he groped for her hand. "Thank you for believing in me . . . and sticking with me . . . and being such a good mom." The corners of his mouth quivered.

Oh, Lord!

That was the nicest compliment anyone had ever paid her.

She swiped her fingers across her eyes and pulled him into a hug. "We'll get through this together, okay?"

"Okay." His voice was muffled against her shoulder, like it used to be in his younger days when he'd been upset and climbed onto her lap for comforting.

"Now let's move forward and trust that God has our backs."

He followed her into the kitchen, and as she finished cooking their breakfast, she sent one more plea to the Almighty.

Because this family—what was left of it— couldn't take many more setbacks.

"Hey, Adam!"

Adam stopped sawing and looked over at Luis through the skeleton of the house they were building on the cranberry farm. Was everybody calling him Adam instead of Stone now?

"What?"

"Your dancing partner is here." Grinning, he

aimed a nail gun in the direction of the gravel drive that led to the site Tracy and Michael had selected for their house.

Adam swung around as Lexie slid out from behind the wheel of a police cruiser.

"I'll be back in a minute." He set the saw down and wiped his grimy palms on his jeans.

"The boss is on her honeymoon. Take your time." Luis winked at him and went back to work.

He met Lexie halfway between the construction site and the parking area as the farm's two border collies galloped over.

"Hey, Shep. Ziggy." Lexie gave them each a pat. "I would have tried calling, but your phone is never on."

"I may have to change that situation soon." He hadn't told a soul about his conversation with Rebecca Oliver, but if they came to some arrangement, Lexie would be the first to hear the news. "Did your mom tell you I stopped by last night?"

"Yes. She left me a note in the kitchen. But this isn't about that. We had another vandalism incident last night—and Brian was implicated."

He furrowed his brow. "When did it happen?"

"Around nine. He says he was with you."

"He was."

Some of the tension in her features diminished. "I thought he was telling the truth. I'm glad my instincts aren't failing."

"I wish I'd called you last night." He massaged

his forehead. "Brian told me the other kid had approached him about another round of vandalism, but you sounded tied up."

"I was."

"Can you tell me what happened?"

He listened as she gave him a quick report.

"I do have one piece of helpful news." As she concluded, Shep and Ziggy raced off, ever diligent at their task of protecting the cranberry beds from bog rats. "We have the name of the accomplice. The juvenile counselor and I will be paying him a visit after school."

"This crime spree could finally be coming to an end."

"I hope so." She slipped on her sunglasses. "While I'm out here, do you want to talk about the date we discussed for this weekend?" A slight undercurrent of nervousness rippled through her query.

Was she afraid he wasn't planning to follow through?

He needed to erase any doubts about that ASAP.

"Yes. That was on my agenda for last night too if we'd connected. I'm sorry I didn't get back to you sooner, but it took me a while to come up with a plan. Being new in town—and somewhat of a hermit up to this point—I had to research restaurants. I think I found a great place."

When he mentioned the name, her lips parted slightly. "That's super high-end."

"The food sounds great."

"I'm sure it is, but . . . that's out of my league."

His league maybe. Not hers.

"You've eaten all over the world. I bet you've had plenty of high-end meals."

"Some—on the job. Not as many in my personal life. And I have an alternate idea for our date. Have you ever been to Shore Acres State Park?"

"No." Did she think that was all he could afford?

"It's a great spot. The gardens are fantastic, and we can catch the end of the tulip display. There's a picnic area overlooking the ocean, and a beautiful secluded cove. If you'd like to take Matt along, he loves to watch the seals on Simpson Reef."

She wanted their date to be a threesome?

Not if he could help it—much as he liked her son.

But . . . could this be Lexie's way of guaranteeing they followed her slow-and-easy rule? It would be impossible to get too cozy with a young chaperone in tow.

However, he had enough discipline to stick to her ground rule with or without Matt. She needed to understand that—and actions spoke louder than words.

"I have a counteroffer. Why don't we have dinner together in Coos Bay Saturday night, and on Sunday we can go on a picnic with Matt to

Shore Acres State Park? A fancy restaurant will help me get my money's worth out of that suit I bought—and they have a small combo that plays dance music on Saturday. You could wear that great dress again too."

Saws buzzed and hammers pounded in the background while he waited for her response—praying she'd give him the opportunity to prove he was worthy of her trust.

At last she nodded. "A dinner in Coos Bay sounds great . . . but why don't we go Dutch? That's what a lot of people do these days."

Not in his world.

Not on a first date.

And though he suspected her offer was motivated more by thoughtfulness than any sort of PC gender equality agenda, it bruised his pride nonetheless.

He straightened up to his full height. "I can afford to take you out for one nice dinner, Lexie." His reply came out stiffer than he'd intended.

Grooves dented her forehead, and she touched his arm. "I'm sorry. I didn't mean to offend you. It's just . . . I understand why money would be tight, and you don't have to spend a fortune to impress me. I'm already impressed—by the person, not the pocketbook. We could eat pizza for all I care. Being with you, not the destination, is the highlight of a date for me."

The sentiment—and her sincerity—helped . . .

but the knowledge that he couldn't take her to a five-star restaurant every night of the week still stung.

"I want to do this." He softened his tone. How could he be annoyed when she was looking up at him with those big blue eyes as if he was the only person in the world who mattered? "A first date should be memorable."

A sweet smile slowly bowed her mouth. "I agree—and I accept with pleasure."

"Six o'clock?"

"I'll be ready. And I'll wear the dress."

"Thank you."

"Well . . ." She took a deep breath. "I should get going." Yet she didn't remove her hand from his arm. As if she hated to break the connection.

He could relate.

"And I need to get back to work." He covered her fingers with his own, fighting the temptation to lean down and brush his lips across her forehead in a repeat performance of Saturday night.

A pulse began to throb in the hollow of her throat, and she leaned toward him. Close . . . closer . . . until a barking Shep and Ziggy zoomed past in hot pursuit of . . . something.

She wrenched herself back. "I'll, uh, see you Saturday."

With that she fled back to the patrol car.

Adam watched while she made a wide U-turn and the cruiser disappeared in a cloud of dust.

Even after he lost sight of it, he remained where he was. He needed a couple of minutes to get his own emotions under control before rejoining Luis and the crew.

But as he finally swung around and returned to the construction project, one thing was clear.

Based on what had just happened, he wasn't the only one who was going to be struggling mightily to abide by Lexie's slow-and-easy rule come Saturday night.

❧ 18 ❧

"Impressive house." Pushing off from the trunk of the car where he'd been leaning, the juvenile counselor indicated the multilevel stone and cedar structure to his left.

"Very. Were you waiting long?" Lexie locked the cruiser and joined him at the back of his car.

"Less than five minutes. What's the story on the family?"

"They own Fisher Lumber, a thriving mill a few miles up 101. A lot of locals have spent their careers there, including my dad and grandfather. Martin Fisher's great-grandfather started it, and subsequent generations built it into a world-class company. Martin took over a few years ago. This is one of the fruits of his labors." She swept a hand over the hilltop home that offered a panoramic view of the sea.

"Yet his kid is a vandal."

"So the evidence would suggest."

"Did you get any prints off the flash drive?"

"No. It was wiped clean. Everybody's seen enough TV cop shows to know how to avoid the obvious traps. Shall we?" She motioned toward the house.

"Whenever you're ready."

She took the lead but stopped at the stone steps leading to the front door as an Audi roared up the long, winding drive.

"Must be Martin." Given his annoyance during their call, it was no surprise he'd cut the meeting close.

"Do you know him?" The counselor shaded his eyes against the late-afternoon sun.

"Only by reputation. I've seen him at various civic functions and exchanged a few words here and there, but he doesn't socialize with the residents."

The Audi screeched to a stop behind the cruiser. The midfortyish driver sprang out of the car and marched toward them, jaw set, tension radiating off him.

"This ought to be fun."

At the muttered comment from the counselor, Lexie braced. She could handle guys like this—but it was never anywhere close to fun.

"Mr. Martin, Chief Lexie Graham." She held out her hand as he approached. In general, she didn't throw her title around, but it wouldn't hurt to remind this guy of her position.

After regarding her outstretched fingers for several beats, he gave them a fast, perfunctory shake.

He did the same with the counselor while she introduced the man, then got straight to business.

"What's this all about, Ms. Graham?"

Ms., not Chief.

An obvious attempt to put her in her place.

She straightened up to her full height and dispensed with the social niceties. "This is a family matter. It would be better discussed with your wife and son present."

"I make the decisions in this family."

"That may be, but we need to speak with your son."

He folded his arms and held his ground.

She waited him out. If he thought he was going to intimidate her, he had another think coming.

When the silence lengthened, a muscle ticced in his cheek. "Fine. We'll go inside. But this better be important. I was in the middle of a meeting, and I don't appreciate having my day disrupted."

As the man shouldered past them toward the front door, the counselor shook his head and hiked up an eyebrow.

She agreed.

If Martin Fisher thought his day was disrupted now, wait until he heard the news they were about to deliver.

He pushed through the front door, leaving them to follow in his wake, and stopped in the center of the foyer. "Diane! Lucas! Get in here." The bellowed summons echoed off the marble floor and soaring walls.

A quick tapping of high heels sounded in the hall, and a few moments later a blonde-haired woman emerged from the back of the house. She looked frazzled—and fearful. "Hi, honey."

"Lucas!" He ignored her greeting as he hollered up the stairs.

A teen who'd inherited the man's square jaw and thin nose appeared at the top of the curving staircase and moseyed down, surveying the visitors.

"All right. Let's get this over with." Martin waved everyone into a spacious living room with a vaulted ceiling. Abstract paintings, contemporary furnishings, gleaming hardwood floors, huge area rugs, and a grand piano on a dais in one corner—it could have been a room from a decorator showcase.

And it felt just as sterile and unlived-in.

"Have a seat." Martin claimed an imposing chair off to one side and sat without waiting for anyone else to settle in. "Now what is this about?"

Lexie linked her fingers in her lap, keeping her posture relaxed. "You may be aware that Hope

Harbor has had a number of vandalism incidents over the past several weeks."

"I read a few lines about it in the local rag."

That would be the *Herald*—and it was far from a rag. But she wasn't here to defend the town newspaper.

"Not long ago, we caught one of the vandals. At first he refused to give us the name of his partner. That changed today." She glanced at Lucas. He was slouched on the couch, arms folded, legs stretched in front of him, ankles crossed, expression defiant.

"What does that have to do with any of us?" Martin made a show of checking his watch.

"He identified your son as the second vandal."

The man's head jerked up. "You can't be serious."

"Yes, I am."

"But . . . that's ridiculous!" He gaped at her as if she had two heads. "What possible reason would my son have to be involved in vandalism?"

"I can't speculate on motive. I only deal with facts."

"Facts? You want facts?" Red splotches marring his complexion, he shot to his feet, stalked across the room, and got in her face. "Let me tell you a few facts. My son is a football star at the high school. He has a wide social circle. He lives in a house with a swimming pool and tennis court. He gets reasonable grades. He takes vacations every year with his mother to Europe and the Caribbean.

315

There is no reason on earth for him to do anything that would jeopardize the privileged life he leads —or our position in this town."

The man was so close she could almost count his eyelashes.

She didn't even blink.

"Nevertheless, I'd like to know where he was last night at nine o'clock."

He didn't move.

Neither did she.

"Fine." He spat out the concession and pivoted toward his son. "Tell the lady where you were last night."

"Here. Doing homework."

"There." Martin swung back to her. "Satisfied?"

"Was your mother home also?" She directed her question to the boy.

"Yeah."

"Did you see your son in the house last night around nine o'clock, Mrs. Fisher?" Lexie shifted toward the blonde.

"I, uh . . ." Her frightened glance bounced between Lucas and her husband. "Well, it's a big house. We don't always . . . see each other."

"If my son said he was here, he was here." Martin dismissed his wife with a scathing sweep. "Aside from hearsay, why do you think he was involved in any of these incidents? Do you have any physical proof? Any witnesses?"

This was where it could get tricky.

"I have no reason to disbelieve the boy who told us your son was the instigator in all of the incidents. He's fully cooperating with law enforcement."

"Who is this kid?"

"I'm not at liberty to disclose his name. He's a juvenile."

"I know who it is." As Lucas spoke, everyone turned toward him. "Brian Hutton."

"How would you know that?" Lexie kept her tone conversational. The more the boy talked, the more likely he'd make an incriminating slip.

"Word gets around at school. Kids gossip."

"I don't recognize the name." Martin moved closer to the teen. "What do you know about him?"

Lucas shrugged. "He and his mom live in that trailer park outside of town. They moved here in January after his loser dad took all their money and disappeared."

"And you'd believe this kid over my son?" Martin spun back to her, tone triumphant.

"He has no reason to lie."

"Sure he does. He's trying to divvy up the blame so he doesn't have to take the rap for everything. Where was *he* last night?" Lucas smirked at her.

"He has an alibi."

"So does my son." Martin's gaze strafed her.

"How could he have an alibi?" Lucas selected a piece of candy out of a bowl on the table beside him. "His mom is working nights this week."

"How would you know that?" Lexie rolled her pen between her fingers.

"Like I said . . . kids talk." He popped the mint into his mouth. "He was home alone last night, as usual. He must be lying about his alibi."

"No, he's not. I confirmed his story."

Lucas stopped chewing. "With who?"

Lexie considered the boy. There was no reason to keep her source confidential. The Fishers would find out eventually if they dug in their heels and lawyers got involved.

"Adam Stone."

"Adam Stone." Martin narrowed his eyes. "Isn't he the ex-con who came to town a few months ago? The carpenter with the long hair and bandana, who looks like a dues-paying member of Hells Angels?"

Anger began to churn in Lexie's gut. "As a matter of fact, he doesn't look like that any-more—not that appearances matter. He's a law-abiding, churchgoing citizen who's paid his dues to society and is building a new life in Hope Harbor."

"Given his background, I'd hardly call him a credible source." Martin sniggered. "For all we know, *he* might have been involved in some of the vandalism incidents."

Lexie bit back the retort poised on the tip of her tongue.

Stay cool. This guy might have more money

than he knows what to do with, but he's a world-class jerk. Don't stoop to his level.

"Lucas . . ." She angled away from the man and gave the teen her full attention. "I believe Brian is telling the truth, and we'll continue to investigate the vandalism incidents until we find the proof we need to identify the culprit. It would be much better for you to be honest with us now so the juvenile counselor can work with you and your family to resolve this in the least disruptive and damaging way. If the situation escalates, you could end up before a judge."

"I think we've had enough of your intimidation tactics." Martin crossed to the archway that led to the foyer and waited on the threshold. "I'm sure you have more important matters to attend to, and I have a meeting to finish."

Lexie stayed where she was. "I'll give you one more chance, Lucas."

"She's right." The counselor leaned forward. "I can help you more if you cooperate."

"Lucas?" Fear laced the single-word query from his mother.

The boy scanned the assembled group, and for the first time Lexie detected a hint of uncertainty in his eyes.

"Look, I had nothing to do with that car, okay?"

The room went silent.

"I don't believe I mentioned the nature of last night's vandalism incident." Lexie watched the teen.

Beads of sweat broke out on his forehead, and he straightened up from his slouch, posture rigid. "You talked about it when you first got here."

"No, she didn't." The counselor's rebuttal was slow and deliberate.

"She must have . . . have mentioned it, or . . . or something." The boy's composure began to crack. "Besides, the flash drive belonged to . . ." His face lost a few shades of color, and he clamped his lips together.

"Lucas . . ." His father strode back into the room. "What's going on?"

"Nothing. They're trying to set me up."

"Based on this conversation, I think it's clear the opposite is true." Lexie swiveled toward Martin. "We found a flash drive belonging to Brian Hutton next to the vandalized car. He gave your son the combination to his locker after they became friends—meaning your son had access to it. It had been wiped clean of prints. All prints. Very odd, if it had been dropped by accident."

Martin glared at his son. "I don't need these kinds of problems."

"Why is everybody making such a big deal out of this?" Lucas swiped some sweat off his upper lip. "I mean, come on. We can pay for—"

"Shut up, Lucas." Martin surged toward the teen, towering over him.

"But Dad, I—"

"Shut. Up." He glowered at his son until the

kid visibly shrank, then turned toward his visitors. "We have nothing else to say until we talk to our attorney. I'll show you out."

Lexie followed the man to the door, the counselor falling in behind her. Martin Fisher didn't offer to shake hands with either of them—which was fine with her.

At the foot of the steps, the juvenile counselor paused. "Those were some seriously negative vibes in there—and not just toward us."

"I'll say. Does the term dysfunctional come to mind?"

"And how." He examined the pristine lawn and perfect flower garden that rimmed the sweeping drive. "Who'd ever guess, standing on the out-side, that there was such discord inside?"

"More proof you should never judge a book by its cover. I'm assuming their attorney will be in touch."

"You don't have a prosecutable case, do you?"

"A judge might be sympathetic to our cause, but I'd rather have some hard evidence." She huffed out a breath. "Without that, it's Brian's word against Lucas's—unless Lucas admits he was the perpetrator."

"I don't think his lawyer is going to let him do that."

"Me neither. But after those two incriminating slips, everyone who was in that room knows he's guilty."

"He won't make that mistake again."

"No kidding."

"He could get away with this, you know."

"I'm very aware of that." Watching guilty parties walk away free was one of the toughest parts of police work. "But I'm not done working this case. We're still searching for evidence."

"I hope you find some."

"Me too. I'll be in touch if there are any more developments."

The man lifted his hand in farewell and returned to his car.

She did the same.

Once behind the wheel, though, she lowered her windows to let in the fresh sea breeze and gave the house another perusal. Even through the thick walls, she could hear the faint echoes of a male voice raised in anger.

A shudder rippled through her as she inserted the key in the ignition . . . and for a moment she felt sorry for the boy who was facing his father's wrath.

Yes, the Fishers had wealth.

Yes, they had prestige in town.

Yes, they lived in a mansion and took exotic trips . . . or at least mother and son did.

But there was a serious fracture in that family.

She put the car in gear and followed the curving drive back to the road, away from the nastiness in that house, toward the dinner waiting for her in the small bungalow where money might not always have been plentiful but love had never been in short supply.

That was what made a home.

And while Martin might have denigrated Adam for his previous appearance and prison record, he could learn a thing or two about compassion and caring from the ex-con.

Accelerating toward Hope Harbor, Lexie put thoughts of the troubled family behind her and indulged in a little daydreaming about her coming dates with that very man. She had another day and a half of work to get through, but once she left the office at noon on Saturday, she was going to forget about law enforcement and focus on being a woman. She might even get her hair done.

And she wasn't going to let anything interfere with what she hoped would be a weekend to remember.

⚜ 19 ⚜

She might have dragged her feet about coming.

She might not belong here.

She might feel conspicuous.

But as Brenda rose to join in the final hymn at Grace Christian on Sunday morning, the sense of homecoming . . . of welcome . . . of acceptance . . . tightened her throat.

Worthy or not, it felt good to be back in a house of God.

Beside her, Brian joined in the hymn, an old favorite he must remember from his younger days—before Jerry banned church attendance.

She remembered it too . . . though it had been a while since she'd felt the Almighty's amazing grace.

The instant the last note of the song faded away, she slid her hymnal back into the pocket on the pew in front of her and nudged Brian. "Let's go."

"But Mom . . . the minister invited everyone to stay for doughnuts."

"We can get doughnuts somewhere else." She took his arm and drew him from the pew. Sitting through the service had been a positive first step, but she wasn't yet ready to meet the minister or socialize with the congregation. That's why she'd chosen a pew near the back. It should be easy to get out fast.

But it wasn't.

As they hustled toward the door, Adam Stone slipped out of the last pew, blocking their escape.

"Good morning." He smiled. "Welcome to Grace Christian."

"Hey, Mr. Stone." Brian's return smile was wide and genuine. Since the police chief's call to let them know the carpenter had verified Brian's alibi, her son had been a lot more upbeat.

"I'm glad you came to services. Are you staying for doughnuts?"

The crowd began to surge toward the exit, and Brenda edged to the side of the aisle. "Not today."

"Aw, Mom . . ." Brian sent her a disappointed look.

"Maybe next week."

"Does that mean we're coming back?"

She'd walked right into that one.

"We might."

"You won't be sorry." Adam shifted away from the crowd and gave her his full attention. "When I came to Hope Harbor, I didn't know a soul except Reverend Baker. And given my background, I wasn't certain what kind of reception I'd get. But everyone here"—he swept a hand around the church—"and in town was welcoming. I'm beginning to respond to their overtures, but I wish I'd done it sooner. A church family can help fill the gaps if you don't have a lot of relatives."

She glanced around. A few of the people passing by smiled at her, seeming to confirm what Adam had said—and a friend or two would be a blessing. Brian wasn't the only member of their family who was lonely.

"I'll give that some thought this week."

"I hope you do."

In the meantime, though . . . they did have *one* friend. If Adam hadn't gone along with the police chief's suggestion, her son might have continued down the wrong path and ended up in front of a judge—and perhaps on the road to a life of crime.

She owed the man more than a simple thank-you for his kindness.

Clenching her fingers around her purse, she summoned up the courage to issue the invitation that had been on her mind for the past few days. "I'm glad we ran into you. I was wondering if . . . would you want to come to dinner tomorrow night? I'd like to thank you in a more concrete way for all you've done for Brian."

A glint of surprise darted through his eyes. "That's very kind—but no thanks are necessary. I was happy to have a helper with the planter project." He gave her son a one-sided grin.

"Are you sure you can't come, Mr. Stone? Mom's a great cook. And we don't have company very often. Like never."

"It won't be fancy." Better be clear she didn't have a gourmet spread planned. "Just meatloaf— but it's my mother's recipe, and it won some prizes in its day. You wouldn't have to stay long. I know you're busy."

"Yeah. We won't mind if you eat and run," Brian seconded.

He looked back and forth between them . . . hesitated . . . and nodded. "I'd be happy to come. Thank you. A home-cooked meal will be a treat."

"Six o'clock?"

"Fine."

"We'll see you then. Come on, Brian." She took his arm and hurried him out the door, toward their car.

"That was a great idea about inviting Mr. Stone, Mom." Brian half jogged to keep up with her. "I bet he'll appreciate your cooking a lot more than Dad did."

That wouldn't be hard. Jerry had rarely had a kind word to say about anything she did. Less and less so as the years went by.

"Your father has issues."

Brian yanked free and stopped, anger chasing away his enthusiasm of moments before. "I can't believe you're still making excuses for him!"

A few people milling about on the church lawn glanced toward them, and she took Brian's arm again, urging him forward. "I don't want to discuss family business in public."

"Fine. We can wait until we get to the car." He pulled free again and stomped ahead.

Bracing, she followed more slowly. This wasn't a discussion she'd planned to have today—but the juvenile counselor had said it was important to air issues rather than let them fester. If Brian wanted to talk about Jerry, it was healthier for him to vent than to keep it bottled up inside.

And he might be surprised at a few of the things she had to say.

Once behind the wheel, she took the lead. "When I said your father has issues, I wasn't making excuses for him."

"That's what you always say." He folded his arms, his expression sullen.

"Brian . . . look at me." She waited until he did. "Your father *does* have issues. Big ones. For years, I thought they were my fault—because he made me feel like they were. But now that we've been apart a while, I'm beginning to see the situation more clearly. I'm not perfect, but I wasn't as bad as he made me out to be. His shortcomings are a lot worse than mine."

"Yeah?" Skepticism scored his features. "When did you figure all this out?"

"After the vandalism incident, I did a lot of thinking. I *have* made mistakes—and one of them was staying with your dad as long as I did. That wasn't fair to you, and I'm sorry you had to pay the price for my cowardice. If I'd left sooner, maybe you . . ." Her voice choked, and she tried again. "Maybe we wouldn't have had this latest crisis."

Some of the fury in Brian's face faded. "It's not fair for you to take all the blame. I made bad choices too." He looked out the window, toward the blue sky beginning to peek through the morning fog. When he continued, his tone was subdued. "You know how you used to think the issues Dad has were your fault? Well, I wondered sometimes if they were mine. I mean, maybe if he hadn't had to worry about a kid, you guys would have done better. Maybe I was the reason Dad was always mad and treated you bad."

"Oh, baby." Pressure built in Brenda's throat, and she squeezed his hand. He didn't need all those undeserved maybes preying on his mind. "You had nothing to do with any of that. Your dad always had a mean streak. He knew how to manipulate, how to turn on the charm if it suited him, but the badness was always there. Our marriage didn't deteriorate because you came along. It deteriorated because he got tired of me. I was useful to him as long as the money kept flowing, but once he met someone younger, with more cash, that was it."

"I bet he never wanted to be a father, though."

True—but no need to phrase it that harshly.

"Your dad didn't want any part of anything that required him to be unselfish or put someone else first. But I can tell you this—whatever your dad thought about being a father, having you was the best thing that ever happened to me."

A sheen filmed his eyes, and his Adam's apple bobbed. "I'm sorry I caused you all this trouble with the vandalism."

"I know you are. And we're going to put that behind us and start fresh. Okay?"

"Yeah. Okay."

After one final squeeze of his hand, she inserted

the key in the ignition, pulled out of the parking spot, and drove away from the church.

But as the steeple disappeared in her rearview mirror, she sent one last prayer heavenward.

Thank you for the blessings and second chances you've given both of us since we arrived in this town. Guide us as we try to establish a new life here that's better than the one we left behind—and please help us persevere if we run into setbacks.

This was what it felt like to lead a normal, happy life.

As Lexie took Matt's hand and bent to study a tulip in the Shore Acres garden, Adam drew in a long, deep breath. Slowly let it out.

It had been a perfect weekend.

A bonding session with Brian while repairing planters yesterday.

An evening of dining and dancing with Lexie last night, worth every penny of the exorbitant bill.

Seeing her again at church this morning—a double blessing. Not only had they stolen a few minutes together after his chat with the Huttons, she appeared to be reopening the lines of communication with God.

Now, a Sunday afternoon with the same lovely woman and her charming son.

Life didn't get much better than this.

"How come they don't smell, Mom?" Matt stuck

his nose into the heart of a sunny yellow bloom.

"Not all flowers smell, honey. Some are just pretty to look at."

"Mamaw's roses look pretty *and* they smell good."

"They also have thorns."

"Oh yeah." Matt straightened up with a grimace. "I don't like thorns. They hurt. Did you ever get stuck with a thorn, Mr. Stone?"

"I've been in plenty of thorny situations." He ruffled the boy's hair. "Now I avoid them."

"Yeah. Me too. Can we go see the seals now, Mom?"

"Sure—unless Mr. Stone has another idea."

"Seals sound fine to me."

"Yay!" The little boy jumped up and down. "They're the best part—after the chocolate chip cookies you made for our picnic, Mom. Come on . . . let's go!" He tugged on her hand.

"I take it he's a veteran seal watcher." Adam fell in beside Lexie.

"Yep. He's very familiar with the routine."

"Let's go down to the beach instead of watching from on top." Matt pulled harder.

"See what I mean?" She grinned.

"I like a man who knows what he wants and isn't afraid to go after it." Adam increased his stride to keep up with the duo.

"Are we still talking about Matt?" Her eyes sparkled with mischief.

"I'll take the Fifth."

"Playing coy, are we?" She waggled her eyebrows.

The corners of his mouth twitched. This flirty behavior was new—and he was liking it.

A lot.

"Come on, Mom!" Matt kept towing her along as the path narrowed, descending from the garden through the majestic fir trees.

Instead of answering her question, he let them get a few feet ahead so he could enjoy the view—of Lexie. Her worn jeans and soft, fuzzy sweater were a 180 from her no-nonsense official uniform —and 180 the other direction from that silky, form-fitting dress she'd worn last night. Yet this look suited her too. And he'd never seen her more relaxed.

Maybe bringing Matt along had been a smart idea. It relieved the man/woman pressure that came with a dating situation.

"You with us, Adam?" She tossed the question over her shoulder while navigating a rocky section of the path.

"Right behind you."

Less than a minute later, they emerged onto a deserted crescent of sand with sheer rock walls on two sides, waves lapping gently on the shore.

"This is incredible. Why isn't anyone else here?" Adam joined Lexie as she dug a pair of binoculars out of her tote bag and handed them to Matt.

"Most people don't want to make the effort to hike down—and back up again."

"Their loss."

A loud barking intruded on the peace, coming from the direction Matt had aimed his binoculars. A quick survey of the offshore sea stacks confirmed the source. Seals were arrayed on the jagged rocks, some sunning, some waddling along, others frolicking in the aquamarine water.

"That's another reason a lot of people don't come down. It can get noisy." Lexie surveyed the seals. "They're well-behaved today, though. We got lucky."

"In more ways than one." He reached over and stroked a finger down the back of her hand.

Her breath hitched, and she lifted her gaze to his. "That's not fair."

"What?"

"Teasing."

He stopped stroking but left his fingers resting against her soft skin. "What do you mean, teasing?"

"Making me want more than you're offering."

"What do you want?"

"What you're doing is nice—but holding hands would be better."

"I agree . . . but I'm trying to play by your slow-and-easy rule."

"I think holding hands falls within that parameter on a second date."

"See? I told you I've been away from this too long." He laced his fingers with hers. "But I'm a fast learner. Better?"

"Much."

"How do you feel about kisses on the second date?" If she could flirt, he could too.

"The forehead kind, like you gave me last night?"

"Uh-uh." He played with a strand of her wind-tossed hair.

"It might be . . ." She swallowed. "Be hard with Matt underfoot."

"He's busy."

She checked on her son. He'd abandoned the binoculars and was picking through the flotsam on the beach.

"I don't know . . ."

Yes, she did.

He could see the longing in her eyes.

"Come with me." He led her to a large boulder that partially blocked the view of the beach and turned her toward him. "Matt will be fine. I'll keep him in sight."

"Do you think . . ."

He pressed his fingers against her soft lips. Now that it was clear her interpretation of the slow-and-easy rule was more liberal than his, he wasn't about to let a sudden, unwarranted case of cold feet delay this inevitable moment.

"All I have in mind is a simple kiss, Lexie.

We're on a public beach and your son is thirty feet away. This is about as safe an environment as you can get. Let's relax and enjoy this. If I'm a lousy kisser, wouldn't you rather find out sooner than later?"

"Why do I think that's not going to be the c-case?" She groped for a ridge in the rock and wrapped her fingers around it.

"Let's test that theory."

Cradling her face in his hands, he stroked his thumbs over her jaw. The warmth of her skin seeped into his fingertips and soaked deep inside, straight to his heart. For several seconds, he savored the feeling of rightness . . . of belonging . . . of connection. Then he slowly lowered his head until everything around them faded away.

At his first, gentle touch, a shudder rippled through her. The kind he might expect from a woman who'd never been kissed. Who was experiencing a bunch of sensations for the very first time. Who was madly attracted to the man doing the kissing.

Not what he'd expected.

His nerve endings began to tingle, and his pulse kicked up another notch. The tingle wasn't an unfamiliar sensation . . . except none of the women he'd kissed in his old life—not a single one—had sent this kind of thrill through him with a mere meeting of lips.

And he wanted more.

With every fiber of his being, he wanted more.

Yet pushing would be a mistake. He might scare her off.

Keep it simple, Stone, or you'll live to regret it.

Yeah, yeah.

But pulling back was going to take every ounce of his willpower.

Just as he'd mustered enough resolve to break contact, however, Lexie blindsided him.

Her arms crept around his neck . . . she rose on tiptoe . . . and the next thing he knew, she'd transformed the simple kiss into an all-out lip-lock.

Whoa!

No way could he resist *that*. If the lady wanted more, he was happy to oblige.

By the time they finally came up for air, he couldn't tell who was breathing harder.

"Oh. My. Goodness." She clung to him as if she needed the support to remain upright.

He could relate.

"Yeah." It was all he could manage.

She sucked in some air, but her eyes remained glazed. "For the record, you are not a lousy kisser."

"I'm glad I passed the test."

"It wasn't a test—but if it had been, you'd get an A+ . . . with bonus points." She peeked at Matt, who was back to watching the seals with the binoculars, and gave him a hopeful look. "He's still busy."

She wanted a repeat performance?

Man, his ego was getting a massive boost today.

"Not that I'm objecting—but what happened to slow and easy?"

"That was a stupid rule. About kissing, anyway."

Tempted as he was to oblige her, he glanced again at Matt, shook his head—and forced out words it about killed him to say. "I think we're at a good stopping place."

"Seriously?" She scrutinized him, the corners of her mouth drooping.

"Yeah."

"Why? I mean . . ." All at once, a flush crept across her cheeks. "Maybe I'm the one who's not so hot at this. It's been years since I . . ."

"Lexie . . . you kiss great. Better than great. World-class. The problem is me. I have a lot of willpower, but if we do that again, your son may end up watching a reenactment of the famous beach scene in *From Here to Eternity*—and he's too young to see that."

"Oh." Her blush deepened. "Maybe later?"

"Hold that thought."

"Hey, Mom! Mr. Stone! I think there's a sea lion out there! Come see!"

She eased out of his arms—but took his hand as they emerged from behind the rock.

And she kept a tight hold on it every minute she could for the rest of their date.

The hoped-for second kiss didn't happen,

though, thanks to a law-enforcement emergency that cut their day short.

But that was okay.

There would be another date. Another chance. She'd made that clear as they parted.

And as Adam drove home in the deepening dusk, he tried to find a name for the new emotion that was warming him to his core, like a cozy fire on a cold winter night.

Contentment—that's what it must be. The emotion might be unfamiliar to him . . . but perhaps this was how people felt at the end of a perfect day.

He could get used to this feeling with no effort at all.

There was just one snag—and hard as he tried to erase it from his mind, it lingered like the Hope Harbor fog that sometimes blocked the sun.

Perfect never lasted.

Not in his world.

He could only hope—and pray—that this time around, God would grant him an exception to that rule.

✺ **20** ✺

"Morning, Lexie. Do you have a minute?"

"Sure. Paperwork can always wait." She pushed the stack of reports on her desk aside and motioned Brent Davis into her office. "Have a seat."

"I'm afraid I don't bring great news on a Monday morning." The city administrator dropped into a chair across from her desk.

"Great news isn't one of the perks of this job." But it didn't matter today. Nothing the man said could dim the lingering glow from her weekend with Adam—and that world-class smooch on the beach. "Lay it on me."

"I just had a call from Martin Fisher."

She stifled a groan.

This was the one piece of news that could dull her glow a few watts.

"About his son, I assume."

"More about you." The man rested his elbows on the arms of the chair and steepled his fingers. "Let me be clear up front that I'm in your corner."

"That analogy is only appropriate if we're talking about a fight."

"We might be. He said you're accusing his son of being involved in the vandalism spree, that you have no credible proof, and if you don't back off, he'll do more than complain to me."

"Like what?" She did her best to control her surging anger.

"He implied he'd bring it up at a city council meeting . . . and talk to the area press. He also hinted at a smear campaign. The goal, I assume, would be to have you removed from office."

"You can't run a smear campaign without mud. I have a stellar career record here and with the State Department. What would he use for ammunition?"

The man shifted in his seat. "Before we discuss that, let me make certain I understand the situation. The boy who admitted being involved in the vandalism—Brian Hutton—identified Lucas Fisher as his accomplice. You have evidence Brian was on the scene of the last vandalism incident, but he has an alibi validated by Adam Stone. Does that sum it up?"

"Yes—and I know where this is heading. Martin Fisher suggested that because of their backgrounds, Brian wasn't trustworthy and Adam Stone's confirmation of his alibi wasn't credible." She linked her fingers into a tight knot on her desk. "First of all, that's garbage. Second, in the meeting the juvenile counselor and I had with him and his parents, Lucas made two slips that proved his involvement. Everyone in that room knew he was guilty."

"But he didn't admit he was involved?"

"No."

"And you have no hard evidence to prove he was, correct?"

"Not yet."

"What's the likelihood you'll find some?"

She blew out a frustrated breath. "Not as high as I'd like. The cases are getting colder by the day. Unless a witness comes forward . . . or we discover some proof . . . or he strikes again and leaves evidence behind . . . it's Brian's word against his."

"I don't think he's going to strike again, do you?"

"No." Not if Martin had anything to say about it.

"Were you planning to have any further contact with the Fisher family?"

"The counselor and I talked again on Friday by phone. We thought it might be worthwhile to pay them one more visit, after everyone's calmed down. As I said, his parents know he was involved. Letting a kid that age get away with multiple crimes sends the wrong message. Lawbreaking needs to be addressed—and punished."

"I agree—but it may have to be addressed by his parents rather than us."

A beat of silence passed.

"Are you saying we shouldn't have another meeting?" She kept her tone conversational. The mayor and city council members had weighed in on her hiring, but Brent was her boss. And he'd been fair to her from day one, trusting her to run the show, staying out of her way. Butting in like this was an anomaly. There must be a reason for it.

"I'm saying Martin Fisher is not receptive to your message, and a meeting might be counterproductive for the family—and for you."

She frowned. "How could it be counterproductive for me? It's my job to see that justice is done when crimes are committed."

"His attorney told him he doesn't have to cooperate, and that further contact from the police or juvenile authorities without any hard evidence implicating Lucas could be construed as harassment."

Ah.

"You're worried he might sue the city."

"No. I don't think he would go that far. The Fishers may not socialize much with residents, but they like the position and prestige of being one of the town's leading employers. I doubt they want to jeopardize that. I'm more worried about you."

They were back to that.

"I'm not. I have an impeccable record and solid credentials. What could he use for a smear campaign?"

"Personal integrity."

She blinked. "Excuse me?"

"Martin saw you and the man who validated

342

Brian's alibi dining and dancing in Coos Bay on Saturday night."

The air whooshed out of her lungs.

Of all the people who could have witnessed her cozy evening with Adam, why did it have to be Martin Fisher?

But once the shock passed, her anger began to simmer again.

"Let me guess where this is going. He told you that if I don't lay off his son, he's going to go public with the news that the Hope Harbor police chief is dating an ex-con—and he's going to suggest that such a relationship isn't good protocol and represents poor judgment. He's hoping that will undermine my credibility enough so people lose confidence in me and you're forced to remove me from office." She had to push the words through gritted teeth.

"He didn't say any of that specifically—but that was my takeaway. This could get nasty."

She vaulted to her feet and paced to the window. Paced back.

"This stinks, Brent."

"I know."

"There's no law here against relationships between law enforcement and felons."

"I know that too—and I pointed it out to Martin. He suggested maybe there should be."

"Too bad. He doesn't make the laws." She combed her fingers through her hair, tension coiling in her stomach. "What he's doing is wrong. Adam's paid his dues. He's a respected, contributing member of this community. He has more integrity in his little finger than Martin Fisher or his son have in their whole body."

"I don't disagree. But you can see how this could be twisted to suggest bad judgment—or worse. Like collusion."

Yeah, she could.

And that stunk even more.

Planting her hands flat on her desk, she leaned toward him. "What do you want me to do?"

"I've never told you how to run this department, and I'm not going to start now. I'm apprising you of the situation, explaining the threat, speculating about consequences. I'll leave the decision up to you."

"I appreciate that—but I'd still like your opinion."

"If you're asking what I'd do in your place . . . I'd drop the case until I had some hard evidence that would hold up in front of a judge. Having another meeting with the Fishers will only make Martin more antagonistic. That won't help you —or his son, I imagine. I expect the kid's under plenty of pressure already."

Lexie studied the man across from her, whose political savvy and ability to create consensus among city officials if there were contentious issues was respected by everyone in town.

What he said made sense.

Even if she didn't like it.

"Fine. No meeting. But I'm not closing the investigation on the vandalism incidents—and if I find anything that implicates Lucas, the meeting *will* take place."

"Works for me." He rose. "Sorry to dump this on your desk before you've had a chance to finish your morning coffee." He motioned toward the disposable cup from Sweet Dreams.

"I've had worse Mondays." Far worse. She needed to remember that—and maintain perspective. This aggravation would pass . . . and Martin Fisher wasn't the last jerk she would run into in her career.

"Keep me informed if anything changes." With a mock salute, Brent disappeared out the door.

Lexie picked up her coffee and took a swig. Nothing but dregs remained. She needed a refill—bad. And she wasn't up for Jim Gleason's toxic brew this morning, even though the rest of the officers and staff swore by it.

A second trip to Sweet Dreams was in order— and she might pamper herself with one of their decadent cinnamon rolls too. If ever there was an excuse to indulge, this was it.

But she intended to put thoughts of Martin Fisher aside while she ate it.

Otherwise, she'd end up with an acute case of indigestion.

•••

Adam hadn't been in the mood for dinner with the Huttons after a long day on the construction site, but as he pressed the tines of his fork against the few remaining crumbs of his carrot cake and swiped up the last miniscule globs of the cream cheese frosting, he had to admit the food alone had been worth the visit.

"This was a delicious meal, Mrs. Hutton. Thank you again."

"Please . . . call me Brenda. It makes me feel younger. And I'm glad you enjoyed it."

"Enjoy doesn't do it justice." And he wasn't just being polite. The meatloaf, scalloped potatoes, broccoli-cheese casserole, and rolls had been the best homemade meal he'd had in years, other than the beef stew that night at Lexie's and the Thanksgiving extravaganza at the Seabird Inn.

"Well . . ." A flush rose on the woman's cheeks. "Let me refill your coffee. Brian, don't you have homework to do?"

"Yeah." The boy polished off his own cake. "But I'd rather hang out with you guys."

"You won't miss much. After this cup of coffee"—Adam tapped the topped-off mug Brenda set in front of him—"I need to go home. A hungry dog is waiting for me."

"Are we still on for Saturday, to finish up the planters?"

"Yes. I also talked to Lex . . . Chief Graham . . .

and the juvenile counselor last week. I know you need to put in some more community service hours, and if you're interested, I think we can set it up for you to fulfill that obligation by working with me on Helping Hands projects."

"What's Helping Hands?"

"It's a volunteer organization that does what the name says—lends a hand to people who need assistance. Some of the chores are simple, like delivering groceries to a homebound resident, and some are more complicated. A few weeks ago I helped paint a house for a family. The father lost his job months ago and hasn't been able to find a new one. To make matters worse, he broke his arm. You might pick up a few useful skills along the way."

"That would be great—and I'd rather stick with you." He rose, empty dessert plate in hand. "I'm glad you came for dinner."

"Me too."

Silence fell as Adam sipped his coffee and Brian dispensed with his plate and glass. Only after he disappeared down the hall did Brenda speak, keeping her voice low.

"I want to thank you again for being kind to Brian. It's made a big difference in his life to have a strong role model." With her fingernail, she worked a piece of cheese off her placemat and rubbed at the greasy blot it left behind. "I wish his father had been half as decent."

He examined the woman across from him. She wasn't old . . . but she seemed worn and tired. As if life had been a constant struggle.

Kind of how his mom had always looked.

Except Brenda had tried to stick up for her son. She might have let her loser husband beat her up, cheat on her, and take her money, but at least she'd tried to protect Brian.

Too bad his mother hadn't done the same.

"You okay?"

At the woman's tentative question, he picked up his mug. "Yes. Just thinking back to my younger years. I didn't have the best father, either. I know how hard that can be on a boy."

"And a mother can't make up for that, no matter how much she loves her son."

"It can help, though. Brian's proof of that. I wish mine had . . ." He snapped his jaw closed. Sharing sordid details with virtual strangers wasn't his style.

Brenda stirred some sugar into her coffee. "I'm not going to pry, but it sounds like your mom wasn't there for you, either. I'm sorry for that. I can't speak to her motivations, but I can tell you a terrible marriage is devastating. If there's abuse, it's worse. It can destroy a person. It almost destroyed me."

"Yet you watched out for Brian. How can a mother not protect her child?" It was the question that had gnawed at him for close to three decades.

"Are you saying yours didn't?" Compassion softened her features.

He gave a stiff shrug. "Whenever my father decided to punish me for some imaginary transgression, she zoned out on booze."

"Even when you were a little boy?"

"Yes. Except . . ."

He stared into the dark depths of his coffee as an obscure memory surfaced from somewhere deep in the murky waters of his youth. He'd been a little kid. Five, six at the most. Not much older than Matt. His mom had gotten him a cake for his birthday. From a bakery. And she'd made his favorite meal. They'd laughed together while she cooked, and she'd given him a couple of hugs. Not once had she touched the bottle of booze she kept under the sink.

Then his father had come home.

And everything changed . . .

"Why does this place stink?" The question roared through the house as his dad slammed the front door of their flat.

His mom froze at the stove while they waited for him to appear—and Adam began to tremble.

Bad stuff always happened when his dad sounded mad like that.

"What are you cooking?" He stopped in the doorway.

"Stew."

"I hate stew. You know that."

"It's Adam's birthday, hon. Remember?" Mom's voice sounded pretend-happy. Like it always did when his dad got mad. Like she was trying to make the mad go away. But it never did. Sometimes it got worse. "This is his favorite dinner."

"I don't care whose birthday it is. I've had a lousy day, and I'm hungry. I'm also the breadwinner in this family—and since I pay for the food, we'll eat what I want. Get rid of the stew and give me a real meal."

"I have some pork chops in the freezer. I'll fry those for you, okay?"

"Do it fast." He pulled a beer from the fridge and glared at the table. "What's that?"

"Adam's birthday cake."

His face got red. "You paid money to a bakery for this? What's wrong with Betty Crocker?"

"I just thought . . . he's never had a real cake. It didn't cost a lot."

His father twisted toward him, a vein pulsing in his forehead. "You've never been anything but trouble from the day you were born, boy. And you cost me way too much money. You know what I think about wasting hard-earned cash on a fancy birthday cake?" He swung back to the table and punched his fist through the middle of it.

Tears welled up in Adam's eyes as he surveyed the ruined cake, and he choked out a strangled sob.

"A sissy too. I'm raising a sissy." His father

strode toward him, fists raised. "You need to toughen up, boy."

He cowered down, heart banging, waiting for the hurt.

It didn't come.

Instead, his mother moved in front of him, blocking his dad. "Leave the boy alone."

"What?" His father looked real surprised, like a character in one of those Saturday-morning cartoons.

"I said, leave him alone."

"Well, aren't you the sassy one tonight. I'll deal with you in a minute. First I'll take care of the boy." He tried to shove her aside.

She didn't budge.

"Go outside, Adam." She kept watching his dad.

"But I—"

"Go. Now. Play with your friends—and don't come back until it gets dark." She gave him a push toward the door, staying between him and his dad while he fumbled for the knob and slipped outside.

He ran through the yard as fast as he could, toward the place he always went whenever it got scary at home—the overgrown arbor in Mrs. McMahon's backyard. Winter or summer, under the arching branches on the old woman's property, he felt safe.

Safer than he ever felt at home.

He stayed there until long past dark. Shaking . . . crying . . . worrying.

When he finally went home, the house was silent. His father was asleep on the sofa in the living room, a bunch of empty beer cans on the floor next to him. His mother was in bed.

Even though his stomach growled real loud, he crept to his own bed and pulled the covers over his head. The house stayed quiet—yet it took him a long time to go to sleep.

When he woke up the next day, his dad was gone to work. His mom was in the kitchen—but it didn't look like Mom. Her face was bruised and puffy, one eye was black, and she was walking funny. Limping, and kind of bent over.

The bottle she kept under the counter was on the sink. It was almost empty.

She didn't tell him what had happened while he was in his safe place—but she never tried to protect him again.

"Adam?"

Pulse pounding, he yanked himself back to the present. "I'm sorry, I . . . I lost the thread of our conversation."

"You were far away . . . in a place that wasn't happy. Bad memories of your mother?" Brenda's features were soft with empathy.

"More of my father." He drained his cup and stood. "I need to get going. My dog will be hungry."

"Of course. I'll walk you to the door." If she

was surprised by his abrupt departure, she gave no hint of it.

On the threshold he paused. "Thank you again for the great meal."

"The thanks are all mine. Enjoy the rest of your evening."

Enjoy?

Not much chance of that after his unscheduled journey to the past.

Instead of replying, he lifted his hand in farewell and escaped to his car.

Once he pulled onto 101, he pressed on the accelerator. Hard. As if speed could help him outrun the memories.

But no matter how fast he went, they kept pace, refusing to be relegated to the shadowy recesses of his mind.

Adam clenched the wheel. Why, after all these years, had he remembered his mother coming to his defense that night?

And if she'd done it once . . . had she done it before? Were there similar occasions from earlier in his life—before she began to drink herself into oblivion while his father took out his frustrations on their child—buried deep in his subconscious?

That wasn't a question he wanted to consider tonight—or ever. The day he'd walked out of prison he'd vowed to leave the past behind, along with all of its hurts and hates and horrors.

Now that one memory had been jarred loose,

however, a handful of other less-dramatic inter-ventions niggled at the edges of his consciousness.

But so what if she'd made a few feeble, tentative attempts to protect him? Most of his life, she'd failed him.

"A terrible marriage is devastating. If there's abuse, it's worse. It can destroy a person."

Brenda's comment from earlier in the evening echoed in his mind.

Adam's hands began to tremble, and he pulled off onto one of the scenic overlooks that lined 101. From this high point, he should be able to catch a glimpse of the twinkling lights of Hope Harbor in the distance, perhaps even spot the top of the lighthouse on Pelican Point that had once guided lost souls to safety in stormy weather.

His mother had never talked much about her past, but he'd picked up enough to know her younger years had been as difficult as his, her family life also plagued with abuse. What kind, she'd never said. But it had been sufficient to drive her to the streets at a tender age too—where she'd hooked up with the loser who'd made their son's life a living hell.

She might have come to his defense a few times early on, but in the end, she'd saved herself instead.

Yet . . . could guilt over that choice have driven her to drink more . . . and ultimately to take the drugs that ended her life?

He wiped a hand down his face.

Maybe instead of hating her, he should feel sorry for her. After all, he'd escaped. She never had.

Maybe he needed to let go once and for all of the resentment buried deep inside and leave judgment to God.

Adam rolled up his window against the chilly evening air and took one last look at Hope Harbor.

It reminded him of the mythical village of Brigadoon from that musical the high school had put on not long after he moved to town. The hamlet that appeared for only one day every hundred years.

A tiny, unsettling shiver raced up his spine as he skimmed the peaceful scene below. The kind he used to get before some petty crime went bad and the walls closed in on him.

Weird.

He hadn't felt like this since the day he arrived in town, filled with uncertainties, trepidation, and doubts about what the future might hold.

Those bad feelings had proven to be groundless, however. Everything had turned out fine.

But as he swung back onto the road and Hope Harbor disappeared from view, he couldn't shake the disquieting fear that he might wake up tomorrow and discover everything he thought was real and good in his new life had vanished into the mist—like Brigadoon.

❧ 21 ❧

"Yo, turd face."

As the familiar voice spoke behind him, Brian's heart stuttered. He'd been expecting this confrontation ever since the police chief and juvenile counselor visited the Fisher family last Thursday. Who knew why the high school hotshot had waited until Tuesday afternoon to approach him?

But he did know why the kid had picked this time and place.

At five o'clock, the soda machine alcove near the high school cafeteria was deserted. Most of the students were long gone. Like he would have been if he hadn't had to hang around to use the high-speed net at school for term paper research instead of the prehistoric—but free—dial-up at home.

He hefted his daypack onto his back, slowly pivoted to face Lucas, and held on tight to the sweaty soda can. "What do you want?"

"I thought we should have a little talk." Lucas strolled over. His posture was casual, but anger smoldered in his eyes. "You broke our pact."

"You broke it first. You stole my flash drive and left it by that car for the police to find."

"Keep your voice down."

"I didn't start this conversation." He tried to

brush past the tall, broad-shouldered kid who outweighed him by at least forty pounds.

Lucas pushed him against the wall. Hard. "I'm not done talking to you."

"Well, I'm done talking to you." His chest heaved, but he didn't move.

"You better be done talking to the cops too."

He didn't respond.

"Did you hear me?" Lucas loomed over him, inches away.

Brian began to sweat. He was still hurting from the last thrashing—and even on his best days he was no match for the muscled football player.

This could get bad.

Real bad.

"Yeah. I hear you." He squeezed the reply past his stiff lips.

"Good." Lucas pressed one palm against the wall and leaned into his face. "In case you haven't noticed, you're like a leper around here now."

Yeah, he'd noticed. As of Friday, he was back to sitting alone at the lunch table.

But that was better than winding up in front of a judge.

"This school isn't the center of the universe." His comeback sounded braver—and more defiant —than he felt. "There are other places to find friends."

"Like doing manual labor with that ex-con who lied about where you were last Wednesday night?"

"He didn't lie—and you know it."

"Who's going to believe a lowlife like him?"

"He's not a lowlife!" Brian glared at the boy across from him. "He's a great guy. Better than you'll ever be."

"Right." Lucas smirked. "Here's the truth, kid. You can hang around all you want with a felon in your free time, but this school will be the center of *your* universe for the next two years. And until I graduate, I can make your life miserable."

"Why would you want to do that?"

"Because I can." Lucas folded his arms. "And because you're a loser."

Brian stared at him. Why had he ever wanted to be friends with someone like this? "You know what? I feel sorry for you."

Lucas blinked. "Huh?"

"I said, I feel sorry for you. And I'm glad we're not friends anymore." He ducked under his arm.

Lucas grabbed his shoulder. Yanked him around.

He staggered. His backpack flew off and slid across the tile floor, and he dropped his can of soda.

"You better believe we're not friends." Lucas's complexion reddened. "In fact, let me show you how unfriendly I can be." He drew his arm back and—

"Hey!" Tiffany Edwards jolted to a stop as she came around the corner.

Lucas dropped his arm. "Hi, gorgeous." He gave the sophomore cheerleader a stiff smile.

She didn't return it. "What's going on?"

"Brian and I were talking."

"That's not what it looked like." She picked up the can of soda that had rolled toward her and walked over, ignoring Lucas. "Is this yours?" She held it out.

"Yeah. Thanks." Brian took it.

"You okay?"

He scooped up his backpack and hefted it into position. "Yeah."

Saved by a girl.

Lucas would never let him live this down.

"What are you doing hanging around so late?" Lucas inserted himself between the two of them, blocking his view of Tiffany.

"I had to take a makeup history test."

"Bummer. You deserve a reward after that. Want to swing by Sweet Dreams for a snack? I've got my new Mustang today. We could take a drive too."

"No, thanks. I have my mom's car—and I need to get home and study." She walked around Lucas until Brian could see her. "You take the bus, don't you?"

"Yeah."

"You missed it. Want a ride?"

He gawked at her. Why would Tiffany Edwards, one of the prettiest and most popular girls in school, offer him a lift home?

She flashed white teeth and a dimple. "It's a simple question."

At her teasing tone, he flushed. A ride would save him a long walk . . . but what would a girl like her think if she saw the trailer park he called home?

"Um . . . I appreciate it, but it's probably out of your way."

"Our house is only a couple of miles from Ocean Breezes."

She already knew where he lived?

"Hey . . ." Lucas joined in, annoyed now rather than flirtatious. "You might want to avoid this guy. Like we all talked about at lunch the other day."

"*You* talked about it. We listened. And I make my own decisions." Her chin rose. "I also choose my own friends—and I don't like bullies who issue orders and ultimatums and treat other people like dirt. Neither do some of the other kids." She turned her back on Lucas. "I'm sorry we haven't been friendlier, Brian. I'd like to try and make up for that. Let me give you a ride, okay?"

"Sure. Thanks. I appreciate it." He walked past Lucas, Tiffany beside him.

All the way to the exit, he kept expecting a shove between his shoulder blades—but they made it outside with no further incident.

"I'm parked over there." Tiffany motioned toward a Toyota.

He followed her in silence and slid into the passenger seat.

She didn't speak again until after she backed

out of the spot and was tooling through town, toward 101.

"Just so you know, a bunch of us talked about the stuff that's been going on with Lucas for the past few months. He was always bossy, but he's gotten a lot worse. We're tired of it—and tired of how he treats people who don't dance to his music. If you want some company at lunch from now on, we'd like to sit with you. Will you give us a second chance?"

"Sure." He smiled at her. "I'm all about second chances."

And as they chatted and laughed during the short ride home, Brian's spirits soared.

This was a miracle.

A bona fide miracle.

Maybe not as dramatic as the one Reverend Baker had mentioned last Sunday about that Lazarus guy being raised from the dead—but getting a new chance at life at Hope Harbor High was a close second.

"Greetings, my friend. Tacos on a Tuesday—what's the special occasion?"

"Why do you think it's a special occasion?" Adam stopped in front of the serving window as Charley grinned at him over the counter and adjusted his Ducks cap.

"Your smile couldn't get any bigger."

Oh yeah. That would be a dead giveaway.

"I had an interesting—encounter—this afternoon." He was dying to tell someone about his meeting with Rebecca Oliver . . . but Lexie was top on his list to hear it. Too bad she had a presentation at some Chamber of Commerce meeting in Coos Bay tonight. His news would have to wait until after work tomorrow.

"Encounter is an intriguing term. You want tacos, I presume?"

"Yes."

Charley didn't ask anything else. That wasn't his way. He was always happy to listen, but he didn't probe. Yet people often ended up telling him more than they'd planned.

Like he was about to do.

"It was a business meeting."

"Ah. BJ's business is certainly growing."

"This wasn't about BJ's business. I took off a few hours early to investigate . . . an opportunity. But I'm not quitting the construction company or anything." Better be clear about that. He had no plans to give up his steady work. "BJ took a chance on me, and I'll never forget that. I owe her a lot."

Charley arranged some fish on the grill and began chopping green onions. "I'm sure she'd understand if a person wanted to follow a passion —as she's doing with her design and construction company."

"I'm planning to do both—for a while, anyway."

The price tag on the small, initial commissions he and Rebecca had discussed wouldn't provide a living—but the dining room table she'd mentioned as a possibility if all went well with these first jobs? That was a big-ticket item. He'd have to find a larger workspace if he took that project on, of course . . . but no sense getting ahead of himself. He could worry about that if it came to pass.

"Testing the waters is always a smart plan." Charley sprinkled some kind of seasoning over the sizzling filling for the tacos. "By the way, I saw the rocking chairs you made for BJ and Eric. You have great talent."

Adam squinted at the taco-making artist. Was that his subtle way of saying he knew what this coded conversation was about?

Maybe.

The man had uncanny insights.

But even if Charley had somehow figured out what was going on, he wouldn't say a word to anyone. The man was nothing if not discreet. Everyone in town knew that, and . . .

". . . sounds great, Paul. But if you ask me, your game would benefit more from practice and prayer than a new putter. It's cheaper too." Father Murphy waved at them as the two clergymen hustled toward the stand. "Greetings, fellow Hope Harborans. Two more orders, Charley."

"Hope Harborans?" Reverend Baker's eyebrows peaked. "That's a new one. Why not Hope

Harborites? It has a more biblical sound . . . you know, as in Levites?"

"I'm well aware of the many references to the Levites in the Old Testament . . . and the one reference in the New Testament." Father Murphy straightened his Roman collar. "And let's not forget the Kohathites and Merarites."

"I'm impressed. You've been studying."

"Very funny." The priest sent his fellow cleric a disgruntled look, then turned with a broad smile. "Hello, Adam. I see you're indulging your Charley's craving too."

"It's the best-kept secret on the Oregon coast."

"I'll second that."

"Make it three," Reverend Baker said.

"Thank you all." Charley gave a mock bow. "Not that I'm complaining about the business, but this is your third visit to my humble stand in the past five days." He added more fish to the grill for the clerics. "Is Anna on vacation?"

"No. Tied up with the Harbor Point Cranberries nut cake business. I'm glad that's taken off . . . but I doubt she'll be able to keep cooking for us much longer." Father Murphy sighed. "There are only twenty-four hours in the day—and we wouldn't want to stand in the way of a growing business. Right, Paul?"

"Right. I think she's trying to find a replacement for us, but good cooks are hard to come by in a small town like this."

Adam's ears perked up. "Are you gentlemen wanting to hire a cook?"

Both of the clerics turned toward him.

"Yes." They answered in unison.

"Do you know someone?" Father Murphy's eyes sparked with interest.

"I might." He hesitated. Would he be stepping out on a limb to suggest Brenda Hutton? She could use a job with regular hours where she was treated better. But despite Brian's enthusiastic endorsement of her cooking, he'd only sampled one meal—even if it *had* been top-notch.

Besides, cooking for the clerics wouldn't provide the full-time job she needed.

It might be better to keep his mouth shut.

"Don't hold back on us, please. We're desperate." Reverend Baker glanced at the man behind the counter. "No offense, Charley. We love your tacos —but variety is the spice of life."

"I'm all for variety." The taco maker laid out some corn tortillas on the counter.

As all three waited, watching him expectantly, Adam shifted.

Too late to back out now. He had to tell them at least a little more.

"I do have someone in mind . . . but I'm not sure it would work out. From what I've seen, she's a first-rate cook—but she needs a full-time job."

"Ah." Father Murphy pursed his lips. "Would

she be interested in housekeeping as well? Paul and I will soon be in the market for that service too. The woman we've been using is moving to California with her husband in three weeks. Between the two of us, we might be able to expand this to a full-time job. What do you think, Paul?"

"I think we should meet this woman."

"She isn't much of a churchgoer now—but she used to be." Adam doubted that would matter to these two, but it was better to lay all the facts on the table.

"Church attendance isn't a job requirement for me—although she'd be welcome at St. Francis." Father Murphy grinned.

"Ditto—but I bet she'd like our doughnuts better."

"Church attendance is *not* about doughnuts." The padre rolled his eyes.

"True . . . but you're serving them now too."

"Excuse me." Despite his attempt to rein it in, Adam's mouth twitched at their banter. "For the record, she did attend services last week at Grace Christian."

"Drat. Foiled again." Father Murphy huffed—then softened it with a wink.

"You wouldn't happen to be talking about Brenda Hutton, would you?" Charley finished filling the first three tortillas and began wrapping them in white paper.

"Yes. How did you know that?" Adam studied the man. Was there any information in town he *wasn't* privy to?

"When she and Brian stopped by for their complimentary welcome-to-Hope-Harbor order of tacos, she brought me some delicious home-made brownies as a thank-you. After the tough road she's traveled, she could use a break. Seems like an ideal candidate for the position."

"Homemade brownies?" Father Murphy was almost drooling.

"I'm sold. How do we get in touch with this woman?" Reverend Baker pulled a small note-book out of his pocket.

"Let me talk to her first." This was moving too fast. What if Brenda wasn't interested—or didn't appreciate having her situation discussed with strangers? Adam didn't want to make any enemies in town. "I'll give her a call tonight and have her get in touch with you if she wants to pursue this."

"Well . . . I suppose that's best." Reverend Baker put the notebook away. "But please tell her we're eager to talk with her."

"I'll do that."

"Here you go, Adam." Charley tucked the tacos in a brown bag and handed it across the counter. "Enjoy."

"No doubt about that. I've never had a taco here I didn't like." Adam counted out his money and passed it to the chef.

"You know . . . it's interesting how our paths often smooth out if we give God a chance to pave the way, isn't it?" Charley maintained his grip on the bag, locking gazes with him. "But too often people let setbacks cloud their judgment. They give up . . . make mistakes . . . take detours that lead to dead ends or get them lost—when what they *should* do is ask for guidance and listen for direction." He released the bag. "I hope Brenda prays about this opportunity."

"I do too." Father Murphy folded his hands and bowed his head. "And I believe there's a homily in what you said, Charley. I should have taken notes."

"Stealing ideas from Charley now, are we?" Reverend Baker tut-tutted.

"Hey . . . I take inspiration wherever I can get it—and I wouldn't be surprised if this theme showed up in one of your sermons soon too . . . not that I'd ever know."

"You're welcome to attend services anytime and take a listen."

"And you're welcome to attend Mass anytime."

"Well . . . I'm off." Adam backed away as the two clerics smirked at each other. The priest and minister were amusing . . . but during the short walk back to his car it was Charley's remark about setbacks that lingered in his mind.

The man had mentioned Brenda at the end . . . but it almost felt as if the counsel had been aimed at him, not her.

Did Charley know something he didn't?

No.

That was crazy.

The man had great intuition, but he couldn't see into the future.

Adam checked both directions for traffic and crossed Dockside Drive. Why was he letting a simple comment from the philosophizing taco chef spook him? He'd walked the straight and narrow since he'd been here, done everything by the book. Life was better than it had ever been.

Yet as he got behind the wheel, a niggling sense of foreboding engulfed him. Like the one he'd felt at the overlook last night.

And even the mouth-watering aroma of Charley's tacos on the seat beside him couldn't revive his rapidly waning appetite.

❧ 22 ☙

As her cell began to vibrate against her hip, Lexie ripped the speeding ticket off her pad and handed it through the window of the sports car to the disgruntled driver.

"On your next visit, stay within five miles of the limit. We can tolerate that. Twenty over is in the danger range, especially for kids on bikes and older residents on foot." She backed away from the car and pulled her phone off her belt.

"Come back again when you're not in such a hurry."

The man muttered a response that sounded a lot like "fat chance" before he put the car in gear and roared away without a backward glance.

She scanned the cell screen, frowning as she put the phone to her ear. If her mom was calling during a workday, it must be important. "Hi. What's up?"

"Am I interrupting anything?"

"I just gave a speeding ticket to a visitor who I doubt will return to our fair town." She walked toward the patrol car. "Is Matt okay?"

"Fine. You know I hate to bother you at work, but I talked to Rose a few minutes ago and she passed on some scuttlebutt I thought you ought to hear."

"I'm listening." She slid behind the wheel and checked the clock on the dash. In five hours she'd be en route to Adam's place for dinner.

Yes!

An unexpected date with a handsome man who sounded *very* anxious to see her was exactly what she needed on a lackluster Wednesday.

"You're not going to like it."

"Just tell me, Mom." This must be the week for bad news.

"There's a rumor floating around town that Adam was involved in the vandalism incidents."

"What?" Her spine stiffened.

"I told you you wouldn't like it . . . and I don't either."

"But . . . but he was a *victim* of one of the incidents!"

"According to the rumor, he did that to deflect suspicion from himself."

"That's ridiculous."

"I agree. Who would plant such a hateful suspicion?"

Only two people she knew had any reason to cast aspersions on the man.

And either of the Fishers could be vindictive enough to pull a stunt like this.

In fact, Martin Fisher had thrown out this very suggestion during their meeting with him. It had been so absurd she'd passed right over it.

"Lexie?"

"Yeah. I'm here. I have an idea who might have started this."

"Care to share?"

"It's connected to a case."

"Oh." Her mother knew better than to push if it was official business. "Well, Rose doesn't believe a word of it—and neither will anyone else in town."

If only that was true.

But once a rumor like this took root, it would be hard to contain . . . more so if the police chief was dating the man in question. That could suggest a cover-up, adding credence to the allegations. Plus, Adam had lived a solitary life until recently. He spent his nights alone at Sandpiper Cove—meaning he had no alibi for any of the vandalism incidents except Marci's car . . . and that one from an admitted vandal.

Apparently backing off on Lucas hadn't appeased his father . . . or perhaps the boy himself was seeking revenge.

"Thanks for letting me know, Mom."

"Do you think Adam's heard anything?"

"I hope not."

"If he hasn't, he will. Soon."

"I know."

"He might appreciate a heads-up."

"I know that too." And it wasn't a chore she relished.

But better that it come from her than a stranger.

"Well . . . you tell him he's got a lot of support in this town. And invite him to dinner again one night later this week."

"I'll do that." Her call-waiting alert beeped. "I need to go. Someone else is trying to reach me. Talk to you later." She ended that call and took one from the *Hope Harbor Herald* editor. "Hi, Marci. What can I do for you?"

"Answer a question. I got back from lunch and found an anonymous tip on the answering machine here at the *Herald*. I think it's a hoax, but superb reporter that I am, I'm investigating. The guy suggested that Adam Stone was involved

372

in the vandalism incidents here in town. Any truth to that allegation?"

Lexie closed her eyes. The rumor mill was cranking at full blast, fed by the vile seeds being planted around town.

"No. It's not true. Adam has been a model citizen since he arrived here."

"That's what I thought. The tip felt suspicious."

"How so?"

"The voice was muffled, like the person was trying to disguise his identity—and caller ID was blocked."

That figured.

"You don't plan to do anything with this, do you?"

"Not a chance. I stick to facts."

"Good. I appreciate the call, though. If you happen to hear anything else, let me know."

"I'll do that."

Lexie punched the end button and slid the phone back onto her belt.

Her mom was right.

If Adam hadn't heard the rumor already, he needed to hear it fast from someone who had no doubt of his innocence.

Namely her.

And much as she'd prefer to wait until their date tonight to share the bad news in the privacy of Sandpiper Cove, it was safer not to put off the unhappy chore. The odds were low he'd hear anything out at the cranberry farm jobsite—but there was a chance he might.

Especially considering how fate had been conspiring against them in the past few days.

Why was there an unfamiliar car parked in front of her trailer?

Brenda eased back on the gas pedal as she approached. The only visitors she'd had of late other than the police chief were the juvenile counselor and Adam Stone, and that wasn't either of their vehicles.

Something didn't feel right.

Still . . . after the upbeat interview she'd just had with Reverend Baker and Father Murphy, nothing could dampen her spirits. If the trial arrangement they'd worked out went well, she would soon have a job closer to home with regular hours, great bosses, and a supportive atmosphere.

She owed Adam big-time for tossing her name in the hat. Maybe she'd bake him one of those carrot cakes he'd scarfed down the night he'd come to dinner.

Smiling, she pulled into her slot and slid out of the car.

But when her slightly overweight, thin-eyed caller rose from the shadowed lawn chair under the sagging awning, her lips flattened.

"Hi, babe."

She froze as the man she'd never wanted to

see again flashed his teeth, yellower than ever from the cigarettes he chain-smoked.

"What are you doing here? And how did you find me?"

"It's not hard to find people with Google. I brought you these." He sauntered forward and held out a bouquet of flowers in a clear plastic sleeve still sporting a price tag from a popular discount store.

She wrapped her fingers tighter around her purse and fought the urge to back away from him. "I don't want your flowers."

"Sure you do. You always liked these kind." He flicked a finger against one of the mums. A few petals dropped off as he held out the past-its-prime bouquet again.

"Excuse me." She walked a wide circle around him and headed for the door.

"Hey! I came a long way to see you."

"You wasted your time—and your gas." She kept walking, gripping her keys in her hand, willing him to disappear.

He didn't.

Instead, his vise-like fingers locked on to her upper arm and he spun her around, his eyes blazing. Like they always did whenever he didn't get his way. "That's not a very polite welcome."

"Let go of my arm." She tried to keep her voice steady despite the earthquake in her stomach.

"We need to talk."

"No, we don't. Get out of my life, Jerry."

"I'm your husband."

"Not for long. Divorce papers are in the works." And they'd be filed as soon as that young attorney in town got back from his honeymoon.

"You want a divorce?" He gaped at her.

"Yes. I have a new life here. A good one. And you're not part of it. Go back to that young chick who lured you away with all her money."

"Look—I'm sorry about that, okay? I made a mistake. You don't need to be jealous of her anymore. She's history."

Jealous? Brenda almost laughed. As for the woman being history . . . more likely her money was history—or she'd gotten wind of Jerry's less-pleasant side and thrown him out.

"I'll say it again. Get out of my life—and don't ever come back."

His fingers tightened on her arm, digging into her flesh. There would be a purple bruise there tomorrow . . . like in the old days. "You're making a mistake."

"No. I'm fixing one. Now let go of me. If you don't, I'll call the police—and I *will* press charges."

He glared at her.

She didn't blink.

Finally, he released her and hurled the flowers at her feet. "Fine. If you change your mind, you have my cell number."

"Don't count on it."

He squinted at her. "What happened to you? You're different."

Yes, she was. Thank God.

"I got my life back. Don't ever bother me again." With that, she turned, walked to the door, let herself in—and locked it behind her.

For almost a full minute, her soon-to-be ex-husband stayed where he was while she clung to the back of a chair and watched through the window, praying her shaky legs would hold her up.

Finally he kicked the bouquet, glowered at the closed trailer door, and stomped back to his car.

Brenda waited for five long minutes after he drove away—in case he changed his mind about leaving. But at last she opened the door and went out to retrieve the pathetic bouquet. Holding it at arm's length, she marched down to the dumpsters where the residents deposited their trash, threw it in with all the rest of the garbage, and let the lid bang shut.

Done.

Finished.

Over.

If she never crossed paths with that user again, it would be too soon. The man hadn't even asked about his son.

Disgust soured her mouth as she walked back to the trailer. That lapse, in itself, spoke volumes about his character. Not to mention the fact that he'd expected a lame apology and limp bouquet of flowers to restore him to her good graces.

What a scumbag.

As she dodged a rut on the asphalt road, the sun peeked out from behind a cloud, bathing the world in light. Kind of like Hope Harbor had done for her and Brian. Maybe they didn't live in the best neighborhood or have a lot of money. Maybe they never would.

But they'd both turned the corner to a new life. One that offered a better, brighter tomorrow.

And they were never going back to the shadowed past they'd left behind.

"Your dancing partner is paying us another visit." From his rung near the top of the ladder, Luis pointed his drill toward the gravel road that led to the cranberry farm construction site.

Adam swung around. In the distance, a cloud of dust signaled the arrival of a car, but from his spot on the ground he couldn't tell if it was a police cruiser.

"Are you sure?"

"Yes. I have an eagle view up here."

Hmm.

Adam weighed his hammer in his hand. Seeing Lexie twice in one day was fine with him—but why would she make a special trip out here when they were going to be spending the evening together at Sandpiper Cove?

Unless she was as anxious to see him as he was to see her.

The corners of his mouth rose, and he set the hammer down. Nice thought. And while she was here, why not tell her about Rebecca Oliver's visit? That would free up tonight for other, more personal, topics.

His smile broadened.

As soon as the cruiser stopped, he walked over to join her. Luis wasn't the type to eavesdrop, but the other workers BJ had brought in for this job might not be as discreet.

"Hi." He stopped several feet from her, fighting the urge to give her the kind of welcome better reserved for a less-public place.

"Hi back." She returned his smile . . . sort of. And her inflection seemed a bit odd. It was hard to gauge her mood behind those sunglasses, though. "Do you think you could finagle a ten-minute break from your boss?"

"My boss won't be back from her honeymoon until Saturday. Luis and I are the acting bosses. So yeah, I can take a break. Is everything okay?"

Instead of answering, she scanned the site. "Is there somewhere a little more private we could talk?"

A surge of unease spiraled through him.

"There's a cluster of rhododendron bushes behind the house. That's the closest spot."

"That works."

He took her arm and led her around the half-built house, toward the bushes laden with buds beginning to show a hint of purple. In another week or two, they'd be a mass of blossoms.

Once they were shielded from prying eyes—and ears—Lexie removed her glasses.

Adam's stomach bottomed out.

She looked seriously worried.

"What's wrong?"

"I need to let you know about a rumor that's spreading through town." She dipped her head and rubbed at the twin creases denting her brow. "I wish there was an easy way to say this."

He fisted his hands at his sides and steeled himself. "Just tell me. I'm used to dealing with bad stuff."

Silence.

"Lexie—what is it?" With every second that passed, his panic ratcheted up another notch.

She sucked in a breath . . . and met his gaze. The anguish searing her eyes, along with the hint of anger and frustration in their depths, clawed at his gut.

"The rumor is that you're involved in the vandalism incidents that have been taking place in town."

Whatever he'd been bracing for, that wasn't it. "What?"

"Seeds of doubt are being planted about you."

"By whom?"

"I have my suspicions—but no proof."

"Do you want to share them?" As far as he knew, he'd done nothing to alienate anyone in town. Why would someone target him?

She hesitated. "I don't usually discuss ongoing investigations, but since you're involved with this one now, I'm going to break that rule."

As she told him about visiting the Fishers, and the family's reaction to her suggestion that Lucas was involved, the left side of his brain did the math.

"It's that Fisher boy or his father, isn't it? This is payback because I verified Brian's alibi."

"That's my assumption."

"This is unbelievable." He raked his fingers through his hair and began to pace. "I was one of the victims, for crying out loud!"

"I know. They covered that in the rumor."

"How?"

At her deflect-suspicion explanation, a wave of despair washed over him. "I can't even fight the insinuations. The only one who can vouch for my whereabouts on the nights those incidents happened is Clyde." He faced her. "Tell me everything you heard."

He listened as she briefed him on the calls she'd received, his spirits diving. The assurance from her mother that the town supported him was the one bright spot, but it didn't help a lot. Once doubt was planted, it was hard to eradicate.

"I didn't want you to find out about this from someone else. That's why I drove out the minute I heard."

As she finished, as the broader implications began to compute, a second shock jolted through him, shaking him to the core.

Lexie was the chief of police. He was a felon under new suspicion. Having anything to do with him—let alone getting involved in a dating relationship—could derail her career.

The bad news she'd come out here to deliver was about more than the rumor.

"It's over, isn't it?" Somehow he choked out the question, stomach twisting like it had the day his father ruined the best birthday of his life. Only worse.

Far worse.

Her face went blank. "What are you talking about?"

"Us. You want to pull back."

"No!" Shock widened her eyes. "I'm not bailing on you. I know you had no part in the vandalism. I just didn't want you to hear about it from someone else. We'll get through this—together."

Relief coursed through him . . . but it was short-lived.

Lexie's career could be at stake here—and the last thing he wanted to do was cause trouble for the woman who was rapidly stealing his heart.

"Were our names linked in any of these rumors?"

"Not that I've heard."

Her cautious response raised his antennas. "What aren't you telling me?"

She hesitated . . . then lifted one shoulder. "It's not a big deal. Or it shouldn't be. I wasn't going to mention this, because I thought it was a moot issue." She proceeded to tell him about Martin Fisher's threat of a smear campaign against her. "I don't think he'll follow through now that we've laid off Lucas. And he's the only person who's seen us together."

But he was the wrong person.

And what would happen if a lot more people saw them appearing together in public as a couple?

What a colossal mess.

"I can't believe this is happening." He wiped a hand down his face.

"Hey." She wove her fingers through his, her tone fierce. "We are not going to bow to this kind of pressure. I'm proud to be seen with you. You're a fine man who's leading an exemplary life. All of the people in this town who know you know that. This will blow over eventually."

But maybe not until after it destroyed her career.

Martin Fisher might never follow through on his threat against Lexie, but the smear campaign against *him* could do just as much damage to her.

He couldn't let that happen.

Gently he tugged his fingers free. "I need to get back to work."

"I do too." She searched his face. "We'll talk more about this tonight, okay?"

No.

Not a smart idea.

He needed to think this through. Alone. If they spent the evening together, it would be too easy to let her persuade him to stick together, regardless of the cost to her.

"Listen . . ." He retreated a step and shoved his hands in his pockets, fighting the temptation to wrap her in his arms and hold her close until all the bad stuff went away. "Why don't you give me a rain check on dinner at my place? We may have to work a little later than usual here, and I need to absorb everything you told me."

Distress etched her features. "It doesn't change a thing between us as far as I'm concerned."

"I appreciate that—and your confidence."

"My feelings for you run much deeper than confidence." Her imploring gaze fastened on his as she made that admission. "I don't want to lose you, Adam. Don't shut me out."

"I'm not. I don't want to lose you, either. I just . . . give me a few days to work through this. Please."

"You aren't going to bolt, are you?" A thread of fear laced through her words.

"No." He wouldn't leave without telling her.

If the townspeople turned against him, however, leaving might be the only way to protect Lexie—and preserve the life he'd created post-prison. He could start over in another town up the coast. BJ would give him an excellent recommendation, and he had Rebecca Oliver's offer on the table. Life would go on.

Even if it wouldn't be the same without Lexie.

Even if leaving her behind would almost kill him.

"I can understand why you want some space—but I'm here for you, Adam. Talk to me before you make any decisions that affect both of us. Please."

He couldn't promise her that. Lexie was the kind of woman who would put the people she cared about first, whatever the cost to herself. And given the strength of his feelings for her, she might be able to sway him. But he couldn't let her undermine her position in the town she loved for him.

"I'll stay in touch." It was the best he could offer.

"Adam?" A male voice called out from the in-progress house.

"I need to get back. Framing is a two-person job. No pun intended."

His lame attempt at humor fell flat.

"Adam?" Another holler from his coworker.

"Coming!" He reached over and stroked his

fingers across her cheek. "Let's give this a few days and see what happens. I'll call you."

With that, he walked away.

Five minutes passed before she emerged from the bushes and trudged to her car, sunglasses once again in place. At the car door, she paused and angled back. He lifted his hand. She responded. Then she slid behind the wheel, made a U-turn, and drove down the road, Shep and Ziggy bounding along behind her with loud barks.

He watched until she disappeared from view—praying she wasn't about to disappear from his life as well.

All the while knowing that was a very distinct possibility.

What a day.

Lexie pulled into the driveway, twisted the key in the ignition to kill the motor, and rested her forehead against the steering wheel.

One peeved motorist after another this morning as she issued speeding tickets. News that a nasty rumor was spreading like wildfire. An emotional meeting at the cranberry farm with Adam. A shouting match to referee this afternoon between two drivers involved in a fender bender.

Summoning up the dregs of her energy, she slid out of the car and plodded toward the house. Aspirin, a cold pack for her head, and a hot bath, that's what she needed. In that order. As fast as possible.

She pushed through the back door to the savory aroma of beef brisket—but even her mom's stellar cooking couldn't tempt her tonight. She'd lost her appetite somewhere along the road on the drive back from the farm.

"Hi, hon." Her mom glanced over from the stove. "Would you tell Matt dinner will be ready in five?"

"Yeah."

Her mother stopped stirring whatever was in the pot. "You don't look too hot. Are you sick?"

Only at heart.

"No. Long day."

"Did you talk to Adam?"

"Yes."

"Had he heard the rumor?"

"No."

"How did he take it?"

"How do you think?" She scrolled through her voicemail, on the off chance she'd missed a call from him during the afternoon.

No new messages.

"Did you ask him to dinner later in the week?"

"No." She slipped the phone back on her belt and continued toward the hall.

"Why not?"

"What is this, twenty questions?"

"Lexie?"

She stopped. Inhaled. Exhaled. It wasn't fair to

take out her fatigue and bad mood on her mom.

"Sorry." She swiveled back. "He asked for some space to think about what's going on."

"Does that mean your date for tonight is off?"

"Yeah."

Her mom removed the pot from the stove, reduced the oven temperature, and motioned to the table. "Let's sit."

"I don't have a lot to say."

"Humor me for a few minutes."

"Where's Matt?"

"Watching a video. He won't interrupt." She pulled out Lexie's chair. "Come on. Tell me what happened with Adam."

Lexie hovered on the threshold. Talking wasn't going to resolve the crisis—but it might help to get a third-party assessment.

She retraced her steps, sat, and briefed her mom on their conversation.

When she finished, her mother looked as worried as Lexie felt.

"I can't begin to imagine how devastating this must be for someone who's been through as much as he has. And being alone might not be the best idea. He needs to be around people who support him."

"I agree . . . but he asked for space. Shouldn't I respect that?"

"Yes—to a point. But in traumatic situations, people can get tunnel vision . . . which can lead to bad choices. If we care about someone, we might need to intervene. Remember how you got that bee in your bonnet about joining the track team in high school?"

"Vividly. I almost killed myself—until you and Dad talked some sense into me."

"But you weren't happy about us butting in."

"True." Far from it. The fit she'd thrown still embarrassed her. "But if you hadn't, that stress fracture I was trying to run on could have caused permanent damage."

"You couldn't see that back then, though. You were focused on the wrong priority and lost sight of the bigger picture. Adam might be doing that too." Her mom cocked her head, expression pensive. "Some concrete sign of support from the town might help restore his perspective."

"Like what?"

"I'm not certain. Let me noodle on it. In the meantime, you might want to show some in-person support."

"Such as?"

Her mother folded her hands on the table and leaned forward. "You're thirty-five years old. Do I have to spell it out?"

Warmth crept over her cheeks. "Fine. I get the picture. But I'll give him a couple of days first, like he asked."

"Mmm." Her mom tapped a finger on the table. "You don't think he might decide to be noble and walk away to protect *you* from any scandal, do you?"

Her mother had voiced the very fear that had been niggling at her all afternoon.

"He said he wouldn't—not without telling me."

"Has he ever lied to you?"

"No."

"Then there's no reason to think he'll start now."

That was true. He wouldn't leave without warning her.

But . . .

"That doesn't mean he won't decide to leave."

"What's your plan if he does?"

"Try to talk him out of it. There are other law enforcement jobs on the Oregon coast within commuting distance. I have no intention of letting anyone—or anything—drive me away from the town I love or the man I—" She cut herself off. It was far too soon to be thinking that, let alone saying it.

"It sounds like you have this under control." With an approving nod, her mother stood. "There's plenty of brisket for all of us. I'll set another place."

"No thanks. I'm not hungry. All I want to do is veg in a hot bath for a few minutes." After she took those aspirin.

"I'll put a plate in the oven for you, in case your appetite picks up later." Her mom gave her a hug. "Hang in, Lexie. If you two are meant to be together, a malicious stunt like this isn't going to change the outcome. I'll keep Matt entertained while you enjoy your bath."

Enjoy?

Hardly.

That description would better apply to the date she'd been anticipating with Adam.

Still—there would be more dates to come once this storm passed.

In fact, if Adam didn't contact her by Friday, he'd find himself on a surprise date come Saturday.

Not the romantic kind she'd prefer—but by the time she left Sandpiper Cove, there would be zero doubt in his mind that no matter what *he* might be thinking, she was sticking with him.

For better or worse.

ঝ 23 ৶

He owed Lexie a call.

Three days had passed since she'd broken the traumatic news at the farm, and their only contact had been via voicemail.

But he didn't know what to tell her.

Adam picked up a broken sand dollar from the beach, weighed it in his hand, and pitched it out to sea as hard as he could. It arced through the air against the blue sky, toward the jagged sea stacks offshore and the distant horizon, fuzzy on this Saturday afternoon. Then it disappeared beneath the dark blue water.

Clyde bounded up with his odd half-hop gait and dropped the ball onto the sand.

"Want to play again, fella?"

He gave a joyful woof and wagged his tail so hard his whole body shook.

"I assume that's a yes." Lips twitching despite his bleak mood, Adam gave the ball another toss.

Clyde took off after it.

"He is a happy pup."

Adam swiveled around to find Luis strolling toward him. Odd timing. Though the man had told him he often took walks on this long stretch of windswept beach, their paths had never crossed.

"Yes, he is."

"A lucky one too."

"I'm not certain about that." He watched the dog maneuver on his bad leg, scampering to corral the ball as it fell. "He'll never recover from his encounter with that car."

"He would have died if you had not saved him."

"But he's crippled."

Luis studied the dog, who'd detoured to play tag with the surf. "It does not seem to bother him. He has adopted."

Once again, Adam's mouth flexed. "I think you mean adapted."

"Yes. Adapted. I always have trouble with

that word." The Cuban's dark irises twinkled with merriment. So different from his early days on BJ's crew, after tragedy had robbed him of the new life in America he'd dreamed of. "Adapting is a valuable skill, yes?"

Adam knew where he was heading with this. Everyone on BJ's crew had heard the rumors circulating about him. Luis had been supportive, but the other workers had avoided the topic. None of them knew him well enough to have a strong opinion, and while they'd been friendly, he'd seen the flashes of doubt in their eyes.

It had been uncomfortable, to say the least.

"I don't know if you can adapt to distrust." He toed a piece of driftwood, dislodging it from the sand where it had settled. A metaphor for his own situation, perhaps? Maybe he should yank out the tender roots he'd put down in Hope Harbor and move on.

As if reading his mind, Luis spoke.

"Running away from difficulties is not an answer, my friend."

At the man's gentle comment, Adam exhaled and gave the sea a slow sweep. "It might be, in this case. You saw how the rest of the crew on the house job reacted to the rumor. I'm tired of being looked at with suspicion."

"They do not know you—and most do not live in Hope Harbor." Luis bent to take the ball from Clyde and gave it another toss. The pooch raced off again, sand flying in his wake. "The police chief, she does not believe this ugly rumor, does she?"

"No."

"Then do not worry about what others think. She is the only one who matters—and not because she is the police chief."

"I can't ignore her position in this town." No sense pretending he didn't know what Luis meant. His friend might never have asked about the relationship between the two of them, but once Luis saw them dance, once Lexie made that first trip to the jobsite, he'd picked up the vibes.

"Because you do not wish to cause her trouble."

"Yes."

"What does she say about this?"

"That we'll get through it. Together."

"And you do not agree?"

Clyde returned, dropped the ball at his feet, and stretched out in the sand a few feet away to soak up some rays. As if he didn't have a care in the world.

Lucky dog—literally.

"I'm not a quitter, Luis . . . but I'm tired of trying to prove myself. I've been doing that for eighteen months, and what do I have to show for it? Nothing. I'm right back where I started."

"No. You are not. You now have a . . . what is it called?" He puzzled over the term he was seeking. "Ah. A track record. You have done much good in this town and made more friends than you know. You should give them a chance to show their support. And it would not hurt to ask for guidance, either, before you make any decisions."

Wasn't that almost what Charley had told him, the day they'd been discussing a job for Brenda with the clerics? The man had talked about how paths often smooth out if we listen for direction and give God a chance to pave the way.

He hadn't done that yet.

And maybe it was time he did. Otherwise, he might make a mistake and take that detour Charley had cautioned against. The one that could leave him at a dead end . . . or lost.

"Thanks for reminding me of that."

"Perhaps that is why I am here today." Luis motioned to the deserted beach. "It is strange we both came out here for a walk this afternoon, is it not?"

So he'd noticed the odd coincidence too.

"You think our meeting was God's doing?"

"Who's to say? But if he counts even the hairs of our head, he surely knows when a man needs to hear the voice of a friend. You will call me if you wish to talk again?" Luis clasped his arm.

"Yes. Thank you."

"It is my pleasure—and no more than others have done for me. Here on this very beach once, in fact." After bending to give Clyde a pat, he continued on his stroll.

Adam had no idea what that last comment about the beach meant.

But he did know one thing. The man's counsel was sound. For three days he'd been wrestling with his dilemma alone. Yes, he'd tossed a few frantic prayers heavenward, but he hadn't focused on prayer—or listening. He needed to do both ASAP.

And as a plan began to form in his mind, he snapped his fingers for Clyde, turned toward home—and powered up his cell.

His Kia was here.

Thank you, God!

Lexie stopped her car farther than usual from the cabin in Sandpiper Cove and took a deep breath. She'd given Adam the space he'd requested, but after three days it was time to break radio silence. Yes, he'd called her on Thursday and Friday—but she'd been occupied. Her return calls had gone to his voicemail . . . and he hadn't responded, even though she'd told him she'd like to hear from him no matter how late he got her messages.

She was done playing tag.

They needed to talk.

Today.

In person.

She got out of the car, straightened her shoulders, strode down the drive to his front door, and knocked.

From inside, Clyde began barking.

The blinds in the window beside the door shifted, and a few seconds later the bolt slid back.

"Hi. This is a surprise." The corners of Adam's lips creaked up, as if lifting them took supreme effort.

Not much of a welcome—except for that swift, telling flare of hunger in his eyes.

"We need to talk."

"I was about to call you." Adam kept his hand on the half-open door.

Apparently he didn't intend to invite her in.

Too bad.

"May I?" She motioned toward the interior. If he said no, she'd have to resort to Plan B.

Whatever that was.

He hesitated . . . but finally backed up.

Lexie brushed past him, inhaling the masculine scent that was all Adam—but froze three feet in.

His clothes were scattered around on the bed, a backpack was half filled, and a sleeping bag was rolled up on the floor . . . ready to go.

He was leaving?

She whirled toward him. "What's going on?"

"Not what you think." He took her arm and guided her to a chair at the kitchen table. "Would you like some coffee?"

"I'd prefer an explanation."

He dropped into the seat beside her. "I need to

get away, somewhere without a lot of memories, to think—and pray. I called BJ a little while ago, and she told me to take a few days of vacation. She's home from her honeymoon and will be back on the job Monday."

"You're leaving today?" Her pulse took a leap.

"No. Tomorrow after church. If I couldn't connect with you by phone, I was going to tell you after the service."

At least he wasn't leaving permanently.

Yet.

And he never would, if she had anything to say about it.

"Adam." She reached across the table and gripped his hand. "My opinion hasn't changed since we talked on Wednesday. What we have needs to be explored. Period. I don't think this rumor will have any lasting impact, but if, by chance, it does . . . and if we get serious . . . I would rather find a job somewhere else than give up on us."

"I don't want to disrupt your life, Lexie."

"You already have—and leaving would disrupt it more."

He propped his elbow on the table and massaged his temple. "You deserve better than this. Better than me. There's a stigma attached to associating with a felon, and even if the current crisis goes away, certain people in this town will never let you forget about my past."

"That's their problem—and I can take whatever they might dish out."

"But I don't want you to have to take it. I can't put someone I lo . . . I care about . . . in that position."

Ah.

His feelings ran as strong—and deep—as hers.

Throat tightening, she squeezed his fingers. "Shouldn't that be *my* decision?"

From the floor, Clyde looked back and forth between them. At last he trotted to her and hopped up, front paws on her legs, and gave her fingers a lick.

"See? Clyde's on my side." She ruffled his ears.

Adam wanted to cave, to tell her he'd weather the storm with her by his side—but he was also holding back, trying to do what was best for her. She could see his struggle in every taut line of his face.

But she knew just how to convince him that what was best for him was also best for her.

Without a word, she rose and circled the corner of the table to stand over him.

"What are you doing?" He gave her a wary perusal.

In silence, she placed her hands on his shoulders . . . leaned down . . . and planted her lips on his.

It didn't take him long to get into the spirit of the smooch.

By the time they finished, she was sitting on his lap, her arms around his neck.

"You don't play fair." His voice was husky as he toyed with a strand of her hair, his smoky eyes hinting at the fire burning within.

"All's fair in love and war, according to the old saying. Don't go, Adam. Stay here. Take your days off if you need to, but do your thinking and praying here—where you belong. With me by your side."

"You make it hard to say no."

"Then don't."

Several silent beats ticked by as he regarded her—but in the end he shook his head.

"I can't make a rational decision with you in my arms. I need to think about it overnight."

Not what she wanted to hear.

But pushing at this point could backfire. Besides, she was privy to a persuasion plan that might eliminate the need for further coaxing on her part.

Better to leave it for now . . . and try to exit on a lighter note.

"Hmph. My pucker power must have lost its punch." She wiggled off his lap and stood.

He rose too and cupped her face with his lean fingers. "For the record, your pucker packs plenty of punch. If I was hooked up to an EKG machine, you'd see proof of that."

"Then I'll keep that weapon in reserve should all else fail." She rose on tiptoe to give him another quick kiss, bent to pat Clyde, and crossed to the door.

"Lexie."

She paused on the threshold. Adam was standing where she'd left him, fingers clenched around the back of a chair.

"Thank you." His two simple words, roughened with emotion, held a world of meaning.

So much for leaving on a lighter note.

Pressure built behind her eyes. "Don't thank me for being selfish. I have a lot to lose if you make the wrong decision."

"Are you certain you know what that is?"

"Yes." Her voice rang with every bit of the conviction she felt.

The strain in his features eased a tiny bit. "I'll see you tomorrow."

With a nod, she left the cabin, pulling the door closed behind her. Her visit might not have produced the definitive outcome she'd hoped for, but Adam was leaning her direction—and that boded well for tomorrow.

Because it wouldn't take much to convince him to stay at this juncture . . . and a whole lot of convincing was on the agenda come Sunday morning.

Wow.

Grace Christian was as packed as it sometimes was on summer weekends when the charming seaside town was filled with visitors.

There must be a local festival somewhere nearby that had drawn a crowd.

From his spot inside the back door, Adam surveyed the crammed pews. For once, his habit of arriving at the last minute was going to work against him. He might have to stand for the service.

A motion to his right caught his eye, and he looked over. Brian waved at him and gestured to an empty spot beside him and his mother in the second-to-last pew.

Saved—even if it wasn't his customary end seat.

Mumbling an apology while doing his best to avoid trampling on the feet of a vaguely familiar couple as he squeezed by, he claimed the empty place.

"Hey, Mr. Stone."

"Hi, Brian." He leaned forward and spoke to the woman on Brian's other side. "Morning, Brenda."

She acknowledged his greeting with a smile.

As the organ struck up the chords of the opening hymn, cutting off further conversation, Adam stifled a yawn. No surprise, given his restless night. After tossing for hours while he mulled over Lexie's suggestion to do his thinking at Sandpiper Cove, he'd almost capitulated.

Almost.

But in the end, he'd decided to drive north and see if he could find an available yurt at one of the state parks. A fresh scene might give him a fresh perspective. She wasn't going to like it—but he'd soften the news with a promise to return in a few days.

After that? It all depended on the mood of the town and what kind of guidance his prayer produced while he was gone.

One thing for sure, he'd be listening hard for direction.

Despite his fatigue, he managed to stay engaged with the service—especially Reverend Baker's sermon on the importance of loving one's neighbor . . . including those who weren't lovable. Like the Fishers, in his case. How could you love people who . . .

". . . in our midst. Adam Stone."

As his name rang from the pulpit, Adam snapped to attention. What in the world?

"Most of you know Adam—or know of the good deeds he's done since joining our church and our community. Most of you also know he served jail time. And most of you have heard the vicious rumor being circulated about him by a person or persons who wish him ill."

Reverend Baker leaned closer to the microphone, as serious as Adam had ever seen him.

"This is a grave disservice to a fine man. We must love and pray for the perpetrator, despite this bad deed, as God has instructed us—but we must also pray for and support the man who has been wronged."

Reverend Baker motioned to the first pew, and Adam's jaw dropped. Father Murphy rose and joined his fellow cleric at the pulpit.

"My friend Father Murphy is here today, along with many of his parishioners, to express solidarity with us in our support of Adam. Lexie Graham, our chief of police, has also asked to say a few words."

The minister stepped aside as Lexie rose from a pew near the front and joined the two men at the pulpit.

A surge of panic set Adam's heart hammering. What was she doing? He didn't want her tainted by any of this!

But based on her determined expression, she'd made up her mind to take a public stand—and it was too late to stop her.

She searched the crowd until her gaze came to rest on him. For a long moment, it lingered . . . then moved on to skim the rest of the congregation.

"Thank you, Reverend Baker, for giving me a minute to speak this morning." Her voice was steady. Strong. Confident. "A public official doesn't have the luxury of separating her civic role from her civilian life. So I want to be totally transparent with everyone here. Several weeks ago, I had the opportunity to meet Adam Stone after he was a victim in one of the vandalism incidents here in town. I was impressed. As I got to know him better, my initial admiration deepened into much more. The feeling was mutual—and just before the rumor hit, we had decided to begin dating."

A slight murmur ran through the crowd, and a vise squeezed the air from Adam's lungs.

Oh, Lexie! What are you doing to yourself?

If she sensed his silent dismay, she gave no indication of it.

"I want all of you to know my decision stands. There isn't one shred of evidence linking Adam with any of the vandalism incidents, and I have absolute faith in his honesty and innocence. I've been your police chief for several years, and I believe most of you know me and my record well enough to trust my integrity. I've always put the safety of Hope Harbor above personal considerations, and I promise you that will never change."

Lexie stepped away from the podium.

Around him, Adam heard a quiet buzz of conversation. Sensed surreptitious glances being directed his way. Felt the hard wood beneath his fingers as he gripped the edge of the pew.

This was surreal.

Why would Lexie put herself—and her job—on the line like this?

What if people turned against her?

What if they demanded she give up her position?

But . . . maybe that was the very reason she'd taken a strong stand. To let him know that whatever happened—good or bad—she was sticking with him. There could be no going back after her public declaration. She had to realize that.

Meaning she'd put herself on the line for him.

The scene in front of him blurred, and he swiped a hand across his eyes.

No one—no one—had ever given him a greater, more overwhelming, gift.

Reverend Baker cocooned Lexie's hands between his before returning to the podium. "Adam is with us today—as he has been every Sunday since he came to Hope Harbor a year and a half ago. Why don't we show him what it means to have the support of this town and faith family?"

The two clerics led the applause while Lexie descended the sanctuary stairs.

At the bottom, she stopped. Watching him. Waiting. For a cue from him, perhaps?

The clapping built and grew until it thundered through the church, and once again the scene grew fuzzy. The resounding wave of affirmation was the sweetest sound he'd ever heard.

When it went on and on, he slowly rose to his feet.

The ovation intensified.

Adam scanned the church. Some of the faces were unfamiliar, but there were many people he knew. Charley, in the suit and string tie he'd worn to the wedding. Luis, far from his home turf at St. Francis. Eleanor Cooper of fudge-cake fame. John from the Seabird Inn. BJ and Eric, just back from their honeymoon. Tracy and Michael from the cranberry farm. Annette and Matt, the latter standing on the seat of the pew and waving instead of clapping, a wide grin splitting his face.

And then there was Lexie.

He squeezed past the couple at the end of the pew and started down the aisle toward the woman who'd transformed his world.

Smiling through her tears, she met him halfway.

And there, in the center aisle of Grace Christian, with applause ringing in his ears, he kissed her.

It was a moment he knew he would remember for as long as he lived.

Rare. Perfect. Sublime.

And he knew this, as well.

He wasn't leaving Hope Harbor.

Ever.

Because after a long and winding journey, he'd finally found home.

❧ Epilogue ❧

"Are you nervous?"

Smiling, Lexie turned toward the man she was going to marry tomorrow, his face bronzed by the sun dipping low on the horizon off Sandpiper Cove. "Nope."

"No second thoughts?"

"Not a one. What about you?"

"Are you kidding? I'm marrying the most beautiful woman in the world . . . I'm getting the best son in the world"—he motioned with his mug to Matt, who was playing a game of catch-the-mole-crab with Clyde—"and I have work that feeds my soul. On this Thanksgiving weekend, my cup runneth over. What's to have second thoughts about?"

"Sharing a roof with your mother-in-law, maybe?"

"Hey, you can't beat a live-in babysitter and cook." He flashed her a grin, then grew more solemn. "On a more serious note, I love Annette—*and* the whole idea of a built-in family. I've spent most of my life alone, Lexie. Having caring people around me every day will be a blessing, not a burden. No worries on that score, okay?"

He sounded sincere, as he always did when this subject came up. *She* might not want to live with in-laws as a newlywed, however wonderful they were—but a man who'd never had a loving family might, indeed, welcome such an opportunity. She needed to let this concern go once and for all.

"Okay. You've convinced me. Besides, after that second-floor Cape Cod master suite BJ designed is finished, we'll have plenty of privacy. I can't believe how different the house looks with a raised roof and dormers."

"It will be a great retreat. And just so you know, I intend to take full advantage of that privacy you mentioned." He brushed the tips of his fingers across her temple . . . traced the curve of her cheek . . . grazed her mouth with the pad of his thumb.

Whew.

The air might be chilly on this last Friday in November, but after that heated touch, she could shed her jacket and never miss it.

"Is that a . . ." Her voice hoarsened, and she cleared her throat. "Is that a promise?"

"Count on it." He set his mug down and tugged her close, resting his hands at her waist. "Now let's talk about tomorrow. Did you decide to wear that silk dress I love?"

"No. A woman needs a new dress for her wedding. But I have a feeling you're going to like the one I found." An image of the knee-length, peach-colored lace sheath with a scalloped hem materialized in her mind.

Yeah, he'd like it.

A lot.

"Bring the other one on our honeymoon."

"To that hideaway you found for us deep in the redwoods?"

"I have a couple of surprise excursions planned."

"Adam . . . I don't need extravagant entertainment. You and me—together—will be more than sufficient."

"I want to take you out for some upscale dinners. We have a lot to celebrate—and I can afford a few splurges, with the commissions Rebecca is sending my way."

"You aren't still fretting about the differences in our finances, are you?" The disparity had bothered him in the beginning, but he hadn't mentioned it much in the past few months. She'd hoped he'd gotten over that needless worry. It made no difference to her.

"Sometimes—but not at this moment." He stole a quick kiss.

"Don't change the subject."

"Why not?" He trailed his lips across her jaw.

"Because . . . because finances are important."

"So is this."

"Adam." She leaned back, out of his reach. "I can't think straight when you do that."

"And this is only a tiny sample of what's to come." He winked, a roguish gleam in his eye.

Oh, man. He knew exactly how to get her hot and bothered.

But she was *not* going to let herself be distracted.

Yet.

"Will you be serious?"

"I am—about you."

She wiggled out of his hold, backed off a few
paces, and stuck her hands on her hips.

He let out a long-suffering sigh. "You really
want to talk about money the night before our
wedding?"

"Yes."

"Why?"

"I don't know. It seems like . . . a loose end. I'm
not certain you're comfortable with the situation,
even though you don't say much about it."

Expelling a breath, he folded his arms. "Okay.
Fine. I'll give it to you straight. Does it bother me
I'm marrying a woman who has a lot more in her
bank account than I do? Yes. Does it bother me
enough to change how I feel about her? No. And
in the not-too-distant future, I'll be earning as
much as she is. Maybe more, once I'm making
furniture full-time. I may never catch up, but I'll
be an equal contributor to the bank account
going forward. Is that a perfect scenario? No.
Can I live with it? Yes. Satisfied?"

"If you are."

"I am. And while we're on the subject of
money . . . I was going to wait and tell you on our
honeymoon, but I'll share it now. A commission

came in yesterday for a custom desk and bookcases for a library one of Rebecca's clients is adding to his house."

When he told her the price tag, she did a slow blink.

"Wow. I'm in the wrong business. Good thing you rented that empty furniture store at the edge of town for a woodworking shop. You're going to need the space sooner rather than later. But how are you planning to juggle this new job, plus your other commission pieces, with BJ's work schedule?"

"I'll worry about that after our honeymoon."

"She hasn't found any potential replacements for you yet, has she?"

"No—and she's going to lose Luis too once he finishes his paramedic training. I can't leave her in the lurch. She was my ally from the get-go."

Lexie moved close again and looped her arms around his neck. "That's another reason I love you, you know. Loyalty is one of your many fine attributes. Shall I name some others?"

"Why don't you demonstrate how much you love them instead?"

She checked on Matt, who was still occupied with Clyde, tipped her head back, rose on tiptoe, and . . .

Her phone began to vibrate.

With a huff, she yanked it off her belt. "Sorry about that. I'm shutting this off when I go to bed tonight and it's staying off until we get back from our honeymoon."

"I like that plan."

"I'll ignore this if you want." She skimmed the screen.

"Is it important?"

"Maybe. It's Jim Gleason. I don't think he'd bother me tonight for anything frivolous."

"Go ahead and take it. I'll watch the mole-crab hunt."

"I won't be more than a minute."

"Don't rush on my account." He brushed a piece of windblown hair back from her face. "I'm not going anywhere."

She watched him stroll away as she put the phone to her ear, relishing that promise . . . and the unexpected blessings that had filled her life with joy.

For who could have guessed, on that April day she'd visited Sandpiper Cove for the first time, what a precious gift this holiday season would hold?

A second chance at love with a kind, caring, generous man certainly hadn't been on her wish list—but come Christmas morning, the best gift under the tree was going to be sitting right beside her.

As it would be for all the Christmases to come.

Adam glanced toward Lexie. Faint furrows scored her brow as she paced on the sand, cell to ear. The call was taking a lot longer than one minute.

Must be trouble.

But he was getting used to that. Dealing with emergencies was part of her job. Part of who she was.

And he wouldn't change a thing.

Five minutes later, as he and Matt tried to corner a mole crab that dared to venture close, she slipped the phone back on her belt.

"These guys are hard to catch, aren't they?" As the crab burrowed beneath the sand, Matt sat back on his heels with an exasperated sigh.

"Yeah. But keep at it. You might get one yet." That outcome was about as likely as a nasty rumor dying a quick death—but it could happen, as his own situation had demonstrated. After that Sunday show of support back in April, the stories circulating about him in town had dried up fast. It had been nothing short of a miracle, as far as he was concerned.

Leaving the boy and dog to their quest, he rejoined Lexie. "Do you need to leave?"

"No." She picked up her mug, peered at the dregs, and dumped them onto the sand.

"Would you like a refill? There's some left in the pot." He'd learned to be discreet about her police calls. If she could tell him about them, she would.

"No. I need to get *some* sleep tonight—and

adding more caffeine to the adrenaline already pumping in anticipation of our big day isn't a smart idea." She gave him a playful nudge, then leaned back against the rock where they always put their empty coffee mugs on sunset-watching nights. "Jim thought I'd be interested in some news that came in over the police radio."

If she'd brought up the call, that must mean she could talk about it.

"What happened?"

"It's kind of sad, actually. Lucas Fisher just plowed into a car after running a red light up on 101, near Bandon."

"Anyone hurt?"

"No—but he was speeding . . . and he had alcohol in his blood."

"Was he drunk?"

"He wasn't over the adult legal limit, but Oregon has a zero tolerance policy for minors. He'll be hauled into jail, fined, and lose his license for up to a year."

Adam gave a soft whistle. "A much bigger problem than the vandalism stuff."

"Yeah. If we'd been able to work with him on that, address some of his issues earlier like we did with Brian, he might have avoided this."

"You tried. His father didn't do him any favors by sweeping the original offenses under the rug."

"No . . . but a DUI charge will be harder to circumvent."

"I'm glad Brian isn't hanging out with him anymore."

"Apparently not many kids are, since he let it slip to a few of them that he was the one who spread the rumor about you."

"Well, maybe this new incident will be a wake-up call for both father and son."

"We can hope. And I agree with you that Brian was smart to cut ties with him when he did. I'm also glad the job with the clerics worked out for his mom. Their new apartment in town is much nicer than the trailer, and now that she's home in the evenings and on weekends, she can keep closer tabs on him. They have you to thank for all of those positive changes."

"Not true." He wasn't about to claim credit for Brenda's success. Her outstanding cooking and housekeeping skills had clinched the deal. "I just happened to be at Charley's the day the clerics were bemoaning the impending loss of their cook. All I did was hook them up."

"That was enough to change two lives for the better. Some people wouldn't have bothered to connect the dots or get involved."

"It was no big deal." He passed off his minor role with a shrug. "But speaking of changing two lives for the better . . ." He draped an arm around her shoulders as the sun inched toward the horizon. "This time tomorrow night, we'll be man and wife."

"I'm counting the hours."

"How long do you want to stay at the reception?"

She gave a soft laugh. "Anxious to start the honeymoon?"

"Yes—and in a great place too. When we were working on the renovations at Seabird Inn last year, I would have laughed if anyone suggested I'd end up spending my wedding night in one of the luxury suites . . . with a police chief, no less." He grinned.

"It was lovely of John to offer that as a wedding present."

"I agree—and I'd like to get there ASAP."

"Me too. But we'll have to hang around the church hall long enough to dance to a few tunes . . . eat some food . . . cut the wedding cake . . . and sample the fudge confection Eleanor Cooper offered to supply for the groom's cake."

He groaned and rested his forehead against hers. "That could take hours."

"But after that . . . I'm all yours. Forever."

"Promise?"

"Yes—and I'll make that official tomorrow. In the meantime, this will have to suffice." She snuggled into his arms and smiled up at him.

He smiled back.

And as he bent to give her another preview of what awaited her at the inn . . . as the distinctive trill of a sandpiper echoed in the background and waves lapped gently against the sand . . . as the setting sun bathed the world in a golden glow . . . a deep, profound, abiding joy filled his heart—and soul.

Maybe he'd spent most of his life treading a dicey and dangerous road.

Maybe he'd made more mistakes than any man should be allotted.

Maybe he'd come close to the gates of hell on far too many occasions.

But today he was living proof that God did, indeed, work for the good of those who love him.

Because here, in the arms of this remarkable woman who filled his life with joy and grace, he'd found heaven on earth.

⊰ Acknowledgments ⊱

Thank you so much for visiting Hope Harbor—where hearts heal . . . and love blooms.

When I wrote the first Hope Harbor book several years ago, I fell in love with this charming town on the Oregon coast—and I hoped readers would too. I'm very happy . . . and grateful . . . to say my wish came true.

Which means there are more Hope Harbor books ahead!

As I wrap up this novel, there are a number of people I need to thank.

My husband, Tom, for his endless support in too many ways to list here without adding multiple pages to this book.

My parents, James and Dorothy Hannon, my original cheering section. I lost my mom very suddenly last August (just seven weeks ago as I write this)—but she is never far from my heart. And I like to believe she's cheering me on still from heaven.

My publishing partners at Revell, who have become friends as well as business colleagues. I am blessed to work with you.

And finally, all the readers whose support has allowed me to tell stories for a living. I ask the Lord to bless each of you every single day.

If you enjoyed *Sandpiper Cove*, I invite you to return next spring for another visit to Hope Harbor in *Pelican Point*, when an endangered lighthouse leads to hope—and love—for two very special couples. And if you like suspense, please watch for *Dangerous Illusions*, Book 1 in my Code of Honor series, coming in October.

❧ About the Author ❧

Irene Hannon is a bestselling, award-winning author who took the publishing world by storm at the tender age of ten with a sparkling piece of fiction that received national attention.

Okay . . . maybe that's a slight exaggeration. But she *was* one of the honorees in a complete-the-story contest conducted by a national children's magazine. And she likes to think of that as her "official" fiction-writing debut!

Since then, she has written more than fifty contemporary romance and romantic suspense novels. Irene is a seven-time finalist and three-time winner of the RITA award—the "Oscar" of romance fiction—from Romance Writers of America. She is also a member of that organization's elite Hall of Fame. Her books have been honored with a National Readers' Choice award, three HOLT medallions, a Daphne du Maurier award, a Retailers' Choice award, two Booksellers' Best awards, two Carol awards, and two Reviewers' Choice awards from *RT Book Reviews* magazine. That magazine has also honored her with a Career Achievement award for her entire body of work. In addition, she is a two-time Christy award finalist.

Irene, who holds a BA in psychology and an

MA in journalism, juggled two careers for many years until she gave up her executive corporate communications position with a Fortune 500 company to write full-time. She is happy to say she has no regrets! As she points out, leaving behind the rush-hour commute, corporate politics, and a relentless BlackBerry that never slept was no sacrifice.

A trained vocalist, Irene has sung the leading role in numerous community theater productions and is also a soloist at her church.

When not otherwise occupied, she and her husband enjoy traveling, Saturday mornings at their favorite coffee shop, and spending time with family. They make their home in Missouri.

To learn more about Irene and her books, visit www.irenehannon.com. She is also active on Facebook and Twitter.